DIVIDED EARTH

DALE E. MCCLENNING

Milton, Ontario
http://www.brain-lag.com/

Brain Lag Publishing
Milton, Ontario
http://www.brain-lag.com/

Cover artwork by and © Jonny Lindner

ISBN 978-1-928011-37-8

Library and Archives Canada Cataloguing in Publication

Title: Divided Earth / Dale E. McClenning.
Names: McClenning, Dale E., 1962- author.
Identifiers: Canadiana (print) 20200257234 | Canadiana (ebook) 20200257242 | ISBN 9781928011378
   (softcover) | ISBN 9781928011385 (ebook)
Classification: LCC PS3613.C55 D58 2020 | DDC 813/.6—dc23

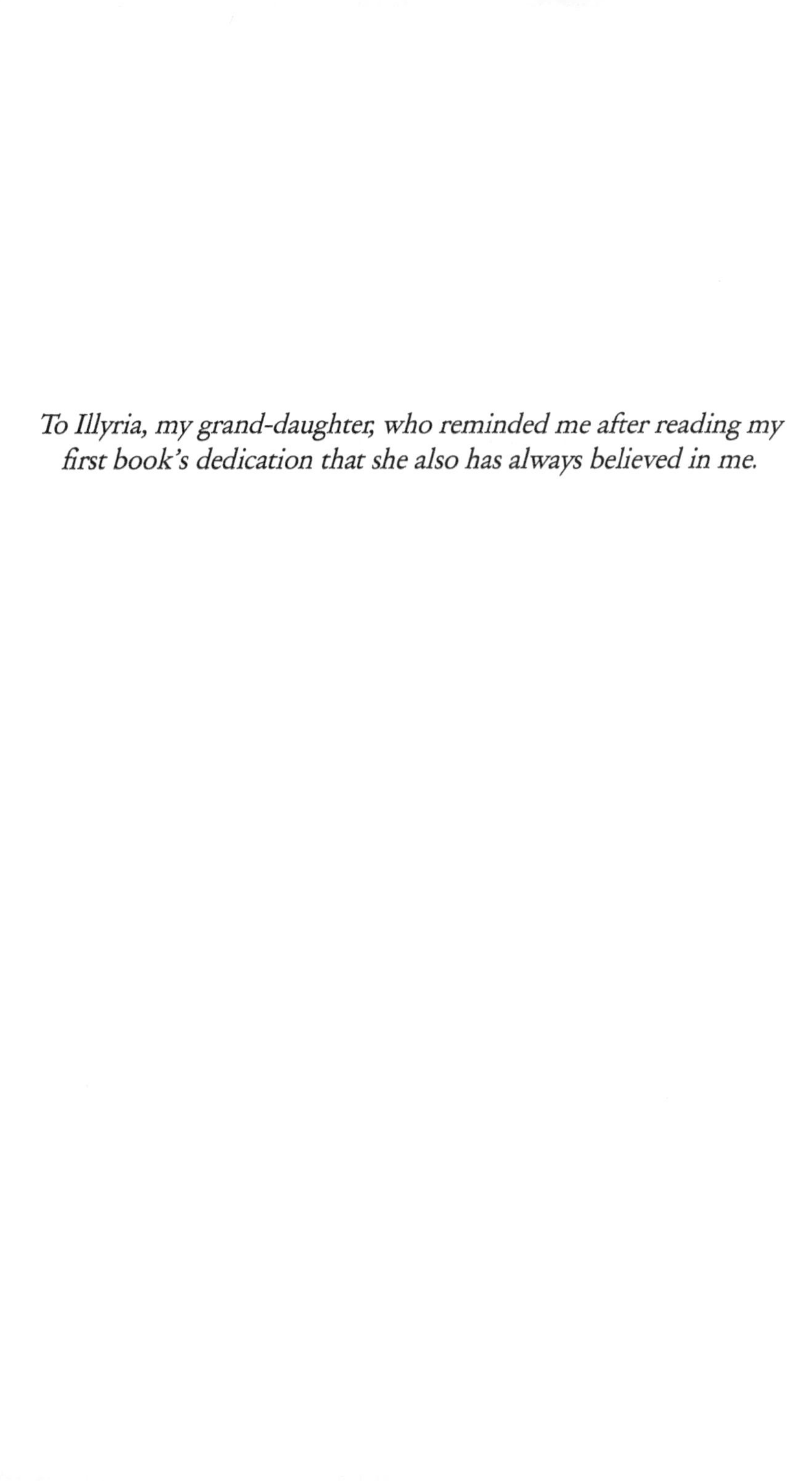

To Illyria, my grand-daughter, who reminded me after reading my first book's dedication that she also has always believed in me.

Chapter One
Back in the U.S. We Are

The waving green wheat fields were a stark contrast to the military facility seen out the front window of the bus. The high, barbed-wire fence appeared to be holding off an invasion by alien plants bent on overtaking the world. As if the world for as far as the eye could see was not enough, the invader plants appeared determined to wipe out the last vestige of the buildings they hated. As the bus drew close, though, it was obvious that wheat was not what hated the complex.

Revelation Base, South Dakota, was perfectly round. Built on the site of the satellite-killer explosion caused by the aliens twenty-seven years ago, the base covered every inch that had been scarred by the explosion. At first, its name had been appropriate. It had not taken long for grass to grow once planted, the radiation of the particle weapon being short-lived by design. Soon after the facility had been constructed, the name had a whole new meaning to those who worked there.

Joseph Gint scoffed at the people camped outside the perimeter fencing near the southern gate of the complex. He shook his head as he talked.

"Don't those Puritans have anything better to do than stand outside the fence and shout at us?"

"I guess not," a man in military uniform sitting in the seat across the aisle said in reply. "Not sure who supplies them, but they don't seem in any hurry to leave. How many are there?"

"I count six," Joseph said, turning his head to continue looking at the protesters.

"Some must have left."

"Yeah, I saw two dozen out there a couple of weeks ago. Maybe they're wearing down?" Joseph's voice tone went higher with a little hope.

"We could only be so lucky." The man laughed. "All I know is that if they throw themselves in front of a tank, it ain't going to stop in time to avoid running over them."

Joseph turned to the man, a smile on his face. "That gives me an idea."

The man laughed harder. "You ain't the first to think of that."

The bus came to a stop inside a fenced enclosure. The side door was opened and a uniformed army corporal entered. Hands that weren't already holding forth identification interfaces pulled them out of pockets or pulled back sleeves to reveal them. The corporal held a small scanner in the palm of his hand, waving it at the interfaces as he passed. Each wave was followed by a small, twinkling beep. Most of the riders were military personnel in uniform. A few, like Joseph, were in civilian clothing. When the corporal came to Joseph and waved the scanner, he chuckled and grew a small smile.

"I don't know, you still look mighty suspicious," the corporal said.

"You're just jealous about losing at darts," Joseph said in reply with a small chuckle of his own.

"I've been practicing."

"Oh! A real game, then?"

The corporal just huffed and shook his head as he continued down the aisle.

Joseph sat and stared ahead as the corporal finished his duty. When he came back up the aisle, the corporal spoke again.

"Darts tonight?"

"Sure. Have to see how much practice you got."

"Loser buys?"

"Ha! Make sure you bring money then."

"You Europeans," the corporal tsked, "so arrogant."

"Who you calling a European?" Joseph furrowed his brow with

the statement.

"The guy born in Europe, that's who." The man smiled as he left the bus.

"Like that's my fault!" Joseph yelled at him as the door closed. The corporal waved at the gate and pounded twice on the vehicle.

"Where were you born?" the chatty man across the aisle asked.

"Netherlands, or Holland if you like the old name." Joseph stuck out his hand. "Joseph."

"Sergeant Edmond Harjo, Logistics." Harjo grabbed Joseph's hand and gave it a firm shake. His hand was larger than Joseph's and had more muscle behind it.

"You're new, I suppose?"

"Just assigned. Asked for it, in fact. Always wondered about this place." The bus glided forward. "They really find alien tech here?"

"Yes and no." Joseph smiled with an internal laugh. "We found pieces of aliens that survived the explosion. None of it worked, of course, but it was still pretty interesting. Led to a lot of new technologies of our own."

"So I heard. What's your assignment here?"

"Particle projectors." Joseph waited for the normal response.

"They let civilians do particle laser research?" The man's voice rose in pitch and his head turned to look at Joseph with his left eye.

"If you're smart enough, they can't do without you." Joseph's grin reached cheesy proportions. As Harjo looked shocked, Joseph added, "It also helps if you have connections."

"Oh," Harjo said, finding his voice, "you the son of some general or something?"

"No." Joseph paused. "My dad is Arhus Gint."

"Wait!" Harjo's hands came up. "*The* Arhus Gint? The guy who talked to the aliens?"

"That's the one. Got all my brains from my mom, though. At least that's what she tells him."

"Wow. Never been this close to an actual celebrity." The bus turned down one of the roads toward the processing center.

"You know," Joseph said, leaning toward the man, "he's still in the Netherlands."

"You're close enough for me." Harjo laughed.

"Actually, most of the research team are civilians here. Best minds, that sort of thing."

The bus came to a stop with a hiss. People started to stand up and grab small bags from overhead racks or from under seats.

"Fine by me. Particularly if you have a few babes in the mix."

"That, you will have to decide for yourself. See you around, Sergeant." Joseph let the man stand first. He grabbed a small black duffel bag from overhead.

"Sure thing. Take care of yourself."

Joseph sat while the line of people exited the bus. Turning over his wrist to look at his interface, he scrolled for the latest base news but grew bored fast.

"Call Wenk," he told the interface.

In a few seconds, Wenk's face appeared. "Hey! You here yet?"

"Bus just stopped inside. Where are you?"

"It's Saturday, where do you think I am?"

"Crawling around some dungeon in your head?"

"Nope. We hit a wormhole and got sent to fifteenth century England."

"Magic?"

"In fifteenth century England?"

"So you have to live by your wits?" Joseph laughed.

"Exactly!"

"You'll be dead in a hour."

"Thanks a lot. Oh, by the way, Mercedes is looking for you."

"You know why?"

"I know why I would want her looking for me." Wenk's eyebrows went up.

"Pff. She's not into pretend, which you clearly are."

A hurt expression ran onto Wenk's face.

"Do you have any real idea what she's after?"

"Not a clue, but she doesn't look mad, so I think you're safe, at least for now."

"Yeah, like that can't change in a heartbeat. Thanks for the warning. See you at the pub later?"

"If I die, sure. If not, who knows. Gonna see if I can find me a wench while I'm here."

"Well, I wish you all the luck finding that pretend girlfriend."

"Even if it's real, it's only in your mind!" Wenk's connection was cut.

"And he wonders why he doesn't have a real one."

Looking up, Joseph saw the last of the passengers leaving. He made his way down the aisle. Once outside the vehicle, he turned to the side, where luggage had been slid onto the sidewalk. Bags were being claimed with military precision.

"The guy probably alphabetized them by name," Joseph said to himself. To test his theory, he walked one-third of the way down the bus to find his red and blue rolling suitcase waiting for him. "Gotta love the military, at least at times."

As Joseph stuck out his hand, a handle extended from the bag to meet it. Bypassing the line of people going into the processing center, he headed toward a gate along the right side of the building. It was white and made of wood in a style intended to mimic the picket fences people used to put around their homes. Once there, he flashed his interface at the port on the gate. A voice sounded.

"You too good to go through the center, Gint?" a woman's voice teased.

"Yes, I am. I run this place, don't you know?"

Laughter answered. "And what would the commander say about that?"

"He'd agree with me, if he was honest. Now, since I have been through orientation three times before, how about you let me through nicely?"

"According to procedure, you are supposed to go through orientation every time you come on base." The woman's voice took the tone of a mother talking to her kid.

"You want me to quote the whole speech to you? I could, you know." Joseph tapped his foot, though he knew the woman couldn't see it. After a few seconds, he added, "I brought chocolate."

The gate clicked softly. Joseph pushed his way through to the other side, letting the gate swing back on its own.

A dark-skinned lady in her mid-forties appeared on his interface. "Is it German?"

"Bite your tongue! It's Dutch."

"Ooh, even better." The woman licked her upper lip.

"I'll put it in your mail box."

"Thanks, sweetie. I'll mark you down after everyone else is checked in."

"Won't want to look suspicious, now, would we?" Joseph smiled.

"Not when there's chocolate involved," the woman said in a serious voice before disconnecting.

Deciding to stretch his legs after the bus ride, Joseph walked past the Personal Conveyance Automatons, or PCAs, and took the path toward the tallest building. The sun was out and a small breeze, for South Dakota, was blowing, so the walk was pleasant. All it missed was a salt tang and it would have been like walking around his parents' house in the Netherlands. Revelry was interrupted by the interface.

"Receive," Joseph said.

"Joe!" Mercedes's face appeared in the interface. She was also twenty-five and had brown hair that curled around her head, stopping just above her shoulders. Her violently green eyes were appropriate for a biologist, though she had the pointed chin and cheekbones of a goddess, a gift from her super-model mother.

"Hey, Merc." A smile was forced onto Joseph's face by Mercedes's contagious smile.

"Welcome back! Got tired of gallivanting around Europe finally?" Mercedes tried to look serious, but was too happy to succeed. "I always wanted to do that, gallivant around Europe for a month."

"You can gallivant around Europe anytime you want. They still let Americans in, barely," Joseph teased back.

"I was never invited." A small amount of faked hurt crossed Mercedes's face.

"If you're waiting for the Common European Concern to invite you, don't bother. They can barely find their ass in the dark these days."

"I meant for someone I know who's from there."

Joseph laughed. "If I brought a female home with me, my mother would die of shock. And I love my mother, so I'd never do that to her."

Mercedes frowned in response, sticking out her lip for an instant.

"So how's the family?"

"Fine." Joseph nodded at a few people as he walked. "Dad's still manually working the farm, though I am pretty sure Mom starts up those prototypes we sent her when he's not looking. The place looked pretty good for as slow as he's getting."

"Did you see your brother?"

"The musician? He wasn't scrounging free room and board from Mom and Dad, so I assume he's doing fine."

"You went all the way to Europe and didn't talk to him?"

Joseph checked the traffic on a street before crossing. "You mean mister 'I don't believe in interfaces'? No way to contact him. I think he does it on purpose so he doesn't have a horde of angry boyfriends on his tail seeking revenge."

"Opposite of you in every way," Mercedes said as she rolled her eyes. "I find it hard to believe your parents somehow ended up with one particle physicist and one musician."

"Actually, what we do is not that dissimilar, just different applications of vibrating media and frequency excitation. It just looks totally opposite."

"If you say so. Where you at?"

"Just approaching MASB now." He pronounced it 'mass B', a name they had given the residence that stood for Minimal Architectural Support Building. It wasn't totally devoid of style, but did not appear to have had much effort applied.

"Hey, stop by after you drop off your stuff. I fixed the software for your laser so it doesn't think a turd is a bug."

"Particle beam," Joseph corrected, "and I need to stop for something to eat first."

"I forgot I was talking to mister sensitive stomach." Mercedes rolled her eyes again.

"Mach three and stomach contents do not mix, I don't care what anyone says. Besides, have you seen what they serve you on those flights?" Joseph's head shook as he turned off the walkway onto the walkway to his building.

"No, no one has ever taken me to Europe. Weren't you listening before?" Mercedes's eyebrows went up in emphasis.

"I'll talk to Wenk about that for you," Joseph said with a wink.

"Don't do me any favors," Mercedes huffed before disconnecting. Joseph shrugged as the front door opened in time for him to enter without losing step. Once in, he took a right turn. Along the wall were old-fashioned cubby holes with names below them. Joseph took a large candy bar out of his pack and placed it in the appropriate slot.

"The things I do for an efficient return," Joseph muttered to himself.

"You got one of those for me?" a male voice said behind him. Turning, Joseph found that the voice belonged to a thin man in his early twenties, dressed in an unnecessarily neat private's uniform.

"And why would I buy you chocolate, Craig?" Joseph shrugged before turning to the lift.

"A guy can dream, you know," Craig called out.

"I'd hate to leave you without any dreams," Joseph said over his shoulder as he walked away.

"Heart-breaker!" Craig said with mild accusation.

The greenhouse smelled of growing plants and flowers. Joseph was amazed every time he walked in how Mercedes could keep some type of flower in bloom at all times. The interior was also more humid than the outside. The plants were 'stacked' with the shade-tolerant ones at the bottom and the sun-hungry ones hanging above. Drains from the higher stacks supplied their excess water to the next level down, adding to the humidity. Mercedes waved from across the plants, barely visible behind a row of vines. It was as much of a greeting that anyone received from her while she was working, so Joseph walked in her direction. She met him on the near side of the pallet.

"Where's my tulip?" she asked right off.

"Your tulip?" Joseph's face crinkled with confusion.

"You went to Holland and didn't bring me back a tulip?"

"You have half a greenhouse of flowers. Why bring you one?"

"It's not the same as getting one." Mercedes tilted her head down and stared at Joseph through the top of her eyes. "I can't believe I have to explain that."

"Everyone else wants chocolate and you want flowers." Joseph spread his hands.

"Chocolate works, too, don't you know?" She raised an eyebrow.

"I thought you wanted to talk about software. I left the chocolate back at my apartment."

"Scientist! No social graces." Hitting Joseph in the shoulder with a dirty glove, Mercedes turned. "It's over here."

Joseph shrugged to himself and followed through the rows of plants to a dense stand of bush beans. The plants were thick enough that he couldn't see the soil underneath them.

"Let's not start somewhere easy," Joseph mumbled.

"When we perfect this stacking system of plants, there won't be room for people to get between rows or individual plants to see if your robots are doing their job. So, yeah, we start here."

"And how are we supposed to know if they're working?"

"I'll know, leave that to me." Mercedes gave her head one shake as she made the statement.

"And," Joseph added, "it's not my robot, it's Wenk's. It's my spaser."

"Spaser?" Mercedes turned toward Joseph with the question.

"Synchronous Particle Amplification and Stimulation Energy Ray."

"Really? You thought that one up, didn't you?" Mercedes crossed her arms in front of her and shifted her weight to one foot.

"You don't like it?"

"Sounds like you really wanted to call it a spaser." She turned back to the plants with the comment.

"Maybe," Joseph said in a non-committal fashion.

Mercedes pulled back some plants. "There. See it hanging on the stem?"

"Ah, it's so cute!" The robot was the size of a large beetle and held a near resemblance to it, with six legs, sensors on the front-top, and the spaser protruding from where the mouth would have been.

Mercedes rolled her eyes. "I've released some pests of various sizes into the plants right after I talked to you. Ready to turn it on?"

"Sure! Let it rip!"

"Computer," Mercedes said into her wrist, "turn on Pest Elimination Robot number one, please."

"I'd be happy to, Mercedes."

"I'll never understand why you turned on the personality program for that thing," Joseph said with a little disgust.

"Someone else around here has to have one," came the flippant reply.

Two small red lights appeared on the top front of the robot. The sensor discs turned back and forth several times in unison and then out of sync. The robot moved along the plant toward the leaves.

"Exactly why do you guys insist on making this thing look like a real bug?" Mercedes asked.

"Because we can."

"Boys and their toys." She shook her head as she said it.

The spaser fired, aimed under a leaf.

"What'd it hit?" Joseph asked.

Mercedes bent down to look under the leaf as the spaser fired again. "Aphids."

"Any leaf damage?"

"Doesn't look like it, but I'll get a better look later."

"Neat and clean." There was a pause as he waited for Mercedes to straighten back up. "You joining us at the pub later?"

"That an invitation?" Mercedes asked with a twinkle in her eye.

"Didn't know you needed one."

"Always nice, you know." Mercedes raised an eyebrow.

"Sure, see you there." Joseph gave her a quick nod before turning and leaving. "What's up with her?" Joseph asked himself as he left the greenhouse.

Chapter Two
The Spark

The transparent displays were covered in data collected the night before. Joseph, Wenk, and Mercedes took turns examining and re-arranging the data. Probabilities and percents were prevalent.

"What's this?" Wenk asked.

"Our bug ran out of power," Joseph said almost under his breath.

"But it had, what, twenty-four kills before then? Not bad." Wenk tried to sound convincing.

"Yeah, it made it a whole six feet before checking out," Joseph replied with a huff. "It needs more power. At this rate, it will take a decade to clear an acre."

"You're expecting a lot from one bug," Mercedes interjected. "A predatory insect would have killed a lot fewer."

"And exactly what are we supposed to do when all our bugs run out of power? Send people out to find them and replace their batteries?"

"We need to be able to send them power from a central location," Wenk said, arms crossed and leaning back on one leg. "I still like our power carrier idea."

"And our simulations show they spend all their time going back and forth from the power carrier. Same with a power line run through the crops, except that the plants also tend to overgrow it and block the bugs from getting power. Plus it would mean a lot more hardware. We need a long-term solution. Figure out how we can send power into the plants without frying them and we got it made." Joseph slapped his head. "Oh, wait, we've been trying to do that for what, two years now?"

"You geeks will figure it out," Mercedes said with a half-smirk.

"You geeks?" Joseph replied.

"Yeah, you geeks. I'm a green thumb."

"Hey, Joseph!" a voice called from across the building. "Your dad's on the news."

"So? What else is new?" Joseph shouted back with a shrug.

"Computer, show the news," Mercedes said. A portion of the screen switched to a view of a large number of people standing outside a stone building. "It's your dad, you've got to watch."

"Not like I haven't seen it before," Joseph scoffed.

"That's the European Council Building, isn't it?" Wenk asked.

"Yeah, Dad said something about them wanting to talk to him." Joseph huffed. "I don't know why they bother. He hates going. They never did buy his 'I'm just a simple farmer' routine, which I think makes him mad."

"I would think it would be an honor to be asked to counsel the Common European Concern," Mercedes added.

"Dad thinks they mostly ask him there to score political points. You know, seen with the great alien whisperer." Joseph wiggled his eyes.

"Shh," Wenk said with a wave at the others.

As Arhus Gint left the building, news crews crowded close.

"Mr. Gint!" more than one shouted. "Can you tell us what the Concern asked you about?"

"Same old stuff," Arhus replied without enthusiasm. He stood like a man waiting for the rain to stop.

"He looks good for nearly sixty," Mercedes said. "Must be all that time out in the sun."

"Can you give us any details?" asked a news 'face' from the front of the crowd.

"I'll let the politicians fill you in on details. Now, if you don't mind, I'd like to go home." Arhus stared at the crowd as if daring them not to move.

"Cantankerous as always," Joseph stated.

"*Arhus Gint!*" A female voice dominated the sound from the scene. The news crews parted to an older lady about four meters from their previous center of attention. "*You ruined my life! You* are the reason I couldn't get on that *ship!*"

Arhus's head turned and tilted downward slightly. "Biel?"

"Yes! Of course it's me! It's still me, here, on Earth, not where I'm supposed to be! *You* kept me here. *You* prevented me from getting on that ship!" The woman pointed with her left hand, shouting with all her being at Arhus as she did so. News 'eyes' moved to get a better view of both parties. The news spokespersons, or 'faces,' stood, their heads tennis-matching between the two participants.

"You would have been killed. I saved your life!" Arhus shot back, scowling.

"You *ruined* my life. You condemned me to a life of nothing, of meaninglessness!"

"Humph. As always, blaming someone else for your problems." Arhus's head came up in a self-assured manner.

"This looks bad," Mercedes said quietly.

"Just some quack," Wenk answered.

"GOD WILL PUNISH YOU!" Biel screamed, pulling a pistol from her clothing with her right hand and pointing it at Arhus. Two shots sounded, accompanied by two holes in Arhus's chest. He crumpled to the ground as panic exploded onto the scene.

"What the..." Joseph stared, open-mouthed. Shock or surprise left people at the scene and those watching from across the world speechless, motionless, and their minds numbed into inaction. Mouths and eyes froze open and breath was forgotten. As they watched, security tackled the woman. She did not resist, but kept screaming.

"God will return and reward me! You are a heretic! All heretics will die!"

A man pushed his way through the crowd. Intercepted by security, a few unheard words were enough for them to let the man pass. Kneeling, the man pulled back Arhus's shirt to look underneath. Arhus made no response to the man, eyes staring up. Someone handed the man a cloth, possibly a shirt, and he pressed it to Arhus's chest, but even on the vid, it appeared half-hearted. When a security officer put his head near the man, a shake was the only response.

Dragged with her feet flailing, Biel was removed from the scene, soon replaced by paramedics in white. The man who had been pressing the cloth to Arhus's chest gave way, but his head was drooped and his steps slow. Two more paramedics carried a body treatment bag and Arhus was slid into it, but Arhus's face never changed. It wasn't until he was moved that those who watched could see the large pool of blood that had been beneath him. In silence, everyone watched for the short time the paramedics worked on their subject before the bag was sealed all the way above Arhus's head.

The sealing of the body bag released the reactions from the crowd. Some still stared, open-mouthed. Others cried individually or with arms around another. Shouts of anguish and rants of anger could be heard while a few just shook their heads and walked away, dejected. News 'faces,' themselves visibly shaken, talked into cameras or tried to interview people at the scene. Talk brought tears. By this time, the whole European Concern council was outside and added their reactions to the crowd, as mixed as those from the crowd. Only two security personnel remained unemotional, their job coming first as they removed the body and tried to preserve the scene.

"Damn!" came from Wenk's mouth.

"Joe?" Mercedes said, turning toward him and lightly touching his arm. "I'm so sorry. Are you…"

More security rushed onto the scene, surrounding Arhus's body and clearing away the news crews against their protests. Joseph remained motionless.

"Joe?" Mercedes continued, squeezing his arm a little tighter. "Are you okay? I mean, if you're not, I understand." The motion of Mercedes's slight chin rise was accompanied by wider eyes. "You need to call your mother."

With a blank look, Joseph tapped his interface. "Call Mom."

The wait was short. "The connection is busy," the interface replied.

"Wow, that was fast." Wenk did a combination of surprised look and eye-roll. "Ask for priority!"

"Priority message," Joseph echoed with urgency.

"I am sorry, no connection is available," the interface said, not knowing the cruelty of the reply.

"Half the people in the world must be trying to talk to her right now." Shaking his head, Joseph canceled the request. "Just like it's always been."

"Joe. I... I really don't know what to say. Please, let's go to your apartment, or mine, or Wenk's, if you want. You need time to grieve and deal with all this..." Mercedes squeezed Joseph's arm with both hands, but then all but let loose.

"I need to be alone." Joseph slipped out of Mercedes's hands and walked toward the other end of the greenhouse. At first, he appeared to have no destination in sight, barely avoiding the pallets of plants, but gradually, he headed toward the workshop at the end of the greenhouse.

"Should I follow him?" Mercedes asked in a weak voice.

"No, let's just let him go for now. Hell of a thing to have to watch." Their eyes tracked Joseph as he entered the workroom.

"I'm worried about him," Mercedes said, looking across the greenhouse instead of at Wenk. "He shouldn't be alone. Not that I think he'd do something, I just mean that no one should be alone at a time like this."

"Just give him time to process," Wenk replied. "He's spent a lot of his life by himself, much of it by choice."

"I never thought he was *that* withdrawn."

"I wouldn't call it withdrawn, exactly. He forces himself to be social, but most of it is an act." Wenk let out a sigh.

"What?" This time, Mercedes turned to look at him.

"He has to work at being social. It turns into an act when others are around. You know, being what others expect you to be. I think it comes from having a famous dad."

A crash of metal parts came from the workroom, causing Mercedes to jump.

"Should I check?" she said without looking at Wenk.

"Naw, most things in there are pretty sturdy and we can fix them even if he does break something." Wenk received a fist to the arm for the comment. Another crash came from the workroom. "Or replace it."

"I was worried about Joe, not your equipment, stupid."

Wenk rubbed his arm. "He's pretty sturdy, too."

"So you're telling me that he's not really himself when he is around us?" The statement appeared to make her worry.

"He's more like himself around us than anyone else. Once, in college, he didn't talk to anyone for days. He didn't avoid them, he just didn't seem to have any need to talk to them. When people started to think him strange, he changed the way he acted. Did you know some evenings, he just sits out in the back forty, staring up at space?"

"No, but I always wondered where he disappeared to. I mean, it's an army base with nowhere else to go. I guess I just assumed..." A sheepish look covered Mercedes's face.

"That he was sneaking off with someone?" Wenk smiled.

"Something like that," Mercedes said, staring at the ground as if she didn't dare look him in the eye.

Wenk laughed. "It's more like he has to balance his time being social with being alone. What makes him a good scientist, I guess."

"I just wish I could do something for him." It was Mercedes' turn to sigh.

"The best thing we can do is leave him alone and not hover. He'll come to us when he is ready."

"I guess." They turned toward the greenhouse exit. "At least he just got to see his dad. It had been almost a year, right?"

"Yeah. Says he's too busy to go more often, for that and lots of things."

"That's just an excuse," she said dismissively.

"Maybe, but he seems to have more urgency than the rest of us."

"Urgency? About what?"

"Who knows? The aliens coming back? I'm not sure even he knows." Wenk opened the door and held it while Mercedes walked out, looking over her shoulder at the workroom door.

Joseph walked out the back door of the workroom into the breeze. The air felt good, like it was going somewhere and would take him with it. Letting his feet decide where to go, Joseph hung his head, barely noticing where he was. The only time he noticed was when he realized he was standing in the middle of a road and decided that was a bad idea. The shock brought other parts of his surrounding to his awareness.

Sound was the first. The wind brought the sound of an argument that was too far to hear the words. His feet chose that direction to move. It took a while for him to notice that he was headed toward the front gate.

When he got close enough, Joseph could see a small crowd of people near the gate making the noise. He estimated fifteen to twenty people, but they were packed tightly together, making them hard to count. They did not seem to have a chant or common statement, placing their shouts in competition which each other.

"Very inefficient," Joseph said with a frown as he walked.

As he drew close, he noted that the shouting crowd had the same demeanor and dress as the protesters he had seen yesterday, only there was a lot more of them. Half a dozen guards stood inside the fence, rifles held in both hands across their chests, staring down the protesters who were bold enough to rattle the fence. One of the guards turned his direction when he was within five feet.

"Sir," the guard said, taking a step toward Joseph, "you shouldn't be here."

"What the heck is going on?" Joseph craned his neck to look around the guard.

"They suddenly got excited. I think it was the shooting. Now, if you'd be good enough to move away from this area…"

"One heretic down! The rest of you next!" came a shout from behind the guard.

"That's your solution, just shoot everyone?" Joseph shouted back, stepping around the guard.

"Sir, don't speak to them…" The guard tried to move in front of Joseph.

"That's what happens to blasphemers!" the man shouted back.

"And somehow a simple farmer was offending God? How pitiful is your god, anyway?" Joseph shouted back, his face starting to turn red.

"Sir, I must insist!" The guard grabbed Joseph by one arm.

"He spoke to God and lied! He deserved to die. He was a heretic!"

"He was my father!" Joseph tried to shrug off the guard as he shouted as loud as possible and shook his fist at the man.

"Shit," came softly from the guard next to Joseph. The man swung his rifle around his shoulder and grabbed Joseph with both hands. "Mr. Gint, it is not a good idea for you to be here. I will be removing you from here now!"

"It's the heretic's son," one of the crowd said, slightly softer than a shout.

As Joseph's view was taken up by the face of the now determined guard, he heard one or maybe two loud bangs. The guard was driven into Joseph, knocking him to the ground and landing on top of him. Joseph's head hit the road hard enough to bring stars into view. The impact of guard's body made his head come back up, at least as far as it could with a soldier carrying twenty pounds of body armor and equipment.

Sirens wailed. As his vision cleared, Joseph heard more bangs and the sound of pulsation rifles, fewer of the latter than the former. The guard on top of him groaned.

"Shotguns," Joseph told himself. "Get your head in the game, Gint, it sounds like your team is losing."

Reaching down along the the body on top of him, Joseph felt around until his hand found a pistol grip. The first tug resulted in no movement of the weapon. Cursing himself, Joseph found the latch and released the weapon. Groaning, the guard on top of him moved, landing an elbow into Joseph's face.

"Not helping," Joseph said to the man as he pushed him off in the direction of the weapons fire. Rolling to his side, Joseph pointed the weapon over the man's body toward the crowd and pulled the trigger.

Nothing happened.

"Damn individually activated weapons." Joseph grabbed the soldier's left hand and brought it to the man's face. "Say emergency activation mode."

A few incoherent words were the only thing heard from the man's lips. The ground just behind Joseph spat up debris, mostly away from him.

"Soldier! Say emergency activation mode. That's an order."

"Emergency activation mode," came rolling out of the man's lips with slow speed. Joseph heard the weapon whine as he felt another hit on the opposite of the guard push both of their bodies.

Holding himself up with his elbow, Joseph swung the pistol over the guard, pointed it at a man in front cocking his shotgun, and pulled the trigger. The green light went straight to the man, the resulting electrical shock creating a black spot in the middle of his chest. He didn't watch the man's reaction before pointing the gun at another armed assailant and pulling the trigger.

His fire drew attention. Seeing several shotguns swinging his direction, Joseph ducked back down behind the guard. Two quick bangs were followed by a third.

"I'm really sorry about that," he said in the guard's direction, "but you're the one wearing body armor I figure your armor can take it."

As he looked up, Joseph noted four drones fly overhead toward the crowd outside the fence. The *zit* of stunners followed in rapid succession. Shouts of dismay now came from the crowd and he started to hear the sounds of retreat. The noise of the drones' engines followed the crowd and the *zit* of their stunners could be heard, along with a few shotgun blasts and rings of metal.

Joseph let his head and arm fall to the ground. Looking toward the base, he saw several vehicles arrive on either side of the gate. He closed his eyes and let go of the weapon.

"Hurrah, the cavalry has arrived. Literally."

Chapter Three
Explain Yourself

The room was sparse and the bed was uncomfortable, or maybe Joseph just hurt too much. The room only had one door. A chair had been placed next to the bed. A well-built, older man in military uniform occupied it.

"You don't look happy to see me," Joseph said with a weak smile.

Commander Michael James Bennett wore a hard stare as he sat in the chair. It clearly was not having its desired effect on Joseph, because the man looked unhappy. Shifting on the bed, Joseph searched for a more comfortable spot, which never seemed to present itself. The pain reliever was starting to take effect but was taking its time.

"What the hell did you think you were doing?" the commander asked with a scowl.

"Going for a walk?"

"I don't want any of your lip!" A finger was pointed at Joseph's face. "Don't think I don't know about your fudging the rules when you see fit. Do you think regulations don't apply to you, Mr. Gint?"

"It's not my fault. I'm a second child, it's kind of our thing." Joseph gave the man a pout.

Bennett glared and shook his head. "I should throw you off the base right now. I can't until the investigation is complete, but I can put you into a cell and let you rot until it's finished."

"Won't that assume I am guilty of something before a trial? I'm sure the Constitution has something to say about that. Besides, I haven't been released by the doctor yet." Joseph looked around the room. "The doctor who seems to be conveniently missing."

"That mouth of yours is going to land you in big trouble one day, mister." Bennett's finger pointed at Joseph and did not waver. "And I would be more than happy to be there when it does!"

A knock came from the door. Joseph's head came up with a start.

"Enter," Bennett said, turning to the door only after saying it.

Captain Fred Allin, Chief of Research and Development, entered the room. She was a stocky woman who looked like she could wrestle a bear and win. She had a square face with a small nose and brown hair cut very short. In addition to her tough exterior, she had a quick mind, evidenced at work as her eyes darted around the room, taking in every detail. Joseph smiled in relief at the sight of her.

"Commander," Allin said easily. "How's my particle physicist?"

"Captain," Bennett said, ignoring the question, "does Mr. Gint normally go wandering around the base and provoking protesters?" He raised one eyebrow.

"Mr. Gint is doing several research projects. I don't lock him in a lab." Allin's voice was firm, but not forceful. She took several steps into the room, ending up leaning her back against the wall across from the foot of the bed.

"Maybe you should rethink locking him up." Bennett turned back to Joseph.

"I want to know what armed locals were doing at our gate." Allin stared at the commander from over her crossed arms.

"We were told to give the locals wide leeway." Bennett stood and faced Allin, crossing his arms. "Mr. Gint doesn't seem to know better than to stir up the locals."

"From what I hear, the locals were already stirred up. Plus, they took the first shots. Was Mr. Gint carrying a weapon when he approached the gate?" Allin asked with a small amount of amusement in her voice and a tilted head. A hint of a smile came and went quickly.

"No, he was not." Bennett took a breath and let it out.

"Then I don't see a problem with his behavior." An exaggerated puzzled expression crept onto Allin's face.

"He shouldn't have been there. He should know better!"

"Do you really think he had the presence of mind to consider that after seeing his father gunned down?" Allin replied, sharpness not totally hidden in her voice. The comment came with a quick look to Joseph, telling him to keep his mouth shut. "And maybe the base should have made sure Mr. Gint was attended to after such a traumatic event. Sounds like a fault of the system, if you ask me." Allin managed to keep a calm expression.

"You're defending him?" Bennett's head came back.

"He's my researcher. It's my job." Allin gave him a smile. "Commander, it is clear that Mr. Gint and the guards were attacked by the protesters, not the other way around. Do you have any records from surveillance that shows otherwise?"

"They do not contradict Mr. Gint's story."

"So unless you have other evidence, I do not see a reason to accuse Mr. Gint of anything." It was Allin's turn to glare.

"Captain Allin," Bennett said while standing, "would you please join me in another room for a minute?"

"Certainly, sir."

Bennett and Allin exited the room. As they did, Joseph saw Mercedes standing outside the door, talking to the guard.

"I am sorry," the guard was saying, "no one is allowed to talk to Mr. Gint."

"I have been here for twenty minutes and all sorts of people have been going in and out of that room, so your statement doesn't seem to be true." Mercedes was actually tapping her foot at the woman.

"Those are authorized personnel."

"And what about the closest thing he has to family here? Wouldn't that be authorized personnel?"

The woman's head jerked back slightly. "You're not his family."

"I said the closest thing he has. What's happened to your compassion? This man has been traumatized! He needs some comforting and it doesn't sound like Bennett gave him any."

Mercedes glared while the woman thought. After a few moments, she spoke.

"Fine, you can go in."

Mercedes watched the door close and slid onto the vacant chair in a hurried movement.

"Are you all right?" She squeezed Joseph's arm and leaned forward, trying to look into his eyes. He didn't face her.

"Yeah, I'm fine. Sore, but the medicine is finally kicking in." Joseph patted Mercedes's hands lightly a couple of times and then stopped. The squeezing continued.

"Look, I know you just watched your dad get killed, so…"

"I don't want to talk about it."

"Did you ever get in contact with your mother?"

"Yes, I eventually got through, though I had to convince a bodyguard I was who I said I was and wait in line behind a couple of heads of state. Unbelievable."

Mercedes was frozen for a second, staring with wide eyes, but found her voice. "It's good to talk about these things, to get them out."

"I said I didn't want to talk about it." Turning his head, Joseph looked into Mercedes's eyes, a hardness in them she had never seen before. "I don't ever want to talk about it."

"But," Mercedes stuttered, "I don't want you doing stupid things because of your grief."

Huffing, Joseph turned away from Mercedes. "You mean like confronting the protesters?"

"Yes!" Mercedes' arms made wide circles. "What the hell were you doing? What were you thinking, going out there?"

"I wasn't thinking, at least about what was happening out there. I heard a noise and I went to check it out." Joseph gave a small shrug, but his gaze was far off out the window.

"When I heard what happened, I went out of my mind!" Clamping her mouth shut, it only took a few seconds for Mercedes to pull back and lower her eyes. Softer, she added, "I'm sorry, I know what you were thinking about. I mean, damn, what you just witnessed would shock anyone into a stupor. I'm sorry. I was already worried about you and then… this happens. You don't have any body armor on! You could have been killed." A tear started to form in her eye.

Joseph patted her hand again, looking down at it. "I'm fine. The guards protected me. How is the guard, by the way? I feel kind of guilty using him as a shield when he was still alive." For his assurances, Joseph's voice sounded strained and forced. His face was stone.

"He'll recover. Lots of bruises and a few stray pellets in him, but it could have been a lot worse." Mercedes appeared to deflate a little.

"They're called shot." Joseph grinned at her.

"Who cares! Oh, why do you have to be so stupid all the time!" Mercedes huffed at him, pleading in her eyes.

Joseph started to talk, but then stopped. He looked up and then bowed his head, letting it hang over his hands. Mercedes could feel the tension in the air, but managed to hold her tongue for a few seconds. When Joseph didn't speak, she let it loose.

"Talk to me! Damn, by now I'd think you'd know I'm on your side, right? Just talk to me, for real, for once. You don't have to keep things bottled up all the time. It's not like I'm going to make fun of you or something. Not me! Don't you know that?" Slower, she added, "People need to talk about these things. It's part of the healing process." Mercedes's breath came harder than normal. She stared at Joseph as she waited.

Joseph raised his head and looked at her. She couldn't read his mind in his eyes. She fidgeted slightly and waited, holding onto his gaze. Silence took the room, but then she saw a shift in Joseph. He sighed and looked down without talking.

"Look, you need to process your dad's death, I know, and I don't want to pressure you with other things. I might not know how to help you get through this like a professional, but I am here and willing to try. At least you could talk to me about whatever it is you're going through." She let up on Joseph's arm some, surprised how hard she was squeezing it.

"It's not what you think," Joseph said softly.

"What does that mean?"

"Dad's death is… shocking… but he's always been in danger." Joseph looked at the ceiling. "It's not like we didn't know it could happen, which is why Mother hated him going to the Concern when they called. There's always been those who hated him. But what happened could be just the start." Joseph turned back to Mercedes and held her eyes.

"This might sound like it has nothing to do with Dad's death, but

I think it does. In fact, I am convinced it does. You may not have bothered to pay attention, but these religious fanatics that call themselves Puritans are slowly taking over, in this country and around the world. The same type of people who I am sure are involved with Dad's death, the bastards. Forty percent of the world now identifies with one of the alien-worshipping religions. The last election, President Tyler barely won a majority. Every year, their numbers grow. They are taking over local governments. They're taking over everything. What happens when we have a Puritan president in charge of the military?" Joseph's voice rose in volume and force during the whole speech.

Mercedes's eyes went wide and then squinted, her head turning. "Surely it can't be that bad. I mean, people have been religious before."

"Not like this, at least since before the Enlightenment." Joseph shook his head. "Have you even read any of their literature?"

"No," Mercedes said with a smaller shake of her head. "Can't say I've bothered."

"Most people haven't." Joseph's eyes got more intense. "They're calling for an end to scientific research, an abandonment of all weapons, and a return to an agrarian society."

"Would that be so bad?" Mercedes' expression was confused. "I mean, it sounds nice."

Joseph tilted his head to the right. "Mercedes, they are coming for us, eventually. To them the military is a group of alien-haters in control of all the weapons. Current and future. What do you think the army is doing at this base?"

"I'm doing agricultural research: intensive farming techniques. You're helping me, remember." The look on Mercedes's face showed she wasn't anxious to know the rest.

"You know killing bugs and weeds aren't the only applications of the particle projectors I am working on, right?" He paused for a second. "Think about where we are at."

"We're on the site of the alien attack almost three decades ago." It came out rote with a roll of her eyes. "So? I don't think anyone else wanted the land besides the army. I was scared myself to come here at first."

Joseph leaned in closer and lowered his voice. "Add to that the fact that some of the material the aliens used for the wings of their fighting units survived the blast and what does that tell you?"

Mercedes drew back slowly, her eyes darting about for a moment. As she drew back toward Joseph, her mouth worked some before sound came out.

"We're developing weapons?"

"Of course we are. It's what the army does."

"To use against other nations?" A small shiver went through her body.

Joseph breathed in and out quickly and moved his arm from under Mercedes's hands to grab a hold of hers. "To use against the aliens when they return."

"Really?" Mercedes's eyes darted around Joseph's face. "How close are we?"

After a frown, Joseph said, "We're doing well enough, for now, but we have a ways to go."

The comment caused Mercedes's mind to go into overdrive. She appeared to have trouble concentrating on anything and her head wandered around a little. When her attention came back to Joseph, it was serious.

"I bet the Puritans wouldn't be very happy about that."

"And if we had a Puritan president?" It was Joseph's turn to raise an eyebrow.

"Okay." Mercedes settled back into her seat. "I think I am starting to understand. But shouldn't the government be paying attention to what's going on?"

"Because the American government is historically so quick to respond to any threat until it gets its nose broken?" Joseph let out a single laugh. "Think about history. When has it ever been proactive?"

"I'm not going to claim to be a history expert, but I think I see your point." Mercedes turned her head and lowered her brow. "We tend to react a whole lot more than act. So what does this have to do with your dad's death?"

Joseph looked away. "I can't prove anything. Yes, his death could be clouding my thinking today, but I've been thinking about this for years."

"Those people out there had nothing to do with your dad's death, they couldn't have." Mercedes's voice was emphatic once more and she leaned forward.

"Really? Maybe not them in particular, but the Puritan movement as a whole, yes. Look at the way they responded to the news. Doesn't that seem a little suspicious? A little planned?"

The question caused Mercedes to think for a moment. "You're proposing some kind of conspiracy theory? Be serious." Mercedes' voice or face did not hold conviction.

Joseph's face was serious when he looked back. "Here's a few facts you might not know. Even my dad didn't know he was going to see the Concern until the day before I left. How did that woman know he was going to be there? And do you know how difficult it is to get a pistol in Europe? That was a slug thrower, the old fashioned kind, with smokeless powder. The only people that have those are criminals and highly regulated collectors. So, am I supposed to believe that some old flame of my dad just happened to show up in the right place at the right time with an illegal, hard to find gun that doesn't register on security devices, to kill my dad all on her own? Defeating all the security that they give him on a regular basis? I don't think so."

"Isn't that how these things usually happen? At least, that's what they told us in school."

"Not anymore." Joseph shook his head. "We have bird-sized surveillance drones driven by specialized AI programs. I've seen some of these systems. Trust me, someone on the inside had to let her get that close. Plus, the way she acted: only drawing the weapon at the last instant, keeping it hidden in an accessible location, standing correctly. She had to have coaching."

"How does that mean the people outside are in on it?" Mercedes's voice was emphatic.

"Think about the timing. I might not have been in the smartest place at the smartest time, but they did bring weapons and they did shoot first. What are people going to conclude? It's going to sound an awful lot like a conspiracy."

"Which the government sure won't like." Mercedes shook her head with the comment.

"True, but that's how people are going to see it."

"And you don't feel at least a little responsible for what happened?"

"For being there? For reacting like a normal human being? Why would I?" Joseph let out a heavy sigh, his whole body sagging. "Besides, what happens next is the important thing."

"Such as?" Mercedes's eyebrows went up.

"Will the Puritans feel guilty and become more accommodating, more tolerant of others? I doubt it. How will the non-Puritan communities react? Is there pent-up fear or anger out there? Or will the Puritans assume the cat is out of the bag and do who knows what?" Joseph's hands waved with his talking.

"Some of that sounds scary, and depressing."

"If I'm wrong, we're all the better for it. But we only have three years until the next presidential election and we need to do something before the floor falls out from under us."

"I sure hope it's not that bad." Mercedes visibly gulped as she again reached for Joseph's arm, seeking support instead of giving it.

The door handle turned and the door opened. Mercedes jumped in her seat, withdrawing her hands and blushing slightly. Joseph turned as Captain Allin filled the doorway.

"You can go now, Mr. Gint, but you'll be watched for your own safety, so I'd behave if I were you." Her eyes told him she would be watching too.

"I think that would be best for everyone," Joseph said in a humble voice as he swung his feet over the side.

"Music to my ears. Ms. Stakes, red is a good color on you." Allin turned without cracking a smile as she returned the way she had come.

"That was embarrassing," Mercedes said quietly after Allin had left.

"Why?" Joseph asked.

Chapter Four
Planning and Preparation

The sound of leather soles pounding on the floor filled the room as Garo entered the office to find Valesco pacing across the seamless white marble floor. The six-foot, three-inch man frowned, his hands held up to his chin, fingertip to fingertip, as he measured the room with his footsteps. Garo stayed near the door, out of the way, in deference to his boss. Not only his height, but the large shoulders and thin waist clearly told of the man's physical power. Garo had been trained by the military, but still held no desire to wrestle the man. After a few minutes, he talked.

"You called for me?"

The question broke Valesco's meditation. The green eyes and full eyebrows looked at Garo.

"We need to move up the time-table."

"To when?"

"Now."

"I will pass the word." Garo gave a small head bow, eyes mostly closed. "Which targets do you want to start with? Easy or hard?"

"Easy." Valesco started pacing again, but his arms flew free this time. "Let's start with Reverend Crystal. Their church is the most vulnerable to a takeover and it will give us momentum. Then we can concentrate on the Church of the Eternal Light and those quacks in Minneapolis. They're relatively small, but a major church in the area. Plus, they control several politicians." Valesco's head wagged back and forth, his eyes wandering as it did.

Garo watched and let the man pace in front of the lead crystal table before asking the next question. "Public or private?"

"Public!" Valesco turned his head toward Garo. "It must look like a reprisal for the Gint murder."

"Some of the advisers still think it will give the heretics a rallying cry. Death of their hero and all that."

"So much the better." A dismissive wave threw the comment across the room. "The more extreme they appear, the more excuses we will have. Remember, the persecuted always come out the victors in popular opinion."

"As you say. I feel better when prepared."

Turning away as if to muse, Valesco shook his head. "The regional captains and sub-captains in each district have already been briefed as to what to expect and how to react. Security forces are already placed, as you know because you put them there. The churches, well, let them be surprised, it will make for better play in the media. But you know all of this." A broad smile grew across Valesco's face. "But I pay you to worry, so I shouldn't be surprised."

"If you are confident, I will attempt to worry less." Garo performed a short bow before leaving.

"And Garo," Valesco said as Garo started to turn. "Do we know who helped the lady kill Mr. Gint?"

"No, we have no information," Garo replied, half-turned.

"Can we get someone to talk to her?" Valesco's eyes went wide with suggestion.

"She's being held under extremely tight security." Garo fought the sweat.

"Almost as if the government had something to do with it?" Valesco raised an eyebrow.

"Or they are afraid for others to know who is involved." Relief came with the suggestion.

"Why would they fear that?" A smile creased Valesco's face.

Garo turned fully to his boss, still serious. "We have rivals who occupy more than just church offices."

"Ah," Valesco said as he cocked his head. "I am sure you are right. I failed to consider that. Keep working on it. And send a message to

Mr. Then that I would like to meet with him at his convenience."

"A Then?" Garo twisted his face in confusion.

"Yes. I think it's time we made him an offer he would be foolish to refuse."

Shishiho looked into the eyes of those seated at the table. A gaze as severe as her thin body showed coiled energy. Most of those seated at the table were younger, full of energy, waiting for direction. Shishiho's chair was positioned on a small platform a dozen centimeters higher than everyone else, forcing them to look up to her. She scanned those eyes several times before speaking.

"How will the Europeans react?" she asked.

"They will look for someone to blame," a voice replied.

"And the Americans?" Shishiho asked.

Several sets of eyes looked away to their colleagues. No one dared to answer the question. A tall man of mixed descent answered.

"They will blame the attack of Gint's son on the Puritans outside of the base. It will draw questions about the Puritans and away from the army." Mr. Smith gave his answer without any hint of nervousness or doubt.

"And do we believe the attack was coordinated with the attack in the Netherlands?" Shishiho asked the questions as if going through a list.

"We have no reason to believe that the attack wasn't precipitated by the young Mr. Gint himself," the man answered.

"Why would he do such a thing?"

"Revenge," a woman in a tight business suit answered. "For his family."

"Maybe." Shishiho took a deep breath. "If he was Japanese, I would be inclined to agree."

"He is half Chinese," the woman said.

"True. And his mother is a substantial woman. I met her once. Not someone who would allow herself to be pushed around."

Scanning the group again, Shishiho let time glide by without conversation. No one looked away or offered comment. They sat and waited.

"The real question is what the Western Pacific Conglomerate should do. Suggestions?"

"It depends on the reaction of the public and the governments…" a man started to say.

"*No*! I want to know what we are to do now!"

Many of the faces showed intimidation. Shishiho's smirk dismissed them as worthless. Mr. Nagoya, an older gentleman, did not flinch.

"Consolidate and place tighter controls on all military weapons," the older man said. "Put them in the hands of people we *know* we can trust."

"Good."

"Secure strategic resources," Nagoya continued.

"To what extent?"

"Whole towns, if needed. Weed out those that are Puritans and move them elsewhere."

"The Puritans are taught to be truthful. It will be easy under interrogation to discover where their loyalties lie," Mr. Smith added.

"Where do we move them?" Shishiho asked.

"Farms. Their leaders emphasize such a lifestyle. They will most likely go willingly." Smith smiled.

"If we start now," Nagoya took back up, "we may be able to secure whole islands and use the water as a barrier from infiltration."

Shishiho stared for a moment. "A solid plan. I place it in your hands, Mr. Nagoya. Don't disappoint me."

"Of course not." Mr. Nagoya stood and bowed deeply.

"Mr. Smith, you will be in charge of finding and moving the undesirables."

"It will be my pleasure," Smith replied with relish in his voice.

"Damn!" Joseph said, looking around the workshop the next morning, fists shaking. "They took my projectors!"

"I think they were concerned you would do something stupid," Captain Allin said as she entered.

"And when was the last time I did something that stupid? Wait, don't answer that. I don't want to know what you'd say." He stared at

Allin, who only stared back like a parent looking at a kid complaining about being in trouble. He leaned against a work bench.

"What the heck did you think you were doing?" Allin asked in an even voice.

"Hey, I didn't know they would get violent. Besides, they said some nasty things about my dad. Was I just supposed to let that go?" Joseph's tone was defensive, but his manner was calm.

"You're very good at hiding things, Mr. Gint, like your feelings." Allin shifted her weight, idly picking up a part, looking at it, and placing it back on the shelf it had occupied. "It's not healthy, in case you didn't know. Go talk to the psychologist about what happened with your dad. You'll feel better."

"I already talked to my mom," Joseph said, waving off the suggestion as he turned toward the bench and rearranged a few items. "At least my brother called. He's headed home to be with her."

"You could too, you know." Allin's voice held sympathy.

"I was just there."

"So?"

Joseph took in a deep breath and exhaled, staring at the wall. "I don't know if I trust myself with the Puritans over there. Besides, I have a feeling that other things will be happening soon. If they do, it might be a good idea for me not to be running around the globe. An even better idea would be to bring my mom here, but there's no way she'd agree to that right now."

Allin moved closer and tilted her head. Her voice was quieter. "What things?"

"I don't know." His mode changing to flippant again, Joseph went back to arranging items on the desk. "It just feels like something is going to happen, maybe lots of somethings."

"By you?"

"No." Joseph laughed. "Not me."

"Then who? And here?" Allin drew closer with every question.

"Not here and I don't know who. It's just a feeling."

"So now you're telling me you're psychic?" Allin huffed as she turned away.

"Just reading the tea leaves, that's all." Joseph's hands went up in surrender, even though he didn't turn to Allin.

"Well, I will leave you with your tea leaves. Just don't stare at them too long."

As she finished, Wenk ran through the door, heedless that someone may have been standing on the other side. "Turn on the news!"

"Computer, display the news," Allin said to the display in a serious tone.

The scene was only too familiar from the day before. Security vehicles, lights flashing, stood outside a gray stone building done in an old cathedral style. A profusion of news crews stood and talked to or hunted down victims to interview. In the center was a male model-looking young man speaking to the viewer.

"Authorities are not commenting, but we have been told now by people who were in the building that Reverend Crystal has been killed by an as of yet unnamed assailant. Witnesses have told us, though, that the assailant made comments that the shooting was in revenge for the shooting of Arhus Gint. This is an unexpected turn of events. As far as our research can tell, Reverend Crystal had no connections to the shooting in Amsterdam yesterday, but if one is found, we will tell you immediately."

"Is this what you were talking about, Mr. Gint?" Allin asked slowly.

"Yes, exactly this sort of thing." Joseph's voice and eyes were sad.

"How could you have known?" Wenk's face was frozen as he watched the screen.

"Anyone who's been paying attention and knows anything about psychology would have known." Joseph's voice had a far-off quality.

"So you expected normal citizens to take matters into their own hands?" Disbelief layered Allin's voice.

"Who says this was done by normal citizens?" The question came sharply, like a professor making a point.

"Then who?" Wenk interjected. "The government?"

Joseph turned and faced the others. "The so-called churches that were started after the aliens left are more than just religious organizations. They're political and economic organizations. They don't just farm, they own the land, the co-ops, even processing plants. That's on top of their people taking over local political offices and working their way up the chain."

"You think they're taking over?" Allin asked.

"Read their literature sometime. And then there is the guy who runs the biggest church, 'Thee Way' as he calls it. As if it's the only church around."

"You're talking about Valesco?" Allin turned from the display to Joseph.

"Yeah, him. If you ask me, the guy has ambitions that don't stop at running a church. Plus he has some twenty million members and is expanding overseas."

"Isn't that what churches do?" Wenk asked, still staring at the screen. "I mean, I'm not an expert, but that's what I heard."

"Before, churches started other churches. This guy is not sharing power." A humph emphasized the statement.

"And that's a lot of power for one man to hold." Allin's head nodded up and down as she made the statement.

"It is. And what kind of person holds on to that much power?" Joseph asked.

"Megalomaniacs," Wenk said weakly.

"This is a lot of conjecture," Allin put in, looking back at the screen. The male model was still talking just to avoid silence. Behind him, a few security forces moved across the view and one guy in the crowd waved his arms at the camera, wearing a big smile.

"May the universe prove me wrong and make me a happy man," Joseph said, looking up. "But if I'm right, there's more to come."

"Wait! You think this Valesco is behind this?" Wenk's attention diverted from the screen to Joseph.

"It won't surprise me if he is behind the attack on the church and my dad."

"Keep those speculations to yourself." Allin's voice had force behind it. "We don't need rumors spreading around this place. Especially by you."

Joseph raised one hand to the air. "I'll behave, I promise. But I reserve the right to say 'I told you so' later."

"If there is an opportunity for you to say that," Allin said as she turned to go, "we might be coming to you. I'm sure the commander is about to want to see me."

Allin strode across the workroom and out the door. Neither man said anything until it was shut.

"Is it weird that I get turned on when she gets forceful?" Wenk asked.

"Weird? No. Inappropriate, definitely." Joseph shook his head.

"Inappropriate is good enough for me." Wenk turned to his friend. "So, now what?"

"We continue our research. And wait for the world to change." Joseph shrugged.

"Not sure I like the sound of that."

"The world has been changing ever since it existed. Most people just don't want to acknowledge that it does and that it's inevitable."

Sighing, Wenk put his hands to his hips. "You can be a real downer at times, you know?"

Chapter Five
The Competitive Advantage

The Church of the Eternal Light was almost entirely made out of glass. Five stories tall at its peak, the light from inside the church shot straight up into the air, a beacon that could be seen for miles when on full power. The whole building had an up-swept shape from back to front, the walls coming to a point directly under the focusing lens for the heavenward light.

At the moment, the church was dark. Being after seven in the evening, people who worked and volunteered there had gone home, leaving a couple of janitors to monitor the cleaning bots, a receptionist, and Sister Monica R'tar, Lead Disciple and unofficial head of the 'gathering' that constituted the church. R'tar walked the halls and rooms, as was her custom after people had left. She smiled as the bots cleaned everything. To anyone who inquired, she would say she liked to see the result of the day's activities though it looked more like reviewing her empire. At times, she closed her eyes and took in the silence that reigned.

"Ms. R'tar," the voice of her receptionist interrupted. Her voice was nervous and her eyes darted about. "There are people here to see you."

"Now?" R'tar said, her eyes coming back open. "Tell them to come back tomorrow."

"I did, but they insist on seeing you now. They say it is important."

"What could possibly be so important?" R'tar closed her eyes, her shoulders drooping.

The assistant stepped closer and lowered her voice. "They say it's about the shooting the other morning. They say there might be a threat to the church."

"Fine," R'tar said with a sigh. "I will talk to them so they will go away."

"They're outside your office." The information given, the receptionist hurried toward the office ahead of R'tar, her short legs moving in quick rhythm.

The Lead Disciple made no hurry to follow. She rarely hurried anywhere, preferring to glide with elegance across the floor, her long dress and hair flowing behind her. It was one of her trademarks. As she came close to her office, she noted three men and one woman standing outside her office. She continued to glide, stopping a little more than a meter from the men.

"How may I help you gentlemen?" she said, using her best pastoral voice.

"Ma'am, we have credible information that there is going to be an attack on this building," the largest of the men said. Like the others, he was dressed in a formal suit, dark with no insignia or markings. The suit jacket hung straight, leaving room between it and his lower body.

"And exactly who is going to attack?" R'tar asked, a heavy dose of doubt in her voice as she looked through the top of her eyes.

"Us." The man drew a pulsator pistol from his jacket and fired two shots into R'tar's chest. Mouth agape, the receptionist behind her desk received two shots also. The man put the pistol back.

"Kill the two janitors and the bots," the man said to the other three. "Make sure you put the message on the wall, then torch the place."

The men and women moved with grim expressions on their faces. The large man held up his wrist to his mouth.

"Package delivered."

With her head held between her hands and elbows on the desk, President Brook Tyler let out a frustrated groan. The five Secretaries making up her cabinet stood in the room looking at each other, none offering a suggestion to the other.

"Does anyone have any good news?" Tyler asked without moving her head.

"At least there were only four fatalities at the church," the Secretary of the Interior, Harrow Adams, replied with intended cheerfulness.

"And the church?"

"A complete loss. The exterior is glass, so didn't catch on fire, but the interior was consumed and the glass, well, let's just say it would be easier to replace it."

"And we are sure this was anti-alien terrorists?"

"They left a message on a wall where they knew it would survive. It said 'God is dead and so will you be.' No one is taking credit, but I am sure that will be coming." Adams cleared his throat and shuffled his feet.

"Not very articulate, but we get the idea. Are we sure this wasn't just someone with a beef against the church?"

"There is no way to tell, at least yet." The man who spoke was Secretary of Security Quintin Melleck. He was taller and broader built than the others. With his body erect, he appeared less disturbed than the others. "An investigation is underway, but local authorities are claiming jurisdiction. That makes it difficult."

"Can't we just take over?" Tyler's head came up, her teeth gritted.

"Our power was severely curbed ten years ago by the Supreme Court. Unless we can show that the group is from another state or international, our hands are tied."

"We have to get ahead of this now!" Tyler pounded her fist on the desk. "I have people screaming at me to do something and the press is talking about how ineffective we are. At this rate, we will be a laughing stock to the whole country in a couple of days. I want ideas!"

Those standing looked at each other. They each looked lost and afraid to speak, except the Secretary of Security, who actually smiled.

"I can call in representatives of our security forces from all over the country. I don't for a moment think this is just some local yahoos working out their frustrations. The attack in Minnesota was too clean, too professional. All surveillance records were wiped. Any group who wanted to take credit won't have done that."

"So you think a national group is responsible for the last two attacks?" Tyler's voice filled with guarded hope.

"And maybe even the attacks on the Gints," the man added.

"That would put the issue firmly in our hands!" Tyler jumped to her feet, pointing at Melleck. "Call your meeting, and get me the answers I want!"

"Yes, Madam President," Melleck replied with a bow.

A small beep from Joseph's interface drew his attention from the simulation he had been staring at for an hour. It was unusual for anything to interrupt him this early in the morning. Closing and opening his eyes once, he turned to the device.

"Receive."

"Your presence is requested at Commander Bennett's office at once," a computer voice stated.

"Acknowledged."

"What did you do now?" Wenk asked without looking up from the micro-welding he was directing.

"I haven't done anything for two days," Joseph protested. As he stood, he snickered. "Maybe they want me to inform on you."

"Me?" Wenk said with a jerk of his head. "The only time I get in trouble is when you start it."

"So what did I start?" Joseph said meritoriously.

"Don't drag me into anything," Wenk said as he went back to the micro-welding.

With a brisk walk, Joseph left the workroom and passed through the greenhouse. He caught a glimpse of Mercedes tending her plants. The sun reflected from her hair as it swirled around her head.

"Sunlight," Joseph said in a distracted way as he exited the building. Once outside, he broke out into a fast jog. "Sunlight. Something about sunlight. Why does sunlight mean something?"

Commander Bennett was sitting behind his desk, head down, concentrating on a flat screen when Joseph knocked on the open door. Bennett waved and pointed at a chair without looking up, waiting until Joseph sat down before speaking.

"First, I want to apologize for before and give you my condolences on the death of your father."

"Don't mention it," Joseph said in a low voice. "And I mean that. Ever."

"I have been asked to attend a meeting in Washington in two days."

"And how does that affect me?" Joseph asked, holding on the first word for a couple of seconds.

"I want you to go with me." Bennett still examined his screen.

"Can I ask why?"

"The meeting is to discuss the recent unrest in the country and propose ideas about what can be done about it. Since this started with your dad's shooting and the *attack* on you, I'm taking you along in case they have questions, instead of having to send someone to dig you up back here."

"Great. An audience with the president could be useful."

"None of that." Bennett pointed a finger and then withdrew it. "We leave at oh-five-hundred Thursday, the airstrip. Be there. Dismissed."

"Yes, sir." The words were very formal, though the tone was not military.

Joseph rose and left the room, not seeing Bennett's eyes once. As he walked past the Staff Sergeant's desk, he asked, "Is he mad at me?"

"No," the sergeant said without looking. "He just hates leaving the base in someone else's care."

"At least it's not personal," Joseph said with a sigh.

"I never said it wasn't personal." The man gave Joseph a meaningful look.

The trip back to the workshop was slower. Thinking about sunlight nagged at his mind, something his brain was trying to tell him but he couldn't hear. The feeling was like a kid pulling on his shirt, trying to get his attention. It followed him all the way back to the greenhouse.

Mercedes's head popped up when he entered the greenhouse. She gave him a inquisitive look, which he answered with with a wave and turn of his head. A smirk and a roll of her eyes followed. Proceeding straight to the workshop, Joseph kept searching for the source of his nagging thought.

"What'd Bennett want?" Wenk asked as he entered.

"He's taking me to Washington."

"Really!" Wenk's head shot up and around to look at Joseph. "How'd you get so lucky?"

"We have to leave at five in the morning," Joseph groaned.

"Who cares! Sleep on the plane."

"Have you ever tried to sleep on a military plane?" Joseph looked at his friend from the top of his eyes.

"Never had the chance, but I'm more than willing to get one. Washington is where all the movers and shakers reside."

"No, just the bureaucrats." Joseph's eyes were focused far off. The answer to his question felt just within reach.

"Hey, you in the same conversation as I am?" Wenk waved his hand in front of Joseph's face. "Where you at?"

"There's a thought I can't quite get a hold of. Something about sunlight." Joseph ignored the waving hand.

"Well, when you come back to Earth, think up a brilliant idea for getting power to these bugs, because they are way too small to put solar panels on."

Joseph waved his finger in the air. "No, not solar." His head came up in a jerk. Joseph turned quickly. "I got it! Wenk, you remember those signals that my dad's friend found the aliens were using?"

"Sure. The one that the aliens hid in the sunlight."

"Yes. What if we use them to send power to the bugs?"

"And let the sunlight transport it?"

"Yes! We can put the transmitter in the lights. Some light reaches deep inside the plant canopy or else we wouldn't be able to see."

"We can put the receivers on the back side of the sensor arrays. Kind of like mounting two birds on one stone." It was Wenk's turn to start shaking his finger. "We don't have any transmitters, though."

"*We* don't," Joseph said carefully, "but the base does."

"Wait." Wenk turned his head to look at Joseph with his left eye. "You mean the secret projects underground I'm not allowed to visit?"

"Yes." Joseph smiled. "But I am."

*   *   *

A small beep from the desk interface drew Valesco's attention. He slowly moved first his eyes and then his hand.

"What is it?"

"A Then has arrived," a female voice said.

"Send him in."

Valesco stood, walking around the desk until he was in front, and waited. It was only a few seconds before the door opened and an older man entered. His hair was colored black and Valesco could make out the signs of surgery to keep the man's face looking young. He walked without a cane.

"Thank you for coming, Mr. Then."

"How could I resist?" The comment left unsaid words hanging in the air. "How may I help you?"

Valesco smirked. "I'm sure you know why you are here."

"You want my parishioners."

"Why would I worry about half a million attendees?" A small smile creased Valesco's face.

"Because while you have been very successful in setting up self-sustaining churches all over the country, they tend to be in low-income areas, while mine tend to be from the wealthier half of society. If you are to expand your church, you have to show you can reach into that part of society, which my people will give you."

"You are more perceptive than they give you credit for, Mr. Then." Valesco walked around the desk in a stalk. Then laughed. Valesco reacted with surprise and gave Then a stare.

"I'm a businessman, Mr. Valesco. I know what's happening, or should I say what you are doing." Then watched Valesco grow tense. "Not that I didn't see it coming, whether it would be you or someone else. It makes sense." Then started to pace back and forth in front of Valesco.

"It only makes sense to consolidate all the churches into one. It's the only way to get rid of all the old religions. And, with the world governments weakened to the point of near non-existence, the time is right." Then flipped his hand. "Of course, I have no interest in doing so. I'm too old. Plus, I have more than I want. I don't need the headaches a world-leading organization can have. But you are different, aren't you?" Then turned toward Valesco.

"If I am called to serve…" Valesco shrugged.

"Of course you are. So you want me to make an announcement handing over my people to you and get out of the religion business."

"And what do you want, Mr. Then?"

It was Then's turn to shrug. "Ten million dollars."

"Is that all?" Valesco raised an eyebrow and he tilted his head.

"No, it's not. I will make a statement telling that I am leaving to a foreign mission field and telling them to go to your church. Not all will go, but most should."

"You will disappear, change your name, change your look, and stay out of the religion business." The statement was flat, factual from Valesco.

"I will move to a beach in Fiji and let the world pass me by. You, on the other hand, will not come looking for me. You will not look into the church finances or start an investigation into what went on before your takeover. You will not look for my accounts or try to sue me in court. You will leave me alone and I will leave you alone."

"And you will not take one more dollar out of your church from the moment our deal is made."

"Agreed, of course." Then stopped and waited. "So, do we have a deal?"

"We do." Valesco held out his hand.

Chapter Six
Success!

Mercedes's face held a slight red color as she wove through the crowds, zeroing in on Joseph and Wenk. They were too busy laughing and drinking beer to notice her approach until she was almost within arm's reach.

"Mercedes!" Joseph said in a slightly slurred, cheerful voice. "Join the celebration!"

"What exactly are you two doing to the lights in my greenhouse? And what are you celebrating besides making a mess?"

"Exactly!" Wenk contributed, worse off than Joseph.

"Exactly what?" It was less a question from Mercedes than an interrogation.

"They're the same thing," Joseph said with a rolling hand gesture. "We're celebrating finding a solution to your bug power problem. Have a drink, on me."

"And what is this solution?" Mercedes ignored the glass of beer pushed her way.

"Joseph came up with this great idea," Wenk started, but received a hit to the shoulder from Joseph.

"We'll tell you when it works," Joseph interjected.

"How does it include tearing up my lights?"

"We needed a power source for the power source. For the power source. Wait, I said that." Joseph twisted his face.

"Sounds like you two have been celebrating enough for everyone here."

"Hey! Two years of brain-drain have to be replenished, right?" Joseph gave her a big smile.

"Are you sure that's why you are drinking?" Mercedes' eyes narrowed at Joseph.

"Why else?" Joseph's head bobbled a little as he talked. "Life's short, enjoy yourself some."

"At least you're not celebrating this A Then guy leaving his church," Mercedes muttered.

"This what?" Wenk's eyes narrowed, but lost focus in the process.

"Guy calls himself A Then. Stupid name, if you ask me. Head of some blah-blah-blah church. He's quitting?" Joseph spent significant effort concentrating on Mercedes as she talked.

"Yeah, calling it quits. Saying he's going to some mission field in Asia. Made the announcement today. Told all his followers to attend Thee Way. I thought you paid attention to this stuff."

"Been busy modifying lights." Joseph's eyes seemed to remember something. "Oh, we took a few of your lights apart."

Mercedes rolled her eyes.

Joseph shook his head. "Valesco must have bought him out, or threatened him."

"Why buy him out?" Mercedes asked.

"Then never was a true believer, just a con artist. Told people what they wanted to hear. His price must have been reasonable. I wonder what con artists get this year." Joseph's head shook back and forth.

"Well, at least no one got killed. I've leave you to your celebrating." Mercedes turned to leave.

"Wait!" Joseph sputtered. "What time is it?"

"It's only nine," Mercedes said with a meaningful stare. "You guys started early."

"I've gotta get to bed. Bennett is taking me to Washington early tomorrow. Don't want to throw up on the plane." Joseph slid off the stool and wobbled slightly for a second.

"I better make sure you make it to your apartment. We'll pick up some anti-hangover drugs one the way." Mercedes grabbed Joseph's arm. "Someone also better make sure your alarm is set with plenty of time."

"You could take me to your apartment," Wenk said, looking wistful.

"You're on your own, Romeo." The comment came with a scowl from Mercedes as she walked Joseph away.

Joseph blinked, trying to make his vision better. It proved to be a futile effort. He stood on the tarmac, small backpack over his left shoulder, and took a deep breath.

"I will never understand why military people like such early morning hours."

"We like to be ahead of everyone else." Commander Bennett was dressed in a flight uniform. He threw something at Joseph, which Joseph managed to catch.

"What's this?"

"Emergency flight suit. Put it on over your clothes. You shouldn't need it, but it's regulation."

"Here's a better question. Where's our plane?"

"You're looking at it."

Joseph's jaw dropped and he stared for a few seconds while his mind remembered how to talk. "We're taking an exo-fighter?"

"You knew I have flight training, right? I have to keep my hours up to stay certified. Seemed like a good opportunity. Plus, it's the quickest way there and back. Now put the suit on."

Bennett walked the fifty feet to where several people attended the plane. Joseph dropped his pack and stepped into the flimsy, plastic body suit. It didn't look like much if there was an emergency, but he told himself it only needed to be used once with success. Sealing the front of his suit, he picked up his pack and walked to the plane. One of the attendants handed him a helmet when he got there. It was thinner and lighter than he expected. The woman helped him seal it to his suit.

"You're in back," Bennett's voice came through the helmet. "You ever flown in one of these before?"

"Nope. Can't say I ever wanted to." Joseph made his clumsy way up the steps to the rear of the cockpit.

"I'll take it easy on you, then. Don't want you throwing up in my plane."

"That makes two of us." Once in, the woman helped Joseph with the straps that held him to his seat and the air lines to his suit. "Thank you, Mother."

The woman smiled back. "When you get to Washington, someone will help you out of the plane."

"Good, I'd hate to be stuck in this thing the whole time. Do I get to fire the weapons?" Joseph said with a lighter voice.

"The only weapons we will be carrying are the pulsators, and that's because they are built in. Their controls are up here with me. You just sit and relax. We'll be on the ground in D.C. in under two hours."

The woman patted Joseph on the helmet and descended. The canopy started to lower.

"And exactly what time of the day will my stomach arrive in D.C.?"

The attendants, assistants, and Joseph sat in the chairs along the wall. The important people, two dozen of them, sat along the rectangular table in the middle of the room. No one along the wall had been introduced. Joseph had not been introduced, questioned, asked for an opinion, or in any way acknowledged.

The uniformed and non-uniformed personnel at the table talked, argued, protested, made points, made counter-points, blustered, sighed, rolled their eyes, questioned, answered, debated, and shook their heads. After two hours, Joseph mostly tried to stay awake. The others along the walls demonstrated a greater degree of patience than him, but ignored him too. All except one young woman in a very neat uniform, blue with a white hat covering close-cropped hair. During the first part of the meeting, she stole several glances his way, but had stopped after an hour or so.

Lunch was never so appreciated. Everyone else along the wall immediately went to the person they accompanied into the room. Joseph headed toward the door to the hallway and the facilities. He made it halfway before the woman in the blue uniform stopped him.

"Mr. Gint, is it?" she asked softly.

"Yes." Joseph couldn't help but smile. It was the first time that day anyone had called him by name.

"I thought I recognized you. I just wanted to say how sad I was about your dad."

"Thank you," Joseph replied, his mood falling. "It's nice of you to say something, I guess."

"I was always a big admirer of how he never varied from telling the truth about the aliens." The woman had kind eyes, her sympathy showing through them. She held out her hand. "I'm Rebecca Amster."

"Wait," Joseph said, taking the hand. "The daughter of Benjamin Amster?"

"One and the same." Rebecca smiled a small, pleasant smile. Her eyes sparkled at the mention of her father.

"What are you doing in the States? And that's an American Navy outfit, right?"

"When the World Council went all but defunct, my dad had to find a new job. The States were one place that was hiring people with experience. And it probably didn't hurt that my dad had a recommendation from someone famous." Her eyes twinkled again.

"Never does." A just perceptible quiver went through Joseph's head and then his expression changed. "How's your dad doing?"

"Fine. He's retired now."

"So you're the baby of the family?"

The woman giggled. "Yes. I was born in the States. Dad calls me his anchor baby."

Joseph quietly laughed along. "So, how did you get dragged along to this boring meeting?"

"I'm the Assistant Adjunct to the Assistant Secretary of the Navy."

"A lot of assisting going on there."

"You have no idea." She rolled her eyes.

"How many ships are left in the Navy?"

"Twelve. Six combat and six support. But we also have command of all air resources that exclusively fly over the oceans, so we have a lot more planes than ships. The support ships handle a lot of humanitarian missions and disaster relief."

"Disaster relief? I thought they could mitigate natural disasters."

"The human-induced kind." Rebecca spoke from the side of her mouth.

"I can imagine." Joseph rolled his eyes. "Say, I hate to run, but I was headed to a room, but we can talk during lunch if you want."

"No problem, I just wanted to make sure I said hello. I'm not sure what I'll be doing during lunch, but if I get a chance, I'll come by."

"Sure thing. Excuse me."

Lunch fulfilled all the expectations of eating at the White House. Joseph looked for peepholes, sure there was a chef lurking in the next room, spying on the guests' reactions. As tempting as the food proved to his tongue, Joseph carefully limited the quantity of food he consumed in an attempt to stay awake for the rest of the meeting. Rebecca didn't make a reappearance and he didn't see her in the meeting room when it reconvened. In fact, a noticeable number of assistants were missing, leaving a number of vacant chairs along the wall. Those sitting at the main table were all there except one. It brought a smile to his face for Joseph to assume the man was the smartest of the bunch.

After lunch, the meeting proved to be a continuation, or re-run, of the morning. From what Joseph could tell, not much was getting done or decided. He noted that each participant tended to see all events through their own specialty. Proposals were made that would primarily be filled by the resources of the person who suggested it. He could not tell if the people couldn't think outside of their own environment or if they were jockeying for power. The result was the same.

Critiquing the meeting helped Joseph stay awake until it was over. With only one short break over four hours, the chance to exit the meeting was welcomed by all. The few who still wished to press their points wore expressions of disappointment when the Secretary of Security ended the meeting. Joseph stood and stretched as much as possible without getting in the way of the others leaving the room. As he did, the Secretary's assistant walked up to him. The man looked more like a bodyguard than the other assistants. His clothes fit loosely on his body.

"Mr. Gint. The President would like to have a minute of your time."

"Of course," Joseph said with some surprise. "When?"

"Now," the man said calmly.

"Of course." Joseph tried not to roll his eyes.

The man led Joseph and Bennett through the hallways to the Oval Office. The rooms they passed were crammed with desks, shared at times by more than one person.

"The President likes the old mannerisms, so call her 'Madam President' when you talk to her," the man said as they walked.

"Quite busy in here," Joseph commented.

"Since the Constitution was changed and Congress was eliminated, the White House is the sole branch of government available to run the country. The scope of the government was reduced significantly. Unless it has to do with international relations or property owned by the federal government, the states pretty much took back control. Still, there are many things that need to be done and people needed to do them."

"Who makes the laws, then?" Joseph asked.

"Laws are made by common consent of the state legislatures. The federal laws are then sent to the president's office for enforcement."

"Sounds like a good way to slow down making new laws."

"To an almost standstill. In here."

President Tyler was standing and talking to several people when they arrived. She gave a quick nod to those already in the room and turned to those entering. "Thank you, Oswald. You may go."

"Yes, ma'am." Oswald, as distinctive as his introduction, gave a quick nod of his head and left.

"Commander, thank you for coming." Bennett gave a quick head bow of his own. Tyler held out her hand to Joseph. "And Mr. Gint. I wanted to take the time to express my regret at the loss of your father."

"Thank you, Madam President." Joseph shook her hand. Tyler gave it two shakes before releasing and turning, heading back around her desk.

"So, what did you think of our little meeting?" Tyler asked.

"A colossal waste of time." Joseph could feel Bennett cringe behind him as multiple emotional waves hit his back. The comment made Tyler stop and turn back toward him.

"How so?"

"No one at the table really understands the enemy." Joseph stood with his hands behind his back, feet spread shoulder-width apart.

"Exactly who are we speaking about?" Tyler asked. "We haven't even identified the anti-alien faction responsible for the attacks."

"And you won't, because it wasn't an anti-alien faction."

"Madam President," Bennett interrupted, "Mr. Gint has some unconventional ideas about our current situation."

From the burning on the side of his face, Joseph was sure a hard gaze was being sent his way, but he ignored it. Walking up to the huge desk, Joseph put his hands on the top and leaned on them.

"Ask yourself one thing. Who benefits the most from the shooting of Reverend Crystal and the destruction of the church in Wisconsin?"

"Those who don't believe that the aliens were God, of course," Tyler said easily.

"Exactly how do they benefit? The people will find another church to attend and the anti-religious factions would only be stirring up resentment against them. In the end, they only hurt their cause, if they have one."

Tyler looked at Joseph, tapping her finger in the air. "You're suggesting that the churches are fighting among themselves?"

"No, I'm suggesting a hostile takeover, in the historical manner, not the business sense. And if they are willing to act against other churches, how long before they come after the unbelievers? They already killed the most famous one." Joseph's voice quivered a little at the end.

"Which church would you think is behind the takeover?" Tyler's eyes narrowed and her head rotated a few degrees to the left.

"Isn't it obvious? Which was the most prepared to benefit from the situation and is reaping the most followers?"

"Madam President, you can't seriously be considering..."

"I can't afford to not consider everything, Commander. This is something I hadn't thought of before." There was a knock on the door. "Come in."

A woman entered. She was dressed in an army uniform. Between forty and forty-five, she had a square, no-nonsense face and piercing eyes that scanned the room as soon as she entered. Unlike current fashion, her hair was tied up in a significant bundle behind her neck. Seeing Commander Bennett, she executed a quick, precise salute. Bennett's salute was more standard.

"Commander Bennett, let me introduce you to your new intelligence officer, Lieutenant Commander Ximena Benitez," the president said with a wave.

"I didn't know we needed an intelligence officer at a home base," Bennett said, sizing up Benitez.

"You didn't, but now you do. Revelation is the most important research center in our country and I am taking every precaution to make sure it stays safe."

"Of course, Madam President." Bennett turned back to the president and made a short bow.

"Mr. Gint, once again, I offer my condolences. Thank you for coming."

Joseph stood up from the desk. "Will you do me a favor?" Once again, Joseph's question caught the president off guard. "Don't wait for all the normal evidence needed to make a court case before doing something. You won't find it. And if you wait that long, it will be too late. For you and all of us."

"I'll try to keep that in mind," Tyler said through a half-squint before turning her back.

With a quiet sigh, Joseph turned, a small amount of longing in his eyes, his head bowed. Bennett led the group out. Benitez feel into step with Joseph. No escort appeared as they made for the building exit. Bennett seemed to know the way. Waiting until they were several turns from the Oval Office, Benitez spoke.

"It's a pleasure to meet you, Mr. Gint."

Joseph looked at her for a second as he walked before responding. "You're not going to offer your condolences?"

"Would you like me to?"

"Seems to be what everyone does," he said with a shrug.

"Does it help?"

"Not that I have found." Joseph looked away.

"I have been reading up on you. You're an interesting character.

Just as a professional courtesy, you understand, were you as 'innocent' concerning that incident at the base as the report says?"

Joseph couldn't prevent a quick glance at Bennett. It caused Benitez to smile.

"Can't say," Joseph responded without emotion. "I didn't see the report."

Benitez let out a small, single laugh. "You know, you would have been good at the intelligence business."

"I thought I was already pretty intelligent." Joseph gave a smug wave of his head.

Benitez smiled. Bennett turned into the front lobby, giving no indication that he had been listening to the conversation.

"When we get to the base, we should have a long discussion. It would be nice to talk with someone who is also paying attention to current events." Benitez stopped when Bennett stopped just inside the front door and turned around.

"Lieutenant Commander, Gint and I came here in a fighter, so you'll have to make your own way to the base. Sorry I can't accommodate you."

"I'd gladly give up my seat for the Lieutenant Commander and take the slow route back," Joseph offered.

"And leave you loose in D.C.? No way, you're coming back with me. Benitez."

"No problem, Commander. See you there."

With a forlorn look, Joseph followed Bennett. "You just like torturing me, don't you?"

"As a matter of fact, yes."

Chapter Seven
Unrest

The street was not filled with cars, but with people. Several blocks away, people also filled the street, walking the other direction. Neither of the groups had filed the proper paperwork at city hall, but the sheer number in both groups made that point moot. The local police, the small number that existed, shuffled their feet in a nervous manner as the two groups walked toward each other.

"Are we going to do something?" an officer asked his superior.

"You really want to stand in between them?" The man pointed toward the crowds.

"No, not really. We are here to keep the peace, right?"

"If something happens, we will do what we can to restore order. Until then, we have no cause to arrest anyone."

Silence covered the two dozen officers as they watched. As the groups drew near, they could see that one group had holographic projection signs above them saying things like 'Justice Now!' and 'People Power.' The other group's messages were more aligned with 'Alien-lovers Leave!' Outnumbered at least one thousand to one, tension filled the officer ranks. The two groups kept walking until they were five meters apart and abruptly stopped. After a few seconds, words started to be exchanged at half volume.

"We might get out of here without too much bother," the officer commented.

"Yeah, if those idiot alien lovers leave before they start something," another officer said next to him.

"What?!"

"Those stupid alien-lovers can't leave people alone. Telling us how to live. This is America, you can't do that."

"I'm not sure I like that attitude." The officer's voice started to sound strained.

"Tough. I get my opinion. You don't have to like it."

The voices from the two groups had become louder, making it hard to hear what any one person was saying. Fists were waved and gestures made. Single steps were taken into the no-man's area between the groups.

"This is not good," the officer in charge said.

Before he could say anything further, individuals from each group charged the other. The sight of the singular acts of bravery inspired the rest to close quarters.

"Good," the second officer said with excitement. "Now we get to kick some a-lovers' butts."

The response was the other officer bashing him in the head with his shield.

"Ma'am, there's a riot in Philadelphia."

President Tyler looked up to see her Secretary of Security, Quintin Melleck, looking into the Oval Office. Tyler's eyes went wide. "What?!"

"Two protest groups met on the streets. Didn't go well." The man walked into the room and closed the door.

"What's local law enforcement doing?" Tyler stood, leaning on her hands on the desk.

"Appears that they are participating," the Secretary said with a downcast face.

"Damn!" Tyler pounded the desk once. "I don't suppose we have a dog in this match?"

"Not yet. Riot is confined to the street. No federal buildings near by."

"What assets do we have there?"

"Not much. Maybe a dozen security personnel."

"Damn it! So we sit by helpless while the town tears itself apart."

"You could make a public appeal…"

"To people who aren't listening? I'd look stupid." Tyler walked from behind her desk and started pacing the room. "How about that information I asked for yesterday? Anything?"

"We haven't found any evidence of one of the churches being involved, but we only started looking. From what little data we have, it appears that Thee Way is very active in recruiting members from the affected churches."

"So there could be something to what Mr. Gint said." Tyler stopped pacing and her head came up with the comment.

"Too early to tell." The statement was non-committal in tone.

"I'm asking for a professional assessment!"

The Secretary looked down, shuffled his feet, set them in a firm stance, and cleared his throat. "It does appear that Thee Way was incredibly prepared for the events, which definitely looks suspicious. If they are involved, they have professional help in hiding it."

"Great! Now we have churches setting up their own security forces?" The questions were coming louder and more forcefully.

"Under local laws, they have the right to employ their own security without much oversight from local authorities."

"But they are national organizations. Hell, some are international." Some light appeared in Tyler's eyes.

"The branches are all organized under local laws and only loosely associated with the national organization, at least legally."

Tyler raised her interface. "I want the Attorney General in here now." She turned back to the Secretary. "We need to find some law that allows us to get into this situation. We need to have forces ready to move at a moment's notice."

"I'll get them ready."

"Then go, do it!"

The Secretary made a hasty retreat from the office.

"Damn country's going to hell. And on my watch!"

A quiet, relaxed meal had been planned. With the power distribution system installed in the greenhouse and one hundred robotic bugs loosed to kill pests and eliminate weeds, Joseph's part of the project was completed except for contributing to the final report. Knowing that another project would be thrown on his desk as soon as their results became public, he had decided to indulge in a three-course dinner and a leisurely evening away from people. If the weather cooperated, spending time after dark with the telescope he had mounted on the roof of a storage building on the far side of the base caused comfort to wash through his mind.

True to what is said about plans, LC Benitez sat down across the table from Joseph halfway through the main course. She had on casual clothes: pants and a button-down shirt of non-military design.

"I wasn't aware we had a date," Joseph said with food still in his mouth.

"We don't, but if it makes you feel better, we can call it one." Benitez wiggled her eyebrows.

"I'm pretty sure you're not my type," Joseph replied, his voice flat.

"What is your type?" She crossed her legs under the table and leaned back.

"Someone that doesn't scare me, for one." Joseph swallowed.

"Given to exaggerating much?" Benitez batted her eyes in an exaggerated fashion.

"No, in fact, I am not." Joseph cut off another bite. "I know a crouching tiger when I see one."

"Don't worry, Mr. Gint, I'm not on the hunt. At the moment, that is." Benitez sat back up to the table.

"Do you practice that? Being scary?"

Benitez laughed. At least it was a pleasant laugh. "Professional hazard, I'm sure. You looked unoccupied, so I thought I could take the opportunity to have a chat."

Joseph swallowed his bite of food. "Official or unofficial chat?"

"Unofficial."

"Good," he said with a sigh. "I don't need to call my lawyer, then."

"And who would that be?" Benitez gave Joseph a look. "From what I heard, I think Ms. Stakes would take the job."

"Well, given the present circumstance, she would be a better defense than any lawyer." The comment caused another laugh from Benitez.

"Touche, Mr. Gint. Can we have one condition? Can we speak plainly, no games, no equivocating?"

"That would be refreshing." Joseph let the comment stand for a few seconds. "As long as this is unofficial, sure. Of course, if this suddenly becomes official, I will deny everything."

"Good enough for me." Benitez smiled.

A waiter came by the table. Benitez ordered a drink. The waiter left. Joseph waited until the waiter was more than a couple of steps away.

"Do you have a sense of history, Ms. Benitez?"

"Meaning?"

"Look at current events. Do you think something is happening in this world, a world-changing event, so to speak?"

"Possible. And it started with your father?"

"My father was the opening salvo. He wasn't really a mover-and-shaker, but he was a symbol of anti-alien feeling. Killing him was a clear signal that the alien-lovers feel bold enough to start taking action."

The waiter came back with the drink. Benitez thanked him. He left.

"You have a pretty definite picture of unfolding history, Mr. Gint."

"Do you disagree?"

"No, I don't." Benitez took a drink. "Passable. If you had access to all the intel that I do, you might feel even stronger."

"I'm not sure I want to know more." Joseph took a bite.

"Do you keep track of the number of people that the alien churches say they represent, Mr. Gint?" Benitez swirled her drink.

"I have a rough idea."

"And do you know their growth rates?"

"Not exactly, but I have a guess."

"Two percent a year." She took another drink. "That's of this country's population."

"Which means by the next election in four years, there will be more alien lovers than not. That's your point, right?" Joseph pointed with a piece of steak on his fork before putting it in his mouth.

"Yes, it is. That doesn't sound like a good outcome. If we could prove that Thee Way or another church was responsible for the attacks…" Benitez tilted her head with a shrug.

"Good luck with that, and by that, I mean forget it. The first thing I would have done, if I was them, would be to put my people in local law enforcement long before I made any moves."

"Sounds like you may have helped them make their plans." Benitez raised an eyebrow.

Joseph only scoffed.

"You are correct. From what I have been able to tell, they have enough people locally to slow down or subvert any investigation. That being said, you are most likely also correct that we will never get the evidence."

"And we are not going to get any help from Europe. They have so many factions of all type, from militant to passivist, they look like a jigsaw puzzle where none of the pieces match. And that stupid Shetter guy thinks he can negotiate his way out of everything." Joseph pushed his plate away, silverware on the plate. "So where does that leave us, in your opinion?"

"In a normal world? Fucked." Benitez took another drink, more than a sip. "Given the normal channels for doing anything, I can't find a way to move against them. The federal government is so weak that we have no tools or even resources to counteract what they are doing. At the rate they are taking over, in ten years they could change the Constitution again and make Valesco, or someone like him, king and we wouldn't be able to stop them."

"So let's do something unconventional." Joseph leaned back in his chair, wiping his mouth with the cloth napkin.

It was Benitez's turn to stare from the corner of her eyes. "Like what?"

"Like something we have the power to do, even if we don't have the authority." Joseph said the statement with so little emotion that it sounded practiced.

"I can't believe that Tyler would do such a thing. She still wants to be re-elected, you know."

"There are things that the military can do by itself, can't it? Consolidate resources, identify and locate critical personnel…"

"Start weeding out the bad seeds?" Benitez's eyes started to light up.

"Especially that. We need to know who we can trust and who we can't. All the way up."

The statement brought surprise to Benitez's face. "Even the president?"

"For sure the president! We can't have anyone knowing about our plans if we can't trust them."

"Huh!" Benitez took a long drink, but appeared to be thinking. "That's going to be tough for a lot of military people to handle. They still have a lot of loyalty to the country and thus the president."

"Tyler's a politician. While she might not be a problem now, it definitely means she might be a liability later."

"*That* sounds pretty close to treason." The comment was joined by a hard stare from Benitez. "But I can't say it doesn't have some appeal to my covert side."

"Not if Tyler is the one who throws in with the alien lovers. Once that happens, if we aren't prepared for it, we've lost." Joseph stared back. He held Benitez's stare for a while, unwavering. She finally broke it.

"Of course, you're right. If Valesco gets his hands on the military and its equipment, he would either disassemble it all or use it to take over the rest of the world. Either way is a bad end for our country. But you know what the other alternative is, don't you?" The question wasn't a question.

"Two separate power groups in one country, one technologically savvy and one agrarian based. A country divided. It's either that or we are forever subject to the will of our alien visitors, their farm to harvest when they please. You really want that?"

"No." Benitez put her glass on the table with a thud. "I will do everything I can to make sure that doesn't happen. By the way, how's your mother?"

"Hard to get a hold of. She's several layers deep in security personnel." Joseph's voice sounded nervous instead of assured.

"Afraid that makes her stand out as a target?" One of Benitez's eyebrows rose.

"Yes, I am. The people in black suits and black vehicles tend to stick out in my opinion. I think she needs to be somewhere safer than our farm. Somewhere with guard dogs instead of Great Danes that threaten to lick you to death, that sort of thing. But since Dad's death she is even less willing to leave."

"You could bring her here." Benitez shrugged.

"Now's not really a great time for me to be out in public." A knowing smile crossed his face.

That made Benitez laugh. "I didn't mean you personally. Someone else, like security personnel."

Joseph's eyes wandered for a moment. "The problem is getting her to listen to that someone, but I think I might have an idea of who. If I can find him."

"I'll leave that to you. Thanks for the drink, Mr. Gint."

The train sounded its whistle as it slowed for the bridge. It really wasn't a whistle, but everyone called it that. Worthia Kerala watched the train in the distance, its long line of cars snaking behind the sleek, silver engine. Even from this distance, she could see that some of the doors on the cars were open.

"Where are you going?" she asked out loud. "Would you take me, too?"

Turning back to the garden, Worthia hurried to hoe the last of the rows. Mother would be expecting her to help with supper preparations soon and she would be mad if the garden wasn't done. Working the hoe around the plants, Worthia cut as many weeds as she could, particularly the tall ones. The little ones she let hide under the vegetables.

Sufficiently finished, Worthia hurried back to the house, took off her shoes, and went to the wash basin to clean her hands and face. She brushed as much dirt from her skirt as she could and quick-stepped into the kitchen.

"Did you finish the garden?" her mother asked as she walked into the kitchen.

"Yes, ma'am." Worthia sat down at the table, where a knife and vegetables waited for her.

"I heard the train. I thought you might be distracted." Her mother gave her one of those suspecting glances. Worthia didn't look at her, but at the knife and vegetables.

"Where do you think the train goes?" Worthia used a voice of general curiosity.

"It doesn't matter," her mother said dismissively.

"But don't we send crops to be sold on it sometimes?"

"That's man business, not yours." Her mother's tone was sharp, the tone she used when Worthia asked questions that she did not consider woman's business. But she had never explained why it wasn't woman's business.

Past experience had taught Worthia to drop the subject. She decided that her mother must not know where the train went. It obviously went east, across the great plains of the country. From her house, all she could see were large fields of grain stretching out to the horizon, but something else must be out there, something.

"You'd be better thinking about yourself and your future," her mother said.

Worthia knew what her mother meant. Being sixteen, she was only two years from the age when girls were married, and one of those would be spent courting. Not that she had a choice who to court. Her parents would decide that. Neither was there anyone she had met that she wanted to court. All the boys seemed to only worry about crops and animals. And religion. Religion seemed to be the only subject worthy of discussions around town. If you were a man, that was. Women were not welcomed in the discussions. A woman's place was the home, taking care of family needs and raising kids. The thought left Worthia empty inside.

The train whistle sounded one last time, an eager whistle as the train increased speed, having cleared the bridge. To Worthia, it seemed like an invitation, one to go places, ones with more than crops and kids and dishes that needed to be washed. Ones where a person could explore the world and find wonderful things to amaze the mind. She knew they existed because the minister insisted they were evil.

The train seemed to be the only door to finding them.

Chapter Eight
Yeah, You

Joseph sat in an unupholstered chair outside of Bennett's office. The door was closed and the light was off. The sergeant was at his desk, typing on his display, ignoring Joseph. Joseph decided that had to change.

"If the Commander wanted me here so early this morning, at least he could be here, too," Joseph said.

"He was most likely delayed. Happens all the time." The man talked without looking at Joseph.

"Still, rather impolite, if you ask me." Joseph huffed, watching for a reaction.

"He is the base commander. He can do anything he wants." There was a sharp tone to the statement.

"What I mean is that I have things to do. You're wasting my *valuable* time having me just sit here."

"It's my time to waste," Bennett said as he walked into the office area, "so don't complain."

The sergeant stood and executed a salute, which Bennett returned. Joseph remained seated, arms crossed in front of him. Bennett walked to his office and opened the door.

"Join me, Mr. Gint. I have a new assignment for you."

Joseph stood and walked into his office with some reluctance, for appearance's sake, and sat in a chair that was just as uncomfortable as the one outside the office. Bennett was slower to take his seat. He turned on his desk display and called up a file before speaking.

"It has been proposed to expand the capabilities of our base," Bennett started. "From your records, I see that before you earned your degree, you spent several years working for the city planning department in Amsterdam."

"It was a job," Joseph replied with a shrug.

"Six years, to be exact." Bennett threw a glance his way.

"I was pretty young through a lot of that time, and it's not like I was designing roads or anything." Joseph started to fidget in his seat.

"And I don't have any C.B.s here, either. In order to get the brass to agree to expand the base, I need a plan. You're all I have, so you get the job."

"So this is a budgeting thing?"

Bennett appeared to consider for a moment, then replied, "Yes, a budgeting thing. Can't get more budget if you can't show a good use for it."

Joseph turned his head while looking at Bennett, disbelief on his face. When Bennett didn't continue, he took a breath and sat back into the chair.

"What exactly are you wanting to put on the base?" he finally said.

"More people, as many as we can. And I want it to be as self-sufficient as possible. Make our own power, grow our own food, that sort of thing. With the research we have been doing, that shouldn't be a hard sell. Call it research application. We also want to plan for some heavy equipment, so we need to keep the airstrip and the rail station."

"So which is the higher priority, the number of people or the self-sufficiency?"

"Both," Bennett said in typical bureaucratic fashion.

Joseph rolled his eyes. "Anything that is non-negotiable?" Joseph asked, bracing himself.

"Our classified research must be maintained, of course. In fact, we might want to make sure we have room for more." The conversation hung vacant for a while.

"If I may ask," Joseph's tentative voice asked, "what exactly will these people be doing?"

"Whatever is needed. I am sure with all the new facilities, there will be things to do." Bennett had a blank expression on his face.

"Nothing so clear as ambiguous requirements," Joseph mumbled.

"That's for you to create, Mr. Gint. I need this in two weeks. Talk to whoever you need, but I need a computer display showing the plan and quantitative numbers. Dismissed."

Joseph managed to rise and leave the office through his shock. He even remembered to close the door and not start muttering to himself until he was outside the building.

"Two weeks? Doesn't expect much, does he?" Looking around the base, a sly smile started on his face. "Then I will give him my best two week effort."

Joseph brought up his interface and said, "Mercedes," before waiting for a reply. It didn't take long for Mercedes's face to show up.

"Joe! What's up?"

"You got plans for lunch?"

"Ah, no." Mercedes's face registered surprise. "Are you asking me out for lunch?"

"I am asking if you could spend lunch talking to me."

"Sure!" Mercedes's face lit up.

Joseph frowned. "What's the big deal?"

"You've never asked me to lunch before."

"Really? Hm, can't remember if I have or hadn't. Not like it's a date or anything."

"I'll take what I can get. And since you asked, you're buying. How's eleven?"

Staring at his interface, giving it commands, Joseph didn't see Mercedes until she was standing next to the table. She had ditched her work overalls for casual clothes that Joseph did his best to not let distract him. Sliding into the seat opposite him, her smile was huge.

"Did you order for me?" she asked.

"Why would I do that?" Joseph looked up from the pad.

"It's the kind of thing a guy will do for a lady," Mercedes said with mostly closed eyes.

Joseph turned his wrist and pulled up the cafeteria menu with his interface, scanning the day's list. His lips bunched up in the corner.

"Chicken tetrazzini?" he said.

"Nice choice."

Joseph manipulated the interface for a moment and then put his wrist down. When he looked at Mercedes, her eyes sparkled. It made him squint and turn his head.

"This is a working meeting, you know."

"I don't know," she corrected as she beamed. "You didn't show up this morning and I haven't been told a thing, so I will interpret events however I please."

Joseph guffawed once before speaking. "Bennett has given me a new assignment."

"You have time for lunch, still, don't you?"

"He gave me two weeks, so I don't have time for much of anything except getting this done."

"So we better enjoy this while we can." Mercedes batted her eyelashes at him. It made Joseph laugh.

"I hate to disappoint you, but I asked you to lunch for information."

"That's one way to describe it."

Joseph rolled his eyes. "Assuming your greenhouse project is as successful as you think it will be, I need to know how much floor space you need to grow enough food for one person."

"For what period of time?" Mercedes started to look curious.

"Full time. All year."

Mercedes's head turned to the side. "You're talking about taking the project full scale? Production mode?"

"Yes." Joseph's finger hovered above the pad.

"In the present mode, three hundred square meters. That doesn't include meat production, of course."

"Yeah," Joseph said, looking at the pad for a moment, "meat production will be a problem. Do you know anything about aquaculture?"

"Sure." The food came on a robotic tray. They each lifted theirs from the tray along with a pitcher of water and place settings. Mercedes frowned. "You really should eat better."

"I'll do that in two weeks," Joseph replied as he set the plate with a bacon cheeseburger and fries in front of himself. "Can you give me some numbers about yields for fish production?"

"Sure, but they aren't your only option." Mercedes broke off a portion of the chicken tetrazzini with her fork. Steam came from inside.

"Meaning?"

"If you have a tank, you can raise other food at the same time, like mussels."

"Mussels!" Joseph's eyes perked up. "I love fresh mussels! Not like I can get them here. I mean the really fresh ones, like at home."

"Plus, there are also sources of protein other than large animals." Mercedes made the comment without looking across the table, placing a bite in her mouth.

"You're not talking bugs, are you?" Joseph cringed.

Mercedes swallowed. "They're a very efficient source of protein."

Joseph shivered. "I don't care what you say, I'm not eating bugs." He took the time to lift the burger and take a bite of it.

"There's also algae. I know it's not very appetizing, but we could grow it as a supplement, putting it in soups, casseroles, stuff like that, where it wouldn't be noticed. The nutrition would be a real boost."

"How much room would we need to grow enough for, say, twenty thousand people?" Joseph asked between a swallow and another bite.

"If it's only a supplement, about the size of a full-sized swimming pool, five-thousand square meters. The best thing is that it practically grows itself. Everyone would only take a little each day, like one bite, because it is so high in iron, though the iron is good for women." Mercedes delicately picked and ate her food while talking.

"Might be worth it," Joseph said after swallowing. "I'll need some numbers to see how all this balances out." He went to take another bite and stopped. "Hey, can we feed the bugs to the fish?"

The comment made Mercedes stop and think. She pointed with her fork as she talked.

"We need to feed the fish, of course. If we use the crickets, we don't have to maintain them as food-grade. Even if they die of disease, which can happen really easy, we could sanitize the bodies and still feed them to the fish. Of course, we still need to feed the crickets."

"Wouldn't we get extra plant material from the greenhouses?"

"Yes, but I don't know if it would be enough. The plants will be perennials and most stop growing after a while."

"What if we supplemented with plant material grown outside?"

"That would work, of course. I could calculate how much we would need."

"That would be great. If you could base it all on space-per-person numbers, that would be even better." Joseph started on the fries.

"What exactly does Bennett have you working on?"

"Maximizing occupation and usage of the base."

"Like how many?"

Joseph looked up and frowned. "That's what I'm supposed to find out."

"And why you?" The question was one of puzzlement, and accusation.

Joseph sighed. "Never tell anyone about your summer jobs."

Chapter Nine
Civil Unrest

President Tyler burst into the situation room. People scrambled about the room, requesting information from interfaces or talking over interface responses. Tyler stomped up to the Secretary of Security, murder in her eyes.

"Tell me this isn't happening," Tyler demanded.

"I can't do that," the man replied in a quiet voice.

"A bomb in New York City! How could this happen? This isn't the twentieth century, you know! They bombed a church?"

"The intended target has not been determined at this time."

Tyler looked at the man like he had gone mad, her mouth open and her eyes wide.

"There's... was... a Catholic church right next to one from the Enlightened Future. The theory right now is that the bombers misjudged the size of the explosive. It could have been meant for either."

"Great!" Tyler threw up her arms. "Now we have *inept* terrorists running around the country. Tell me we have something on any of the other incidents."

The Secretary appeared to relax a little. He swung his hand at the screen in front of him, moving the images until stopping at one.

"The CEC has announced that while the security guard who killed himself was once a member of the Enlightenment, they think the main driver behind the death of Mr. Gint was a small, radical group that call themselves The Sword. They've arrested six members, which happens to be a significant number of their followers, by the way."

"So the pressure is off the Enlightenment?" Tyler asked.

"Mostly, but the damage was already done. Europeans have even less of a taste for violence than Americans. They've lost some thirty percent of their members just in the last week."

"Do we know where they went?"

"Not yet. Too early to tell. We have only tracked their withdrawal from the Enlightenment at this time."

"And what about the attack in South Dakota?"

"Isolated incident. The protesters were most likely emboldened by the news of the shooting and reacted on impulse."

"Those are the kind of impulses we don't need. And the others?"

"Nothing more yet. We still can't find any evidence that Reverend Crystal's shooting was more than a one man job and Minneapolis is not sharing information."

"The riot in Philadelphia?"

"Spontaneous combustion."

"You're not making me feel any better." Tyler looked from the corner of her eyes as her chest heaved. "You make it sound like we have no control over the situation."

The conversation was interrupted by a voice from behind. "Sir, you really need to see the feed from New York City."

The Secretary waved at the display and changed to the NYC feed. It was filled by a scene of people marching through the street, smashing windows and causing general destruction.

"Do we know which side these people represent?" Tyler asked.

"They're in an alien-friendly part of town," the Secretary said after looking at his interface, "so I think we can make an assumption."

"Damn! This is getting out of hand. We need to get troops in there!"

"Not without the invitation of the governor."

"Get the governor of New York on the interface!" Tyler yelled. She watched the scene as the connection was made. The governor's face replaced the scene. "Governor, your city is going to hell."

The man in the view shrugged. "We've seen worse."

"Worse!" Tyler was lost for voice for a few seconds. "When?"

"New York City has a long history, President Tyler, which you should know. We've seen a lot here and we'll make it through as we always have."

Tyler recovered some of her composure. "Governor, I can have troops in the city in a couple of hours."

"That won't be necessary." The governor remained calm.

"They're destroying your town!"

"We have a lot of town. I'm sure there will be plenty left tomorrow."

Tyler stared, unable to speak.

"Thank you for your concern, President Tyler. We will be fine. Now, if you don't mind, I have matters to attend to."

The image disappeared from the display. Tyler stood there, not moving. The others looked at her, waiting.

"I'll be in my office," Tyler said as she stomped out of the room.

Valesco stared at the large display, smiling. The door to his office opened and closed. The sound of footsteps were followed by Garo standing next to him.

"They're concentrating on our competition's assets, correct?" Valesco asked.

"Of course. They were given very specific targets."

"How convenient for the city to put two of our competition's churches next to each other."

"Two birds with one stone, so to speak."

Valesco stood and smiled for a moment. "And the follow-up riots?"

"Ready to go tonight. We'll be targeting a historic church. Should increase tensions exponentially."

"And the governor?"

"Being a good boy, playing by the script." It was Garo's turn to pause. "He wants to be elected again."

"Politicians are so easy to manipulate. Our man in Minnesota is holding firm?"

"Yes. His dedication to our cause is commendable."

"He will be fully rewarded," Valesco muttered in an automatic way.

Both men watched the display for a while. Garo shuffled his feet. The question came after a few moments.

"Are we moving too fast?"

"We are not looking for a fair fight, my friend, we are looking for overwhelming force. After the riots, we will begin our work in less obvious ways, but we must create the right amount of… incentive for people to act." Valesco nodded as he said the last phrase.

"And we will provide the incentive." Garo smiled.

"It *is* our calling."

William Bridge slammed the front door as he entered. It brought his wife running, short of breath.

"Bill! You scared me!"

"Are the kids home?" Bill's face was reddish and clenched.

"Of course they are. You don't think I'd let them out, do you?"

"Have them pack. One suitcase each. I left the car out front." Bill made his way to the bedroom.

"Why? Where are we going?" His wife followed.

"Out of New York City!"

"What? What are you talking about? We can't just leave."

Bill turned, his face even redder. "They're killing the faithful out there! Anyone they think is a Puritan. Our lives are in danger. Our kids' lives are in danger! We have to leave and we have to leave now!"

"But Bill, we can't just leave."

Bill grabbed his wife's shoulders with his hands. "Honey, they are three blocks down the street," he said with a more controlled voice, "and moving this way. We have to leave before they get here. They're burning buildings and smashing cars. If we don't leave now, we'll be one of their victims."

"But where will we go?" His wife's eyes looked vacant.

"Out into the country." William let go of his wife and took several steps and changed direction multiple times. "My brother says there's a church settlement out there, fifty miles out of town. I'm sure they will take us in. Heck, we probably won't be the only ones going, so we better get there before the rest. Now pack the kids. Take only what we need."

"But, but, my pictures… The things Grandma gave me…"

"Only what we need! Do you hear me? It has to fit in the car."

"What about Carrie's stuffed animals? You know she won't want to leave them."

"Tell her we'll come back for the rest."

With a look of shock, his wife said, "But that's a lie."

"If we don't get out of here soon, it won't matter if we lied or not. Now come on, let's go!"

Despite the importance of any particular assignment, people found themselves huddled around displays, watching the news. Joseph, Wenk, and Mercedes watched a large display in the common area of the residence building that showed the day-after view of New York City. Not much was said as they watched the view scan the wreckage from the previous night. Fires still burned. Brief scenes of a hospital crowded with the injured were shown. These brought the most gasps from the watchers.

"This is unbelievable," Wenk said softly.

Joseph looked around the room. At least one hundred people, some in fatigues, some in lab coats, all gaped at the screens. A few pointed and appeared to ask questions of those around them. It didn't appear to Joseph that any answers were given. "You would think military people would be less shocked by such scenes."

"This doesn't happen here," Wenk replied with conviction. "It only happens in less civilized countries."

"Still, all the news from Indonesia the last few decades should have given some exposure," Joseph said in a calm, scientific voice.

"Like I said, less civilized countries."

"It's different when it's your home," Mercedes interjected. "Besides, you're a few weeks ahead of the rest of us."

The comment caused Joseph to lower his head and shuffle his feet. After a moment, he said, "I guess you are right."

"I'm sorry!" Mercedes quickly turned toward him, hands raised to her mouth. "I didn't mean to be callous. It just popped out."

"No, you're fine," Joseph said, lifting his head. "You're right. Your folks live in New York City, don't they? These things have been spreading to affect more and more people like waves in a pool."

"I think we're all going to have problems dealing with what is happening." Mercedes seemed to deflate as she lowered her hands. Joseph took a breath and gently put his hand on her shoulder.

"Where are your parents now?"

"I'm not sure. They live in New York City, but not that part of town. Still…" Her eyes grew distant.

"Have you tried to call them?"

Mercedes's eyes became alert as she refocused on Joseph. "Yes, but I didn't talk to them personally. They've always had such busy lives. I guess everyone is trying to call somebody these days. What about your mother?"

"I'm working on getting her to a safe place." Joseph's voice was soft as if not to be overheard.

"My folks are fine, by the way, in case anyone was interested. Won't stop calling me actually." Wenk turned from the screen.

"Good for you. Count yourself lucky they're nobodies," Joseph replied flatly.

As Mercedes took a step away to better view the screen, Joseph's attention went back to Wenk, who was again captivated by the scenes on the display. With one elbow in the opposite hand, he tapped a finger on his face as he watched.

"This is what it must have been like for people watching the news when the aliens were here." Wenk's voice had a hollow, far-off sound.

"You've never really seen this sort of thing before, have you?"

"No. I never paid attention to Indonesia. I really didn't want to know and it eventually went away." Wenk slowly turned his head, watching the display as long as he could. "You know why this is happening, don't you?"

"I have an idea, one I am sure no one wants to hear," Joseph tried to reply as gently as he could.

Wenk leaned in closer, scanning his eyes quickly back and forth before speaking. "That incident outside the gate, it's not connected, is it? People make their own decisions, right?" Wenk's voice was barely audible and shaky.

"True," Joseph said firmly and silently, "though there is no way for me to say that things aren't connected, and I don't mean in the philosophical manner."

"Why would they do this?"

"Have you ever studied why wars happen?"

"Can't say I ever wanted to know." Wenk leaned back into a more normal stance.

"My dad was real big on the subject after the aliens left. He was concerned about how the world would react when the aliens left. If you examine world history closely, many leaders were not above starting a crisis so they could step in and solve it, taking the reins of power in the process."

"So you think someone is doing this so they can, what, win the next election?" Mercedes's face twisted in disbelief.

Joseph shook his head. "The person doing this doesn't care about elections, except to legitimize their rule afterwards. This type of person takes power by one kind of force or another. The end justifying the means."

"Won't the authorities stop them?" Wenk tried to sound hopeful.

"They rarely do. If the person can get the masses behind him, the authorities will be too scared to do anything. Look at the people in this room. They are shocked to inaction and they are the military. Do you really think the military is going to fire on crowds of people?"

"No," Wenk said, shaking his head. "I can't imagine they would."

"So the other guy has already won." Joseph let out his breath.

Wenk looked back at the display for a few seconds and then back to Joseph. "What are we supposed to do?"

"That depends if we can get the president to act or not. It would be a lot easier if Tyler would get involved. If not, we're on our own."

"You really know how to make someone feel good," Wenk said with disgust. "Tyler has to do something."

"I'm sure she'll do something. Let's just hope it's the right something." Joseph looked around the room. "You okay here? You need me to stay?"

"Nah," Wenk said with a laugh. "I think all us cripples can take care of each other."

"Watch out for Mercedes coming back, will you? I think she is going to need people around her for a while. At least until we hear that her parents are all right. Can you do that for me? I need to get back to my project." Joseph's thumb did a hitch over his shoulder.

"Sure! Comfort our local super model? No problem." Wenk's expression was not as confident as his words.

"Thanks. Call me if you need me for anything." Joseph slapped Wenk on the shoulder as he turned to go.

"I must say, I am not extremely comfortable with this idea." Bennett looked at Benitez with skeptical eyes over his desk.

"Planning can't hurt anything." Benitez sat on the non-padded chair as if it was the most comfortable in the world.

"It's not the planning I have a problem with. It's any execution that comes afterwards. We have no authorization to move supplies to this base."

"That is not exactly true. We have authorization to move anything that is 'necessary and proper' to our base if available at a depot. Have you looked at the list of items at our depots? They're loaded to the brink with just about everything you can imagine. Santa would have a field day." Benitez gave him a smile she must have stolen from a cat.

"Ancient holidays notwithstanding, we also don't have that much room to store things here," Bennett huffed.

"But if we have more than we can store, we then have a need for more storage capacity."

Bennett stared. "That's a tricky game you're playing."

"You think anyone is actually watching?" Benitez laughed. "They have more important things to worry about and not enough people to worry about them as it is. Plus, I know that many of the governors are asking the government to release that material to the states." Benitez leaned forward with the statement.

"At which point we'll never see them again." Bennett waved his hand with the comment. "I understand what you are saying. I don't suppose you have a depot in mind to start extracting things from?"

"Washington state is the most active in this... re-procurement as they call it... push. We should start there." Her head nodded up and down as she spoke.

"Fine. Make up a list and a shipping schedule." Bennett shook his head. "I'm still not clear how this is my Chief of Security's business."

"Keeping this base safe is my business, which means having plenty of supplies." Benitez leaned back in her chair.

"You're keeping abreast of New York, I assume?"

"Of course."

"How bad is it?"

"It looks bad, but it could have been a lot worse. In my opinion, it was intended to scare people more than anything." Benitez talked in a calm tone.

"You make it sound like this was planned."

"When you examine the targets of the destruction, it's hard to not make that conclusion. Fires tend to be all consuming, raging out of control across whole blocks. These were more controlled, burning down assets and homes of those associated with the two churches that were bombed."

Bennett drew back, his head pressed back while maintaining eye contact. Then his head turned slightly and his left eyebrow came down on his eye.

"I don't know if that sounds scarier or not. You're saying someone orchestrated this riot. Do you have proof?"

"No. That would be hard to get halfway across the country. From the way events unfolded, my professional judgment comes to no other conclusion."

Scoffing, Bennett replied, "You're starting to sound like Gint."

Benitez offered no reply and her expression remained fixed. Fully erect, she looked at Bennett with quiet confidence. After moments of silence, she said, "I will have those documents to you today."

"Very good. Dismissed."

Chapter Ten
Reactions

Calmness prevailed in the situation room. Most of the attendees sat at the central table. A few of lesser ranks flitted around the room at various jobs. Brook Tyler looked at the men and women who sat before her. Outwardly, they looked calmer and more rested than she did.

"It's been four days since the riot. What do we know?"

"Madam President," Quintin Melleck started, "local authorities have arrested eight people in connection with the riots. We are not sure if they are also being questioned about the bombing because the authorities are not sharing information."

"Are these ringleaders or just participants?"

"As far as we can tell, participants."

"What about those who planned the bombing or led the riots?"

"We are not receiving that information," Attorney General Tallenson commented. "Since no federal assets were damaged…"

"We cannot demand the information, I've heard." Tyler's voice was still sharp. "And the last two days?"

"There has been no terrorist activity or talk of further plans," Melleck stated.

"So, has this run its course? Are people going to settle down?" Tyler's stare dared people to talk. The silence that followed gave her an answer. "I heard people were leaving New York City. Surely you must know something about that."

Clentin Carmichel, Secretary of Information, spoke for the first time. "The names of those that we could find who were leaving the city are all registered at one Puritan church or another. Those families affected by the riots but not affiliated with one of the churches show a trend to move deeper into the city."

"Deeper?"

"Manhattan, Long Island."

"Putting an obstacle between them and the Puritans?"

"So it would seem. Madam President," Carmichel continued. "The same thing is happening on a smaller scale in other cities. It appears that people who are moving to new locations are now inquiring about the church affiliation of that neighborhood before deciding to live there."

"So you are saying it has only taken three weeks since the death of Arhus Gint for people to start segregating themselves?"

"It would appear so, ma'am."

"This could be a good thing, ma'am," Melleck interjected. "It should reduce tensions in the neighborhoods."

"Are you saying that a society segregated between the religious and non-religious people is a good thing?" Tyler's voice went up in volume with the question. "Do you really think it will help promote peace and understanding between the two?"

"I think it will lower tensions for the time being. I am not making a statement if it is good or bad in the long run." Melleck gave no ground while looking at the president.

"So we are going to solve our present problems at the expense of our future?"

"Madam President," Harrow Adams, Secretary of the Interior, said, "if we don't find a solution to the current situation, we might not have a future. People are still demonstrating around the country, but at least it's peaceful. I don't think there is one college campus that hasn't had at least one group of students marching through it."

"Students march for anything," Tyler dismissed with a wave. "It makes them feel like they are doing something. I'm more worried about the people with bombs."

"I think the nation was shocked by the events in New York City," Tallenson said. "Everyone I know was. It made the country pause and consider what it was doing. Gave people some perspective. I mean, by God, we're not Indonesia, you know."

"What is the situation in Indonesia?" Tyler's transition to the new subject was made without emotion.

"The events in America and other countries have emboldened factions in the country," Wo Standington, Secretary of State, said in a neutral voice. "I am confident that we will see more fighting soon. At least four smaller factions have increased rhetoric about their dissatisfaction with the current government."

"No one's satisfied with their current government," Tyler spat out. "It's a coalition of seven different groups, none of whom were even close to being happy with the result. I assume the agitating factions are the ones that were expunged?"

"Yes. There is also one faction in the coalition that has become more vocal about their dissatisfaction also."

"A pile of garbage all around," Tyler said just loud enough for people to hear. "As long as there is no threat of their conflict spilling over, I don't care what happens there."

"Our contacts with the Western Pacific Conglomerate indicate that they are keeping a close watch on the situation. I am sure they are even less willing for the situation to cause trouble outside of Indonesia." Standington eyed Melleck as he made the comment.

"Should we contact them?"

"Not at this time, ma'am. It would cause the Conglomerate to believe we think they are weak." Melleck looked back at Standington.

Tyler huffed. "Weak they aren't. Any other areas of the world we need to worry about? Or are we the only part of the world losing its mind?"

"Europe has quieted down but is still a soup of different groups and demands," Standington continued. "I wouldn't count on Europe settling down anytime soon, but they don't appear to be exporting their unrest here. The rest of the world has seen very minor, local declarations by all the normal voices, but nothing that raises alarms or concern. I hate to say it, but we seem to be the center of this church thing."

"I want some celebrities on the interfaces asking for calm and understanding. People need to be quieted down. We can do that, can't we?" Tyler searched the faces of those at the table.

"We have friends that will be happy to help," Carmichel said with a smile. "They love having their faces on viewers sounding benevolent."

"Just try to make it look like it was their idea. And let's have no more riots for a while, okay, gentlemen?" Tyler stood up and walked purposefully out of the room.

"Very nice," Valesco said as he stared at the display in front of him, showing membership numbers. The number slowly ticked up with time.

"Better than projections," Garo responded.

"And how long will it last?"

"At least two weeks, from our models. We shouldn't need any more incentives before then."

"How is Minnesota progressing?"

"A large portion of the increase is from there."

"Wonderful!" Valesco smiled as he turned. He placed his hands, fingertip to fingertip, on his lower jaw. "I assume the next incentives have been prepared?"

"They are ready now. They only lack the command." Garo smiled as if the thought caused him pleasure.

"We will wait. I wouldn't want the president to lose too much sleep. At least not yet. Has the government formulated a response?" Valesco smirked in anticipation.

"Our man says that they are proceeding with some 'announcements' by celebrities to help calm the people down." Garo laughed while talking.

"Is that all?" No laughter came from Valesco.

"Yes. They are helpless and floundering in their own ineptness."

"The states did that for us, removing most of their power." Valesco clapped once and rubbed his hands. "Has there been any progress infiltrating the military?"

"There we are having problems." Garo's hesitant walk toward Valesco exuded worry. "The military organization is patently anti-alien, as can be understood, given recent history. Most of those who believed in the aliens either left the military in protest of what the military did when the aliens were here or they were removed for various reasons. We have to start from the lowest levels. Even then, true believers have a hard time hiding their feelings. Most have been moved to jobs of little consequence."

"Keep trying, but if there is no real progress in a year, terminate the program. By then, we will need our resources in other places."

"As you wish," Garo said with a sigh of relief.

"That doesn't mean I am happy with your results in this area." Valesco turned and gave Garo a stare, one that seemed intended to kill. "Do not fail me in any other area. Understood?"

"Understood, sir."

The computer calculated while Joseph set his head on his table and tried not to fall asleep. The soft ding of the doorbell brought his head up.

"Come in," he said without enthusiasm.

Wenk walked through the door. He was looking at his interface while he walked, as was his frequent habit. He didn't look up until he was at the table. A frown formed on his face when he did.

"You look awful."

"Thanks for the encouragement," Joseph responded.

"Where you been?"

"All over the place, then mostly here." Joseph laid his head back on the table.

"The project for Bennett?"

"Yes," Joseph said in a drawn-out fashion.

"You late?"

"Me? Never."

"What you doing?" Wenk walked around the table to look at the display. He studied it for a while. "Optimization program."

"Running different scenarios. Having it optimize all the parameters at once was too complicated, so I'm running each one separately, then making my own adjustments."

"Land usage per... Is this the base?"

"Ding, ding, ding, we have a winner!" Joseph made the statement with his head buried on his arms.

"You really need to get some sleep," Wenk said with a serious look at his friend.

"I want to get done early." The comment was more of a groan than anything.

"Do you really think you're going to make good decisions as slap-happy as you are?"

"I want to get done early. Wait, I said that."

"Do I have to get Mercedes in here?" Wenk put his hands on his hips.

Joseph looked up. "That's low, that's really low. Hit a man when he's down, why don't you?"

"Friends take care of each other, remember? Now go get some sleep and don't force me to use the Mercedes gambit."

"Fine, *Mother*, I'll get some sleep."

"Now." Wenk pointed at the bedroom door.

"Yes, now." Joseph stood up and shuffled toward the bedroom.

"Have you eaten anything?" Wenk asked as he turned to watch.

"Don't push it, bub." Joseph pointed into the air.

Wenk watched as Joseph entered the bedroom and closed the door. Once closed, Wenk sat at the table and examined the display, reading the accumulated tables. He pulled up the ever-changing model of the base and then switched it to past, completed models.

"Wow, he's doing the whole base!" he said quietly to himself. "Hmm, yeah, the airstrip is going to be a problem. It really needs to be moved unless you want jets flying through those buildings there." Wenk flipped to another model.

"What? What the hell?" He looked at the tabs under the model. " 'Maximize food production.' That explains the cows and pigs. Hmm, too inefficient, though who doesn't love a good steak? Ah, that would be Quinzie. She'd make friends of the cows and then not let anyone slaughter them. Probably organize them into a union that demanded equal treatment." Wenk laughed at the thought. Then his face changed. "You know, most of the army guys think she's weird. I wonder if she would go out with me? I could tolerate vegetarian for a meal or two."

*   *   *

Joseph rolled to a sitting position and sat on the side of the bed. Rubbing his head and eyes, he looked at the clock. Not remembering what time he had lain down made it hard to know how long he had been asleep, but the clock read eleven. Pushing off, he stood and walked to the door. On the way, he realized how badly he needed a shower.

The open door revealed Wenk at the table, studying the display. A few memories came back as he walked to the table.

"You still here?" Joseph asked in a groggy voice.

Wenk looked at himself. "I guess so. Pretty sure I'm not dreaming."

Joseph scoffed. "How long I been asleep?"

"About four hours." Wenk kept his eyes on the screen.

"Why you still here?"

"Kind of lost track of time. And this is fun!" The computer came to the end of its calculations and displayed the results. Wenk moved numbers and boxes around and restarted the calculations.

"I'm going to take a shower," Joseph said with a slow voice, turning.

"Good idea. By the time you're done, I think I'll have this ready for you."

"Thanks, I think," Joseph said in a half-awake manner.

The shower felt good and woke him up. The shave also felt good. Fresh clothes completed the experience. Spraying his shoes to freshen them was clearly a good idea. Once he was done, Joseph felt like a person again. Then his stomach grumbled and reminded him of other needs.

Walking back into the living area, Joseph was happy to find that eleven had meant in the morning. He made his way to the refrigerator only to find it empty of anything that looked like food or drink. Taking a glass from the cupboard, the last one, he filled it with cold water. His stomach protested again.

"In a minute," he told it. "What you got?" he asked Wenk as he walked to the table again.

"I'm not sure what your goals are, but I have some pretty neat layouts here." Wenk pulled up one of the models. "We need to lose the livestock."

"Yeah, they take up too much room," Joseph replied. "I kept them as a possibility just in case it worked out somehow."

"Yeah, well, you can produce a whole lot more food without them, that's for sure. What exactly are you wanting? People or produce?"

"Both, according to Bennett." Joseph took his second long drink.

"Just like a bureaucrat." Wenk shook his head. "If you stick to plants, you get the most results."

"You really think people are going to convert to pure vegetarians?"

"Probably not, but it would give us something to trade with the locals. Are you really thinking of growing crickets? I don't think people will be thrilled with that." The scowl on Wenk's face gave emphasis.

"They're to feed the fish." Joseph finished the water. "I need food. You coming?"

"Ah, sure. I guess I can stop doing this for a while." Wenk's tone made his reluctance clear.

"What about your day job?"

"Writing a report? Boring! This is way better."

"Isn't someone waiting for that report?"

"No one's screaming yet, so I got time." Wenk shrugged as he said it.

Joseph chuckled. "My friend, you have a funny sense of urgency."

"Hey," Wenk said, standing up, still watching the display, "is it like anyone really cares about the greenhouse project?"

"They very well might in the very near future! Not to mention Mercedes." Joseph pointed at the display.

"Oh, good point." A small amount of panic ran across Wenk's face. "Guess I should finish the report, huh?" Wenk's expression changed to one of guilt.

"Yes, but after lunch. I'm starved."

As they made their way from the apartment, a thought hit Joseph. "I seem to remember I had some chicken wings, but when I looked in the fridge, they weren't there. You know anything about that?"

"They were really good."

"You ate my chicken wings?" Joseph asked in disbelief as Wenk headed down the hallway.

"Hey, you know how much I love chicken wings. If you didn't want me to eat them, you shouldn't have left me alone with them." Wenk raised his chin.

"Weren't you the one who told me to get some sleep?"

" *You* listened."

"You owe me a dozen chicken wings."

"Ha!" Wenk stepped into the elevator with a long stride. "Good luck collecting on that!"

Chapter Eleven
My Little Runaway

The train was slowing down, but not quite as much as Worthia had thought from watching it from her home. She crouched in the long grass next to the track, a pack made of a sack with ropes attached on her back.

"There's no going back now, girl," she told herself as she watched the train. She had changed into some pants her brother had outgrown for better running, but she had kept the skirt, stuffing it in the pack. She just couldn't bring herself to throw it away, telling herself it could be used for many things as an excuse to keep it.

Picking an open train car, she started running. Sprinting to full speed, the train car still slowly slipped away from her. Realizing she was not running fast enough, she quickly formulated another plan. As the next open car came near, she removed the pack from her back and threw it into the car as the open door approached. Unencumbered, she was able to run faster, pacing the rail-car. The cargo car was an old-fashioned one that had a handrail and step on the outside. Grabbing the handrail with her right hand helped keep pace with the car. In one movement, she grabbed the rail with the other hand and jumped to put her foot on the step.

She missed. Holding on with both hands, she pulled herself up and away from the ground, fearing an entanglement that would cause her to fall. Frantically kicking her legs, she managed to get her left foot onto the step and stand on one foot. Sighing in relief, she took a deep breath and looked up.

The bridge was a lot closer than expected. The heavy metal fencing along the side was fast approaching and did not look to leave room for someone to stand outside the train while on the bridge. Gulping, Worthia did a shoulder roll into the open door, rolling over once completely before stopping. The metal fencing rushed by as she lay on the wood floor.

Taking several deep breaths, Worthia tried to force her heart to beat slower. Turning her head showed her pack within arm's reach. Looking upwards, she said a prayer of thanks.

"I made it," she said softly.

"And what do we have here?" an old, male voice said from the back of the car. Rising onto her elbows, Worthia looked in the direction of the voice. A large crate occupied most of the back half of the car, but room was left between the crate and the walls, enough for someone to walk along. It was just then that she noticed the smell, one like straw that had been left in the barn too long and desperately needed to be cleared out. She coughed once. Footsteps started coming around the crate.

"Well, my, my, my. We have another rider, don't we?" The shape was hard to make out with so little light making it behind the crate. It appeared to be as tall as a man, but was loosely defined, as if he was wearing a lot of worn clothing. "And a girl to boot! I don't get many visitors on these trips. Where are you going, honey?"

"East," Worthia replied, keeping her eye on the moving pile of clothes.

"Well, then, you're on the right car. Curious having a girl on the train. Let's take a look at you."

The man who came from behind the crate looked old, older than her father. It could have just been the ragged clothes and unwashed appearance, but Worthia doubted it. His mouth was full of black and missing teeth, his face held more dirt than her brother's shoes, and the smell increased as he drew closer. Worthia took a quick glance outside, out of reflex, but the train was picking up speed rapidly, having navigated across the bridge. Jumping from the train would be dangerous, plus she would never catch another on this side of the bridge.

"How old are you, girly?"

Worthia remained silent.

"Oh, come now, talk to me. I never get anyone to talk... or other things. Tell old George about yourself."

The man kept coming, not fast, but not stopping. Worthia stayed where she was. There was nowhere to run anyway. She thought hard about the situation.

"Here, let George take a close look at you. You might have hurt yourself getting in the car, mighten you? I'll just have a quick look."

As the man got close, he tried to pounce on Worthia. Bringing up her feet, the man landed on the bottom of her feet while she grabbed his wrists with her hands. Twisting to her right, she pushed with her feet. The man's face filled with surprise as he fell out the door, quickly disappearing from view.

"Didn't count on me having brothers who liked to roughhouse, did you?" she shouted out the door with spite.

Breathing deeply for the first time after the man was gone, the stench overwhelmed Worthia, causing her to gasp. She crawled, coughing, to the opposite side and breathed in fresh air. Once she had recovered, she removed her shoes and set them at the back end of the door. Then she recovered her pack and moved to the front end of the door. The wind was getting stronger, too strong to lay in front of the opening. The front of the car was occupied by another large crate, an area as wide as the door in the middle the only unoccupied space.

Moving between the wall and the crate, Worthia made a pillow from her pack and lay down, the skirt proving its worth in the pack as a pillow. As she lay her head on the pack, weariness washed over her. It was still early in the evening, but her eyes felt the need to close. An hour would pass before anyone missed her at home and by that time, the train would be too far for anyone to consider chasing it. As the small bit of wind that made it between the wall and crate fluffed her hair, Worthia relaxed and fell to sleep, somehow more at peace than she had been for months. By the time the door automatically closed, the sensors detecting a sufficient drop in odor in the car, she was fully asleep.

*   *   *

The slowing of the train car woke Worthia. She dug a large amount of sand from her eyes as she rose.

"What time is it?" Looking around, she noticed the doors were closed, but strong light sneaked in through the cracks. "Could I have slept all night?"

Picking up her pack, Worthia removed her water bottle and took a long drink. She thought about the food, but decided to wait. The train felt as if it was coming to a stop. Standing, she tried to look out the space between the doors, but it was not wide enough to show anything meaningful. Sitting back down so she wouldn't fall when the train stopped, she decided she could only wait.

"If the doors don't open here, I'll just have to wait on the next stop."

The train stopped with a small jerk. Next, she heard air escaping from underneath the train, then silence. The silence seemed to stretch on, but then she heard voices outside the car. She told her panic that it was fine, because she needed someone to open the doors anyway, but her panic refused to be totally persuaded. Soon, an electronic-sounding click came from the door next to her and it opened.

"Okay," a deep man's voice said, "get in there and find out what the heck they sent us now."

A young man in a green outfit jumped into the car. He was about as old as Worthia's oldest brother, maybe twenty, and was very fit. The outfit looked like a uniform with pockets on the front of the shirt and he had on some kind of boots.

"Let's see," the young man said, looking around, "we have... whoa!"

"Whoa what?" the voice called from outside.

"You gotta see this to believe it!" The young man approached Worthia and held out his hand in a gentle manner. "It's okay, darlin', no one is gonna hurt you here. Let me help you out."

The man did not smell like the old man had and he was definitely cleaner. He smiled, a kind smile, and stopped his hand about two feet from Worthia, waiting for her to take it. She didn't feel anything threatening from him, but reminded herself to still be careful. Slowly taking the man's hand, she let him help her to her feet and lead her to the door.

"What the...!" said a man standing in front of the door on the ground. He was bigger than any of the five others who stood around him and his clothes had some stripes on the shoulder. "How the hell did you get in there?"

Even with the language he used, he didn't seem mean or harsh. Worthia had heard that people spoke with more cursing outside in the world, but had never been exposed to it.

"Help her down, boys. Can't leave her in there."

All five of the younger men rushed to help Worthia down from the car. It shocked her at first, but then she took hold of two hands and they lowered her to the ground. All the men stared like they hadn't seen a girl before. It was a little unnerving.

"Sergeant, is that my construction supplies?" came another voice from beyond the circle of guys. The big man turned, the others following with reluctant looks in their eyes.

"Won't know until I unload it," the sergeant replied.

"Well, I sure hope so, I've been waiting days for that stuff and I was told it was readily available. Now..." The voice stopped when the man came into view. He was as old as the sergeant, older than the others, but wasn't dressed in green. He wore blue jeans and a collared shirt that had three buttons at the top. Plus, he wasn't wearing boots, but some kind of soft, low shoe. The thing that caught Worthia's attention most was his eyes, more exactly around his eyes. They didn't look the same as everyone else's. The man sighed, tilted his head, and put his hands on his hips.

"Okay, which one of you mooks ordered a girl?"

The question brought laughter from the young men around her. It was pleasant laughter, not mean, but she still felt her cheeks getting warmer.

"I think you ordered the wrong model, though," the man continued. "This one looks too new." More laughter followed.

"Looks like a runaway," the sergeant said. "First refugee we've had on a train, though."

Worthia's mind went into full throttle. "Yes! I'm a refugee. I request sanctuary!"

"There you go," the man said. "She said the magic word. Now we can't put her back on the train. So, Sergeant Harjo, what are you going to do with her? She came with your cargo."

Worthia took a deep breath and slowly let it out. Her nerves seemed to settle.

"I was hoping you'd take her to the induction center for me?" the sergeant said and raised his eyebrows. "Unless you want me to slow down unloading these cars by having one of my men do it."

The man tsked. "The things I do for you. Fine, I'll take her, but you get moving on these cars! And if my material shows up, make sure you put it where I can get to it."

"Of course, Mr. Gint." The sergeant turned to her and swooshed his hand. "Little lady, if you please."

Hesitantly at first, Worthia walked past the young men toward Joseph. He smiled at her and bowed.

"Pleased to meet you, Ms..."

"Kerala, Worthia Kerala." She smiled at the man's formality. "Pleased to meet you, Mr. Gint."

"Joseph," came the reply as Joseph rose and started walking away from the train car, inviting Worthia to join him with a wave.

"That's a biblical name," Worthia said as she walked.

"Jewish, actually. My dad's best friend is... was... a Jew and I was named after him."

"Oh, did..." Worthia stopped before asking the question.

"Worthia is an unusual name, one I'm pretty sure I haven't heard before. Is it a family name?"

"Sort of. My mother likes making up meaningful names."

"And let me guess. Worthia means 'worthy of' something?"

"Yes," Worthia said, taking a breath before speaking more. "Worthy of God."

"So you're a Puritan?"

"Is it that obvious?" She gave him a weak smile. "I was raised a Puritan."

"But you don't know if you want to be one?"

"I don't know anything else, but then, I haven't been told anything else."

"Is that why you left?"

"No." She took a couple of steps before answering. It did feel good to have someone to talk to who wasn't telling her she was wrong all the time. "I'm sixteen and in two years, I'd be expected to marry."

"At eighteen?" The amount of surprise in the question was huge.

"That is when girls normally get married, at least in our community. I really didn't want to end up married to some farmer, so I decided to leave."

They exited the rail yard. Beyond were roads and new-looking buildings. Almost everyone wore the green uniform-like clothes. A few wore long white coats.

"Where are you from, then?" When Worthia didn't answer right away, the man said, "Give me a state at least."

"Idaho," Worthia replied tentatively. She didn't notice that the man had stopped walking for a step or two. She stopped and turned toward him.

"Idaho?" The man laughed. "You are a long way from home, aren't you?"

"It's no longer my home," Worthia said with a firm voice. "If I'm not to stay here, wherever I land will be my home."

The man laughed and started walking again. "Give credit to a girl with determination. You know, I have a friend that I think you and her would get along famously."

Worthia waited to talk again. They seemed to be headed toward a white building closer to a set of gates. "Can I ask you, what is an induction center?"

"It's like a greeting center, where new people go first to get registered and such." The man turned and smiled at her. "Don't worry, I know the woman who works there and she's really nice. Particularly if you give her chocolate."

"I don't have any chocolate. It wasn't allowed. Too expensive, they said."

"Oh, don't worry." The man laughed. "I keep her supplied in chocolate most of the time."

"Where will they send me?" Worthia shook a little with the question.

"I'm sure they'll keep you here. Not like we have established somewhere to send refugees. You're lucky, we haven't received that many yet."

"Is there work here? I can work for my stay."

"Work? Heck, more than you can shake a stick at, whatever that means. My mother said it all the time, though when she shook a stick at you, it wasn't work, it was because you did something wrong. First, though, you have to receive an education."

"My parents taught me what was necessary at home."

"Necessary?"

"It doesn't seem that they felt much was necessary." Worthia looked at the ground while she said it.

"Don't worry, we can catch you up on your studies. Here."

The man opened the door, letting Worthia walk inside first. The room was nothing like she had seen before. There were tables and chairs, pictures that floated in the air, people milling about, and lots of sound. Everything was clean and there was no smoke from fires. In fact, the room was warm, even though there was no fireplace or stove.

"Madge," the man said when he walked in, "I have a refugee for you."

A dark woman walked around a table and came toward them. "And where did you find this little one?"

"She hopped a train ride from out west."

"Oh, dear child, why'd you do a thing like that? You could have been hurt." The woman's round face looked concerned.

"I would like sanctuary," Worthia said.

"Sanctuary? What could you possibly need sanctuary from?"

"Don't worry," the man said, "when you hear her story, you'll agree."

"Bless you, child, come this way. I'll get you all processed right away and then we can get you into a shower and some proper clothes."

"With hot water?" Worthia asked.

"Of course, of course, honey. Where have you been living?"

"Madge," Joseph interrupted. "How are we doing on living space for the new entries?"

Madge got closer to him as she spoke quietly. "With all the new people the army's been sending us, we're starting to have to ask people to take in the new arrivals. It would really help if you would get some new apartments made. People aren't used to being so crowded. But don't worry, she's just one little girl. I'm sure we can find a spot for her."

"Thanks, I appreciate it. She seems to be a smart kid."

"You just let Madge take care of things." Madge gave him a slap on the shoulder and turned to Worthia. "Now come on, dear. We have a smidgen of paperwork to fill out and then we'll get you that shower and new clothes."

Joseph watched them go for a few moments and then went back outside. Once there, he called up the living area statistics on his interface. Madge was proven correct. Even though they had only had a handful of refugees, the extra military personnel were straining their capacity. "And I have a C.B. battalion coming. I hope they bring tents or something. If not, we will have to take the planes out of the hangar and bunk them in there. Things are not going smoothly at all."

Shaking his head, Joseph walked back to his apartment, which was doubling as his office. Personally checking on the contents of the train shipments now would be too early and only irritate Harjo, as much as he wanted to. "I hope they contain concrete mix and rebar. Windows would be nice, too." By the time he reached his building, he had found nothing on his interface to make his day better yet.

On a whim, he checked the new entry status. Worthia's name stuck out. As he scrolled through the information, he noted that a resident assignment was on hold pending an opening. He felt his stomach drop at the thought of not having a place to assign her. He took a breath and let it out.

"Oh, hell, why not. Computer, add my name to the list of voluntary apartment sharing for Worthia Kerala."

"Your name has been added, Mr. Gint."

"Thanks." Joseph walked into the building. "Not like that isn't going to raise a few eyebrows."

Chapter Twelve
Darn College Kids

The last to Benitez's office, Joseph entered without caring about his tardiness. He was the only one located in another building, so it seemed like a foregone conclusion that he would be last. Bennett stood looking out the window while Harjo lounged in one of the chairs. Dirty boot marks on the desk indicated that he had already been reprimanded by Benitez once. Joseph took a seat next to him and gave the man a friendly elbow.

"Good, we're all here. Commander?" Benitez sat, leaving the last chair not behind the desk.

"Thank you, LC." Bennett turned to face the group. "I am getting a lot of questions from above about what we are doing here, ordering these supplies. They want to know why we are ordering so many construction materials."

"We are having refugees from Puritan areas come into the camp," Joseph started. "We had one the other day who hitched a ride on the supply train."

"I was meaning to ask you about that Puritan you brought in," Benitez said as she turned to Joseph. "You think that was a good idea? You sure she is not some kind of spy?"

"At sixteen?"

"Could happen."

"You talk to her, decide for yourself." A huff accompanied Joseph's statement.

"I plan to. Anyway, with all the army personnel that have been sent here, our official occupancy rate has been exceeded," Benitez added.

"Do we have numbers to support this?" Bennett asked.

"I can send them to you anytime." Benitez activated her interface. "Good thing we have a budget item for construction."

"That's lab construction, not apartments." Bennett pointed at the LC.

"It's a multi-purpose building," she answered easily. Joseph smiled.

Bennett gave both of them a stare, then looked away. "If I didn't know better, I would think you two are in on this thing together. Scratch that, I'm sure of it."

"You're the one who assigned me," Joseph retorted.

"And you requested a construction battalion on top of everything. What is wrong with local construction crews?"

"We haven't had time to apply the new security screening protocols to them. We barely have time to screen the new personnel." Benitez crossed her arms.

"Screen for what?"

"Terrorist links."

Bennett gave her a stern look, then said, "You mean Puritan membership."

"Potato, po-tah-to."

"Look, the brass is not going to overlook all this. With the riots over, they are paying closer attention to all military bases and personnel..."

A corporal opened the office door and took a step into the room. "Sorry to intrude, sir, but I really think you want to see the news feeds right now." The corporal disappeared out of the office.

"Now what?" Bennett grumbled as he activated the desk display. A news 'face' stood in the center of the view. A mass of students marched behind her.

"Yes, this is one of only dozens of campus protests that have sprung up today all over the country. The students say they are demanding the truth from the government. What truth they are demanding is not clear."

The scene changed to focus on the students. At least six across and forming an endless line, students marched while waving homemade signs, shaking their fists, or pounding improvised drums made out of anything that resembled one. As they marched, they shouted mostly in unison.

"We want the truth! We want the truth! The truth and only the truth!"

"And who is going to give it to you?" a voice yelled.

"Not the government!" the crowd shouted back.

"And who will give it to you?"

"The *people*!"

The cycle of chanting continued. Some of those who marched looked to be enjoying the outing more than the chanting, howling random or nonsensical phrases, but most appeared deadly serious as only college students could. A few older people could be seen, though there was no hint if they were professors, interested bystanders, or outside instigators. The camera quickly bored of the scene and switched to the campus security that watched the march. Their number was noticeably fewer and their main function appeared limited to making sure no one was run over by the march.

"How many campuses are marching?" Benitez asked.

"Thirty-two," replied a computer voice.

"Saved by college students," Joseph said with a chuckle.

"That's not funny, Mr. Gint!" Bennett shouted.

"Interesting timing," Benitez commented to no one in particular.

"What does that mean?" Bennett switched his attention to her.

Benitez straightened in her chair. "The noise over the riots has died down. People have seemed to stop reacting to what happened. Then, all of a sudden, dozens of campuses are overrun by protesting students on the same day like clockwork. This doesn't seem suspicious to you?"

"It would be easy to communicate to each other and coordinate the events," Joseph said.

"But getting them organized in a week or two? No way. They had to start planing before the riots."

"Meaning?" Bennett asked.

"Meaning my new screening protocols are definitely needed. We can't afford to let any untrustworthy individuals on this base."

Benitez calmed herself. "Plus, I would wager it means the president is having a stressful day, which means the brass will be distracted for a while."

"Isn't there some of the construction that a local company can do if they are strictly supervised?" Bennett took his seat on the far side of the desk and placed his elbows on it.

"Yes, if I can use some of those extra personnel to supervise," Joseph said before Benitez could get in a word. "Of course, they would need to bring a lot of their own equipment. By the way, where are my C.B.s?"

"On their way," Bennett replied with a flat voice. "It is taking them longer because they are bringing their own equipment."

"I hope they bring their own living quarters, too."

"I think they are bringing 'temporary housing.' "

"Great! We can make it permanent!" Joseph's eyes brightened.

Bennett and Benitez rolled their eyes while Harjo chuckled.

"I still want to go over the master plan." Bennett switched off the news feed. "*Not* that I am authorizing it. Parts of it I find concerning. Other parts I'm not clear exactly what is called out."

"Pick a time and I will be there," Joseph said with a smile.

"Count on it." Bennett looked at Harjo. "You haven't said much. Anything you'd like to offer?"

"I need a bigger rail yard!" Harjo said with enthusiasm.

"Don't worry," Joseph said with a shake of his head in the sergeant's direction, "it's in the plan."

"Then I like the plan already." Harjo gave him a wide grin.

Multiple displays showed versions of the same scene: college students marching across campuses. Valesco smiled as he watched all twelve displays at once. "Beautiful how the sheep respond, isn't it?"

"Makes one think they should be on the payroll," Garo responded. The comment caused Valesco to let out a laugh.

"That would ruin some of the fun, my friend," he said, half turning his head. "Just watching all those students do our bidding while thinking it is their idea, that's poetry. Never knowing they were talking to a computer program and not each other just makes it that much more delicious. This is why people need us!" His hands went wide. "They rush to follow so easily, never asking why or who, just doing! Can you believe that for so long, they have been wandering aimlessly in this world, no purpose but their own delights? Think of all the lost time, lost effort. Think how much better the world will be with someone to make their path clear."

"And they will love you for it," Garo said with a chuckle of his own.

"People have always wanted to be led. And those who don't, well, we will have no use of them." One hand flipped over his shoulder as Valesco watched the displays. "Are the preparations ready for Los Angeles?"

"Of course. We are scheduled to start tonight."

"I want that sycophant of a preacher dead, I want his staff dead, and I want that ugly excuse for a house of worship destroyed so nothing is left standing! I don't know what the architect was thinking when he designed that thing, but if he was standing in front of me, I would shoot him, too!"

"I could arrange that."

Valesco waved with his right hand. "I think I shall show a little restraint. Inform me when it is done."

"Of course," Garo said with a bow.

"So beautiful."

"It's really nice of you to let me stay here," Worthia said as she looked around the apartment. "It's so huge for one person."

"Not a problem," Mercedes replied as she closed the door. "I'm afraid you're going to have to sleep on the couch, at least for a while. I only have the one bed."

"I'm used to sleeping with my sisters," Worthia said with a shrug.

Mercedes laughed. "Wow, you did live a sheltered life. The fact is that the bed is really only big enough for one person. In fact, it's not that much bigger than the couch, which is actually pretty comfortable, by the way." Mercedes gave her a grin and a small chuckle.

"I'm sure I'll be fine." Worthia walked over to the couch and felt the cushions. "It feels strange."

"It's not stuffed with anything you're used to, I'm sure. Here, you can put your things in the closet." Mercedes led the girl to a closet off the bathroom and opened the door, moving some things off of two shelves and pushing them on others. "I have too much stuff, really. Sometime we can sit down and figure it all out."

Worthia put her small pack of items on one shelf. She looked into the bathroom and stared.

"You ever see indoor plumbing before?" Mercedes asked.

"Sort of, but nothing like that. And it's so big!"

"Ha! That's a small one. Here, take these sheets for the couch. It's now officially yours."

Worthia rubbed her hands on the sheets. They felt soft, softer than anything so thin should feel. The sheets were colored a pastel pink.

"Thank you again. I can't believe you are doing all this for me."

"Well, I couldn't let you stay with Joe. After I heard he had volunteered to take you in…"

"He's very kind." Worthia walked absent-mindedly to the couch, still rubbing the sheets.

"Kind?" Mercedes gave her a puzzled stare. "More likely he didn't think it through. You realize why staying with him would be a bad idea, don't you?"

"He is a guy, but I am not of marrying age yet and I have older brothers. It would be like having another one, right?" The statement ended with an unsure crack of the voice.

Mercedes could not contain her laughter. Putting her hand to her mouth, she tried to stifle the laughs, but only partially succeeded.

"Did I say something funny?"

"Around here, if a gal and guy live in the same apartment and they aren't related, people assume they are sleeping together." Mercedes noted confusion on Worthia's face. "Having sex?"

"Oh!" Worthia's cheeks blushed. "But they are supposed to be married, right?"

"Not necessarily. In fact, not usually."

"I have heard of such things. There are boys and girls who will hide up in the barn to… be together… but it was frowned upon, greatly. I don't think Joseph would ever do that."

"No, he wouldn't, but sometimes we have to protect him from himself. You hungry?"

"No, thank you, I was fed." Worthia gave Mercedes an analytical look. "You like him, don't you?"

Mercedes sighed, one that lowered her shoulders when it was over. She looked down instead of at the girl. "Yes, I do."

"Does he know?"

"Know? Who knows? Sometimes I'm not sure he lives in the same world we do, and other times I almost think he's going to say something." Mercedes looked off to the side at nothing.

"How long have you known him?"

"Five years, ever since being stationed here." Mercedes looked up, recovered her composure, and smiled. "But that's my problem and not yours."

"You should ask to court him," Worthia said firmly.

"Ask to court him?" Mercedes said the words slowly, as if they were in a foreign language.

"Yes. He's old enough, just ask him if you can start courting."

A smile came across Mercedes's face, followed by a giggle. She put her arm around Worthia and gave it a gentle hug.

"Little sister, you might have a great idea there! Now let's get you settled."

"My friends!" Valesco paced across the stage while he maintained eye contact with the camera. His arms were spread wide in front of him. The church was full. All the churches to which the signal was sent in real time were full beyond state-regulated capacity. "We all have seen the events in the last few weeks. Attacks on God-fearing churches! Attacks on God-fearing people!

"Now, I know some of you are asking, is this the end times? My friends, these are the end times, but not our end times. God will not allow his people to end. These attacks are the last, desperate gasps of a dying society. The old society. The Godless society! What we are experiencing are not death wounds, but the birth pains. The birth pains of our future!"

Amens, hallelujahs, and clapping issued from the crowd. Faces started to lose their worry. Valesco stopped in the center of the stage, arms to his side and hands straight in front, palms up.

"What we are seeing is the birth of a new nation, a God-fearing nation. Those who only pretend to be believers will be burned away. The true believers will remain because God has ordained it!" He pointed up in the air. "For too long, man followed the false teaching of men, written in books as if that made them true. But now we know what is true. We saw it with our own eyes. God spoke to us! God walked on the Earth. Now we know our place before God and we know what he expects of us!"

More clapping, with greater enthusiasm, spread through the crowd. The noise was filtered to a low level for the broadcast so Valesco's words were not lost.

"God does not need fancy technology. God does not need high-rise buildings. God does not need armies and planes. And neither do we. God needs only for us to accept him, and to care for each other and this world He has put us on." With arms crossed, Valesco's words were gentle, loving.

"That is why we have been establishing farm communes across this country: so that the faithful can rediscover the world that God has placed in our care. We were not made to live in concrete and glass cages. We were not meant to work in front of displays." Valesco's voice got louder. "We were meant to work the earth and meet each other as people, not images.

"Now, I know, you ask, what about those who do not believe?" Pacing began again as his clenched fist pumped. "I firmly believe, my brothers and sisters, that many, if not most of them, do not understand our message. Their minds have been *poisoned* by society. If we can only tell them, personally, friend to friend, the truth of God, they will come to enlightenment. All people desire the truth of God. It is in our nature because we were created by God. How can we not respond? How can we not love Him?"

Applause and enthusiasm rose from the crowd.

"And the few, you ask, that do not respond to His message." Again the volume dropped. "Sadly, my friends, I must tell you the truth, because the truth is what God would have us say at all times. Sadly, my friends, I must tell you that they will have no part with us. They must be cast out." His hand swept across his body before reaching for the crowd. "But do not blame yourselves, my friends. They bring this doom upon themselves."

That same evening, the Church of God's Covenant in Los Angeles was the location of a board meeting. A board meeting meant that wine and gourmet food flowed for the privileged few who knew about the true nature of the church. Outside the building, a team of individuals wore clothing that made the eyes wonder where their shapes started or stopped waited.

As wine glasses clinked inside, one of the intruders approached with a laser glass cutter. Once inside, the intruder quick-stepped his way to the security office, knowing it would be unoccupied. The rest entered and waited until the leader's interface blinked twice. The group of five quietly wound through the building, then the leader stopped and held up a fist. After a quick shake, air-powered slug-throwers were drawn. Three fingers came up and started to disappear one at a time. When the last finger was gone, the group burst into the room and fired. The pastor and the board members didn't even have time to know what was happening.

"Check the bathrooms," the leader said. Two members of the group exited the room. "Set the bombs."

The rest of the team left the room, moving to the structural supports of the building. As they did, the leader walked to the front of the building. After turning off the outside lights, she removed a small can of spray paint from her belt and wrote "God Is Dead!" on the sidewalk. Throwing the can in the bushes when complete, she didn't have long to wait for the entire team to join her.

With one wave of her arm, the team ran across the dark parking lot and through the bordering trees to their waiting ride. Five minutes later, the Church of God's Covenant was falling to the ground.

Chapter Thirteen
Factions

"We caught a break!" AG Tallenson shouted as he burst into the Oval Office.

"About time!" President Tyler responded, looking his way.

"One of the board members at the Church of God's Covenant is retired military."

"I don't think 'retired' warrants federal involvement," Security Secretary Melleck said, concern on his face.

"He wasn't just retired, he was placed on the recall list, which technically means…"

"He's still a federal employee," Tyler finished. She took a quick breath. "Get an investigation team there *now.* Our best."

"I know just who to send." Tallenson smiled as he turned.

"We still might want to be careful…" Melleck started.

"The hell with careful! This is our chance to get into the middle of this crap and we're going in with both feet! Alert any security forces we have in the area and contact the local authorities and tell them we are sending people to investigate the deaths." She gave Melleck a hard look.

"Yes, Madam President." Melleck turned and activated his interface, his hands shaking slightly and a worried look on his face. As he exited the Oval Office, he sent a one word message.

Trouble.

*   *   *

"With the investigation just underway," a news 'face' was saying into the camera, "we have now learned that one of the victims was a retired military man with reserve status. The federal government has announced that they will be taking over the investigation of the man's death."

"About time!" an older man, head topped with gray hair, at the sports bar said to the display. "Now get back to the game!"

"We don't want no federals snooping around here, Gary!" a middle-aged man all but shouted.

Gary turned his direction. "What have the locals done to solve any of the bombings or riots, huh, Mike? Probably in cahoots with the terrorists, it would seem to me!" Gary gave a gesture with his right hand.

"Like local security is going to let someone blow up buildings?" Mike stood up and walked toward his antagonist. "What are you, ex-military?"

"Sure am! And proud of it!" Bracing his hands on a chair and the counter, Gary looked to be ready for action.

"Stupid military that got people killed thirty years ago?" Mike swaggered within three feet.

"The military that stood up for this country and didn't just roll over when the aliens showed up, like the World Council did!" Gary got up and stepped within inches of the other. Faces were starting to turn red.

"At least no one in Jerusalem died!"

"Yes they did, you idiot!" Shouting like a drill sergeant, Gary all but spit in Mike's face, the moisture felt but not running.

"Idiot? I'll show you who's the idiot!"

The sports bar had experienced no brawls since opening. Tonight's would be the cause for major redecorating.

The ding from the interface prevented Joseph from pulling out any more hair. He had only lost a few strands, his hair stubbornly holding onto his scalp.

"What's wrong now," he said as he pulled up his interface. A message awaited him requesting his presence in Bennett's office.

"Oh, good, being called to the principal's office again. Wonder what I did wrong this time." As Joseph stood, he caught his reflection in the window glass. It showed his uncombed hair. He stared at it for a second, then waved at it.

"Nah, forget it. Why pretty up if I'm getting yelled at?"

The walk from his apartment to Bennett's office gave Joseph the opportunity to stretch his muscles. Doing so reminded him of how long he had been staring at the computer display without moving. It also reminded him of how long it had been since he had eaten, but that would have to wait. He did grab a quick cup of coffee as he walked through the administration building, loading it up with cream and sugar to increase the calorie count.

When he entered Bennett's office, he found Benitez already seated. Captain Allin was there also, standing in a corner, leaning against the wall. Joseph tried to remember if he had ever seen her sitting, other than at meals. He took a seat.

"Washington called. The president is getting pretty worked up with this alien church situation, particularly since it appears that the attacks on churches may have been executed by rival churches. So far, there is only circumstantial evidence, but it's enough to make people nervous." Bennett taking a breath gave room for Benitez to interject.

"Why… how exactly are we involved in this?"

"Tyler is calling in advisers, again." Bennett almost sighed with the comment.

Joseph rolled his eyes.

"No, this time it is different. And this time, she explicitly asked for you, Mr. Gint."

The statement caused Joseph's head to jerk in surprise. "Me? Why?"

"You haven't been quiet concerning your feelings about the alien churches. Plus, the fact that your father was considered something of an expert on the aliens doesn't hurt, either. I am sending you and Benitez to Washington for this meeting. I want Captain Allin to send any technical research data she thinks will be needed for the meeting."

"Like… what?" Joseph asked.

"I've talked to her about that already. She will provide Benitez with the information. Your secondary job, Mr. Gint, will be as a technical adviser, if needed."

"Okay." Joseph turned his hand palms up and shook his head a little in a dazed manner.

"What is the meeting to accomplish?" Benitez asked.

"The president is looking for policy on how to handle the churches and the situation. If they are at war, we need to formulate some kind of plan to deal with them."

"Arrest their sorry asses?" Joseph suggested.

"Harder than it sounds," Benitez said, tilting her head his way. "The infractions are local, the one killing being the exception, and local law enforcement has a bad history of not sharing. Plus, the fact that they might be compromised by one of the churches. These churches represent a large number of people in their areas. That means we can't just accuse them of something without proof."

"So you are saying the situation is also political," Joseph said.

"Yes, that is what I am saying, at least until we can get concrete proof of who is responsible. Right now all we have is… guesswork based on innuendo."

"Great! Decision making based on all unknowns. Sounds like Washington's standard operating procedure. At least I won't have to take a jet this time." Joseph sat back into the chair.

"You think I can't fly one?" Benitez asked, one eyebrow raised.

"There's nothing in your file about being able to fly a jet." Joseph almost laughed with the statement.

"You've seen my file?"

"I'm planning the future of this base. I've seen everyone's file. At least their skills and training, that is."

"I didn't realize you had access to that." She gave him a squinted stare.

"You only have to know how to fill out the forms." Joseph took a breath and let it out. "Besides, I'm not sure my stomach could take another trip. We're not on speaking terms as it is."

Bennett's stare allowed no contradictions. "You leave tomorrow morning, oh-six-hundred. Make sure you have everything you need with you for three days. Dismissed."

"Three days in D.C.," Joseph said as he stood up. "I can't wait. No, wait, I can, if that's an option?"

As they walked out of the office, Joseph fell into step with Benitez. "By the way, I would like to use, or you to use, some of your, shall we say, resources?"

"To do exactly what?" Benitez gave him a sideways stare.

"Locate someone for me. Someone who tends to disappear rather well."

"Exactly who is this person?"

There was a short pause allowing several steps. "My brother."

"You worried about him?"

"Johan? Ha, no, he can take care of himself. I need him to talk my mother into doing something for me."

Joseph looked around the room, matching people to the faces and names on his interface. He didn't look happy. He had been listening for an hour while the too-small room got warmer from the bodies crowded into it. Some had begun to sweat.

"Bureaucrat, bureaucrat, bureaucrat..."

"Stop mumbling," Benitez said quietly.

"This group is depressing. They don't understand."

"We don't understand what, Mr. Gint?" a man at the end of the table said in a stern voice. He was dressed in a three-piece suit that was long out of fashion. It was blue pin-stripe and made Joseph wonder what antique store he had bought it from. The man tried to act like he was running the meeting, which had not gone well with a few others in the room.

"You don't understand who you are dealing with," Joseph said with no surrender in his voice.

"We are dealing with religious fanatics."

"*No!* You are not!" Joseph pounded his hands on the table as he stood up. "You keep talking about laws and investigations and proof. These people don't care about laws or proof. If they did, they wouldn't be blowing up churches! They are the rising power base in this country and they mean to make the country into what they want. They don't care about the existing laws. Their excuse is that they are on a mission from God, but the real reason is the same it has always been. *Power!*"

"We have to operate within the confines of the law..." the man countered.

"Then you have lost already. The federal government has been weakened to almost nothing. These groups aren't afraid of us. They aren't afraid of the law because they own the law."

"You have proof of this?"

Joseph threw up his arms and threw his head back, unable to speak.

"We have circumstantial evidence," Benitez interjected, "and we know that many of the local law enforcement, particularly the elected ones, are members of the churches."

"That doesn't prove..."

"What the hell do you want? It laid out on a silver platter for you?" Joseph all but shouted. With a huff, he sat back down and gave the man a stare.

"We are here to find a legal, reasonable solution to the current problems," the man restarted. "We cannot fly off on emotion. Now..."

Joseph called up his interface and manipulated the display. After a minute, he moved his wrist over to Benitez to show her something. She frowned in response, then stood up. Joseph followed her.

"Where are you going?" the man asked.

"We are done here." Benitez moved purposefully to the door. Once outside, she turned toward the Oval Office. Without a word, she made her way until she reached the secretary in front of the office.

"I need to talk to the president right away."

"I don't know," the secretary said tentatively. "She's busy with this special meeting..."

"It's about her special meeting."

"Oh, okay. I will see if she will see you."

The woman talked to her desk interface in a hushed voice, looking over at Benitez and Joseph once. Then she turned to them.

"She can see you now."

Benitez did not wait an instant to enter the room. Inside, they found the president by herself, closing down her interface.

"Lieutenant Commander," the president said as she stood.

"Madam President. I need to talk to you about this… group… you have called."

"What about it?"

"Did you know that the man in there trying to take charge belongs to one of the alien churches?"

"We don't limit a person's religious affiliation when it comes to governmental jobs…"

"He's a member of the church that is causing all the trouble!" Benitez calmed herself after the statement, took a breath, and said, "Sorry, ma'am."

Tyler just stared for a second, then turned and took a few slow steps, her hands behind her back. "You're saying that we can't count on an unbiased look at the circumstances."

"I'm saying we can't count on him not sabotaging the whole effort."

The comment caused Tyler to spin around and look through a squint. "Do you really think he would do that? You are assuming an extensive organization."

"We can't afford not to assume that, Madam President."

"So you're saying we have to purge all church goers from the committee? Alien or otherwise?"

"It would be for the best. It would also assure unbiased action."

Tyler scoffed. "From your perspective, but I'm sure the churches will see it differently."

"President Tyler," Joseph cut in, "what is happening is a war among the churches, though some don't know they're in one yet. It is a reasonable assumption that Valesco is behind these attacks, seeing that his organization is one of the few not attacked yet. And given it is the largest in the country, it would have been the natural target of such attacks, if they would have been instigated by anti-alien factions. They remain not only unscathed, but have benefited the most from the attacks. He is trying to take over all the alien churches. Once he is done with those, he will move on to the traditional churches. By the time he has done that, he will control more than half of the people in the country and if we aren't prepared, we're fucked!"

Tyler looked at Joseph while bringing her hands in front of her just below her chin, tips together. She waited a few seconds before answering. "Young man, you will understand when I say that I can't take your opinion as an unbiased appraisal."

"Then let me bring in someone who can tell you from personal experience."

"Someone in the meeting?"

"No, but we can have them here tomorrow."

"Just how expert of a person is this?"

"She lived in one of the Puritan agricultural communes until recently."

Benitez gave him a look as he talked.

"Fine. Make an appointment for tomorrow with my secretary. Good day."

Tyler's turn was a clear dismissal. Joseph and Benitez made their way out of the office. As Benitez scheduled the appointment, Joseph worked his interface.

"Are we talking about who I think you're talking about?" Benitez asked.

"Who else?"

"You think she can handle the meeting?"

"She's a smart kid. I hear she's blazing through her studies even for being so far behind. They say she'll catch up in a year. Heck, she might even be smarter than me!"

"That wouldn't take much," Benitez said with a huff.

"You been talking to Mercedes?"

"You been keeping tabs on your little friend?"

"Of course," Joseph said, then looked a little uncomfortable. "I feel a sense of obligation. You know, like a big brother."

"Heaven help her if you're her big brother." The comment came out more as a laugh.

"Now I know you've been talking to Mercedes."

Looking around the room with wide eyes, Worthia stared with an open mouth. She went over all the details multiple times.

"This room is really old," she said.

"They've done a good job at preserving it. The whole building, actually. Can't even see the modern equipment. Of course, it helped that it's really small." Joseph sat on the couch with his feet on the coffee table, even after the look from Benitez.

"The stuff we used on the farm was made the same way as antiques are, but this stuff is the real thing! How old is that table?"

"A few hundred years, I think. I really wouldn't know, I wasn't born here."

Worthia started to look worried. "How... how am I supposed to do this?'

Joseph took his feet off the table and sat up, leaning toward the girl. "Just tell the truth. Don't hold back or try to figure out what she wants to hear. Tell the plain, simple truth. If you don't know, say so. Don't try to spare her feelings, either. She needs to know what it is like."

"Okay," Worthia said, shaking her head. "I just hope she doesn't get mad at me."

"She'd be madder if you don't tell her. Speak truth to power, as the old saying goes."

"Didn't people used to get their heads chopped off for doing that?" Worthia asked.

"Don't worry," Joseph chuckled, "that got outlawed centuries ago."

The door opened and President Tyler entered the room. Everyone in the room stood. Tyler moved directly to the little group at the couches.

"President Tyler," Joseph said, "I would like to introduce you to Worthia Kerala, late of Idaho, now of Revelation Base, South Dakota."

"A pleasure to meet you, ma'am." Worthia did a curtsy.

"A pleasure to meet you, young lady. I am told you were recently a member of a farm commune?"

"Yes, ma'am. Near Dubois."

"Can you tell me about it?" Tyler sat down on a couch. The rest of the group followed suit.

"What would you like to know? I mean, it was a farm with crops and animals and people."

"Everyone there worshipped the aliens?"

"We were taught they were God." Worthia nodded her head as she spoke.

"And what do you think?"

"I... I've never been told differently until recently."

"Did you run away because you didn't believe?"

"I ran away because I didn't want to get married in two years and knew there had to be more than what the commune offered. I didn't know what that was, but the way the pastor talked, there had to be something."

"And how did your pastor talk about non-believers? About me, for instance?"

Worthia bowed her head a little, not looking at Tyler. She took a breath and held it for a second before letting it out.

"It's fine, child, I've been called some pretty awful things." Tyler smiled with the comment. Worthia raised her head.

"He called you the Whore of Babylon."

Tyler reacted as if she had been slapped in the face. She gasped and her eyes went wide.

"He calls you other things, too, like the Devil's Bitch and the Camel."

"I get the idea," Tyler managed to get out. "What about unbelievers in general? How are they looked at?"

"The military is called the Army of the Devil or Army of Demons. He would tell people that the government wanted to take their children away and indoctrinate them, brainwash them into not believing. He would say that if we didn't stand firm, if we didn't reject everything outside of the church, we would never make it to Paradise and be condemned to Hell." Worthia's voice shook a little with the statements, as if their distaste affected her as she said them.

"And that talk didn't scare you from running away?" Tyler's voice wavered a little with the question.

"It sounded like manipulation to me. I mean, if the aliens were God, was he really so weak that we were on the brink of being overrun and condemned?"

Tyler let out a chuckle of relief. "I think you're right, it sounds like manipulation to me, too. Thank you for talking to me."

"Thank you for letting me come here. It's amazing!"

"It can be daunting, but yes, this room is amazing. I try to live up to it every day." Tyler stood and shook Worthia's hand before turning to Joseph and Benitez. "You've given me a lot to think about. I'll need time to process this. Thank you for coming."

As the three left the room, Benitez stared at the shocked expression on Joseph's face. Worthia just looked relieved.

"What's wrong?" Benitez asked Joseph.

"That's it? Give me time to think?"

"What did you expect?"

"Action. We need action!"

"You expect too much." Benitez gave a small huff and looked away. "You just turned that woman's world sideways. Give her a few days."

"Can we go see things?" Worthia asked excitedly.

"You mean sight-see?"

"Yes, if that is what you call it. Sight-see. That sounds right. I want to see sights!"

"Why not," Joseph said with a shrug. "We're here and it will be educational. Besides, I guess we need to wait a few days for people in Washington to think."

Chapter Fourteen
Arrangements

The slap was hard, knocking the woman to the the ground from her kneeling position. She didn't react except to slowly rise back to her knees. Tears showed in her eyes, but no whimper came from her lips. The tears were not from pain.

"You got sloppy!" Valesco screamed at the woman as he bent over her head. "You left the paint can. A paint can!" Another slap from the other direction struck the woman.

"I'm sorry, I didn't think it mattered. There were no prints."

"But there was trace threads from your gloves. They may be able to trace those to the special gloves you insist on wearing. How are the right people supposed to get blamed if they trace this back to you?"

Valesco paced away from the woman and stopped, his back to her. His hands tapped against each other behind his back as he rocked back and forth a little.

"What are we to do?" Valesco asked.

"I will leave the country. Asia. I have heard that our efforts there need people. If they connect the gloves to me, I will disappear into the mountains." The woman put on a brave face, making every effort to stop the tears. She waited for a reply from Valesco, who let it drag out.

"Better than killing you, I suppose. Fine. Garo, make it happen. I want her out of the country quickly and quietly."

"I will not let you down again, sir."

Valesco slowly turned and walked to the woman, putting his face directly in front of hers. His expression like stone, he stared into the woman's eyes.

"If you do, don't make me send someone after you."

"Yes, sir," she replied with a shaky voice.

After the door had closed from the woman leaving, Valesco turned to Garo, a determined look on his face.

"How is recruitment going?"

"Good. We continue to gather the lion's share of the displaced flocks." Garo smiled at his metaphor.

"The federals are getting involved sooner than we planned. I think we need to step up our efforts."

"That will make what we are doing more obvious."

"We have to take that chance. Besides, Washington is gelded."

"It will be done, sir."

Joseph paced his room, a track of five meters long. Muttering to himself all the time, his arms waved or counted in the air. The first ding of the doorbell went unnoticed, as did the second. The knock finally got his attention. Startled out of his mental trance, he went to the door and opened it.

"Mercedes?"

"Hey, Joe." She made her way into the apartment without being invited. "I waited all day for you to leave your apartment. When you didn't, I figured I'd have to come here."

Joseph took a deep sigh. "I've been… thinking all day about the changes planned for the base. So many things to try and prioritize. Every time I think I have number one, I think of another."

"Have you eaten?" Mercedes smiled as she asked.

"Ah… I don't remember."

"I'll take that as a 'no' then. Come on, my treat." Mercedes gave an encouraging wave with the statement.

Joseph sagged, closed his eyes, and then opened them again. "I guess so. Not like I've come to any conclusions anyway."

"You mind if Worthia comes along?" Mercedes asked while Joseph spun around several times as if trying to think of what he was forgetting.

"I guess not," he said absentmindedly. "Maybe I should brush my hair."

"Wash your face off, too," Mercedes said to his back as he walked to the bathroom. "It will make you feel better."

Joseph came back with brushed hair and a fresh shirt. He even applied some deodorant.

"You cleaned up. I feel privileged."

"I didn't want to embarrass you." Joseph waved his arm for Mercedes to proceed first.

"Thank you, kind sir," she said with a giggle. With exaggerated emphasis, she added, "You do care."

"Or maybe I just care about you not telling me what an embarrassment I was."

"Don't ruin a moment, no matter how little," she said with a fake scowl. Joseph closed the door behind them. "Worthia hasn't stopped talking about her trip to D.C. since she got back. It's all she talks about."

"It was fun. She was so excited I think I laughed the whole time. Besides, I had never been to the sights either." The elevator met them with an open door.

"You didn't go while in college, on break?"

"No, I studied in college." Joseph gave her a sideways glance. "And beat off all the women after me."

Mercedes sputtered while the elevator started to move. "Right! Tell me another one I don't believe."

"You don't believe women were after me?"

"I don't believe you'd beat them off." Mercedes laughed after giving Joseph a glance and seeing his cheek turn red.

"I'm not sure if that was a compliment or not."

"From me? Guess."

The elevator stopped at the ground floor and opened the doors. Joseph let Mercedes go first.

"Prearranged the elevator?" Joseph asked as they walked to the front door.

"Of course. Why not?"

"Kind of an assumption, wasn't it?"

"Well, at least one of us was going to supper."

The sun was still up, but getting low. A small breeze blew across the base and pushed cirrus clouds across the sky. The sidewalks and roads were occupied, but not crowded. Joseph looked up at the sky.

"Going to be a clear night tonight." Joseph started toward the cafeteria.

"Good for star-gazing?"

Joseph missed the hint in her voice. "Yup. You ever do that sort of thing?"

"Only as a kid. No telescope, mind you. Never had anyone to show me how to use one."

"Really? I thought everyone had done it at one time at least." Joseph's forehead furrowed.

"I spent a lot more time looking down than up." Mercedes raised her eyebrows at him.

"That makes sense." Joseph walked for a while, not saying anything. "You want to go tonight?"

"I thought you'd never ask!" Mercedes said with faked shock, hands clasped together in front of her. "Why, I'd be happy to star-gaze with you. What time do you want to pick me up?"

Joseph gave her a look and then shrugged. "Ten. It will take time to set up the scope once we get there."

"Ten it is, then." Mercedes stood to the side of the cafeteria door and let Joseph open it for her.

"You know, women do open doors for guys these days."

"I'm buying, you can open the doors." She flipped her head as she spoke.

Joseph let out a laugh, but held his tongue as they entered. When they got inside, Mercedes led him to the left and into the area that used a hostess and servers for the tables.

"Oh, fancy," Joseph said.

"Make it special when you can," Mercedes responded.

Once inside the restaurant, they were led to a table where Worthia was already seated. She smiled broadly at Mercedes when they got close, causing Joseph to give her a curious look.

"How you doing, kid?"

"Great," Worthia replied with a giggle.

Joseph held out the chair for Mercedes, who accepted with graceful lady charm. It earned an approving look from Worthia. Joseph sat across from the women. A waiter walked up and handed them menus. Worthia didn't open hers, but placed it on the table.

"Not eating?" Joseph asked.

"I already know what I want. Had to do something while waiting for you two."

Joseph gave her a small smile and quickly looked at the menu and made a choice, placing it on the table also. Mercedes took longer before slowly closing the menu and placing it on the table. The server did not take long to take their order, using paper and pen to write down the order. The restaurant considered their use part of their charm. With the orders made, the server took the menus and left. During the process, Joseph noticed several glances from Worthia to Mercedes.

"Is there something going on I should know about?" Joseph asked.

"If there is, you'll find out," Mercedes responded with a smile.

"Okay, now I know there is something going on." Joseph looked at both women individually, then focused on Worthia. "And what is your part of this, young lady?"

"I'm the witness," Worthia responded with a smile.

"Witness to what?"

"Witness to the fact that I asked you a question and witness to your answer," Mercedes interjected. "From what I am told by our friend here, a witness is typically used."

"Is this a legal thing?" Joseph drew his head back as her asked.

"Legal, no. It's sort of a social convention."

"Okay," Joseph said slowly, his eyes going back and forth between the two.

Mercedes straightened in her chair, leaning a little forward and placing her hands, folded together, on the table in front of her. She cleared her throat and looked into Joseph's eyes.

"Joseph Shenen Gint, I formally request permission to court you."

"You... do what?"

"Court you. An activity that is intended to lead to marriage."

"I... I know what courting is, I'm from Europe. I just didn't know anyone still did it anymore." Joseph stole a quick glance at Worthia.

"Maybe they should."

Joseph sat, not speaking for a moment. Finally, he closed his mouth, cleared his throat, and spoke.

"Does this courting come with rules?"

"There used to be quite a few, but I decided on only one basic rule. The only person you are to see socially, or any way that falls under the romantic area of life, is me until we decide to stop courting."

"That shouldn't be hard," Joseph said under his breath. Mercedes waited, watching Joseph's head turning aside.

"Well?" she finally asked with a gentle voice.

"Ah, wow," Joseph stuttered. "I would have never expected this. I mean, not that it's you, but just the whole courting thing, you know, has kind of thrown me. Not that I dislike the idea of courting, I'm just saying it was kind of out of the blue, you know…"

"I would like a yes or no."

Joseph looked at Mercedes. Slowly, a smile came to his face and his eyes sparkled as he looked in hers. His shoulders settled.

"Yes."

Worthia stopped herself before she stood up and whooped at the top of her lungs.

Chapter Fifteen
And Again

"This is getting to be a habit," Joseph said as he walked the halls of the White House.

"Stop being right all the time then," Bennett replied.

"Darn bad habit of mine."

"The situation in the cities is getting worse," Secretary Melleck said. "People are dividing up between church and non-church groups…"

"You mean alien churches," Joseph put in.

"Not exactly. There are small factions of historic churches, mostly Catholic and Baptist, that are forming their own communities. We believe that they are uncertain about both sides or are trying to form a middle ground."

"Afraid their religion will make them a target to the non-religious?" Benitez asked.

"Very likely."

"They never had to worry about that before." Joseph looked at the people also walking the halls. Many more were military than when they had been there before.

"Times change. At least with all the upheaval, there is plenty of housing to move into." Melleck laughed. "We're in here."

The room was the largest conference room they had ever occupied. It had an oval table and paintings of presidents, museum quality. There were four windows on one side, one with a door to the outside. About half of the high-back, padded chairs at the table were already taken. Bennett, Benitez, and Joseph took seats just off of center as indicated by the thick-stock paper name-tags.

Joseph recognized some of the faces, but not many, particularly the military ones. A few were governors, others were CEOs. Joseph leaned toward Bennett.

"Do you know these guys?"

"Commanders of major military bases, mostly. We seem to be lacking the top brass, but that I don't mind. Of course, the navy could have sent someone."

The president walked in, followed by a group large enough to fill the rest of the seats. Everyone stood and sat back down after she took the central seat closest to the windows. It took a minute for all the shuffling to stop.

"Thank you all for coming. As I am sure you are aware, the situation in our country is getting worse. It appears that people are voluntarily segregating themselves between church and non-church people. Hostilities are common between these groups, but mostly concentrated on some of the alien-worshipping churches. The local governments, for the most part, do not seem to be handling the situation well, blaming the attacks on anti-alien feelings. In fact, a few seem to be letting the groups fight between themselves. We need to decide on a course of action not only now, but for the future."

Tyler's pause gave room for others to comment.

Melleck's was the first voice. "I know it is not a desired state, but letting the groups separate should reduce the number of incidents between the groups."

"And increase the long-term antagonism between them," a man at the end of the table said. Joseph recognized him as the mayor of Boston. "If we let people separate themselves, we risk turning the country into a two-state nation."

"It's either that or let Valesco take over the whole country," Joseph stated.

"Your opinions are well known, Mr. Gint," Melleck replied in a sharp voice.

"Did everyone get the same briefing?" Joseph asked, eyebrow raised. "Does anyone truly doubt that Valesco isn't making a move to take over all the alien-loving churches in this country? Especially in those states that aren't doing anything about it? After he does, how long will the other churches last?"

"You're talking about a national coup," Melleck shot back. "That seems highly unlikely."

"They won't need to stage a coup. All they need to do is be fifty-one percent of the votes to elect Valesco as president and they win."

Murmurs went through the group. Many of them looked as if they had not thought of the scenario before. Tyler looked scornful.

"You assume he wants to run for president," Tyler said.

"You read the extracts from his speeches, didn't you? Does that sound like someone who wants to take over everything or not?"

"Speeches are one thing…"

"You did not take his most recent speech as a call to war?" Benitez asked. The question hung in the air as a condemnation of a negative answer. Instead of speaking, people looked at each other, knowing the answer in each other's eyes, but not saying it out loud. Joseph was the exception.

"Unless you are ready to convert, we need to accept that a two-nation state will exist in the future. That assumes you are willing to fight for yourselves, if it comes to that."

"What you are proposing is illegal," a voice from the other end of the table said.

"I'm talking about survival: survival of our history, survival of our technology, and survival as an independent species when the aliens return. If we allow Valesco to take over, the whole country will bow down before the aliens and they will farm us for all eternity. Is that what you want, to be some alien's crop to harvest? I, for one, do not."

Silence ruled for a few minutes. People contemplated or processed. Most waited for Tyler to say something. Eventually, she cleared her throat.

"Given these… facts… the question is still, what do we do? How do we prepare for… the changes that are coming?"

Conversation started fast and furious, though not loud. Debate between attendees started. Joseph sat quietly, arms folded across his chest, back pressed against the chair. Bennett watched others, mostly the military personnel.

Benitez spoke. "Excuse me," she said and then waited for some of the noise to die down. "The first thing we need to do, Madam President, is to vet those we allow in the conversation."

Tyler's head cocked slightly to one side. "Vet? You mean make sure no one is connected to one of the churches?"

"We cannot afford for any word of what we do to get back to those with whom we may end up in conflict."

"Surely you don't think there is a traitor in our midst, do you?"

"Like someone who, up to two years ago, was a member of Thee Way? Whose name was never totally removed from the member list? Who has regularly made calls to a service that directs the content to Thee Way? Just who might that be, Mr. Melleck?"

Gasps went through the room. Tyler turned to Melleck, mouth open.

"Quintin, is this true?"

"You have no right monitoring my communications!" Melleck said to Benitez with scorn. "I can talk to whoever I want."

"But you can't warn them of an impending federal investigation, at least legally."

"Mr. Melleck!" Tyler said, recovering her composure. "Explain yourself."

"I don't need to explain myself to you or anyone here," Melleck said, his face turning hard with a scowl. "You are all heretics! You profane the name of God! I would be glad when I am no longer in your presence!"

"Secretary Melleck, you are relieved of duty." Tyler spoke into her interface. "Security! Make sure Mr. Melleck does not take anything that is government property and remove him from this building, immediately. On second thought, make sure he takes nothing with him."

Melleck stood, gave the group a hateful look, and stomped out of the room. People watched him leave, shock still on their faces. Tyler shook her head and looked down at the table.

"At least we know what, or should I say who, was hampering our investigations. I hate to think how much information he has, how many decisions he has influenced, that can be used against us."

"Madam President," Benitez said softly, "we need to vet everyone else in this room or anyone that will be involved in our future plans. I myself am willing to go first, if that helps others feel more comfortable."

"How are we supposed to do that?" was asked.

"I'm pretty sure the Western Pacific Conglomerate can help us. They appear to be ahead of the curve on this issue."

"Heather, please get Chairman Shishiho on the comm." Tyler leaned back in her chair. In front of her was Benitez, Bennett, and Joseph.

"Lieutenant Benitez, I will ask them to send anything to you."

Benitez nodded in return. After a few minutes, a face came on the display.

"Chairman Shishiho, thank you for talking to me."

"Always a pleasure, Madam President." Shishiho did a barely perceptible head bow.

"I'm sure you've heard of what is happening in this country."

Shishiho closed her eyes and nodded her head sideways.

"We find ourselves in an unconventional situation. One where we need to be able to tell friend from foe. I am told you have had some success in creating a method for doing this."

There was a second of no movement or speaking. "Yes, Madam President, we have developed a method which we have been using for our own… sorting. We will be happy to share it with you. I fear this is an enemy that many of us have in common."

"Thank you, Chairman. I will have my people provide contact information to your office where the information can be sent." Tyler paused a second. "We have been so busy here that I have not had time to think about what other countries around the world may be facing. Once we get a plan settled, it might be a good idea to have a conference with the major states as to what needs to be done."

"I agree." Shishiho talked without emotion. "If you wish, I will start the conversations and present the idea of the conference."

"I appreciate your help in all matters." Tyler executed a small head bow. "Your diligence and preparedness is a model for us all."

"You are most gracious, Madam President. Good day." Shishiho made another small head bow before disappearing from view.

"That went well," Bennett commented with some surprise while Benitez worked her interface.

"I just hope we are not handing the initiative to the WPC," Tyler grumbled.

"With the state of the nation, we can afford to give the initiative to someone else. Plus, it gives you coverage on what the rest of the world is doing," Bennett pointed out.

"That's true. I just hope we don't regret it."

"Information sent," Benitez stated.

"Good. Please let me know when it arrives and give it to..." The woman paused. "Use it on the Deputy Secretary of Security and if he passes, have him start using it on those at the meeting today and then the rest of the White House Staff."

Tyler took a deep breath, let it out, and leaned back in her chair, staring at the ceiling. She started to swivel.

"Now all we have to do is come up with some kind of plan for the country," Tyler said to the ceiling.

"Madam President," Joseph said softly. "I have actually started on a plan."

"You have?" Tyler sat up and then let her shoulders sag. "Why am I not surprised? Of course you have one. Give me the bare bones."

Joseph cleared his throat and shuffled in his seat before talking.

"As I see it, there are a few basics we need to do first. Obviously, military equipment needs to be kept away from the Puritans. Luckily, most of it is already in storage on military bases, except for vehicles and personal weapons presently in use. Plus, we have some convenient locations to put things that are inherently hard to get to."

"Such as?"

"Guam and Hawaii are the two obvious ones. We can move all the naval ships to Hawaii and most of the planes not currently in use there or to Guam with little effort. The large energy weapons could also be sent to Guam. I really don't think we want to use them on the population."

"Of course not," Tyler agreed.

"After that, we are talking about military bases, equipment, personnel, industrial capacity, power, non-Puritans, and strategic resources."

"You didn't mention things like food." Tyler's voice was halfway between pointing out the obvious and worry.

"There is no way we will be totally self-sufficient. Given that fact, it would be reasonable to retain some capacity in which the Puritans will require trade between us and them. The most obvious thing, and easiest, is medicine and medical expertise."

"Excellent thinking!" Tyler slapped the table.

"I believe we have to start thinking about bases as enclosed cities. Military stores will have many of the items we need to protect and we can salvage abandoned bases for construction material on other bases. But in the long run, we need to think about larger cities."

"Let's talk about military bases for now." Tyler swept her hand in front of her. "To implement this in cities, won't we have to do full scale testing of the population to make sure we have no spies?"

"Yes, Madam President," Benitez said. "We may need a whole new group of experts for execution of the plan. With the population naturally dividing at this moment, I think we have some time before we need to begin, but once cities are secured, it will be necessary."

Tyler wagged her eyebrows. "That's a nasty thought. I understand the need, but screening our own people into desirables and undesirables has nightmarish connotations."

"A fact not lost on those of us who have been thinking about this," Joseph replied.

"We want the truth! We want the truth!"

The cries echoed between the buildings as they had been doing for weeks. Students sat on the commons, chanting their slogan. A few ran around, delivering bottled water or food. Those who did not participate walked far around the seated students.

Inspector Clarence Brudding stepped up next to a campus security officer. He scanned the scene, noting the dozen campus security officers spread evenly around the group, almost the whole campus complement. It was considered a small school and had not had an incident bigger than a loud argument before the protest happened for as long as anyone could remember.

"You in charge here?" the inspector asked.

"I'm in charge of these twelve guys standing around that group." The man pointed toward the center. "Whoever's in charge of them, who knows?"

"You'd think they'd get tired of chanting."

"Just an excuse to not attend class," the man said dismissively.

"Maybe, but you know they are violating four different city ordinances at the moment, not counting sleeping here at night and who knows what else when no one is looking."

"They're not hurting anyone, so we leave them alone."

Brudding turned to the man. "You call that law enforcement?"

"Hey," the man said, turning toward the inspector, "what you want me to do about it?"

"I want you and your men to leave. We are in charge here now." Brudding went back to looking at the students.

"Says who?"

"Check your interface."

The man did, registering surprise as he did so. In response, he clicked the interface and then said, "Okay, guys, we're out of here. Meet at HQ."

With some looks at each other, the security officers made their way from the commons at a slow walk. When the students noticed, they cheered, though their demands had never included for security to leave.

"Stupid kids," he said to himself. Activating his interface, he lifted it to his mouth and said, "Move in now."

In response, two hundred law enforcement officers ran onto the commons and surrounded the students. Those outside the circle stopped and watched. Brudding waited until every officer was in place and spoke into his interface again.

"I will give you one chance to disperse," his interface projected to the crowd of students, "before I arrest you on violation of city ordinances 1044-A, 1044-B, 1157-F, and 1157-G. This will be your only offer to stand down and slowly make your way back to your dorms in silence. You have thirty seconds to comply."

The students looked around in disbelief. Then, the one who had been leading the cheer straightened his back and raised his arm. "We will not leave! We demand the truth! We will not leave! We demand the truth!"

Students inside the circle stood, eagerly cheering along until all chanted in unison. After thirty seconds, a beep came from Brudding's interface.

"Oh, good. Move in!"

Drawing stun batons, the officers advanced. The chanting suddenly stopped as the students realized that their numbers or their passion meant nothing to those advancing on them. They stood and waited in silence until the first of the officers reached the group and extended their batons. The whole outside layer of students fell in unison. Then the screaming started.

Some students charged the line of officers, only to be stunned into unconsciousness, their bodies twitching for a few seconds before lying still on the ground. Others ran toward the center of the ground. The opposite movements caused some to be knocked to the ground, a prime location to be trod upon. The ones in the center started to be piled upon by their fellow students. The officers moved inward, stepping over or pushing bodies away with their feet, stunning those on foot or prone. The screaming from the center increased in volume. Students panicked and tore at each other. Some were trampled by their fellow students, creating a pile in the center. The only mercy came when the officers stunned the students, preventing them from hurting each other more.

In two minutes, it was over. The officers moved outward and waiting emergency crews came forward to find the injured. Those not selected by the crews were cuffed by the officers and carried to waiting vehicles. Those around the common gave them a wide berth, pointing and talking, identifying those who were carried away. A few made records of the event.

"Now that's what I call a statement," Brudding said to himself. He checked the time. "An efficient statement."

Scenes of the action were carried around the country as fast as electrons could move. The interfaces of other protesting students lit up with the images, causing horror and disbelief. At the Arizona Institute of Higher Learning, Maz Urden watched with particular outrage.

"Look!" he shouted to those around him. "Look what they are doing! They are trying to quiet our voices with violence!"

As his face grew red, Maz looked around and singled out three security guards laughing at something and pointing. Maz felt his blood boil.

Breaking into a dead run, Maz body-tackled one of the guards, punching him as they fell. His movement caused a handful of others to follow. Before they could react, each agent was set upon by two or three students, all raining violence upon them. The sight of their success inspired others to do the same, attacking any security personnel in the area. Once satisfied with the first agent, Maz stood up and waved his hand in a forward-motion gesture.

"Come on! Let's go!"

With a cheer, the students ran toward the college administrative buildings. As they did, drones appeared in the sky above them. The *zit* of stun rays reached the ears of the protesters and bystanders, who ran from the drones and the protesters. Students started to fall. Some picked up rocks and made inaccurate throws at the drones. They became the next to fall. The size of the group made sure that some of them reached their destination, but a pathway of bodies gave evidence to their trail. Once at the administration building, they found the doors secured. The drones continued to reduce their numbers as they turned and looked for options.

The delay ensured the failure of their efforts. The last of the students stood with fists raised as the drones pacified them.

As if it was chain lightning, violence spread across American campuses. Students who had been peaceful for two weeks turned violent, delivering beatings and destruction to any symbol of authority. Security personnel who had been respectful and tolerant for two weeks became targets and defenders. Chit-chat became war cries. The skies filled with drones. Jail cells and hospital beds were filled.

News reports filled the airwaves. They contained pictures, personal interviews, opinions, and statistics. Names of students appeared in lists on campuses and on the airwaves. Parents made frantic calls and posted bail. Some brought their children home. Others left them in jail.

Soon after the campus riots there were many calls for action, actions as varied as the people who gave them. Only a few called for the federal government to intervene and then on the side of the students. No governors echoed the calls. No religious leaders called for help. But that didn't prevent the reports in the news from blaming the president for the violence.

Chapter Sixteen
More Committees

The meeting convened with most of the same attendees as before, though the subject of their conversations was the campus riots. When Tyler entered, the conversations stopped. Though they had been called for a specific purpose, all waited for her to start her subject of choice. With the criticism being thrown at her administration, changing the meeting topic would have surprised few.

"Thank you all for coming again. I regret that our last meeting had to be dismissed, but it was inevitable, it appears. I would like to start with a question.

"Are we all agreed that, given the current events, we should be concerned first with securing our military hardware and bases from any form of attack or confiscation?"

Heads nodded. No one seemed to disagree, even those not associated with the military.

"Good. I have created a list of critical military bases. Please do not argue about one you personally want to preserve. The list was chosen by necessity, coverage of the country, and defensive capabilities. Admittedly, some on this list are not particularly defensible at the moment, but can be made so easier than others." Tyler swiped her interface, sending the list to all there.

"You may also notice the lack of depots on the list. That is for two reasons. The first is that all combat equipment will be moved out of the depots. Secondly, by the time construction material and other material needed for the bases is delivered, we will have removed most of what is stored at these locations anyway. Any 'civilian' equipment that is left over can be given to our future secured cities."

Tyler swept her head back and forth as she talked. "There will be no arguments about saving jobs or commands. Commands will be moved to new locations. Also, I have a feeling that with the heavy recruiting the churches are doing, there will be fewer workers for every location if we do not consolidate."

"Madam President," the Admiral of the Navy said, "I don't see any continental navy bases on this list."

"The Navy will be moved to Hawaii and Guam. Ports inherent to bases on the list will be preserved. Port capabilities in other locations will be incorporated later."

"What exactly does that mean?"

"We are not going to worry about that at this time." Tyler gave him a look from the top of her eyes.

"Madam President," came another interruption, "this list is not very big. Are we really going to get all of our personnel and capabilities on this short of a list?"

"Personnel, yes. We will inherently lose some capabilities, but quite frankly, we have kept more than we need. Also, some are not practical for the foreseeable future. Let's face it, people, we will not be fighting a land war against another major country, let alone more than one in more than one location. There are functions we definitely want to preserve, like communications, research, and development. We must still prepare for the future while letting go of the past."

"What if these... churches... get advanced weaponry from other countries?"

"I will be talking to the leaders of the other major factions about this very issue. But for now, we must get our house in order."

"Madam President," Warrence Donnest, the new Secretary of Security, asked, "how are we supposed to get all our personnel on these bases?"

"I am glad you asked. Mr. Gint, if you please." Tyler turned her head Joseph's direction.

Joseph stood up and looked over the group, fighting off a 'what the heck am I doing here' look on his face. Stern, serious faces stared at him from both sides of the table. The image of sharks gathering for the kill would have been an apt comparison.

"Morning, gentlemen and ladies. If you will examine the information sent to your interfaces, I have made preliminary estimates of the number of personnel at each base in the future. This includes not only military personnel, but research and governmental people in some cases. I realized that these numbers exceed the current listed capacities of all bases, though not the historic numbers in some cases. The obvious solution is that the bases must expand their capabilities. A plan must be created for each base to optimize their usage. Since I know this can sound like a nebulous statement, I have brought an explanation."

Joseph manipulated his interface. The central display embedded in the table came on, at first showing only a white screen. After a few seconds, a three-dimensional hologram of a base appeared.

"This is Revelation Base in South Dakota as it appears today. As you can see, the structures of the base do not cover a significant portion of the grounds. Now, this is the future plans for the base."

The scene changed. It was the difference between a small town and a fully developed city. The changes caused gasps of surprise.

"Are you serious?"

Joseph was too nervous to track the origins of questions. "Yes, we are very serious. This plan has been made to maximize the occupancy and self-sufficiency of the base. Of course, not everything can be made at the base that it needs, but its vulnerability to being cut off has been reduced considerably."

"And why is your base so important?" Joseph was sure the question was asked by one of the civilians.

"Because we are the location of research into systems which we can use in the future to defend ourselves from the aliens when they return."

"You're assuming they are returning."

"Wouldn't you?" Joseph let the statement settle for a while. When no one argued, he continued. "I am sending a copy of the program I used to perform this optimization to each of the stations. I can't take credit for its total creation. A friend of mine helped and she'd probably kill me if I didn't give her credit. You will need to enter your own base information, but after that, it shouldn't take long to find an acceptable solution."

"Thank you, Mr. Gint." Tyler gave him a quick head nod and turned back to the group. "This is priority number one for the military."

"Aren't we going to do anything about the campuses?" came from a general.

"We have not been invited. Our presence would probably only make things worse. We need to concentrate on the bases for now. Any other questions?"

To Joseph, everyone looked overwhelmed except for Bennett, but he had a head start on being overwhelmed. Tyler nodded once.

"Dismissed, then."

"Is it done?"

Construction Battalion Colonel Suz Natora turned to find Joseph standing behind her. She huffed in response, restraining her reply.

"You back already? Thought you would be there another day."

The eye-roll from Joseph was the only reply she needed.

"We have completed a twenty-story, two hundred and fifty unit residential building in record time and all you can ask is if it is done? Look at this thing! It's a work of art! And did I mention the record time?"

Natora stared at Joseph with her head cocked to one side. At least her hands weren't on her hips, Joseph noted.

"It's a good start," he replied without commitment.

"Start? What's that mean?"

"It means," Joseph said, tilting his own head, "that by the time we get the furniture in and the systems working, half of those apartments will be spoken for. The rest won't be vacant long."

Natora stared for a few seconds. Straightening her head, she took a more upright stance.

"Exactly how many people do you expect to be based here eventually?" She adopted a defensive posture.

"Twenty thousand, give or take." The easy response was in contrast to the jaw-dropped response of the colonel.

"Twenty thousand!" Natora said when she could find her voice. "This base can't support that many people!"

"Correct!" Joseph said with a cheerful wave of his finger. "That's why you're the lucky winner of the next project, construction of a new power plant. The details have been sent to your interface."

"Power plant?" Natora fast-handed her interface and stared as it called up the plan. "You've got to be kidding me. How am I supposed to build a reactor?"

"That part we will get from another base. All you have to make is the building." Joseph gave her his best Cheshire Cat smile.

"And what about the electrical distribution system and power lines?"

"On their way, too."

"You know," Natora said, shaking her head and looking back at Joseph, "you're going to need other things like water and sewer treatment."

"Of course, but first we will need power. The research guys are already complaining about not having enough."

"This plant of yours, it's going to make a lot more power than you need."

"For a while, yes. But all our new buildings will be strictly electric, out of necessity, so we'll need a lot of power. Besides, it's cheap." He gave her a full-shoulder shrug.

"Didn't they have natural gas around here at one time?"

Joseph gave the woman a blank stare.

"I know, ancient history. But, I mean, you have to feed something to the fusion reactor."

"We can always use water for the hydrogen," Joseph said with a shrug.

"True, just thinking. What's your timetable for this one?" Natora furrowed her brow at him.

"ASAP, of course." Joseph clasped his hands and rubbed them together. "We got a lot to do in a short time."

"You have those civvies doing stuff too, I see." Natora's thumb pointed over her shoulder.

"Warehouses only, at least for now."

"Sure, give them the easy part." A huff came with the statement.

"Give them the non-critical, easy-to-make-sure-they-don't-do-something-to-sabotage-us part, you mean." Joseph's expression told the woman he was serious.

"You don't trust them that much?"

"Not yet, and given the choice, I would rather not have to. There's plenty to be done, so right now, it's not an issue."

Natora gave him a squinting stare. "You want to tell me what this is about?"

"Nope, and the less you have to worry about, the better. But don't expect too many excursions off the base." A half-smile went with the statement.

"I didn't know there was anything around here to excursion to."

"There isn't really. But don't worry, I know people want entertainment. We've been working on that, too."

"It would be nice. Hey, by the way, when do we move out of our temp digs?"

"As soon as you build yourself new ones."

"How did I know that was going to be the answer," Natora said as she shook her head.

Mercedes looked up at the clear sky. Stars twinkled beyond the tall grass. At least the grass blocked the night breeze as they lay on the ground.

"Too bad Sirius is in the southern hemisphere," she commented.

"Why?" Joseph asked.

"It ruins a lot of jokes when you're out stargazing." A small lean of her body brought her shoulder in touch with Joseph's. "I can't believe the southern hemisphere gets the brightest stars."

"I can't believe someone locked the door on us," Joseph said with a little grouch in his voice. "Who locks the door to an unusable building?"

"Maybe someone started using it for something. Besides you, that is." A small giggle followed the statement.

"I just can't believe someone would want to mess with our dates. I mean, why..." Joseph stopped and rolled over onto his side. "You didn't lock that door, did you?"

"Me? Why would I do that?" Mercedes raised her eyebrows.

"Because the floor on the roof is hard?"

"Are you implying something? Like I have some scheme or something?" She gave Joseph a sly smile.

"Ah, nope," he said, closing his eyes while he shook his head. "I'm not implying anything, I am just going with the flow."

Mercedes laughed. She brought her hand up to rest on the right side of Joseph's face. When he opened his eyes, he found hers staring into them.

"I do have a real question about this courting stuff."

"I didn't think I made it complicated, but okay."

"How do I know when I can kiss you, or… whatever?" To Mercedes's confused expression, he said, "Look, you've been the one to initiate most of that, but I wouldn't want to violate some ancient courting right and mess things up, so I thought I would ask."

Mercedes's head moved back and forth a little as if trying to decide if he was serious. "Whenever I let you," she finally said with a smile.

"Hmm, I guess I'm going to have to try my luck, then."

His luck held.

Chapter Seventeen
Friends and Enemies

"About time you came around again." Wenk lifted his stein and took a drink. "With you working so much and spending time with Mercedes, I barely see you anymore. Not that I have anything against Mercedes, you understand." Wenk's hand came up in a flat-vertical defensive position. "Anyone who can land a girl that good looking deserves to be distracted. It just kind of leaves me out here wandering around alone."

"Why don't you get a girl of your own?" Joseph took a drink of his ale, smaller than the ones Wenk was taking. "Preferably one that lives alone, so she can move in with you and free up an apartment."

"Yeah, right. Because skinny techies are in such high demand." Wenk scoffed and took another drink.

"Maybe you should talk to Worthia," Joseph said easily.

"She's a little young, don't you think?"

Joseph scowled. "Not date her, stupid. Ask her to find you a girl. She likes playing matchmaker."

Wenk laughed. "Matching you two up wasn't hard. Mercedes's been stalking you for a few years now. You just didn't notice. In fact, I think you're the only one who didn't notice."

"Comes from having a famous father." Joseph's head turned down to the table between them. "Having had that is. You run into so many people who just want your attention as a connection to your dad that you start to ignore them. You shove it all aside with other things that probably shouldn't be shoved aside. It's easier just not to feel with all the hate that gets thrown your way by people who don't even know you or your father or what he really did. Push the emotions down, don't talk about it. Then when he died, it was easier just to close the door to it all, not think about it, not talk about it. Maybe that's being disloyal, but it's how I learned to deal with it all."

"Hey! Buck up!" Wenk hit Joseph in the shoulder. "You've taken the situation and done something positive with it. Also, you've done pretty good by yourself, professionally, even if it took a while."

"Yeah, don't know if I finally got lucky or if it's my just desserts. But I'm serious, Worthia's a smart kid. She might be worth you asking her. And she'd get a kick out of it."

"Have you been watching the news lately?" Wenk turned from looking at Joseph.

"You're not trying to change the subject, are you?"

"You used to follow everything that went on. Now that you're so busy, didn't know if you'd been keeping up. Where's our wings, by the way?" Wenk looked around the room. The number of people sitting at tables or walking around gave no encouragement of his wings' coming arrival.

Joseph sighed. "No, I haven't. Haven't had time. Been trying to get all the stuff for the base moving. We finally got another of the construction companies cleared, but Benitez is making us inspect all the material they bring in to make sure it's up to spec or doesn't contain explosives, I'm not sure which. I've had to order extra just to keep the flow moving. Not that we won't use it, just a pain."

"Everyone seems to be fighting." Wenk leaned forward, one hand still on his mug. "Okay, not literally, but it's all over. Churches fighting churches, non-church people fighting church people, some people just fighting to fight. Seems everyone has gone crazy all over." His arm was flung up, making a semi-circle until over his head and coming back down.

"People are scared. The aliens' arrival turned the world upside down. Most people had stopped believing in God and then they show up."

"But they never claimed to be God." Wenk shook a finger at Joseph.

"They claimed to be something close enough." Joseph took a drink. "Besides, it depends on your definition of God. If you believe they seeded this world with humans and guided history, isn't that close enough?"

"But why fight each other? It makes no sense. Not like the aliens set up some kind of games and the winner gets to go with them. They only took like twenty-five thousand people and we have way more than that. Plus, who knows if they will ever come back?"

"Movements mean power." Joseph assumed his instructional stare. "When the World Council lost power, it created a power vacuum…"

"And nature hates a vacuum." Wenk nodded his head.

"Of any kind, evidently. People recombined into new groups and that created new types of power." Joseph shook his head. Raising his mug to his lips, it stopped and returned without losing any liquid.

"Which is all well and good, but when they start messing with the ultra-ball games, I draw the line!" Wenk swept his hand across the table.

"What?" Joseph looked up at his friend, his head shaking a little as if slapped.

"Yesterday's game. The coach for Seattle wouldn't let the Puritan players on the field. That angered the Puritans on the other team, which was most of them. The whole thing turned into a big riot with the fans joining one side or the other. Not sure anyone even knew why they were fighting. Hundreds of people went to the hospital."

"And it wasn't even Europeans." Shaking his head back and forth, Joseph sighed. "Americans are picking up our bad habits."

"This is serious. If we can't even play a game without people fighting, that's awful."

"We've been doing it for hundreds of years. America finally caught up."

Wenk gave him a dirty look. Joseph took a breath and spread his hands.

"Look," Joseph said, "I'm sorry. I understand what you mean. All this pent-up anger and frustration over the last twenty-seven years is coming out. With the governments who would have provided the support systems for people to deal with their feelings all but destroyed, there was no outlet but each other."

"Then all I can say is it's a good thing I like you."

"What?" Joseph's head jerked back.

"I figure you're the one guy I could take." Wenk smiled.

"Really? I have like fifty pounds and two inches on you."

"But I am a fourteen level fighter specializing in exotic weapons. And there's magic." Wenk smirked as he took another drink.

"Oooh, I'm so scared. My quantum armor and splaser pistol is more than a match and you know it." Joseph laughed. Their wings were delivered to the table.

"About time. With all the extra people around, service is getting slow." The comment came too slow to be heard by the delivery tray.

"Don't worry. That new construction company is going to build a new cafeteria first thing. I'd like them to start on increasing the size of the rail-yard, but people need to eat. Who knew?"

"Selfish of them, I know. What capacity?"

"Six hundred."

Wenk's eyes went wide. "That is a serious cafeteria."

"Not only that, but the building will be made so that more apartments can be built on top."

"Okay, enough about business. This is supposed to be about fun. Eat up, I've been practicing darts. You're going to be in trouble." Wenk took a wing with purpose.

"Like I'm supposed to believe that?" Joseph huffed. "Be real."

"Did you know that off-year elections are next week?" Wenk said through a mouth of chicken.

"No, haven't paid attention." Joseph took a wing before they all disappeared.

"Local offices only, but that could be bad, right?"

"Yeah, for lots of places. Not like we can do anything about it, though."

Gabrielle Sanchez walked up to the polling station, a grade school on any other day. Because it was early, she was not surprised at the small number of people coming and going. The scene was the same as every previous election, with signs littered on both sides and two older people not closer than five meters from the door giving out flyers in a last ditch promotion for their candidate. The exception this year was the two men standing just outside the door. They were broad-shouldered and tall, more than a foot taller than she was, with grim expressions on their faces. They were dressed in flannel shirts and jeans, but stood with their feet spread shoulder-width apart and their arms crossed. Just looking at them sent a shiver through her. Taking a breath, she put her head down and walked toward the doors, feeling the pressure of their eyes on her as she neared the door. As she did, one of the men stepped in front of her.

"I hope you're voting for the right person," the man said.

"You're not supposed to talk to me about that," Gabriel said without looking up. Her voice shook as she talked. "You're not even supposed to be this close to the door."

"A lot of things are changing. You want to be on the right side of things. Be on God's side."

"Please get out of my way," she said in a weak voice.

"Just making sure people understand what's going on here."

"Look, I have three kids I'm raising on my own. I don't care about your religion, all I care about is taking care of my kids."

"Then you need to do the right thing. For the good of your kids."

The man moved. After a pause, Gabrielle walked into the building. Inside, she made her way to the polling room. She found the same equipment as there had been the last time, but she also found more of the large men. They moved like they were working the polls, but she saw how they watched all those who voted. As tall as they were, they could see into the voting booth and how the people were voting.

Stunned, Gabrielle stopped walking. There was a police officer in the room, but he didn't seem to be doing anything about the situation. Eyes darting from side to side, Gabrielle walked to the wall and leaned her shoulder against it. Opening a pamphlet, she pretended to read while watching the room. One of the big men was watching an older man vote.

"You don't want to do that," the large man said.

Stunned, the older man turned. "You can't tell me how to vote."

"I can tell you if it's a good idea or not," the big man said easily. Then he grinned. It wasn't a kind grin, more like one you would see on a villain in a movie.

The older man huffed, moved his body in between the large man and the voting machine, and made his choices. The big man gave him an evil glare.

"We won't forget this."

Gabrielle walked over to the police officer. He didn't acknowledge her until she stopped next to him. He looked bored.

"Aren't you going to do something about that?" she asked with a nod of her head.

"Why would I?" the man said back.

Inside, Gabrielle panicked. As she lowered her eyes, she saw a small pendant of the number one inside three circles and recognized it as the symbol for Thee Way Church of God. Turning to hide her shock, Gabrielle made for the exit in a hurried walk.

"Ma'am, ah, ma'am, you haven't voted yet," came a voice behind her.

Without stopping, Gabrielle exited the room and made for the building exit. As she moved between the two men standing guard, they ignored her, watching those coming in instead. It wasn't until she was off of the school grounds that she remembered to breathe. Her body shuddered and she wrapped her arms around her. The town she had lived in for so long suddenly felt strange, like an alien planet. She looked at the people around her, noting small pendants on many of them.

"Now what do I do?" she asked herself as she walked.

"That felt kind of pointless."

"What do you mean?" William Bridge asked his wife, turning to look at her as they walked from the large community hall building.

"There was only one candidate for each office. Why even vote?"

"We're part of a community out here. These people are our friends. Don't you think they would like to know that their friends voted for them, showed them some support?"

"I guess so." His wife took his arm as they walked, but her head was still hanging forward. "It's just so different here."

"It's better here! Clean air, bird song, nature. The kids have so many animals to play with, Carrie doesn't even miss her stuffed animals. And we're safe!"

"I know, but does it have to be so primitive? I mean, a few more modern things would be nice."

"It's a new community. I'm sure those things will be coming." His tone was dismissive. "Plus, with the constant stream of new people coming out here, that's probably about all they can deal with at the moment. You should know that from work."

"I do. Those poor people are as clueless as we were when we came out here. It's kind of sad."

"Look," William said as he put his arm around his wife's waist, "we're building something here, something to last. Something our kids can inherit. A good place to live. We should be happy."

"I guess," his wife said with a weak smile.

The door opened and closed softly. Mercedes tried to walk across the room without making any sound. She only got halfway.

"You don't have to come home, you know," Worthia's voice said from the other side of the couch. "You can stay the night if you want."

"What are you doing up?" Mercedes assumed a motherly voice.

"I like watching the construction lights." Worthia sat up and looked over the couch. "I'm a big girl, I can take care of myself."

Mercedes grinned and walked around the couch to sit next to the girl. A hug seemed to be in order, one where she swayed a little. Worthia hugged back.

"I know you can, but I still feel responsible for you. You've been here, what, five months? That's not a lot of time to adjust. Besides, I worry about you."

"Thank you so much for all you do for me, but at home, I would be an adult soon. I would be expected to run a home of my own. I think I can sleep inside the apartment by myself." She disengaged from the hug and looked at the older woman, who sighed with a slight nod.

"I never had a sister, you know..."

"As you have told me several times." Worthia gave her a look kids give parents who can't help repeat themselves.

"…and I just don't want to do anything wrong. If anything would happen to you, I don't know…"

"On the base? Really? What's going to happen here?"

"I don't know, but I don't want to find out." Mercedes gave her another quick hug. "Now, you get to sleep."

"Wait!" Mercedes grabbed her arm. "Was it romantic?"

"It's always romantic," Mercedes said with a dreamy look.

"Tell me about it!" Worthia sat up straighter on the couch. Mercedes started to talk, stopped, and then gave her a friendly glare.

"No way, young lady, or you'll be up all night. Maybe I will tell you tomorrow. Now, good night." Mercedes tossed the girl's hair before getting up and walking to the bedroom.

"Spoil-sport," Worthia said with a frown as she lay back down on the couch.

Chapter Eighteen
The Times They Are Changing

"**Y**ou know, they've shut down that new church, Church of the True God, I think. They say it's for health reasons, but I mean, really, that building? And now they claim that they found radon gas in the basement. If you ask me, since that Razmon guy won the election, I think he's out to shut down all the churches except the one he goes to."

Gabrielle tried to keep busy as she was forced to listen to Barb talk. The woman sat on the edge of Gabrielle's desk while she did so, but she didn't take up much space, so Gabrielle couldn't say she was in the way. Not that she minded talking to Barb, it's just that she seemed to like to talk more than work and Gabrielle needed her job. Actually, she needed a better paying job but could find little time to look for one.

As she raised her eyes from the papers on her desk, she noticed her boss coming out from his office into the general area. Forcing down a gulp, she put her hands on her lap to hide the slight shake that threatened to start. He was heading her way.

"Barb, does the True God Church have a policy with us?" she asked, looking up at the lady. Barb's face got a stunned look as she stopped talking.

"Well, no, not that I know of," Barb said in a quiet voice.

"Then I don't see how I can help you. Excuse me, I have things to attend to."

Barb rose from the desk, confused until she saw Mort approaching. Clearing her throat, she started to say something, but then beat a hasty retreat to the back room. Mort ignored her and walked up to Gabrielle's desk.

"Can I talk to you in my office for a moment?"

"Ah... of course." Panic went even higher as Gabrielle rose from her chair. Thoughts of being fired, and the bad things that came after that, ran through her head. Her hands kept clasping and unclasping each other. Mort had turned and started back to his office, so he didn't appear to notice.

Gabrielle followed Mort into his office. Once inside, Mort closed the door and indicated a chair with his hand. He was smiling the whole time. Not an evil or devious smile, but a pleasant one. Gabrielle told herself that it was a good sign, but the panic inside of her refused to believe it.

Mort casually walked around his desk and sat down, placing his hands on the desk in front of him, clasped together. He still wore the smile, one she had seen him use with customers. He took a breath.

"I need to apologize to you, Ms. Sanchez."

The comment took Gabrielle by such surprise that her hands stopped shaking and she looked wide-eyed at the man.

"I never really noticed how hard you work around here, harder than, shall we say, other people?" Mort indicated with his eyebrows out of the room.

"I... thank you, sir. It's very nice of you to say," Gabrielle managed to mumble. She didn't know if she dared to look the man in the eye.

"I was thinking that we should move you up to a full agent."

Unable to believe her ears, Gabrielle stared at the man with her mouth open. He let her adjust to her shock, continuing to smile. After what seemed like a long time, she managed to say, "Thank you, thank you so much."

"Well," Mort said as he leaned back in his chair and gave her a wink, "we do want the right kind of people representing this agency."

Gabrielle saw Mort's eyes shift quickly down to her shoulder and back during the statement. She knew what he had looked at. She had gone to church Sunday and a lady had come up to welcome her. As she did, she had placed a small pendant on her dress, a one inside of three circles. It had seemed prudent for Gabrielle to always wear it. The service hadn't been that different from the church she had attended with her grandmother when she was little and the kids had loved their class, though the cookies might have had something to do with that. When she talked to the teacher afterwards, something the woman said she did with all new arrivals, the woman had also told her that they had a food pantry on Monday nights where she could get free food. It was definitely on her list for tonight. The kids were already dreaming about what they would find there.

"Of course," Mort continued, "there will be a salary increase with your new position, which we will start during your training."

Gabrielle's head started to spin. She wanted to tell herself to wake up and stop dreaming. Knowing she probably looked silly didn't help her rise out of the fog in her head.

"Are you okay?" Mort asked. "I haven't overloaded you, have I? At least, if I have, it's in a good way."

"No! No! Thank you so much. I... I can't thank you enough." Gabrielle stood and held her hands to her chest.

"You earned it. Now go, process."

Mort smiled even broader as Gabrielle turned to leave. She walked back to her desk in a daze. She just sat and stared for a moment, then looked around the room.

"Maybe this religion stuff isn't so bad after all."

"How bad is it?" President Tyler asked, looking as if she dreaded the answer.

"Valesco's church dominated the elections, particularly in the small towns and rural areas. There are rumors of irregularities, but at the moment that's all they are. No one has filed a complaint and no one has asked for a recount."

"And they won't," Secretary Donnest said. "We weren't looking before the election, but Valesco's church goers make up the majority of the election board members. It caught us by surprise."

"Yes," Tyler responded, "Valesco has been playing a very long game and is ahead of us. The question is, can we catch up?"

The men sitting in front of her looked at her and then looked at each other as if daring the others to speak. Adams took a deep breath and dared.

"At this time, I would say that we can't. By the time the next election comes around, he'll have a clear majority."

Tyler leaned back in her chair and got a thoughtful look on her face. The chair swiveled through quarter-turns in both directions. The men waited.

"It would seem then, gentlemen, that we need to either get on the bus or change routes." The chair stopped and Tyler looked at the men. "Anyone here want to join the bus?"

No one spoke. Some looked shocked at the suggestion. Tyler waited, no hints from her face or eyes as to what she expected from them. After thirty seconds, they had all settled down and still said nothing.

"I will take that as a no. So, what do we prepare for and how do we prepare?"

"Are you talking about not holding elections?" AG Tallenson asked.

"Do you really think in three years we will be able to have a fair election?" Tyler shot back.

"If things keep going they way they are," Secretary Donnest said, "no."

"Does that give us the authority to pre-empt them?" Adams asked, the shifting in his chair showing his discomfort with the suggestion.

"And you don't think Valesco isn't staging a coup at the moment?" Donnest asked. "If half the stories I've heard are true, he's rigged most of the local elections. Next year, the state elections processes will be starting. Two years from now, he very well might have control of the states, followed by the White House."

"But you are talking about a total abandonment of the documents we live by," Adams countered.

"Valesco will make documents meaningless. Tell me, if you controlled the states, wouldn't you call a constitutional convention and give yourself more power?" Donnest raised an eyebrow with the question as the volume of his voice went up. "How many times have we seen that in other countries in the past?"

"But not here!" Adams insisted.

"First time for everything." Donnest shrugged. Adams seemed to have no response to the statement.

"Back to the question at hand," Tyler interrupted. "We're already securing military bases, but we need to think beyond that. There will be at least some population that will not surrender to Valesco, particularly if we give them an alternative."

The comment caused hard thinking in the men, evidenced on their faces. A few pulled up their interfaces and made quiet inquiries while others just thought. Tyler waited, elbows on the arms of her chair and fingertips together.

"Wherever we choose," Donnest spoke up, "we have to be able to secure the location. That might take some work for some cities."

"You mean like fencing them off?" Secretary Standington asked.

"Or wall it off. Fences are a good start, but walls would be better. Of course, they take longer, so we might start with fences and then install walls."

"We're really going to talk about walling off cities?" Standington asked.

"If we don't, preventing infiltration will be impossible. Unless you allow shoot-on-sight orders." The statement brought horror from Standington, directed at Donnest. "Just saying."

"Also, we will want to control all of the highest-technology capabilities, which the Puritans would probably destroy anyway. Luckily, many of these are concentrated in certain areas of the country or we can easily move the additive manufacturing or part treatment methods."

"The question then becomes where we place this manufacturing," Tyler pointed out.

"True. Our historic tendency to place our large cities on the coast where they will have access to shipping helps us there—New York City and San Francisco being two prime examples of not only being large cities but being islands, thus being natural barriers to incursion. Too bad Puerto Rico is independent. It could have been useful."

"I see where you are going. But we can't rely only on islands for all the people."

"No, but it helps, since they will not need as many defenses as other locations, like Chicago."

"Defenses? I would really hope it doesn't come to that," Adams said.

"Which cities are critical?" Tyler asked.

"Chicago," Adams said. "Denver, Seattle, Miami, San Diego, Dallas, Cleveland, Boston, Phoenix, Pittsburgh, Baltimore…"

"That's quite a list," Secretary Carmichael said.

"Yes, we may need to cut down the size of the city we protect, or at least start smaller and expand later," Donnest said.

"If there is a later," AG Tallenson said.

"Lucky for us, there is a lot of wasted space in cities," Adams said. "So to speak, that is. A lot of the businesses will not be needed or even exist by then, not to mention what will happen to the sports teams. If we concentrate on converting to residences and factories, for the most parts, I think we will be able to get a very large population even in smaller sections of the cities."

"We also need to think about securing other locations that are not as populated but easily defended," Donnest said.

"Like?" Tyler asked.

"Long Island comes to mind. I am sure there are other islands that could be selected."

"Yes. I will need a full list."

The discussion was interrupted by a door opening and an aide sticking her head into the room. "Madam President, you want to turn on the news."

"What's going on?" Tyler asked.

"Indonesia is in full-scale revolt."

As Donnest's fingers manipulated his interface in furious strokes, Tyler activated the desk display.

Chapter Nineteen
Elsewhere

The line was moving slowly, though Hasan Kok did not know where it was going. Everyone was in the line, so he assumed it was the right place to be. A woman stood on top of something so that he could see her from the waist up. She was shouting to the people in the line.

"We will no longer be ruled by puppets of the military! We will not longer be ruled by dictators who continue to keep this country in the past! The people will rule! We will take back our country. Kill the dictators! Kill the military!"

The crowd echoed some of her shorter sayings. The speech confused Hasan. He couldn't remember when the country wasn't ruled by a dictator with military support.

As he moved, he saw that someone from inside a building was handing people in the line items. When he was close enough, he saw weapons being passed to those in line. At his turn, the man handed Hasan a pulsator rifle. Hasan just looked at the weapon in his hands, pushed along by the line. The people in front of him were gathering about another man standing on a box.

"Point your rifle straight up unless you are pointing it at the enemy," the man was saying. He turned the rifle he had to the side, pointing at it with his finger. "Here on the side is the on switch. Red means it will shoot, no red means it will not. Do not turn it on until you see the enemy. Do not shoot your companions. Once it is on, point the end at the enemy and pull the trigger. Simple as that. If it won't fire, you need a new battery. A dropped rifle will be the quickest place to get a new one. The release is down here."

The crowd moved out, Hasan with them. He had never held a gun before and was sure most of the crowd hadn't either. Not knowing where he was going didn't matter. People cheered as they ran and he was caught up in the exuberance.

After a few blocks, they heard the distinct sound of pulsator fire. Hasan stood for a moment while the rest turned and ran toward the fire. He followed, not quite the last person to do so. He tried to see what was happening ahead, but couldn't tell.

It wasn't long before fire started to fall among the runners. Several fell to the ground. The others kept running. Some of the fire came from the roofs ahead of them. Hasan fired a couple of shots at the roofs, but it had no effect on the fire coming their way.

The man next to him fell to the ground, smoke coming from his body. Hasan hit the ground, shaking. Fire fell around him and the others. A larger pulsator sound came, followed by an explosion just ahead of him.

"What was that?!" Hasan yelled.

"Heavy pulsator," someone called back.

"What do we do?"

"We have to take it out!"

Fire continued to fall around him. Hasan moved behind a body near him. Next to the body was a rifle that was different, mounting a scope. Putting his rifle down, Hasan picked up the new rifle, raised it to his shoulder, and pointed it at the roof. Inside, the scope was black. Bringing it back down, Hasan turned it to the side and turned on the rifle.

Lying on the ground, Hasan rested the rifle on the dead body and pointed it at the roofs. Scanning across the roof slowly revealed a person in military fatigues. A red circle appeared in the scope, moving and circulating, until it settled around the person. When it stopped, Hasan pulled the trigger and watched the person drop with a hole in his chest.

"Sweet!" Hasan exclaimed before putting his eye once more to the scope and scanning the other roofs. Another set of fatigues appeared and another person dropped. The last shots seemed to come from above. Rolling onto his back, Hasan pointed the rifle straight up. After a scan, all he could see was the barrel of a gun. Focusing on that, Hasan waited for the circle to stop and pulled the trigger. The gun barrel flew backwards from sight.

"Yes!" As he sat up, he noted the number of people who were not moving. The heavy pulsator was still firing, taking out people with every other shot.

Moving to one knee, Hasan brought the gun to his shoulder and pointed it at the heavy pulsator. He sighed in relief to see the weapon pointed in another direction. Placing the gunner in the sights, he waited for the circle and fired. A hole appeared in the man's head. Smoke came from it as the man dropped, a wild pulsator shot going into the air as he did.

"Come on," someone ahead of him shouted. "Let's go!"

Before he stood up, Hasan took the battery from his first rifle and put it in his pocket. Lifting the sniper rifle, he joined the others as they ran forward. The first man stopped at the heavy pulsator, turned it in the opposite direction, and started firing. Hasan ran to a vehicle and stopped behind it, panting. Fire started coming from the other side of the vehicle. The heavy pulsator answered. Explosions followed.

"What the hell am I doing?" Hasan said out loud.

"We're winning!" the man at the pulsator said. "We're winning!"

Just then, a pulsator burst hit the man and a large hole formed in his chest. The man looked down at himself just before falling off the weapon. He was immediately replaced by another.

"Get moving!" the new man at the pulsator shouted. "You stand still and you die."

Hasan took a deep breath, turned, and ran around the vehicle.

The Indonesian soldier ran into the room, panting. A burn mark on his arm was evidence of a shot that had come too close. As he doubled over, trying to get breath into his lungs, a general walked up to him.

"What are you doing here?"

"There were too many of them. We were overrun," the man managed to pant out.

"That is not acceptable! Where are the rest of your troop?"

"Dead. Most on the line, the rest between the line and here. We were pursued all the way."

"What?! You led them here!"

"What else was I supposed to do?"

"Defend your line!" The general drew a pistol and fired into the man's head. While the body was still falling, the general turned to the rest of the room. "Situation report!"

"Forces are collapsing on all sides," came back a voice.

"Why can't we hold ground?"

"Weapons are degrading from firing so much," a different voice said.

"Lock down the building."

"They're in the building!" a panicked voice said.

"Call in any available forces." The general walked toward the door.

"Sir! Where are you going?"

"To defend the base, of course." With pistol drawn, the general walked out of the room.

Everyone in the cafeteria was watching the displays, scenes from Indonesia their only subject. People fought and died. Buildings burned. It wasn't clear who was winning.

"Where are they getting the views?" Joseph asked.

"Overhead satellites," Wenk replied.

"Explains the perspective. Hard to tell the sides apart from above."

"Yeah, particularly when the rebels put on army helmets."

"You think they are doing it on purpose?"

"Confusing the rest of the world on purpose by putting on helmets? Sounds kind of farfetched, isn't it?" Wenk's tone made it hard to tell if the question was serious or not.

"Just a question," Joseph said with a shrug.

"Where's Mercedes?"

"Said she couldn't watch, made her sick to see people killing each other."

"Needs to game more," Wenk said while nodding.

"And eat into my time? No way."

"You could game with her."

"Gaming is not what I want to spend my time with her doing."

Wenk laughed at his statement.

"Hard to imagine, I know."

"No, it's not when you have a supermodel girlfriend."

"Yeah," Joseph said in a drawn out manner. "The supermodel thing is pretty distracting."

Wenk huffed. "Anytime you get tired of being distracted, I'll take over."

"That would be up to her, not me."

"Oh, well." Wenk shrugged. "'Twas a nice dream."

"LC," Joseph said as Benitez walked by. The woman turned. "Any idea who's winning?"

"No one," was all she said before turning back the direction she had been walking and continuing.

"That's not very helpful," Joseph said quietly.

"I think she was talking philosophy," Wenk said.

"And when was that ever helpful?"

"Don't let a philosopher hear you say that," Benitez answered.

"What are they going to do, philosophize me to death?"

"I'm not sure that's even a word." Wenk's face turned about itself.

"Be picky," Joseph spat out.

The friends continued to watch in silence. People continued to die. Buildings had holes blown in them. Jets came overhead and fired into crowds. Missiles took out the jets, which fell into more buildings. Smoke started to fill the air and obscure the view.

"Not like in your simulation games, is it?" Joseph asked.

"No, it's *just* like in our simulations. That's the scary thing."

They stood there for maybe another hour before the scene got so confused that they couldn't tell what was happening. No information signals came from the capital. No one claimed victory. The city and the country burned in more places than could be counted.

Chapter Twenty
It's Called Progress

"At least the cold weather is over." Joseph walked up to Colonel Natora with a smile on his face. Wind whipped around his face as if trying to wipe it away.

"You mean the really cold weather." Natora shifted her coat on her shoulders to draw it closer.

"Yes. In comparison, this is mild."

"At least we can work outside." Natora brought her interface to her mouth. "Bring in the next batch of concrete, we'll need it soon."

"What's Wenk doing out there?" Joseph pointed at the pour site.

"He made some modifications for the concrete bots over the winter. Testing them now. If it works, should halve the time to make each floor."

"Sounds good. I have an idea about next winter too." Joseph rocked on his heels.

The comment caused Natora to turn his direction, a suspicious look on her face.

"Imagine a giant, air-filled bubble on top of the building that moves up as the floors get completed. Temperature control inside should allow pouring concrete in the winter. Of course, you'll need to put the windows in before it moves up."

"That bubble of yours exist yet?"

"Not yet, but I am trying to convince the research guys to make it. Could have multiple uses. Just need the funding approved." Joseph looked around the work site nonchalantly.

Natora scoffed. "Let me know when it exists and then we'll talk." She turned back to the construction site. "You didn't come out here to tell me about imagined bubbles, did you?"

"No, I didn't. As soon as you guys are done, I need you to build a new airstrip."

"What's wrong with the old one? It's plenty long, that's for sure."

"It's in the middle of the base. Makes people nervous to have planes landing right next to their bedrooms."

"Wimps." Natora laughed. The sound was carried away by the wind almost as soon as it left her mouth.

"When's the power station scheduled to be up and running?"

"Two weeks, assuming all goes well. The wall will be cured before they hit the on button. Kind of a pain to leave the building open, but only way to get the reactor in."

"You've done a great job getting this ready." Joseph took a deep breath and let it out. "I know we've been driving you guys pretty hard since you arrived. If there's anything I can do to make your guys feel appreciated, let me know."

"Getting into these apartments will go a long way," Natora said with a nod of her head over her shoulder toward the new resident tower, where most of her men were working. "Some have been away from their families for a long time. Any chance of getting some leave?"

"Unless their families are on a base already, it would probably be better if their families moved here. You've seen what it's like around the country, right?" Joseph's voice went up slightly as he finished the sentence.

"Yeah, but that's a big move for some of them. What if they don't want to come?"

"We can't make them, that's for sure. I would feel better if you would float the idea first. You're going to be busy here for quite a while, years in fact. I would think they would prefer to be together the whole time. Plus, it would be a lot easier than running across country every few months."

"I'll ask. Can't promise."

"And you call yourself an officer," Joseph said with mock derision.

"No, the military does."

Joseph stood for a few moments without talking, then said, "I have no answer for that one. Later, Suz."

Gabrielle sat down on the old couch in her living room. The sounds of gleeful children echoed through the doorway. She smiled at her visitors, Hensley and Martha. They sat comfortably on her new couch, friendly smiles on their faces.

"The kids just love your daughter," Gabrielle said as she settled back. "They talk about her all the time when we come back from church."

"She's wonderful with children," Martha replied. "It's her gift."

"Can I get you something to drink?" Gabrielle asked, leaning forward.

"No, we're fine, thank you," Hensley said. "We just wanted to have the chance to talk to you about something."

"Sure." Gabrielle sat back into the couch. An inner voice sounded warnings in her head, but she told it to behave. All the church people had been good to her and the kids.

"We've been, well, concern isn't exactly right, more like sympathetic about you raising your kids all by yourself. It must be hard with work and all." Martha spoke in a gentle voice, head slightly forward.

"We've adjusted, and my children are the most important things to me, so I don't mind putting time into them." Gabrielle's smile turned a little strained.

"Do you know where the father is? I mean, he has some responsibilities too, doesn't he?"

"He left when Cal was only a few months old. I woke up one morning and he was gone with all his stuff. He had been complaining about Cal crying all the time, but I think he really didn't want to be saddled with so many kids."

"Have you heard from him?"

"No, not since he left." Gabrielle shook her head.

"Haven't the courts done anything? I mean, shouldn't he be helping support them?" Martha nodded her head as if to make the statement true.

"I never had enough money for a lawyer to file a case. And he seems to be good at avoiding being found." Gabrielle sighed.

"That's what we were afraid of," Hensley added. "You know, it's much better for children to have a mom and a dad at home. It's what God intended for the family."

Gabrielle nodded her head politely.

"We, the church, like to do everything we can to take care of our families. We're all brothers and sisters in God, so it's only natural."

Gabrielle could feel her nervousness grow. Her head turned a little without intent.

"That's why we thought about your situation for a while and we've come up with a suggestion. Do you know Cam Turrunik?"

"A little," Gabrielle said tentatively. "Why?"

"We, the church that is, think he would be a good match for you and your children."

Gabrielle felt like someone had hit her with a board, one that imparted shock only. "You... you're saying I should consider dating him?"

"No, dear, we think you should marry him."

Head spinning, Gabrielle remembered all the things that had been said in church about husbands and the family. The church was big on the husband being the head of the house and the wife submitting to the husband in all things. It was the 'all things' that bothered her. And now they wanted to pick this person for her.

"Well, it's very nice of you to make such a suggestion," Gabrielle said without looking at her guests.

"It's more than just a suggestion, dear," Martha said. "We think you should *seriously* think about this." The look in Martha's eyes made it clear it was much more than a suggestion.

Gabrielle swallowed with difficulty. She looked down. Her hands started to fold onto each other. She tried to talk, but her voice just croaked softly. Clearing it, she looked back to her guests.

"Can you give me a little time to think about this? I mean, it's kind of sudden and I don't want to just spring it on the children."

"Of course, dear, take your time. We just want to make sure you're happy."

*   *   *

Her guests gone, the kids changing for bed, Gabrielle sat with her head in her hands.

"What am I going to do? Where can we go?"

Gabrielle called up her interface and started checking news reports. She focused on locations where non-church people were going. Denver seemed like an idea, but even that wasn't totally safe, from the reports she saw. She looked for half an hour before a solution came to her.

"Mommy," a child's voice came from behind her. "Are you going to read a story to us?"

"Of course I am, honey," Gabrielle said, turning around. "Would you like me to read you the one about the rabbits?"

"Yes, yes," the little girl said with enthusiasm. Gabrielle scooped her up into her arms.

"And tomorrow we are going on a trip."

"Where, Mommy?"

"To see your grandma." Gabrielle carried the girl toward the bedroom.

"I thought Grandma died?"

"That was my grandma. I'm talking about your grandma." Gabrielle tossed the girl's hair.

"I didn't know I had another grandma."

"Everyone has at least two grandmas, silly. Now let's get you to sleep. It's a long way to Grandma's house."

The car ride had been almost six hours, but the military base was in sight. There appeared to be a lot of activity near the gate. Gabrielle took it as a good sign. Parking near the entrance, she turned to her kids.

"Mommy has to go ask for directions. Stay in the car, okay?"

"Can we get out?" came a young whine. "I'm tired of riding."

"Soon, baby, soon. Mommy will be right back. Stay here and be good."

Gabrielle exited the vehicle and walked to the guardhouse at the gate. The man did not look happy to see her.

"You can't park there," the man said.

"Can you help me, please? The church has taken over our town and I am trying to escape them. Can you provide us with shelter?"

"A refugee?" the man asked with resignation.

Gabrielle nodded.

"I'm sorry, lady, but this base is being closed. We're even scavenging the building for materials."

"My vehicle is low on charge." Gabrielle's voice added some panic. "I don't know how much further I can go."

The man sighed. "I need to talk to my superior."

The man went into the building. After a moment, he came back out. "Please wait by your vehicle," he said before turning away from Gabrielle.

Walking back to the car, she noted that the kids had their faces plastered against the vehicle glass. She gave them a smile. A window was lowered by the youngest.

"Someone is coming out to help us," she said when she was close.

"Is it an army guy?" Cal asked.

"We'll just have to find out."

After a few minutes, a man in uniform walked up to her from inside the base.

"Can I help you?"

"Yes, please. We need to get somewhere safe and are almost out of charge. I thought the base would be safe, but the man said it is being shut down. Can you please help us?"

The man looked at the little family and then looked back at the base. When his gaze came back, he shook his head.

"I have a convoy leaving soon. It's an all-day trip and won't be the most comfortable, but I think there is room for you, if you wish. It's all that I can do."

"Thank you, thank you. We'll take it."

The man took a step back and pointed. "Go through the gate and follow the red arrows on the road. There's a heavy equipment convoy leaving soon for South Dakota. You can go with them, but you better hurry."

"Thank you very much!" Gabrielle quickly got into the vehicle, started it, and drove onto the base.

"Where we going, Mommy?"

"We're going on a very special ride."

The road was not long. A line of seven huge vehicles stood behind another gate. Gabrielle stopped near the first one and got out of the car. A woman waved from the open window of the vehicle.

"You our passengers?"

"Yes," Gabrielle called as she got out of the car.

"Well, get your stuff and get in here. You're just in time."

Working quickly, Gabrielle hustled the kids out of the vehicle and then their luggage from the back. She had the kids pull their luggage to the vehicle while she brought the rest. A side door opened and a young man jumped out to help them put the luggage in the rear of the huge vehicle. The kids climbed into three rows of seats, one in each seat. Gabrielle climbed in with Cal. The young man closed the doors and went back to the front of the vehicle.

"Is this an army tank?" Cal asked.

"No, honey, it's not, but it is a military vehicle."

"Yeah! We're in the army!" Cal cheered.

"I'm tired," Mona, the middle girl, said. "Can I lay down?"

"Sure, honey." Gabrielle wished she had a pillow to lay her head on as she stretched across the whole seat. "Are you okay, Shanna?"

"Yes, Mother," the girl said with a pained voice. "Can I just sit here by myself?"

"Of course, dear." Gabrielle turned back to her son, who was bouncing on the seat with excitement.

"This is convoy leader. Status," the woman in the front passenger seat said into her interface.

"Vehicle Two, green," came over the interface.

"Vehicle Three, green."

"Vehicle Four, green."

"Vehicle Five, green."

"Vehicle Six, green."

"Vehicle Seven, ready in two minutes."

"I want a green in two minutes," the woman said. "Convoy, start vehicles."

A whine started from the vehicle they were in. The sound got faster and higher with time until it was too high to hear. The vehicle's rumble was so slight that it could be missed if you didn't pay attention. The woman looked at displays on the vehicle before placing her interface to her mouth.

"Base, Convoy 1-6 away in one. Request gate open."

The gate in front of them pulled to the side with a slow, grating motion. As the gate finished opening, the interface sounded again.

"Vehicle Seven, green."

"Acknowledged. Base, Convoy 1-6 moving out. Is the first leg verified clear?"

"First leg is verified clear, Convoy 1-6. Have a good trip."

"Roger, base." The woman put her interface down.

"Are we carrying tanks?" Cal called out to the woman.

She laughed. "No, we're hauling heavy equipment. It's going to take the rest of the day to get there, so you better get comfortable."

"What are we going to see, Mommy?" the little boy asked.

"I don't know, honey. I've never been this way before."

"Do you like cows and sheep and horses and big rivers?" the woman asked.

"Yeah!" shouted Cal.

"Well, you'll see all that and more if you keep your eyes open."

"I can't wait!" Cal turned to the window. The vehicles gained speed as they pulled out of the base and drove down the highway.

"What was that about the way being clear?" Gabrielle asked.

"Just want to make sure we don't have to deal with any protesters or fanatics on the way," the woman said. "Each leg will be checked before we get there."

"Are we carrying anything dangerous?"

"I'll not allowed to say." The woman turned back forward.

Gabrielle slid over to Cal and wrapped her arms around him as she felt a shiver go through her body.

Night had settled in by the time the vehicles pulled up to the base gates. Mona was the only one fully awake, having slept through most of the trip. Gabrielle stirred the kids. Once Cal knew they were at a military base, he awoke quickly. Shanna dragged herself up from the seat.

"About time you got here," a baritone voice came from outside.

"When you're hauling stuff this big, you can't hurry too much. Hey, we have refugees for you, Sarge," the driver called out from the window to someone Gabrielle couldn't see.

"They get here any way they can," the voice said back. "I'll make sure they get where they need to go."

"They got luggage in the back. Trunk's popped."

"Thanks."

Gabrielle looked at the woman in front. "Aren't we going to the base?"

"You have to go through the induction center first," the woman said. "It's like a welcome center. They'll make sure you have a place to stay and know where you can go and not go."

"Oh, okay. Thanks."

"You'll want to get out my side."

Gabrielle herded the children to the right side of the vehicle. As she reached for the door handle, the door opened. It revealed a tall man with wide, well-muscled shoulders, thick-muscled arms, a thick neck, and the v-shaped body of an athlete. On top of all those muscles was a head with short cropped hair and kind, gentle brown eyes. Even though it felt chilly outside, he only wore a short-sleeved shirt and vest against the cold. Gabrielle's mind kept picturing him without his shirt. She told her mind to stop it, but it wasn't listening.

"Here, let me help you," the man said. Gently, he lowered each of the children from the vehicle. Lastly, he raised his hand to help Gabriel down. It was large with thick fingers, but held hers gently as she climbed down.

"Thank you," Gabrielle said with a slight shiver, not from the cold.

"Do you see that white building with the lights on?" the man asked, pointing.

Gabrielle nodded.

"You need to go there first. Do you need help with your things?"

"No, no, I think we can manage. Thank you for your help..."

"Sergeant Edmond Harjo, at your service." The man did a short bow. "You need anything, you let me know."

"That's very nice of you... Sergeant. Take your luggage, kids, we need to walk over there."

Gabrielle led the children down the concrete path to the building. She took one look back to find Harjo watching her, then turned back before he could see her blush.

"He was nice," Mona said.

"Yes," Gabrielle said with a grin, "he is."

Chapter Twenty-One
We the Few

"I want to thank Ms. Shishiho for setting up this call," President Tyler said to the interface. "I also want to thank all of you for attending. I know this meeting has taken a while to arrange, but I am sure it will be worth it."

"We are all concerned about world events," Bahir Kattan of United Arabia said. "We are also concerned about the rise of the alien churches. Though small in our part of the world, we do not wish for a rival."

"Agreed," Mambou Tammil, head of the African Confederation, said.

"First things first," said Lucien Shetter, head of the Common European Concern. Tall and thin with a sharp nose, Shetter looked typically British down to the pipe peeking from his front pocket and the ever-present hint of tobacco scent. "Do we have reliable intelligence about Indonesia?"

"Yes, we do." The voice belonged to Shishiho. "The new junta is holding elections for the republican government they have approved. The military, or what was left of it, has been dismantled. The cities are still in chaos and reconstruction has not started, except for individual efforts. There is another issue, though."

"Which is…?" Tyler asked.

"From what we can tell, the church known as Thee Way is making substantial efforts at recruitment. With the current power vacuum, they are having much success."

"Any hint that they helped start the insurrection?" Tyler asked.

"No, but that is most likely due to our inability to look for evidence in such a chaotic situation." Shishiho's expression did not change with the statement.

"Not good news either way," Shetter added.

"Any other hot spots we need to worry about at the moment?" Tyler asked. "We are not aware of any, but our information may be incomplete."

No one spoke up, but sat calmly as if unwilling to give away information. Tyler sighed.

"Look, we have to start trusting each other if we are going to get anywhere. With all... most... of our governments suffering from limits imposed the last couple of decades, we can't afford to sit silently and not share information. And if these churches are starting to fill power vacuums, we need to rely on each other to be fully informed." Tyler let the statement permeate.

"Agreed," Shishiho said after a moment. "Even though we have firm controls over our interests, we do not need to suffer attacks from sources of which we are not aware. The Western Pacific Conglomerate will share all information equally in the hopes that everyone else will do the same."

The statement reduced the tension in all faces. Several nodded. Tyler smiled in admiration to Shishiho.

"Central and South America," Isabella Ruiz, Head of the Confederation of the Americas, started, "while not religious, is still heavily influenced by past Catholic Church norms. We have seen little in-roads by the alien churches except in some of the large cities. We have noticed, though, increased community services offered by the churches and are concerned this might create an atmosphere of acceptance by the general public. At the moment, our budget is too small to start competitive services and we are looking for other counter-measures."

"United Arabia has not seen any incursion of these churches because of their association with Jerusalem and past Euro-Christian ideas." Kattan's face changed, lowering slightly. "Our strategists, though, warn that if they can breach this divide using pre-Christian historic connections, their growth could be very rapid. We are monitoring public sentiment in this area."

"The African continent has mixed situations," Tammil started after a short pause. "We have many regions that are less prosperous than the rest of the world, making them vulnerable to such groups. We have noted a large number of such churches starting in these areas, but they appear to be keeping themselves small, maybe to avoid examination. In contrast to Ruiz's experiences, churches are starting in the rural areas and not the cities. This makes it hard to have reliable information. We have started a media campaign to convince people not to revert to past social forms, but agricultural living is still looked upon fondly."

"Adjusting their strategies for the areas, it seems," Tyler commented.

Once again, the conversation quieted. Eyes slowly moved toward Shetter, who at first showed no tendency to speak. As the eye pressure increased, Shetter shifted under the scrutiny and finally spoke.

"To be honest, Europe is a mess. You know about the events of last year. It appears that our crackdown of the Enlightenment Church did not have the desired effect. Attendance of all churches is actually up and the Catholic Church has taken a hard-line stance against the alien churches, calling them heretics and calling for closing of their churches. Priests have become more vocal, but I am not convinced the strategy is working. This has given cause for the alien churches to portray them as authoritarian and cruel. I am worried that the Catholic Church has entered a downward spiral of their own making that will lead to their destruction, but only the future will tell." Shetter looked down before continuing, tapping his finger on something out of view.

"The other worrying aspect is that we also have a very vocal anti-alien movement growing, using the death of Arhus Gint as its centerpiece. It has all the earmarks of the extreme right-wing groups of the past and we are worried that some holdouts have redrawn themselves into these groups. If either or both of these groups acquire weapons, things could become bloody fast."

"What measures are you taking to prevent this?" Tyler asked. The question was calm, though the looks in the monitors were not.

"There is not much we can do. Almost all of the power resides within the local governments. We are trying to keep them abreast of the dangers. Some listen, others don't. We are using diplomacy and negotiation as our main tactics." Shetter's eyes finally rose to the others, though they were more lost than anything.

The atmosphere of the meeting got darker in response. Several turned to their displays and spoke a few words. Others spoke to subordinates behind them. None appeared to approve of Shetter's words. Shishiho showed the least concern, but then she always did, looking at Shetter for a time before turning from him. She spoke before Tyler could.

"The issue we need to address is what we do in response to these efforts. We must each decide how much can be done in our own areas and we must be realistic about what can be done. I know that the Conglomerate has more power than any of your governments. Thus, we are willing to assist in areas of the world that are not covered well by any of our groups. Not that we are seeking to expand, but may have resources we can bring to bear where yours may be needed at home."

"You mean the Indian Wasteland and the Swept Russian Steppes?" Tammil asked with a laugh. "You can have them. They are more trouble than they are worth."

"Thank you, Shishiho," Tyler said with a voice that left doubt it was fully convinced. "It appears that U.S.-Canada and Europe will be busy with our home issues. I think we all need to be willing to ask for assistance when required without worrying about sovereignty. I think threats from the new sources cause more concern than old rivalries."

"Yes," Ruiz added in a quick voice, leaning forward, "I agree. We need to be helping each other and not fighting each other or else we won't survive."

The others nodded in agreement. Tyler took a breath of relief.

"Back to the issue. What do we do in response?" Tyler asked. "Any suggestions?"

"Maybe we would like to know what America and Europe are doing," Tammil said, his voice at half-volume and low.

"Of course," Tyler said, as if expecting the question. "I just wanted to give others a chance to speak. We are securing ten critical military bases, moving all weapons and critical equipment to them. They will be built up to hold as many personnel as possible. We are also identifying critical cities that can be secured for the general population that is not associated with the alien churches. This process will take longer, of course."

Tyler looked at Shetter. The man visibly gulped before talking.

"We are taking a more complete approach," the man responded. "We are not resigning any of our countries to church control. We will find a way to keep our control over the countries while allowing people freedom of religion."

"You are a fool," Shishiho said.

Shetter blanched.

"I must agree," Tammil stated. "With all the trouble you have been having, expecting to control the situation is naive."

"We represent all the people in our countries, not just the ones who agree with us." Shetter's chin notched up and became stiff.

"We trust," Tyler said, "that you will at least secure your weapons from the general public."

"Of course," Shetter said, taken aback. The other delegates did not look convinced.

"We all must secure strategic resources," Shishiho continued, "whether that is facilities, sources, or people. We must also make sure that our cities are not starved for the resources they need, particularly food. Each of us must examine our situations and decide how we are to deal with these issues."

"That will be primary in all of our plans," Ruiz stated. She leaned back into her chair and raised her chin with the statement. The easy reaction appeared to indicate that it had already been considered by her administration.

"I suggest we reconvene in a couple of months to communicate how our situations are progressing," Tyler said. "Agreed?"

Heads nodded in all displays.

There were about two dozen of them. Joseph watched from behind the fence as they waved their signs and shouted, bringing up painful memories. They were dressed plainly in jeans, pullover shirts, and work boots. Most were men less than forty years old. Allin walked up beside him.

"Don't they have anything better to do?" Joseph asked.

"Apparently not. Planting must be over."

"It only takes one person to watch a robot plant."

"Good point, though it may take more than one to fix it."

"Good point. I really want to ask them if they don't have cows to milk or something."

Allin laughed. "That's why it's mostly men."

Joseph turned his head and squinted. "Milking cows is woman's work?"

"Sure, haven't you heard of dairy maids?"

"Where were you when my mother was sending me out to milk the cows?" Joseph turned back to watch the protesters.

"You had cows?" Allin asked in surprise.

"I did live on a farm, you know." Joseph's head wagged back and forth a little.

"Doesn't mean you had cows."

"We're Dutch."

"Oh," Allin said with a suppressed laugh, "that explains it."

They stood for a while, watching people walk back and forth in front of the gate. On their side of the gate stood six guards armed with pulsator rifles. To Joseph, the guards looked like they would have liked someone to charge the gate just for the fun of shooting them.

"We need you back in the lab," Allin said.

"You clear it with Bennett?"

"Yes. He said that with the plans set, he can get someone else to execute them. Didn't say who." She gave a shrug with her head.

"So I am out of purgatory?" Joseph's eyes widened.

"Yes, you've done your penance and can walk into heaven." Allin smiled.

Joseph sagged. "About time. Thank you, thank you, thank you." He turned and put his forehead on the woman's shoulder.

"Don't thank me yet until you see what the people down there want."

"Don't care," Joseph said, shaking his head while still on her shoulder. "As long as I am out of that nightmare."

"Oh, come on, it can't be that bad."

"Nothing showing up on time, everyone complaining, always getting told you are spending too much while being told it's not going fast enough? Trust me, I'll take grumpy researchers any day."

"Well, then, you get your wish."

Joseph took his head off the woman's shoulder and once again watched the protesters. "I just don't understand what they think they're accomplishing."

"I know what you're not accomplishing," Allin said in a calm voice.

"Oh." Joseph did a small jerk and a turn. "You meant now?"

"Yes, I meant now." Allin turned her head and gave him a stare.

"All right, slave-driver." Joseph made of point of slumping off toward the research building.

"Double-time!" Allin called.

"So, what we got?" Joseph asked as he entered the particle beam lab, rubbing his hands together.

"Oh, look, the hero has decided to join us," a technician said before turning and walking away.

"What's his problem?" Joseph directed the question to Wenk, who was standing in the small group.

"He just missed you," Wenk said with a half-smile.

"Yeah, he missed you taking your part of the load," a woman standing next to Wenk scoffed. Joseph made a mental note that he would have to brush up on everyone's names.

"Hey, wasn't my idea to play builder man." The comment didn't appear to persuade anyone. "Anyway, what's going on?"

"Follow me," Wenk said with a wave, walking toward the secure testing area. He opened the door to one of the concrete test cells. Inside, Joseph found a projector set in a stand pointed at a transparent material.

"Is that some of the wing material they found on site?"

"Yep, one of a shrinking batch of samples."

"Shrinking?" Joseph's head did a fast swivel to Wenk. "Isn't that stuff just about indestructible?

"Just about. Watch what the laser does."

"You know that's not a laser?" Joseph asked dubiously.

"Combination laser and particle beam projector, I know. It's just easier to call it a laser." Wenk waved his hands as he spoke.

"But the laser is only there so we can see it. The particle beam does all the work."

"Potato, potato."

Joseph's head came back in question. "You just said the same thing twice."

"Exactly. Now, watch."

Wenk handed Joseph a pair of goggles and put his on. It seemed silly to Joseph, but he put his on too. Walking around to the rear of the weapon, Wenk flipped a switch. The hum of the weapon charging came to Joseph's ears. After a few seconds, Wenk flipped another switch. A blue light shot from the end of the projector to the wing material. In under a second, the material started to dissolve, a blue lined hole growing larger as it did. Wenk turned off the beam and the hum started to die away.

"Holy crap!" Joseph stared at the wing material as it continued to dissolve. "You guys did it!"

"Sort of," Wenk said without enthusiasm.

"What do you mean sort of? I'd say you just destroyed that wing!" One of Joseph's hands gestured toward the sample.

"This is the only unit that has demonstrated the ability to destroy the material."

Joseph stopped and gaped. He looked at Wenk, then at the weapon, and then back to Wenk.

"How many units are there?"

"Six, supposedly identical. Yet this one is the only one that works."

"What's different about it?"

"Don't know. Frustrating as hell." Wenk sighed.

"I assume you took it apart and put it back together, checking all the dimensions and material?"

"Yep."

"And nothing?"

"Nothing."

"Then you missed something."

"Obviously."

"And I get to find out what?"

"You're the expert. Where do you want to start?" Wenk raised his eyebrows.

Joseph wagged his finger at the device. "I want to take a full spectrum of the output before we do anything else."

"Done that already. Want to see the results?"

"No, I want to do it myself." Joseph's finger was still moving.

"You think we did it wrong? I mean, a full spectrum is a full spectrum, right?"

"I'm going to need two phase-measurement units," Joseph said as if the question had never been answered.

"Two? What for, and better yet, how in the heck are you going to use two at the same time?"

Joseph straightened up, turned to his friend, and smiled.

"I'll show you."

Chapter Twenty-Two
No Man an Island

The truck stopped at the gate. Two men got out and walked up to the gate. A "NO TRESPASSING - I MEAN IT!" sign took up a large portion of the gate.

"Should we open it?" one man asked.

"Can't you read?" the other man asked in disbelief. "Besides, don't you know where we are?"

"Anvil's land," the man replied with more calm than the other man. "But you can't even see his place from here. How's he supposed to know we're even here?"

"Trust me, he knows. He always knows. His cabin is up there on the hill where he can see people coming. Right now, he's on his way down here with that rifle of his. All we have to do is wait."

The two men waited, the one turning around and taking in the countryside, looking down the road in both directions, and peering into the woods to see if anyone was approaching. The other man just stood and waited.

Ten minutes later, a man appeared just past the trees that started at the base of the hill. He was clothed in camouflage and carried a rifle equipped with a large scope. It was too far to tell details of his face.

"What you want?" came a booming voice.

"Mr. Moser! How you doing? We haven't seen you in a long time. Just wanted to make sure you're alive."

"Well, I am. So now that you know, you can go." The man made no move to come closer.

"We missed you during the election."

"Don't care about your gov'ments. Don't care how you run your town. Stay off my land and we'll get along."

"We'd like to invite you to our church. Most everyone from town meets there on Sundays and Wednesdays. You sure are welcome to attend."

"Don't care about your church neither. Me and God have an understanding right here. I'm going to keep to mine. I suggest you gentlemen do the same."

With that, the man turned and disappeared into the woods. The men stared for a few minutes before the one turned back to the truck.

"We're just going to leave?" the other man asked.

"Not much left to do."

"You think he's still there?"

"I'm sure he is. Just like I'm sure he's looking at you through that scope of his right now." The man opened the truck door.

After a quick glance, the other man turned and walked back to the other side of the truck. He looked nervous as he entered the truck.

"You really think he'd shoot us?"

"Count on it," the man said as he started the truck.

The blue light ate through the concrete blocks, throwing dust into the air to be sucked into the overhead vent. Some of the dust was red, still glowing from the heat induced by the weapon. The pre-drilled holes in the top of the blocks spouted dust and heat as the beam reached their location. The beam only stayed on for fifteen seconds before the last hole spouted dust. Automatic systems turned off the beam's power. The blocks continued to glow for a minute. When the dust was cleared and the temperature had dropped, the door to the test cell opened.

Joseph came through the doorway, followed by a cautious Wenk. Going immediately to the instrument panel, Joseph checked the data recordings.

"We got it all, every channel," Joseph said. He pushed on a button and a data chip ejected from the machine. With the chip between his fingers, Joseph headed out of the lab.

"I still don't know why we couldn't have recorded the data outside the cell," Wenk said.

"Data corruption, my friend. I'm not taking any chances of data corruption." He flipped the chip in the air. "This is going to show you what you guys have been missing."

"Why do you talk like you already know what's on it?" Wenk followed him to the computer unit in the control room. Joseph inserted the chip into a slot.

"Computer, run analysis program," Joseph said. He waited as the computer created graphs, then pointed. "There you go."

"What is it?" Wenk asked.

"Two wave-forms, one out of plane of the other."

"Out of plane?"

"Well, that's the simplistic way to describe it. The real answer takes a lot of math. Basically, the two particle streams set up counter-acting pulls on the material, causing it to rip itself apart while the particles destroy it once apart. Like a one-two punch."

"Did you somehow know we'd find this?"

"It was the most likely possibility," Joseph said with a shrug. "The other possibilities would have been harder to find, so I'm glad I was right."

"Harder? We spent weeks just setting up to find this one. I'd hate to see what it takes to find the others."

"A lot more equipment, that's what. Now comes the hard part. Computer, log data and send to archive and my unit."

"Hard part?" Wenk asked with a huff.

"Yeah, figuring out what in this unit is causing this to happen."

"Wait! You mean you don't know how this is happening?"

"What do I look like? God?" Joseph gave him a cheesy smile.

"Don't even kid about that," Wenk said with a shiver.

All conversation stopped as Tyler walked into the conference room. She didn't look around as she made her way around the table to her seat. In her wake were four assistants and one secretary. One assistant carried inactive visual and audio recorders. The equipment was eyed by all in the room, drawing worried looks.

"Gentlemen," Tyler said as she sat down, heedless of the mixed genders of the attendees. "It has been a year since our last meeting. I believe an update is in order."

People turned and looked at each other, then turned to look back at the president. "Is there a reason for the cameras?" a general asked.

"They are not for this meeting. They are a holdover from the previous meeting." There was a dismissive note to Tyler's voice.

"As long as they stay off," the general noted.

"Then who would like to begin?" Tyler looked around the table.

The representatives from the ten bases looked at each other, still nervous. Bennett smiled at them.

"I'll start. Modifications to Revelation Base are going well. We have installed point defenses at the gates and at intervals along the fence. Good thing we put in that second power station or we wouldn't be able to power them. The new buildings are going up quickly. We're most the way through an eighty-five story residential building that should relieve our housing issue, for a while at least. I sent the modifications for the construction bots to all the other bases. We are keeping any 'protesters' away from the base, for security reasons. We've also moved the civilian construction crews onto the base, at least those that would come and are not Puritans. We didn't have to force them, they were more than happy to get to a place of safety."

Bennett listened to the other nine reports. They were all similar, though not as advanced as his base. There was also a report for the non-selected bases, three of which had been closed and two others which had been disassembled to supply material to the selected bases. All weapons had been moved to one of the bases, Hawaii, or Guam. Other material was still being moved off of non-selected bases, but was expected to be completed in six months. Bennett was staggered thinking about the logistic assets involved in the moves. With the reports over, Tyler turned the meeting over to Secretary of Security Donnest.

"We established a list of cities to consider for protection. Several are no longer under consideration. We lost Miami because of the elections last fall—they elected a Puritan mayor and he has installed Puritan lackeys in city offices.

"Under further consideration, we've added a few more locations to our list. We kind of forgot about Canada." The comment was accompanied by a blush. "These included Vancouver Island and Nova Scotia. There are a few others we would like to add, but we're trying to not bite off too much at once, though no one wants to see their home not on the list. While we can sympathize, we do have our limits."

"What about the populations?" Tyler asked.

"The population continues to voluntarily segregate themselves. We are planning the cities' defenses around the locations that the non-Puritan populations have been occupying. Plans are being created to demolish the buildings in-between the two factions. Most mayors are only looking at this as preliminary planning, though they don't argue with separating the two factions at all."

"And 'sorting' efforts?" The emphasis could not be missed.

"At the moment, we are doing government and essential locations like hospitals and power stations in or near our cities of interest. The Puritans or those with Puritan leanings that we find are reassigned or fired under some pretense. It takes a while, but it is progressing. I can't imagine that they haven't seen a trend, but that was inevitable. No backlash as of yet; they're not taking us to court over the firings."

"Good. At least that should help keep the peace for now."

"Let's hope so." Donnest said the words almost like a prayer.

"Yes?" Valesco looked up from the flowers he had been examining in his garden. The garden was immaculate and always had something in bloom.

Garo cleared his throat. "We are sure that some cities, ones we did not capture in the elections, have started removing our people from offices."

"So they have started making their move sooner than we expected. Did someone warn them of our plans?" Valesco brought a flower to his nose and inhaled deeply.

"Not one of our people, no."

"You are certain?"

"Yes. We conducted interviews. Those affected said the authorities have imposed a test. Some did not even know why they were given the test. The questions seem to vary between individuals and there are sensors, but they have not seen any machines in use."

"I assume you are looking into this?" The question was layered with implications.

"Of course, but the procedure is held under very tight security. Our people in the agency in charge were the first to be weeded out."

Valesco took another sniff before throwing the flower into the bed. He moved to another plot and picked a different variety.

"This is inconvenient. We can't move our time-table up at the moment. Someone is causing us pain. Do we have any idea who is responsible for such an inconvenience?" Valesco sniffed the flower, made a distasteful face, and threw it away.

"We are not certain, but analysis would indicate it may have stemmed from comments made by Joseph Gint at Revelation Base."

"The son of the witness?" Valesco turned, a hard stare on his face.

"The same. Our intelligence indicates that he is quite insightful." Garo stood his ground, not daring to waver.

"Interesting. It may be that I have a worthy opponent. I want our file on him, everything we have. Doesn't his mother still live?" Valesco's demeanor changed abruptly to calmness, something Garo had experienced many times, but still found unnerving.

"Yes, but she has disappeared."

"Disappeared?" Valesco turned back to his assistant, a look of curiosity on his face.

"Joseph has an older brother, Johan. He seems to be good at... staying out of sight, electronically speaking. We had a man on him, but he lost him after only a couple of days."

"So we assume he knew he was being followed. Another interesting person in the same family, but totally different." Valesco clasped his hands together. "This gets better and better! I don't think I've had this much fun in years!"

"Sir?"

"A challenge, Garo, a challenge!" Valesco slapped the man on the back. "Do you know how rare it is to find someone who can see the big picture, who can think ahead? Add to that the challenge of remaining anonymous and you have a real game!"

Garo remained silent, but held a concerned look on his face.

"Keep looking for the brother and the mother. Don't do anything, though. Anything untoward happening to them could incite Mr. Gint further. It will be interesting to see if they join him at the military base." Valesco went to the next flower bed.

"Yes, sir." Garo was able to prevent shaking his head as he left the garden, though he couldn't help but feel apprehension. He activated his interface. "Find Mrs. Gint and her son, but do not engage. Remain unseen."

Valesco selected another flower. He picked the flower, raised it to his nose, and took a deep breath.

"What is the old saying? 'The game is on,' Mr. Gint." He crushed the flower in his hand and tossed it into the bed.

Chapter Twenty-Three
As Constant as Change

"What do you think you're doing?" the woman shouted at the man directing the demolition unit after stepping out of the onlooking crowd.

"Tearing down a house, what's it look like I'm doing?" The foreman didn't even look away from the work.

"You can't do this!"

"I have an order from the city to take down these houses, so yes, I can do this." The foreman waved at the demolition bot to move in.

"This is a historic Chicago neighborhood. You can't just tear it down."

"Look at these things!" the foreman shouted, finally turning to the woman. "The inspector says they're condemned, going to fall down by themselves if we leave them. That's unsafe and that means they come down."

"But they could be repaired! You are destroying history!"

"Why do you people only care about things when we go to take them down?" The foreman put his hands on his hips. "If you want to preserve it, you should have bought it and fixed it up. But no, you want someone else to take care of everything, take on all the responsibility. Well, lady, you waited too long. They're coming down, all the way to the dirt." The foreman turned to the crew. "I want all the bots moving. And get this person out of here! She doesn't have the proper safety equipment on."

Two men moved in and grabbed the arms of the protester. The woman jumped up and down as she was forced back into the small crowd.

"You'll see. We'll stop you. You can't destroy our city!"

The demolition bots moved into the homes. Wood splintered and walls fell to the efforts of the five-ton machines. The bots were methodical, taking down each wall in turn. Even the falling bricks and blocks could not stop the hardened machines. Within a few minutes, what once was a home was dust and rubble. As the demolition bots moved on, the loaders moved in, scooping and grabbing piles of rubble and placing them in waiting trailer beds. In less than an hour, all that was left were foundations, empty basements, and the sight of the demolition bots moving down the row of houses. Backhoes moved in to remove the remains.

The truck stopped outside the gate. Three men got out this time. The third man, in a suit instead of the jeans and flannel shirts of the other two, walked to the gate. He scanned the trees in front of him.

"Where is he?" the suited man asked.

"Don't worry, he'll be here," the driver answered.

"I find it incomprehensible that you gentlemen have not been able to resolve this issue," the suited man said as he stood, feet shoulder-width apart, hands behind his back.

"I don't understand what's the big deal," the driver answered. "He's just one guy and doesn't come into town but a couple of times a year at that."

"He's a pagan, and all pagans must be brought to the truth of God one way or the other. Even one pagan can end up infecting the community and will not be tolerated. Do you understand this?"

"Of course, sir. We just thought we would give him more time."

"From my understanding, more time will not resolve this issue." The man peered with more intensity. "I think that is him."

"I told you people to go away!" a voice came from the tree line.

"Mr. Moser. I am a federal agent. I need to talk to you." The suited man walked up to the gate and put his hands on it.

"Come any closer and you won't be talking at all."

"I am still outside the fence, Mr. Moser. Please, meet me here and talk to me or I will have no choice but to enter your land."

"You can't come on my land without a warrant."

The suited man pulled a paper from his coat. "I have a warrant, Mr. Moser. Now please come talk to me."

"I didn't know you had a warrant," the driver said.

"Shut up, you idiot."

Anvil stood for a moment, then walked toward the gate at a leisurely pace. When he was about twenty feet from the gate, the suited man resumed talking.

"Mr. Moser, we need you to come into town to clear up a legal matter."

"Talk to my lawyer then," Anvil said, stopping.

"We need you."

"My lawyer has full legal power to do what I need. If there are papers to sign, he'll sort it out."

"Mr. Moser, please be reasonable..."

"I don't need to be reasonable. You said your piece, now scoot." Anvil waved with the tip of his rifle and then turned to walk back.

"Mr. Moser... Mr. Moser..."

"I told you, he's quite contrary," the second man said.

The suited man watched Anvil walk back toward the woods. "Gentlemen, close your eyes."

"What?" the driver said.

"Just do as you are told." The suited man turned to watch both men close their eyes while raising his interface. When both sets of eyes were closed, he said, "Now."

A red beam burned its way from the far hillside, striking Anvil in the back of the head and continuing through his skull to exit the front. Anvil stopped for a second, then dropped the rifle and slumped to the ground.

"Open your eyes, gentlemen."

"What happened?" the driver said as he observed Anvil on the ground, face down.

"It appears someone shot Mr. Moser," the suited man said calmly.

"Who?"

"I didn't see and neither did you." The man walked to the

passenger door of the truck. "Your problem is solved. Don't make us solve another one."

"Haven't you slept?" Bennett asked Joseph as the younger man entered the office. In contrast to Bennett's normal pressed uniform appearance, Joseph's clothes were wrinkled, his hair was a mess, and his eyes had bags under them. At least he didn't smell.

"This is actually me after sleep, just not enough of it."

Allin followed on Joseph's heels, looking better than him but not quite as pressed as Bennett. She sat down without being invited.

"Please don't tell me that you're yanking my researcher. Again." She gave Bennett a stare.

"Only temporarily and at the president's request."

"How long?"

"A couple of days at most."

"Does the meat sack get a vote in this?" Joseph asked, raising his hand.

"No!" came two simultaneous voices.

"Just wanted to know."

"May I ask what the meeting is about?" Allin asked.

"Securing locations and resources."

"And why does the president want Mr. Gint?"

"Because he started all of this? How should I know?" Bennett threw up his arms. "We're in the military. The president makes a request and we comply, if possible. You remember how that works, Captain?"

"Yes, I do, sir. I was just wanting to know why my asset was being pulled across the country at a crucial research time."

"Maybe she thinks I need the sleep," Joseph said with a laugh.

"I'm not the one forcing you to work all those hours," Allin said in a bland voice.

"Sure." The word came out in an exaggerated tone. "Dangle the shiny bangle in front of the scientist and not expect him to lose himself in the effort."

"You're an adult. Besides, you have your own personal life monitor to rein you in, thus you should be the last person complaining." Allin looked up and away from Joseph.

"Another person with demands on me," Joseph said with a sigh and side glance.

"You're tortured, I'm sure," Bennett put in. "Just make sure you clean yourself up before you leave tomorrow. You *are* meeting the president."

"I'm sure my personal assistant will take care of all those details to everyone's satisfaction but mine." Joseph frowned with the statement.

"Glad to hear it. How is the research coming, by the way?"

"Slow," was all Joseph said with closed eyes.

Allin took in a breath to take over the conversation. "We are dismantling and measuring the parts of the subject projector, even those that Mr. Gint assures us are not involved. We made measurements of a non-performing projector and did not find the same characteristics, as Mr. Gint predicted. But we took three weeks to set up the instruments, so we might as well."

"How long before you know something?"

"I can't say." Joseph took back the conversation, though he still did not look at Bennett. "We also seem to be using a lot more power than we are getting out, which makes us wonder where it is going. But we'll solve that mystery too."

"I look forward to it. Dismissed." Bennett looked down at his interface.

"I see Washington hasn't gotten any prettier since I was here last." Joseph followed Bennett into the conference room. "Same cast of characters?"

"Don't know, only know we were invited." Bennett led him to a seat at one end of the table. There were only a couple of other people present, military types of course, but others soon followed. Tyler was the last to arrive.

"Thank you for coming," Tyler said as she sat down. "I called you in here because we have been receiving disturbing news from some of the rural areas. It appears that Thee Way Church of God is getting militant. We have reports of people being killed. The details are not clear, of course. I find this very disturbing. I didn't know they would go this far."

"We've been seeing an increase in movement of non-Puritans into safe areas," Donnest said. "We are trying to be prepared, but the movement of people is beyond the capacity we have at the moment. We have been converting buildings as fast as possible, but it's not keeping up."

"Would it be faster to tear down old buildings and put up new ones?" someone Joseph couldn't see asked.

"We don't have the resources to rebuild everything. Maybe with time, we can selectively destroy and rebuild larger buildings, but we're overwhelmed at the moment."

"We still need to get started," Joseph put in. "My friend has made some modifications to the construction bots that make them twice as fast. Even if we only do one building at a time, if we don't start, we will always be behind. I know that means some people will have to wait, but they are already waiting. I would suggest starting with the older, shorter buildings, since these will be the least efficient and allow the greatest increase in usable space."

"I agree." Tyler looked around at the people at the table. "The military bases can take up some of the slack, if they have room. We can even move people across country if we need to."

"That will take significant efforts as well. It all seems like a nightmare that won't end, but we will do our best." Donnest shook his head. His sagging shoulders made him look like Joseph felt.

"We can't abandon the populations. See to it. How are we doing securing the cities?" Tyler looked at Donnest.

"We are clearing space in between the two faction areas. We expect the real opposition will come when we start building fences or walls. Some cities are starting with fences, some have plans to go straight to concrete structures. It will take massive amounts of material, so securing this material will be critical."

"Like Berlin all over," Tyler said with a disparaging tone, "but across the whole country. I hate to think what history will say about my presidency."

"Taking care of the general population is needed, but there is a more pressing issue." Joseph leaned forward on the table.

"And what would that be, Mr. Gint?" The president looked

annoyed through the top of her eyes.

"We need to secure people important to our future, the ones who will lead the required scientific research and development, if we are ever going to prepare for the return of the aliens. If we don't do that, all our preparations are useless."

"Aren't we already doing that?" Tyler looked dubious.

"We are only thinking local. For instance, we have top-grade astronomers at an observatory in Tibet that we have not secured, unless other countries have grabbed them already. There are others in less exotic locations, some in cities with Puritan mayors and some in remote rural areas. I believe we should secure these people immediately to protected towns, if not military bases. They might be upset at the interruption to their research, but leaving them to the Puritans would be worse."

Tyler looked at Secretary of State Wo Standington, who gave back a blank look.

"Do we even know who these people are?" Tyler asked the table.

"I have made a list," Joseph sent files from his interface.

"When did you have time to make that list?" Bennett asked.

"It helps me think to work on other things for a while." Joseph shrugged.

"No wonder you're so tired."

"Ah, no, that has nothing to do with it." Joseph smiled.

Chapter Twenty-Four
New Kid in Town

Everyone was standing. A large oval table with name tags and inlaid displays waited for the delegates. Not even the entourages sat, waiting for their respective leaders.

"This is getting stupid," Tyler huffed to Donnest. "Everyone is so worried about losing prestige by being the first to be seated that we're all standing here like idiots. What's the point of having a face-to-face conference if no one sits at the table?"

"So, we do something," Donnest said. Tyler glared at him for a second, but then took a breath and relaxed.

"I guess so." With upright shoulders, Tyler walked over to Shishiho, standing among her own support staff. The staff parted to allow entry and Tyler executed an abbreviated bow to Shishiho, who nodded in return.

"This posturing is getting us nowhere," Tyler stated.

"What do you propose?"

"Let the two of us walk to the table together and sit at the same time. Then we can invite the others to the table."

A rare smile creased Shishiho's face as her head tilted to the right. "A wise suggestion. Shall we?"

Together, the two women moved to the table. They were placed on opposite sides, causing Shishiho to slow her walk so their arrival at their chairs was simultaneous. Tyler could feel the looks of the others on their backs as they drew back their chairs and sat in unison.

Without delay, Lucien Shetter, Head of the Common European Concern; Mambou Tammil, Head of the African Confederation; Isabella Ruiz, Head of the Confederation of the Americas; and Bahir Kattan, Representative of United Arabia, all took their seats. Each delegate was book-ended by one assistant on either side. Seating accomplished, the delegates waited for the host, Isabella Ruiz, to speak.

"I hope all of you had a relaxing evening," Ruiz started in an easy voice. "I myself have great hopes for this meeting. From my intelligence, Thee Way has absorbed almost all of the attendees that have left the other churches. They have not turned their attention to the non-alien churches yet, but I figure this is only a matter of time. Personally, I feel that our preparations will be highly critical to dealing with events in the future."

"You can live in your paranoia," Shetter said with a sharp voice, "but we in the CEC still believe in the rule of the people! This isolation being planned here is a surrender to harmless events. Who cares if all the alien churches combine into one church? They still are not a majority and the majority will never agree with them. People are too intelligent these days!" Shetter's hand moved with his words, lightly pounding the table twice.

"Harmless events?" Shishiho's voice was sharp. "I don't call churches being burned down and people being attacked and even killed as harmless. Europe is in chaos."

"A temporary situation," Shetter's nose rose a little. "Law will prevail, it just takes time."

"You talk of law but there is no law in Europe." Scoffing, Shishiho turned her head away from Shetter.

"You mean there is no authoritative rule like in the Conglomerate." Shetter scoffed back.

"At least we don't let our people die before we do something." Shishiho's voice was calm, given the subject.

"People will see reason, even the churches, once they have expended their energy." Pointing his finger into the air, Shetter's hand waved back and forth in a slight quiver.

"So you are going to sit by and do nothing? You would continue to put your people in danger?"

"With time they will come to the logical conclusion."

"The common people haven't needed to truly think for themselves for almost a hundred years." Shishiho's voice and stare were sharp. "The World Council saw to that! They regulated everything. Sure, life was comfortable, but comfort makes a person soft. People who don't have to struggle forget how to fight for themselves."

"The people don't need to fight for themselves! They still have a coherent government to defend them! Us!" Shetter pounded the table. "Are you proposing that they take up arms? Are you advocating fighting in the streets?"

"It may come to that," Shishiho said, maintaining the stare.

"Ridiculous! Handing out arms to common people? You might as well hand away the government while you do it. We have the responsibility to show people how they should live, what they should accept in others. You are all power-hungry dictators who are afraid of losing their power. We will not be a part of this!" Shetter stood up, fist on the table.

"And we will not be a part of you." The voice came from just inside the doorway. Everyone turned to see three people entering the room. At the lead was Conna Stewart, whose regal walk was crisp if somewhat hurried. Short and slightly plump, she was dressed in all white that all but reflected the light around her. Following close behind was Allepo Gulliano and Bogdan Horvat, both diplomats known to the others from meetings with the greater European community. They walked directly to Shetter, who turned toward the group and laughed.

"Just what we need, a British princess leftover from the past."

"Queen, Shetter, not princess." Her words gave Shetter no quarter. "My mother abdicated six years ago to run off with that artist from the Caribbean. And while my title may not mean anything politically, my family not only owns a lot of property, I still have the admiration of many in the country. That translates into influence. I am here to tell you, Mr. Shetter, that you do not represent the opinion of everyone in the CEC."

"That is a matter that should be discussed in a CEC meeting, not here." Shetter used a firm voice.

"It *has* been discussed in a CEC meeting and *you* have not been listening, so I am here at *this* meeting to represent four countries to the rest of the world." Conna pointed at the table with one finger as she talked.

"And exactly who do you represent?" Mambou Tammil asked.

Conna turned to those seated at the table, her expression softening as she looked at them. "I, of course, represent England. Mr. Gulliano represents Italy, and Mr. Horvat represents Hungary. They, and Germany, have consented to let me talk for all of us to make the process faster."

"You have no authority here!" Shetter was yelling, pointing at the ground with one hand. "All countries in the CEC have designated the central authority to have control over their political administration and representation. For the good of all!"

"We withdraw from the CEC," Stewart said with a wave of her left hand. "All four of us."

"You can't withdraw, there is no process for withdrawing from the CEC."

"Our agreement to join the organization implies the power to withdraw. Simple logic." Conna raised one eyebrow.

"Logic? What? I... I don't accept your reasoning!"

"It doesn't matter what you accept or not accept. *You* no longer represent us. Our representatives are being withdrawn as we speak."

"Mr. Shetter," Tyler interrupted. "If you have no intention of participating in the actions of this group, then you have no place in this group."

Shetter reacted as if he had been slapped across the face. He stared at Tyler, but then looked at the other delegates. Shishiho would not meet his eyes, but looked away. Straightening his shoulders and inhaling, he pulled down on his suit jacket.

"It would appear that I do not. Good day to you all."

Turning back toward the door, Shetter stomped out of the room directly through the three representatives. His attendants followed close behind. Conna, Aleppo, and Bogdan took the seats they had vacated.

"Welcome to the table, each of you," Shishiho said in a calm voice.

"Thank you, all of you," Conna said with a head bow. "I believe that we have been keeping up with what this com... group has been discussing."

"If you don't mind me asking," Tyler said, "how?"

"We have our sources inside of Shetter's administration." Conna smiled. "You don't think we totally trusted the man?"

"Of course not," Ruiz replied with a smile directed at Conna. Turning to the rest of the table, she took in a breath. "With that unpleasantry behind us, I suggest we start."

Chapter Twenty-Five
Hostile Intent

A single man stood in the middle of the mountain road. The lead vehicle stopped four meters from the man, kicking up dust and gravel as it did. The cloud hid the view of the doors opening, but not the sound of them being closed. The cloud dissipated as a man in black, close-fitting clothes, leather shoes, and sunglasses walked in front of the vehicle.

"I am a state law officer," the man said. "I suggest you get out of the road."

"An' I suggest y'all go back where you came from." The man held a shotgun in his hands across his chest. He was dressed plainly and had a handmade straw hat on his head.

"We are here," the officer continued, "to enforce the new state law that makes it illegal for private individuals to own guns, firearms, projectors, or any other type of weapon. And since you live in the state of Tennessee, that includes you."

The man laughed. "My ancestors have been carryin' guns here since they crossed the mountains and settled this land hundreds of years ago. You really think we're goin' to give them up now because some pol'tician tells us to?"

"If you don't, we will take them."

The comment caused another laugh. "I would like to see you try."

Both men stared at the other, not moving. People from the vehicles walked forward. All were armed, but waited for their cue from the man standing in front of the lead vehicle.

When movement came, it was almost faster than one could see. The officer's hand flashed to under his arm to draw a pistol. The gun of the other man rotated in his right hand to point at the officer and roared first. The officer was thrown back by the solid slug, though minimal blood appeared on his shirt. A woman in black, closer to the vehicles, raised her pistol and shot a red beam, hitting the local man in the shoulder.

As if directed by a conductor, several dozen people appeared from behind trees, their weapons rippling in fire that swarmed across the agents. Many went to the ground either by impact or for cover. Fire from the rifles continued, hitting the vehicles and people that were exposed. Return pulsator fire burned the trees and, on occasion, the person behind it.

"Central," a woman behind a vehicle shouted into her interface. "We're taking fire. The captain is down. I repeat, the captain is down."

"Understood. Reinforcements are on their way."

"Take these fuckers out!" the woman shouted.

From the top of the third vehicle, a large pulsator rose. Turning to the right, it sprayed particle pulses into the woods from right to left. Pine fragments in size from splinters to small trees exploded into the air, most smoking or on fire. The fire from the woods stopped quickly, but the sound of frantic running could be heard. The woman came from behind the vehicle.

"I want all sensors on. Every tree, every rock is now considered a hiding place. Get the wounded into the last vehicle. The rest of us are going forward. These hillbillies are going to pay for this! Now move!"

"Madam President, there's reports of fighting in Tennessee." Donnest had entered the room quietly, closing the door behind him. He wore a solemn expression as he talked.

Tyler closed her eyes and shook her head. "I feel like I'm failing." Her voice sounded worn. She rubbed her forehead with one hand.

"I see nothing that we can do. The Tennessee legislature passed a law forbidding citizens from owning firearms and state officials are enforcing it."

"In Tennessee, of all places. And I suppose it will all be over before anyone could bring the law to federal court."

"If it can even get there. You know that if there is no successful challenge to the law, the other states will eventually pass similar ones…"

"As a first step to controlling the population, yes, I know. Damn, I hate the government being so neutered." Tyler's fist hit the table. She looked sideways, twisting her head in a circle. "We barely have enough troops to cover government assets and almost no power to investigate things. Why do we exist if the states stripped so much power from us we can hardly do anything?"

Donnest stood on the other side of the desk and placed his hands on the edge. Leaning down to just higher than Tyler's head, he looked at her through his eyebrows.

"We can't let this distract us from what we are doing. It's only going to get worse. We need to take care of what we can take care of."

Tyler looked at him with weary eyes. "But Shetter is right, at least partially. We are abandoning part of the population."

"But we have no power to help them." Donnest spoke slowly. "Unless you want to do something… off the books."

"No!" Tyler shot at him as she leaned back and waved her hands in front of her. "Then we would be as bad as they are. That's not an option."

"It may solve our problem, or at least give us more time."

"And if we fail, we give them more ammunition to use against us." Tyler shook her head violently. "No! I won't hear of it. We'll just have to do the best we can."

Donnest straightened, took in and let out a breath. "Yes, Madam President."

Secretary Adams walked into the room without knocking. "We have another problem."

Tyler looked at him through the top of her eyes, eyebrows slightly up. "Why am I not surprised."

"The western states are starting to take federal land, using eminent domain claims in state court."

"Eminent domain? On the federal government? Really? How 'eminent' can it be?"

"They're parceling up the land and placing communal farms on them."

"And exactly where are the people for these farms going to come from?"

"As far as we can tell, the cities." Adams had a dubious look on his face.

Tyler huffed.

"I hope they add a healthy dose of education to those moves. Most people don't know jack squat about farming," Donnest added, shaking his head.

"I think it's more symbolic than anything, or maybe a way to clear some of their people out of the contended zones. I'm more concerned about them just taking the lands outright." Worry shot through Adams' voice.

Tyler looked at Donnest. "Do we have the forces to protect our undeveloped portions of the states?"

Donnest closed his eyes and shook his head. "No."

"Then," Tyler said, turning back to Adams, "tell the states that as long as they give us a fair price, we will consider all transfers of unimproved lands to the states. Might as well get something out of the whole mess and we will be hurting for cash with all the changes being made, particularly if we have to help the cities set up defenses."

Adams' head jerked back a little and his brow furrowed. He opened his mouth to speak, but said nothing as he turned, watching Tyler the whole time. He finally found his voice.

"Are you sure we want to do that?"

"Yes!" The word came out fast and forceful. "If we lose control of all state and local governments to this church, they'll take the land anyway. Also, we wouldn't need to worry about the parks and nature preserves and can concentrate on other things. I know this cuts right into your department, Harrow, but you need to concentrate on what can be done for all the people moving into the cities." She gave Adams a sympathetic look.

Adams shifted his feet before clearing his throat. "Yes, Madam

President. I'm sure you're right. If you'll excuse me?"

"Of course. I'd like to keep to one disaster per department a day, if possible, gentleman," Tyler called out the open door as Adams left.

A small crowd of people stood outside the base gate. A few in front wore the uniforms of local law enforcement. Another group inside the gate watched Commander Bennett walk through the personnel gate and toward the small crowd. He had left his interface on so that those inside could hear. Having been warned by Bennett, Joseph paid particular attention. When he got close, Bennett spoke.

"State your business at my base, Sheriff."

"We have a warrant here for the arrest of one Joseph Gint," said the uniformed man in front of the group, waving a folded paper.

"What for?"

"Murder."

Believing that there was no way Bennett would hand him over to the crowd did not prevent Joseph from sweating a little. He hadn't thought about the incident since right after it happened.

"You have no jurisdiction on my base." Bennett's voice was flat and casual. He stood with ease with his arms crossed.

"Carl wasn't killed on your base, he was killed out here!" The man waved the paper in an angry manner.

"The base actually extends beyond the fence line into the fields, so yes, the incident did happen on the base. We just allow farming of the land for free. Goodwill and all that."

"He's still in South Dakota and in our county. Citizens of the United States are subject to United States laws." The man's face was turning red.

"Mr. Gint isn't a U.S. citizen, he is Dutch. And, as a foreign citizen, he is subject to the courts of the federal government, not the local government. Thus, once again, you have no standing to issue your warrant." Bennett paused. "Is there anything else?"

"We will not allow you heretics to murder our people at will!" The statement brought a chorus of cheers and assent from the crowd behind the man.

"And if you try to enter our base without our approval, our

automatic defenses will cut you down like the wheat that surrounds us." Bennett stood silent, letting the statement sink in before continuing. "Look, I am sure you are doing this because of outside pressure, so you can tell them that there is no way I am going to let you prosecute anyone from this base, military or civilian. With the lack of available activities around here, you probably won't see them in town anyway. We can have an adversarial relationship or we can at least tolerate each other."

"And why would we tolerate heretics?" Despite his words, the man's face started to lose its redness and his tone became softer.

"Because we are going to need things that you produce. We could get them shipped in from somewhere else, but I am sure your local economy would benefit by providing goods to our base. Quality goods, of course, not ones that have been tampered with."

The statement caused the man's face to react, both in horror at the suggestion and fear at the fact that Bennett had already thought about the issue.

"Clearly," Bennett continued in a business-like voice, "we are not going to produce things on this base that you already produce. Wheat, oats, corn, pork, beef, and chickens, to name a few. We will also need lumber and clothing. You might not have those in supply, but you may have someone who would like to become our supplier for such goods. In return, we can talk about items that you need around here or could benefit from. We could even talk about providing shipment for goods to markets in large cities, if you so desire."

The man looked thoughtfully at Bennett, his head nodding up and down slightly as he did. He brought his hand to his chin and stroked it. He spoke in a lower voice.

"You may have a point there. A mutually beneficial arrangement would be better than an adversarial one, for both of us. I never expected you to hand over Mr. Gint anyway, but it was... heavily suggested that I try."

"You can be sure I will be confining Mr. Gint to the base." Bennett smiled as if he enjoyed the idea. "Not that I expected him to wander off anyway."

"For his own good, I would say that's a healthy suggestion. I cannot guarantee his safety if he was to leave." The man raised a knowing eyebrow.

"As I suspected. But I anticipate all courtesies given to other people associated with my base."

"Of course. You're our neighbors and we are taught to be kind to our neighbors, even if they are... don't agree with what we believe." The man smiled.

"Glad to hear it." Bennett smiled back. "I will appoint a person to act as liaison for setting up goods transactions. They will make contact with you when they are ready."

"Sounds fair enough to me. Nice to meet you, Mr. Bennett." The man held out his hand, which Bennett shook.

"Commander Bennett. Nice to meet you, too, Sheriff."

Bennett walked back to the gate. The crowd murmured to each other, but quieted as the sheriff told them what Bennett had said. A few still looked upset. Joseph took a guess why. He didn't see anyone who looked like they were from out of town, but knew that didn't mean anything.

Joseph took a breath and turned from the scene to find Sergeant Harjo next to him. He smiled at the man.

"How's the family?" Joseph asked.

"Doing great," Harjo said with enthusiasm. "Kids seems to be adjusting well. Cal loves the base, climbing on all the vehicles and pretending he's in the army. Even marching with the troops, or tries to, that is."

"And the wife?"

"She's great!" Harjo got a twinkle in his eye.

"Good to hear. Glad they landed well."

"How about you?" Harjo asked.

"Me? Oh, I'm doing fine."

"No, I mean when are you and Mercedes going to tie the knot?"

Joseph's head jerked back. "That hasn't even been discussed. Things are going just fine, if you ask me."

"But hasn't she been 'courting' you for, like, two years now?"

"So? What's your point?"

"Seems like a long time." Harjo gave the air an innocent stare.

"I've been busy."

"Yeah, right." Harjo gave Joseph a laugh and walked away. Joseph stood his ground to allow distance between him and the man.

"Nice job pacifying the mob," Joseph said to Bennett as he walked by.

"Something you didn't think about before you acted, was it?" Bennett gave him a meaningful glance.

"I wasn't exactly in the state to think about it, but no." Joseph didn't look at the man.

"You're lucky the people pushing this weren't from around here or this wouldn't be over."

"If they were from around here, this would have happened a long time ago, wouldn't it?"

"Most likely true, but it would have been worse." Bennett took a breath. "So, lesson learned?"

"Yes, sir!" Joseph suppressed the urge to salute.

"Good. I hope it sticks. Now, go back to work." Bennett walked away.

"Do you have to say that like it's a punishment?" Joseph called after him.

Chapter Twenty-Six
Growth and Adjustment

"**R**eport!" came the command from behind the desk.

"Recruitment is within two percent of projections..." Garo started.

"Meaning that they are two percent below goals?" The question was more of an accusation.

"Our planned integration efforts have proven to be insufficient to handle the number of people in our projected goals..."

"And whose fault is that?"

Garo said nothing.

Valesco looked up from his screen for a few seconds and then looked back down. "What percentage are we at?"

"We have claimed nearly eighty percent of the attendees of the other churches. We have not started on the traditional churches, though there has been small numbers of recruits from that area, too." Garo tried to steady his nerves as he talked. The sharpness of Valesco's questions grated across his body.

"When does the plan have us starting on the traditional churches?"

"Two to three more years, depending on variables."

Valesco drummed on the table with his fingers. He took in a sharp breath, held it, and let it out with force. Garo's nerves took another hit. Clenching his jaw, Valesco rotated his head and then looked up at Garo.

"You know, they are already erecting fences in some cities."

"Yes, I have seen the reports."

"Well before predicted."

"Yes, sir." Garo gulped.

"And we attribute this to what? Our own stupidity?"

"Maybe people were smarter than we expect."

Valesco's stern gaze suddenly changed to full-bodied laughter. He leaned back into his chair and threw his head back, spinning the chair as he did so. Garo stood in shock, his eyes going rapidly back and forth as if looking for something he missed.

"I told you this would be great!" Valesco roared as he spun. "How I love a good game. It makes it so much more *fun*."

Garo felt his head spin. He spread his feet a little farther to help remain stable and blinked to clear his vision.

"Relax, my friend," Valesco said with cheer as he came back around. "You look like you're about to faint. If everything went to plan, it would be boring. This! This has added some spice to the game. I have seen the numbers and we couldn't possibly move faster. If they hadn't acted so soon, we would have all of the cities under our control in a few years. This way, the game will keep going, maybe for decades!"

"And that makes you happy?" Garo said slowly.

"Garo! What would life be without adventure?" Valesco stood up and walked around the desk. "If our predictions were perfect, there would be no surprises. And what would life be without surprises?"

"Safe?"

"Do you think I would have started all this if I wanted safe? Buck up, my friend." Valesco gave the man a one-armed hug. "In a few years, we will be in charge of all the churches in the country and on our way across the world. Once that happens, then we can worry about the unbelievers."

"Even after we secure the U.S.," Garo said in a soft, tentative voice, "we will need our resources here to address the rest of the world's churches."

"Meaning that the cities and military bases will only be that much more of a challenge. Then we will see if they are willing to fire on their own people, and if they do, they will deliver popular sentiment into our hands, right?" Valesco said, looking directly into Garo's face.

"I can't say that with certainty, sir."

The metal poles cemented into the ground had been suspicious. A line of metal poles could not stop anyone from moving from one area to another. But when the poles, concrete now set, had been joined by top and bottom cross-pieces and steel fencing rolled across the frame, it became too much. People gathered and yelled at the workers, prevented from approaching by military personnel. At intervals, strange looking devices were placed on top of a pole. Wires were strung across the top of the fence from one device to another. The last straw for the on-lookers came when a sign was secured to the fence. In large letters, it proclaimed:

WARNING: TOUCHING OR TAMPERING WITH
THE FENCE WILL RESULT IN BODILY HARM

"What the hell do you think you are doing?" yelled a woman as she stepped forward from the crowd. "You can't keep us out of that part of the city!"

"You don't like those people anyway," a soldier said, gesturing over his shoulder.

"But what if I want to go downtown?" the woman insisted.

"To do what, start a riot? Not going to happen."

"We're citizens of this city, too!"

"No, you're Puritans who want to impose your beliefs and way of life on everyone else. You want to set up your own governments to impose new laws, just like you've been doing in the countryside. We are the true citizens, the ones who believe in the original documents that started this country."

"We are just exercising our freedom of religion!"

"*No!* You are imposing your religion and preventing other people from their freedom. This fence will ensure that we get to keep our freedoms."

The woman turned to the crowd. "Are we going to stand for this? Are we going to let them take away our city? Or are we going to stand up and stop this?"

The crowd cheered, raising their fists in defiance. The woman turned back toward the fence, waving her arm in a large gesture to bring the crowd forward. As she did so, blue particle beams cut ruts into the ground, kicking up dust as they went. Startled, the crowd took a step backwards.

"We are authorized to use deadly force!" the soldier shouted. "And make no mistake, we will use it! I suggest you disperse!"

The woman scowled, but said nothing as people started to turn and walk away. She was the last to leave, giving dirty looks the whole time.

"That could have gone worse," the soldier said, mostly to himself.

"And why did you bring the girl?" Bennett asked as they walked the halls of the White House.

"Because she is smart, probably smarter than me," Joseph replied.

It brought a contained laugh from Bennett.

"No, I'm serious. You know anyone else that can go from lower grade school level to college in less than two years?"

"So what's she going to specialize in?"

"Don't know. Probably everything."

"What does that mean?" They turned a corner.

"She's smart enough to do multiple fields and unrelated fields to boot. Nothing seems to throw her. Gets embarrassing at times." Joseph smirked.

"But why is she *here*?"

"Because one of the things she does really well is read people."

They walked for a while before Bennett spoke. "That could be useful."

They were directed to the Oval Office. Inside, they found Donnest, Adams, and Tallenson with the president. Stopping at the door, they were waved inside. Bennett looked around uncomfortably. About the time they were seated, three more people came in, two military officers and the mayor of New York City, and the door was shut. Worthia sat in the back.

"I wanted to get a smaller group together this time," Tyler started, "because I have something I want to talk about without getting two dozen opinions at once. Those here seem to agree with each other most times."

Tyler got up from her chair and started to pace behind her desk. Her fingers were tip-to-tip under her chin.

"The next election will start in a year. The gains that Valesco's church has been making in the local and state elections have me worried. He already controls half of the states, at least, particularly the plains and western ones. Most of our big cities are divided between church and non-church people, as some in the room know only too well." She gave a quick look to the mayor. "With barriers being erected in the cities, I doubt we can count on much of the vote outside those barriers. Because the presidency is a popular vote, I think you can see where I'm going with this."

"You're afraid they're going to have a candidate that will win," Donnest said.

"Yes, I am."

"Do you really expect the country to hand itself over to a religious organization?" Tallenson asked. "All we have to do is make the case that if they vote for Valesco's man, they are handing the country over to the church."

"It might not be that easy. If they run someone else, one of the mayors for instance, they can claim we are just fear-mongering. If Valesco then comes out and states that he exercises no control over the person, I'm afraid people will believe him and not us."

"They have not made inroads to the non-church population," Donnest put in. "Almost all of their membership increase has come at the expense of the other alien churches. We still are not fighting any greater contingency than before."

"That we know of!" Tyler took a breath and put her hands to the sides of her head. "Plus, we have another year before the election. What might be true today might not be true then."

"We can always cancel the election due to the upheavals in the country," Tallenson offered. "We can say it is for people's safety. That wouldn't be a stretch."

"No! I won't do that! I would be called a dictator or a usurper." Tyler's pacing got faster.

"Then want do you want to do?" Adams asked.

"I want to talk to Valesco. I want to try to find out exactly what he is up to and what he expects in the next few years."

"You can't be serious," came from Joseph.

"He will see the move as weakness," one of the other generals said. "He will take it as a sign that you are worried and be more likely to push his agenda in the next election."

"Not if we approach him right," Tyler countered. "We can make it sound like we are concerned for the integrity of the election. It just takes the right phrasing…"

Most of the other people in the room stared wide-eyed. Joseph's mouth was open. Bennett looked like he had been slapped, or might need to be to get him out of his stupor.

"…Benson, I want you to work on the right approach. Format a statement so we get this right…"

"You want to talk to him?" Tallenson asked. "The man destabilizing the nation?"

"She wants to cut a deal," came a young female voice from the rear of the room. The force behind the voice had contempt in it. "She wants to cut a deal to try and stay in power."

"Young lady, I'm not sure who you are or why you are here, but your opinion is not required here." Tyler gave Worthia a stare of equal contempt.

"She's right!" Joseph stood up. "You're going to make a deal with that… scum!"

"I am president of the whole country, not just of you!" Tyler drew up in indignation. "I represent everyone, not just the people in this country. That means I talk to everyone!"

While others looked at Tyler with shock, the three military officers looked at each other.

"This would be a disaster," Bennett said to the other generals.

"I agree," the woman in a formal blue uniform said. "She knows too much about our plans. If Valesco had that intelligence…"

"So, what do we do?" the other man asked.

"There is still a line of succession," Bennett answered.

"What are you talking about over there?" Tyler asked.

Bennett stood. "Madam President, in light of current events and your response to them, I am afraid for the safety of this nation. We are placing you under arrest."

"You can't do that!" Tyler said amid gasps from her staff.

"Actually, if we believe you are endangering the common good, we can." Bennett activated his interface. "I need a security detail in the Oval Office at once."

"This… this is treason!" Tyler stammered.

"No, Madam President," Donnest said while standing, "what you were about to do is treason by consorting with an enemy of the state. There is no doubt in any of our minds that Valesco is staging a coup, and your desire to deal with him makes you an accomplice to the coup."

"What? What? You're insane!" Tyler watched security walk in. "Arrest these men, all of them."

The two security guards, who wore military uniforms, looked at the generals with questions on their faces. The woman in the blue uniform approached them.

"Take the President into custody and lock her in an isolation cell. No contact with anyone but us for now. Understood?"

One of the guards appeared to almost grin as the two moved, one to either side of the desk, to secure the president. Each grabbing an arm, they forcefully led her out of the room over her protests. Everyone else watched until they had left.

"We have to make an immediate statement," Tallenson said. "And we have to instill a successor. That would be you, Donnest."

"Me?" Donnest said as if the thought just crossed his mind. "Wait, I was just deputy secretary two years ago. Me, the president?"

"It's the order of succession," Adams said with a laugh. "Now you know why I never wanted to be Security Secretary."

"But, I mean, are people going to buy this?"

"We will make a statement that President Tyler was consorting with the enemy and is being held incognito. Those we care about will understand. Those in that alien church, who cares." Tallenson shrugged.

"I'll contact a judge we can trust and get Warrence sworn in. Then we'll work on the statement, though I think we will need to tell the people in the building something right away." Adams turned to his interface.

Donnest activated his interface quickly and spoke into it. "Lock down all outgoing communication until further notice from me. No one leaves until we talk to them." He lowered his interface. "I didn't want the news feeds getting word before we want them to."

"Good thinking." Tallenson turned to the group. "The Cabinet has things to do. Until then, you can go back to the other things you've been worrying about. We'll let you know about any other changes."

"Can you trust everyone in this building?" Bennett asked.

"They've already been screened, so yes. There are a few Tyler diehards that we may need to let go, but I don't think anyone is going to blab just yet. Good day, ladies and gentlemen."

Still dazed by the events, Joseph followed the military personnel out of the room. Worthia joined alongside.

"See what you did," Joseph said, grinning.

"I... I was just pointing out..."

"Relax. You did a great job."

"But I just got the president arrested."

"No, she got herself arrested. You just saw through her scheme." They turned down a different hallway than the one they had come in.

"But I... Like, wow, did all that just happen? I don't know if I can take these trips to the White House. I'm not used to this much excitement. Did I just really..."

"Yeah, kid," Joseph said, putting his arm around her shoulder, "you did. I had faith in you and you did good."

"Faith in me? What... what are you talking about? Did you expect something like this to happen?" She gave him an open-mouthed stare.

"No, but I trust your ability to read people. Good thing I had you along, too."

Worthia closed her mouth and shook her head. A frown formed on her face. "So I'm just a tool to you, huh?" she asked with a little sarcasm.

"No, but you're a useful tool." Joseph gave her a glib grin.

Worthia scowled. "Thanks a lot. By the way, where are we going?"

"No idea, I wasn't aware of another meeting."

"That's because it was just called," Bennett said over his shoulder.

"With what happened, it seemed like a good idea for the military to be told what's going on."

"There you go, thinking again," Joseph said with a snide voice that had a drawl.

Their destination proved to be the Situation Room with a dozen people in military dress inside. The screens were alive with faces of more military personnel.

"I think I'm going to develop a complex," Joseph said quietly to Worthia.

"Now?" Worthia replied.

"General Samuelson," a man said as he saluted the woman who had been in the meeting.

"Report," she replied.

"We've contacted all ten bases. Seven are ready. The others will be soon. Other bases are hooking in to listen only."

"Good. Let me know as soon as we're up."

"Yes, sir." The man turned back to the displays.

Joseph and Worthia took up a position that looked out of the way. Bennett and the other two generals walked over to the main display, which had been divided into ten sections. Seven were occupied and the eighth became that way as they walked up. It only took a few moments for the other two to join the event.

"Thank you all for coming," Samuelson started, slowly scanning the views as she talked. "The President has been arrested for planning to consort with the enemy. She is being placed in solitary confinement. I fully expect the new president to declare a state of emergency before the next election is scheduled to happen. This should not surprise any of you. With the breakdown of dependable local government, we all knew this was coming sooner or later. As of this moment, you all should look at your bases as independent entities responsible for your own survival.

"That survival is your top priority. Your second priority is the protection of citizens from forces that would take away the freedoms that they have enjoyed as citizens of this country. Make no mistake, I fully expect to eventually end up at war with the Valesco church and the local governments that support him, but hopefully this will not occur for some time. In the meantime, our mission is to create secure areas. I also expect in the near future to assist in the protection of the cities we have selected as important to our future. Do not overextend your efforts. We will continue to communicate regularly, as communication will be critical. Any questions?"

"Will the president be put on trial?"

"I seriously doubt we will have time for that and it would serve no purpose. When the information she has is no longer crucial to our operation, she will be released."

"Are the cities going to be allocated to particular bases for protection?"

"The cities have already been sent initial units for the establishment and maintenance of protection. Their situation will be monitored and additional units will be provided if it is deemed prudent. Once things are better defined, I am sure additional facilities will be established in the cities, particularly the ports."

"Sir, I saw that Washington, D.C. is not on the list of cities to be protected."

"You are correct. We are only taking the bureaucrats we like with us."

The comment drew some chuckles.

"Since we will be losing the Pentagon, where will we be moving headquarters?"

"Headquarters will be moved to Denver, Colorado for many good reasons, one of which is not how much I like my skiing."

More laughter came from the screens.

"She's really good at this," Worthia whispered to Joseph.

"It's her job, isn't it?" he asked, confused.

"I mean setting people at ease after giving them disturbing news. She basically told them they're on their own for a while."

"They're military, shouldn't they be prepared for that?"

"Doesn't mean it's not disturbing. Look how anxious you get if Mercedes is late for supper."

"That's different. It's self-preservation. If I goof up somehow, she'd kill me."

"No, she wouldn't," she said with a pinched face, "she'd just make you pay for it later."

"Like I said, self-preservation."

"Is there some reason we were dragged to this meeting?"

"So we don't wander off and get in trouble?"

"Speak for yourself," Worthia said with a huff.

"Mr. Gint, would you join us, please," Samuelson's voice interrupted.

Joseph jumped up and walked toward the woman.

"Since we have all the bases represented, please catch them up on your research."

Joseph looked at Bennett, who nodded. He gave the man a sarcastic 'thanks for nothing' look before turning to the displays.

"We have managed to develop a particle projector that can destroy the angel wing material in a very short amount of time. This weapon was developed unexpectedly and as of now, we only have one working copy, the original. We have tested and dismantled the working unit and managed to reassemble the unit and repeat its performance. We are in the process of creating a second unit based on our measurements of the first unit. We are also investigating an excessive power usage by the unit. So far, no credible reason for the excessive power usage has been found."

"When do you expect to be able to reproduce the unit and make it available?" was asked when Joseph stopped to take a breath.

"I am not even going to guess at that until I am sure we can reproduce the weapon."

"How hard can that be?"

"We are talking about some very precise manufacturing and engineering that is not understood as well as our current weapons. I am also worried about the excessive power usage. If the extra power is why the projector works, we will have to find out exactly where the power is going to reliably reproduce the results or it may be hit and miss."

"How big is the unit?"

"Bigger than a couple of guys can haul around. Of course, it is experimental at the moment and we have not started any efforts to reduce the size or weight, if it is even possible."

The questions went dead. Joseph stared at the display for a few moments and then turned back to the general.

"Thank you, Mr. Gint. Can you and the young lady wait outside for Commander Bennett?"

"I guess so." Joseph shrugged with the statement.

Worthia joined him on his way to the door.

"I guess that answers my question," she said softly.

"So why don't you try 'How soon is the meeting going to be over' so we can get out of this place?"

Chapter Twenty-Seven
The Resistance

"I am very vexed."

The statement unnerved Garo, being completely unprepared for it. It unnerved the man next to him even more. He was small with a sharp, pointed nose and thin face. Garo liked to call him Mr. Bird.

"I am vexed," Valesco continued, "that the Church of God's Covenant in Phoenix is still functioning. Can anyone explain this?"

Garo said nothing, but looked at Mr. Bird.

"We have been concentrating our efforts on the small churches," the small man said, visibly shaking. "After the attack on their branch in Los Angeles, they added quite a bit of security. We felt that once we had the other congregations in our flock, we could concentrate all of our efforts on the remaining church."

"Not thinking that we would be losing some of those congregations to the Covenant church?"

"Well, at least we know where they are." The man turned his head sideways to Valesco.

"So you are saying you are allowing them to get stronger just to make it more of a challenge?" Valesco walked up to the man and stared down at him.

"Ah… yes?"

Valesco smiled. A small snicker could be heard.

"You are a brave man. I admire bravery in my people." Valesco turned and walked away. "Of course, you know that if you do not succeed, it will be your head. Literally."

The man forced down a huge gulp. His shaking increased.

"I won't let you down, Mr. Valesco."

"For your sake, I hope you don't." Valesco stood for a moment, then turned back to look at the man and Garo. "Why are you still here?"

With a jump, the man turned and ran for the door. Valesco waited for the door to close before speaking.

"Let's hope he has more courage when it comes to the competition."

"I have contingency plans in place already," Garo said.

"Of course you do, because you, my friend, know what you are doing and are efficient. If I could clone you about a hundred times, this would all be going much smoother." Valesco walked back around his desk. Garo resisted giving his own assessment of the progress.

"Can I talk to you about another subject?" Garo asked.

"Yes, of course," Valesco said with a wave.

"The presidential election is coming up in two years. Have you decided on a candidate for the office of the president?"

Valesco laughed a full, belly laugh. "Do you really think they will hold elections?"

"Why not?" Garo asked with a blank face.

"Because they will be worried they will lose." Valesco emphasized the last word. "They will use all the ongoing hostility as an excuse, I am sure."

"Will the people stand for that?"

"Some will, some won't, but it won't matter. In two years, we will be moving on the traditional churches and tensions will be even higher. You didn't expect the military establishment to just roll over and play dead, did you?" Valesco finally turned to look at Garo. He had one eyebrow raised.

"I guess I expected them to respect the rule of law."

Valesco lowered his head to look at Garo through the top of his eyes. Garo stared for a few seconds until understanding dawned, and then nodded his head up and down.

"They don't expect us to honor the law and will feel freed from doing so themselves," Garo stated.

"Exactly." Valesco laughed again, spreading his arms. "Of course, it's not like we haven't given them cause, is it? Besides, this makes things so much more interesting. If they 'played by the rules' the whole time, we would win in no time." Valesco turned back to his display.

"Your propensity to consider this a game worries me," Garo said in a flat voice.

"Do not worry, my friend." Valesco walked around the desk and put his arm around Garo's shoulders, patting the opposite shoulder. "We are going to win. It's inevitable. We have the people on our side. If they shelter themselves in their cities, we will just starve them out. What can they do?"

"I don't know, and that's what worries me. Plus, the fact that they will have all the real weapons." The arm did not leave Garo's shoulder, staying longer than it ever had before. The action worried him.

"If we had weapons," Valesco said, with a pointing finger at his chest, "then we would be labeled as rebels and they would be justified in shooting us. By allowing them to have all the weapons, they will be the only ones who will be condemned by using them. Thus, we will win, one way or the other." Valesco withdrew his hand and turned to walk back around the desk.

"What if they decide to use the weapons anyway and wipe us out?" Garo stared after Valesco.

"Then they will be condemned by the rest of the world. Who knows what would happen after that? Maybe the world would worry about the U.S. using the weapons on them next and decide to attack." Valesco's free hand flew back as if throwing something behind his back. "If they kill us, I am sure someone will exact our revenge."

"I would rather it not come to that."

"It won't, it won't." Standing behind his desk, Valesco placed his hands on his chest and turned back toward his friend. His eyes were large and had an accompanying smile. "Don't worry. And enjoy the excitement!"

*   *   *

"Welcome to the club." Conna Stewart's voice held enthusiasm and warmth.

"Thanks. Not sure I'm ready for this, but I guess I wasn't given a choice." Donnest fidgeted in his seat as he looked at the monitors holding the other heads of state.

"You have come a long way. I am sure you will make your people proud. It is often the hidden flower that blooms the best." Shishiho gave a small smile.

Donnest returned a small nod. "At least I am up-to-date on all the briefings Tyler attended. I am sure, though, you have questions." Donnest sat back into the chair and placed his arms on the rests. His hands gripped the chair.

"Do you feel that Tyler had been compromised before she was placed in custody?" Isabella Ruiz asked in a direct manner, after giving Donnest only a second to relax.

"No. We believe she was just nervous about the election. Nothing in her schedule would indicate that she had contact with the Puritans." Donnest's eyes darted between the monitors to gauge the reactions.

"Will this disrupt any of your preparations?" The question came from Shishiho.

"We do not believe so. Actually, I think it is a great relief to people not to worry about the election." Donnest's head twitched in a tic and he took a small intake of breath.

"So you will not be holding elections in two years?" Shishiho raised an eyebrow.

"We can't predict the future, but we expect the situation to become such that safety during the voting process could not be guaranteed. Of course, we could be proven wrong."

The comment brought an approving smile from Shishiho.

"I have heard rumors that your seat of government will be moving. Can you tell us where it will go?" Mambou Tammil made the statement with such ease that it belied the contrast to the fact that he had the information at all. Donnest took a breath and decided not to ask where the information had come from.

"We will be moving to Denver, Colorado. We plan to be moved before the election, or when the election would have been held. It will depend if we feel the city is secure."

"Why not use a more secure city?" Tammil asked.

"Denver is central within the country. It is also isolated compared to other large cities, so the Puritans will not have a large population base in the immediate area, as would be the case on the east or west coast."

"Sensible." Tammil nodded his head.

"That is quite a distance to move," Ruiz commented.

"The federal government was significantly downsized when the Constitution was changed. Compared to, say, one hundred years ago, we're barely moving a department's worth of people. Plus, Denver has much nicer weather." Donnest gave a cheerful smile. A few polite laughs could be heard.

"Then to other matters." Shishiho lifted her shoulders the barest part of an inch that was left to lift. "London, Budapest, and Rome have been added to our list that we are calling the Twenty-One. These shall be the major seats of government in their areas. Do you have the rest of the list, Mr. Donnest?"

"Last I knew, the list included Hong Kong, Cairo, Tokyo, Seoul, Nanjing, Rio de Janeiro, Beijing, Lagos, Taiwan, Panama City, and Berlin. That only makes fifteen that I know about."

"The other six are Jabail, Tyumen, Sydney, Havana, Luanda, and Colombo."

"I assume when you say Colombo, you really mean the whole island?"

"Of course." Shishiho smiled. "It is the only area around the Indian continent that is of significance. Any other cities in a faction's area will be their responsibility to choose. I assume you have already chosen yours?"

"Yes. Our list includes Chicago, parts of New York City, San Francisco, Toronto, Quebec, Dallas, and such places."

"Not Miami?" Ruiz's face showed concern.

"We lost Miami in the last election."

"Hmm. That is going to affect a lot of people down here."

"That may be why it was targeted by the Puritans. Quite frankly, it caught us off-guard." Donnest shifted a little, but was getting used to telling people about Miami.

"I am sure there will be other surprises as time goes on," Shishiho said easily.

"What is the latest on continental Europe?" Donnest asked.

"Nothing has changed yet," Stewart answered, "but I am sure there will be changes coming."

"What about Scandinavia?"

"Sweden is one big corporation and controls the whole peninsula as if it were a kingdom. I seriously doubt the Puritans will make inroads there for a long time, if at all. I know the CEO-slash-owner and he believes in a firm grip. All his family is the same way. They might just believe they are actual royalty." The disdain in Conna's voice was impossible to miss. The last sentence was all but spit out of her mouth as she slightly turned her head. The comment brought laughs from almost all in the meeting. Shishiho was the exception.

"Are we worried about the small islands at all?" Donnest's voice almost cracked. "Just asking."

"None are big enough to affect the rest of the world. Plus, they are pretty insular, particularly the tourist islands. They have to be to avoid overcrowding." Shishiho smirked with the comments. "They can suspend tourism any time they want."

"We have several islands on our list," Ruiz added without Shishiho's derision, "such as the Falklands and Grenada. With islands being easy to defend, it is tempting to add more, but we need to concentrate on main population areas at the moment."

"I understand, we are in the same boat. What about religious areas?"

"Mecca will be defended, of course." Bahir Kattan's eyes lit up and he leaned forward toward the display. "Jerusalem is not of any significance since after the aliens left, the riots turned most of the World Council buildings into shells and the city is not defensible anyway, per design when it was rebuilt after the Nuclear War. Welcoming and accepting, you know. We are looking at other locations, but since we have so many, it will come down to hard choices. Not everyone will be happy with us. Thankfully, the percentage of people who still practice religion is small. I assume some will volunteer to protect their own sites. In fact, they may prefer it."

"What about Tibet? It still has a significant, culturally unique section of population. Are we thinking of taking any action?" Donnest almost cringed as he looked toward Shishiho.

Shishiho huffed, turning away her eyes. "Tibet wanted its independence and has it. They can take care of their own problems, just like the islands that asked to remain primitive. We will spend no effort on them."

Donnest wasn't the only one who flared his eyebrows. He looked at the others with some discomfort, but most seemed resigned to the inevitable, saying nothing. After some silence, he decided to speak.

"I know some of you may be nervous about my new administration. Please know that a minimum of changes have been made. Please feel free to contact my office whenever you feel it is needed. I will be appointing a new Secretary of Security soon. Thank you for all the information you have shared today. I look forward to other meetings with you."

"They can't do that!" A man slammed his second beer onto the counter while staring at the six o'clock evening news display.

"Do what?" the man sitting next to him asked, absorbed in his nachos.

"They arrested the president! Our duly elected, people selected, President of *the* United States. We voted her in! They can't arrest her."

"What did they arrest her for?" The second man still showed no enthusiasm.

"They say consorting with the enemy. The enemy my ass! We ain't even at war. Who's the enemy?"

"Who do you think?" the man said with a huff before eating another nacho.

"Well, I don't know." The man turned to his companion with his head cocked to one side. "Why don't you tell me?"

"The Puritans. Don't you know the government don't like them?" The man talked with a full mouth.

"You mean us?" The man's eyes went wide open.

"Yeah, us, I guess."

"How the hell are we the enemy?"

"Don't know, but why do you think they're building that fence? They want to keep us out. And why do they want to keep us out? You figure it out." The man went back to his nachos, which were almost gone. "Distracting a man from his nachos so he don't enjoy them," he muttered.

"Are we going to let them get away with this?" the man bellowed. He stood and looked around the bar. "Are we going to let them get away with putting our president in jail? Well, are we?"

"*No!*" came from about half of the patrons.

"So let's go do something about it!" The man waved his arm toward the door.

"Yeah!" came the reply.

"You can't leave without paying!" a waitress yelled at the departing crowd. "And you didn't even leave a tip!"

The small crowd walked down the sidewalk. Questions from onlookers resulted in more joining their number. After a few blocks, there were enough that they marched down the street instead. Their presence made the drivers unhappy, but most were smart enough not to anger the ever growing crowd. Those not smart enough regretted their lack of foresight and dents left in their vehicles. By the time the fence was in sight, the crowd had risen to over one hundred. The gate constructed across the roadway on the other side of an intersection became their destination. As they neared, two guards appeared in the road on the other side of the gate. Drones appeared overhead one or two at a time until a dozen hovered overhead.

"Stop! What's your business here?" the older guard asked when the crowd was twenty feet away.

"You put our president in jail!" the man from the bar shouted.

"That wasn't anyone here in Chicago and we had nothing to do with it," the guard said in a loud voice.

"You work for the government!"

"So do a lot of people." The guard's voice was loud, but not threatening.

"We want our president back!"

"Like I said," the guard said, shaking his head, "we don't have her. You need to go to Washington, D.C. and talk to them."

"We're talking to you!"

"Disperse now!" was the only response.

"We're not dispersing. We're taking our town back. Come on!"

Before the man could finish his first step, two pulse stunners and the drones opened fire. The guards swept the oncoming crowd while the drones targeted individuals in rapid succession. Bodies dropped on the road slower than the stun pulses hit the people, but fast enough to inhibit progress by the crowd. Bodies on the ground started to block the progress of those behind. Still determined, those left standing walked over or around those on the ground. The pile got bigger and wider. Sirens started in the background on both sides.

When the pile reached three people high, those behind stopped. They had not made more than five feet of progress. They looked at each other as if asking what they should do.

"Disperse now! Don't make us arrest any of you. Go back to your families." The guard kept his voice even and unwavering.

As the sirens turned into security vehicles coming down the intersecting roads, the crowd melted away, some more hesitant to go than others. When the security personnel exited their vehicles, they shooed away the last of those still conscious. A man in an officer uniform walked to the front of the pile.

"What the heck do you think you are doing?" he asked the guards.

"Defending our post," the man replied.

"Your damn post shouldn't be here in the first place!"

"Not my call."

"You army guys think you can shoot whoever you want." The officer waved at the pile.

"They're only stunned."

"You better hope so or we'll be bringing charges." He turned to his men. "Get some ambulances in here and check all these people. I want each one to receive a full medical examination!"

A large vehicle pulled up on the other side of the gate and more military personnel got out, taking up positions around the gate and adjacent fencing. A man with captain bars walked up to the guards.

"Good job, men."

"I am sure the hell glad you're here, sir," the man replied without taking his eyes from the scene on the other side of the gate.

"Don't worry, you did the right thing. Just wish I could have been here to get some of my own licks in."

"You're welcome to the next batch, sir." The man allowed his voice to hold some quiver for the first time.

Even though it was late, Garo hurried into the office to the waiting Valesco. He was not surprised to see the man watching the news feed.

"Did one of our people do this?" Valesco pointed at the display.

"No, it was spontaneous." Garo took up position on the opposite side of the desk.

"It's too soon. Our people in Chicago need to get the situation under control. We don't need mobs running around taking on the military. At least, not yet." Valesco waved at the display, which vanished.

"I will make that abundantly clear to our people there." Garo used a firm, no nonsense voice.

"Of course you will. You're a good man, Garo. What would I do without you?" Valesco smiled.

"I hope to never find out." Garo gave his own smile, though it held a bit of nervous tension.

Chapter Twenty-Eight
News

Rubbing his head didn't make it feel better, but it was all Joseph could think to do. The pain was in the inside.

"Working too hard?" Mercedes asked gently as she kissed his head and proceeded around the table, placing a platter in the center as she did. "Maybe you need a day off."

"Maybe I need a month off." As he raised his head, Joseph took a deep breath. The light, flowery scent of the candles on the table competed with the aroma of the dish Mercedes had just put down. Somehow, they complemented each other. "How do you do that?"

"Do what?" She sat in the chair opposite.

"Coordinate the smell of the candles with the food." Joseph ran his fingernails through his hair.

"I do know a thing or two about plants, dear." She gave him a sweet smile.

Joseph looked at the table with the crystal glasses, gold-trim plates, and gleaming silverware. The table was even covered with a linen tablecloth.

"Is there some event that I've forgotten about?" he asked.

"Can't I just make a nice meal for the man I love?" Mercedes broadened her smile.

"I guess you can, it just feels like more."

Mercedes used the serving utensils to place food on their plates. "There is something I would like to talk about."

Joseph gave her an 'I thought so' smile.

"Your mom and dad were legally joined, right?"

"Yes."

"But were they married?"

"They didn't have a ceremony, if that's what you mean, but they refer to themselves as married. The term is really more imprecise than it used to be."

"Have you ever thought about getting married?" Mercedes put the utensils down.

"You mean a ceremony, like a religious one?" Joseph's head turned to his right.

"Or a non-religious one." Mercedes gave him a small tilt of her head.

"Not really. You know me. I'm not much on ceremony."

"But how do you feel about them? Ceremonies, that is." Mercedes played with the food on her plate.

"I've never been to one. Wait, that's not right. I went to a Jewish one, which was kind of strange, but I doubt you're talking about one of those." Joseph hadn't picked up his fork yet and spoke with his hands.

"No," Mercedes wrinkled her nose, "not really. So why did your parents get a legal union?"

"They said it was for us kids, to make us feel like a permanent family. Weren't your parents married?"

"Yes, but it was more of a social event. With my mom being a model, they had news crews and everything. Doesn't sound very romantic to me, but the demands of famous people, you know." Her eyes wandered around the top of her vision.

"So do you want a ceremony? I mean, when you get married or joined or whatever." Joseph still hadn't touched his silverware. Mercedes continued to play.

"Well, I was thinking more of the kids. I mean, you want kids, don't you?" A small amount of panic showed in Mercedes' eyes.

"Yeah, I do. I mean, my mother would never forgive me if I didn't have kids. Not like my brother is going to have any that he brings home or knows about. She has been looking forward to being a grandmother for several decades, I think."

"So you think we should 'make it legal' if we ever have any kids?"

"I guess that would be best. I mean, it makes it a lot easier with all the legal things required with the kids. And I think it makes them feel more secure." Joseph nodded his head with the comments.

"So we need to think about it." It was more of a statement than a question.

"When we come to the bridge, yes, we should think about it." Joseph looked at Mercedes, whose head was slightly bowed as she was giving him a shy smile. He furrowed his brow. "Wait, you're not saying we've come to the bridge, are you?"

Mercedes laid down her fork, reached across the table and took both of his hands in hers. She looked down for a second, but then looked into his eyes, hers twinkling.

"Joe, not only have you come to that bridge, but you've already paid the toll."

Joseph remained frozen for more seconds than he could remember later.

"I'm here. What you need, Madge?" Joseph took his eyes off of his interface long enough to look at the woman. This early in the morning, his interface tended to want lots of attention.

"You got visitors." Madge looked like she could barely keep herself from bursting out with something. With a questioning look, Joseph turned the direction Madge pointed. When he did, he wanted to pinch himself to make sure he was awake.

With quick steps, Sindie ran up and gave her son a hug. His brother, relaxing in the background, made a weak single wave and a half-smile.

"Where have you guys been?" Joseph managed to ask through the hug.

"Had to keep Mom safe," Johan said.

"You wouldn't believe where we've been," Sindie said as she let go of the hug. "The places your brother knows! I thought we raised him better than that."

"We weren't found, were we?" Johan asked.

"I'm not even sure we knew where we were half the time." Sindie gave him a stern look, but then smiled. "But he did get us here safe, so I guess I should be proud of him."

"I don't care how you got here, I'm just glad you made it." Joseph walked over to his brother and held out his hand. "I owe you one."

"Yeah, you do. How many does that make you owe me?" Johan shook his hand.

"One. And that doesn't count how many times I bailed you out of jail."

"Twice, only twice. And I paid those back by…"

"Something we don't need to mention." Joseph turned. "Madge, you done with these guys?"

"Heck yes. Not like I have to worry they're Puritans. Especially that good-looking one there." She gave Johan a wink.

"Shit, already? Come on." Joseph's head lolled as they turned.

Joseph led them out of the building and across the compound. Sindie took his arm.

"So, I hear you have a lady. So when are you making it official? When do I get grandchildren?"

"Well, are you committed to that order of events?"

"What?!" Sindie tugged at his arm. "What are you saying?"

"I'm asking if it matters which comes first, because we have an option here, if you really want the grandkid first."

Hugging resumed, with a little dancing thrown in and some cheers for effect. Johan laughed, though it wasn't clear at who.

"Where is she? I have to meet her now!"

"She's working in the new greenhouse, setting things up. We can go there now, I guess." Joseph tried to sound nonchalant. His mother had enough enthusiasm for everyone.

"Of course we have to go there now! I have to go see her and how far she is along. Women need to talk about things. This is her first, isn't it?"

"Yes, it's her first. It's this way."

Mercedes seemed to be as excited to see Joseph's mother as Sindie was to see Mercedes. It didn't take long for Joseph and Johan to feel out of place. After watching for a few minutes, Joseph turned to his brother.

"You want to get a drink?"

"And how. Mom's really crimped my style in several ways." They both turned toward the door.

"I feel so bad for you. No, wait, I don't. This way."

As they walked out of the greenhouse, Johan said, "Now, you know, I really owe you."

"For what?"

"For giving Mom a grandchild. Really takes the pressure off me." They walked the surrounding sidewalk.

"You sure you don't have one somewhere you could dig up?"

Johan laughed. "Not that I know of, or want to know of. So, when's the wedding?"

"Soon. Mercedes is still working out the details. She wants to have a ceremony, though not a religious one. She said something about 'traditional Roman'? Not sure if togas are involved. I sure hope not."

"You're still like this? I thought you would have changed by now." Johan shook his head.

"Why would I change? Besides, you are just in time to sing for the wedding."

"I don't do weddings." Johan, walking with his hands clasped behind his back, gave a woman in military uniform an eye as she walked by. It was returned, if briefly.

"You're not leaving, then?"

Johan huffed. "Do you know how dangerous it is to be a person with the last name of Gint out there at the moment? I was lucky to get Mom here unobserved."

"Well, we are setting up a whole city here on the base. One thing that we are short on is entertainers."

"Well," Johan said as his head turned, eyeing another woman, "I might try the local environs for a while. It could prove interesting."

"Just don't get me in trouble." Joseph rolled his eyes.

The new dining hall was used for the reception, and though it had a capacity of six hundred people, it was packed. Joseph shook his head every time he scanned the crowd.

"Didn't know you had so many friends?" Mercedes said.

"You sure they're not yours?"

"Some of them." The conversation was interrupted by Mercedes' mother coming up and giving her a hug. "I'm sure glad you could fly in."

"And miss my girl's wedding? No way in hell." The woman disengaged from the hug only to let Mercedes' father, noticeably a few years older than her mother, give her a hug. After the hug, he turned to Joseph and shook his hand.

"I have heard so much about you, son," the man said after three enthusiastic pumps. "Mercedes has talked a lot about you."

"And you are still happy to see me. That's a good sign for future holidays."

The man laughed. "I have also heard quite a bit about your work here." The man smiled a knowing smile, but then held up his hands. "No details, of course, but lots of good things."

"Now you're really making me nervous," Joseph said with a chuckle. A small tap on his shoulder caused him to turn and find Worthia standing next to him. She gave him his biggest hug of the night.

"I'm so happy for you! And Mercedes!"

"Thank you, little one. Guess you can be happy with a job well done."

"Mercedes did all the work." She gave Joseph a smirk of a smile.

"And I had nothing to do with it?"

"Nope, not from what I hear."

They both laughed.

"Well, then, at least no one can blame me." Joseph gave her another hug.

"Oh, if there's any blame, you'll get it," Worthia said with a giggle.

"Thanks a lot." Worthia moved on to Mercedes. Wenk stepped up and shook Joseph's hand.

"About time, you idiot," Wenk said with a smile.

"Everyone's a critic."

"You guys talk about baby names yet?" He gave Joseph a hopeful look.

"Yes, and Wenk is not one of them."

Wenk's smiled turned into a frown. "Now I am hurt. You could have at least left it in the running." The comment was accompanied by a laugh.

"You're the one that just called me an idiot. Just proving it."

Wenk moved on to Mercedes, giving Joseph a momentary break. After Wenk hugged Mercedes, he and Worthia walked off, holding hands. Joseph leaned toward Mercedes.

"When did that happen?" Joseph asked with a nod.

"When you weren't looking. Claimed you were busy, if I remember right."

"I was busy. He's like ten years older than she is."

"So?" Mercedes shrugged.

"Guess she likes the short, skinny, nerdy type."

"Not what she told me she likes." Mercedes looked away.

Joseph gave his wife a strained look and then turned away. "I don't even want to know."

"That's okay," Mercedes said, patting his shoulder, "you probably don't want to. Besides, that's girl-talk anyway."

"And what exactly have you told her about me?" Joseph turned back to look at her.

"Only the good things, dear." Mercedes kissed him on the check. She was rescued from saying more by the approach of Captain Allin.

"Congratulations, you two." Allin gave them both a hug, then turned back to Joseph, pointing her finger. "I'll give you one week off and you have to take it."

"You can negotiate that with my new boss," he said with a thumb toward Mercedes.

"Already done," Mercedes replied, then furrowed her brow. "New?"

"So let me guess, my life has been scheduled until I die already."

"Just some of it. But don't worry, I'll take care of the rest." Mercedes gave his arm a body squeeze.

"Oh, good, one less thing for me to worry about." The statement lacked feeling.

"What's the baby going to be called?" Allin asked.

"We're keeping that as a surprise," Joseph replied.

Allin frowned. "We'll talk later," Allin said to Mercedes as she left.

"Seems to be the question on everyone's mind," Joseph said out of the side of his mouth to Mercedes.

"Not like a baby is born on the base every day, you know."

"Sure, but it just doesn't seem like a question you ask at a wedding, or am I misinformed?"

"You're the one who waited so long." Mercedes grumbled.

"You were the one courting me. I thought it was your responsibility." Joseph tried to look innocent.

"Riiight. No initiative on your part."

"I just didn't want to mess up a good thing."

Mercedes grabbed Joseph by the suit and turned him toward her, a coy smile on her face as she looked up into his eyes.

"You did just fine," she said just before kissing him.

Chapter Twenty-Nine
South of the Border

Council of State President Igle Perez couldn't see because he had a blindfold over his eyes. Strapped to a chair that didn't move, listening and talking were his only options. His initial inquiries brought no response, but then he heard footsteps approaching.

"If you are thinking of ransom, I hate to inform you that I am poor and the government will not pay any."

The footsteps stopped. The person was close enough for the man to hear their breathing and smell their sweat.

"We don't want money, we want your cooperation."

"Cooperation? With what?"

"Your city, and your country in fact, has not been very friendly to our interests. We think this needs to change."

Perez laughed. "You're Puritans, aren't you? Even though we may not go to church, we are Catholics here. We don't need your alien-worshipping church."

The man walked around the governor to whisper in his ear. "And what would Francesco think of your opinion? Maybe we'll ask him."

"Francesco? You have him too?" The question didn't hold worry.

"Yes." The word was drawn out like a hiss. "We do."

The governor smirked. "I feel it fair to tell you that if you torture him, he'll most likely enjoy it." More laughter followed.

The man walked around to the governor's front and slapped him hard. "Do you think this is a game?!"

"No," Perez said, adjusting his mouth. In a serious tone, he added, "You should see very quickly how much a game this is not."

Perez could not see the man raise his hand again, but he heard the splintering of wood as multiple doors were bashed in. He heard the *zit* of pulsators and the screams of men as they reacted to the invasion. There were rapid footsteps in the room.

"What do we do? Kill him?"

"We are not authorized to kill him," the man who had slapped him said.

"This can't be for nothing!"

"No! No killing him!"

"But..."

The comment was cut off by the *zit* of a pulsator. Several more followed, then booted feet approached. The blindfold was removed to reveal security personnel.

"Are you all right, President?" an officer with captain's bars asked. The woman started cutting his restraints.

"Yes, I am fine. What about Francesco?"

"We have men retrieving him also. We activated the trackers as soon as we knew you were missing."

Perez looked at the men on the floor. They were dressed in common clothing, but did not have the deep tans most people sported around town.

"Are they dead?"

"We didn't want to take any chances."

"Good. At least this way, the courts will not be involved." Perez stood and flexed his muscles. "Do we know who they are?"

"Working on it." The woman stood at attention, muscles tensed.

"I want to make a statement as soon as Francesco is safe." Perez started walking toward the hallway. He followed the directions of the security personnel in the building until he was outside. A full-sized vehicle had parked in front of the building.

"President Perez," another security officer said as he approached the vehicle, "we just received word that Francesco has been rescued. He's fine."

"Good! I want a full city-wide broadcast from here. Set up now."

"Yes, sir." The man saluted and turned to talk to others.

Perez straightened his clothes as best he could. He used the vehicle window to look at his hair, but then decided it would be better if it was ruffled. Clearing his throat, he stepped back so the building would be behind him. A security officer with a camera eye walked in front of him, a small display on his arm. As he watched the display, he held up three fingers on his other hand. After a few seconds, one finger was curled under, then another, and finally the last one. The officer nodded.

"Friends. I have just been rescued by our security forces from kidnappers. Foreign kidnappers. Who were these people and what did they want? I can tell you that because they told me. These people were Puritans, bent on pushing their influence on our island, and they are not above using violence in doing so.

"Friends, you know that I am not a violent man. I prefer to use discussion and reason to resolve our problems. But these people who would use violence against our people just to peddle their religion have gone too far. Cuba will not stand for this!" Perez's arm pumped up and down.

"As of right now, I declare all Puritans criminals. I call on all Cubans to help us identify these Puritans and bring an end to their ways of violence. Their property and churches are now forfeit. I do not advocate violence, but, seeing as they are a violent people, I realize that violence may be required to bring them to heel.

"Do not overly endanger yourselves! I am directing the security forces to detain all Puritans and check all of their locations for weapons. We will not allow these people to dictate to us how to live or what our society will become. We do this for our children. We do this for Cuba!" Perez said, his finger pointing into the air.

The light on the camera eye went out and the officer withdrew. The captain of the security force walked up to the president.

"Sir, are you sure you want to do this? Do you even have the authority?"

"Yes," Perez replied sharply to the woman, "I am very sure I want to do this. And as for authority, it is a national emergency, so I have it. We will not allow this stain to spread across our island. It will stop here and it will stop now!"

"But the people, they... it may be chaos." The words were said softly.

"The people need to be involved. They need to feel ownership for protecting their island. This way, there will be no questions about whether it was right or wrong. We will band together, making resistance to the Puritans even stronger. Take me to the legislature. I need to talk to them about a new law."

"Yes, sir." Ushered inside the vehicle, which then rolled away, a display was soon filled with the face of a woman in a formal business suit.

"President," the woman said, "I'm glad to see you're not hurt."

"Thank you, Ulinda. I need to talk to you about sponsoring a new law."

"Exactly what kind of law?" The woman's face was curious, but cautious.

"One that makes the Puritan church illegal. Do you think we can do that?"

"Religion is not regulated by the state. But if they were not a religion…" The woman's eyes drifted away as if in thought.

"I will make an executive order declaring them a terrorist group. You will have it in a few hours."

"Then I see no problem making their organization illegal, once that is done." Ulinda's composure returned to firm. "You will make sure to include all of their affiliates and any other organizations that are only fronts for the church?"

"Of course. Don't worry, I will have my best people on the wording to make sure there are no loopholes."

"Then I see no reason why we can't get this done by, say, the end of tomorrow?" A smile grew on the woman's face.

"It's a pleasure doing business with you, Ulinda." Perez smiled back.

"It is an honor to serve, sir." The woman gave a small head bow as the picture disappeared.

Footsteps interrupted Valesco's thoughts as he paced backstage.

"What is it now?" he asked in a gravelly voice.

"There is news from Cuba, sir," the man said. There was a pause.

"Well?" Valesco's head came up. "What have those idiots done now?"

"The president of Cuba has declared our church a terrorist organization. The legislature has outlawed the church."

"And why would they do that?" Valesco turned to the man. He was young, well-groomed, and sweating profusely. His eyes wandered around and he stuttered.

"Because... our people kidnapped him and tried to make him cooperate." The man's voice went up in tone at the end of the sentence.

Valesco's eyes flared along with his nostrils. His face started to turn red. Approaching the man, his chest puffed out as if he would explode. As he drew close, Valesco let the breath out and calmed himself. Turning, he pinched the bridge of his nose with his forefinger and thumb. The young man relaxed and hoped it was sweat going down his leg.

"If our idiot in charge there manages to get away, make sure he is shot and thrown into the sea. Anyone else in that organization that is found will be taken to headquarters and held. Is that understood?"

"Ye-yes, sir." The young man quickly turned and left.

"And now," a voice came from the other room, amplified by a sound system, "the person I am sure you have all been waiting to hear from. Our spiritual leader, *Valesco!*"

Pushing his way through the doors, Valesco entered the corner of the stage of the fifty-thousand seat stadium. Every seat was filled. People cheered, clapped, waved flags and banners, or blew horns. The sound was thunderous. Valesco made his way to the podium to be greeted by the grinning master of ceremonies. A quick handshake and the man departed to his seat. Valesco grabbed both sides of the podium and started in a soft voice.

"My friends." The noise started to die down. "I am humbled that you asked me to speak at this convention today. I am not a political man myself, but I guess they needed someone used to addressing large crowds."

Some laughs and brief cheers followed.

"I am heartened to see so many people here, so many people participating in our country's political process, especially after the politicians in Washington, excuse me, Denver, have declared that elections will not be held."

Boos filled the auditorium for a few seconds.

"They forget that this country is not theirs, it is the people's!" Valesco's voice grew louder. More clapping followed. "This is not their election, this is your election. The people get to choose their leaders, not the military system!"

Cheering and clapping filed the air. People whooped and waved their flags and banners. The news crews covered every angle of the event.

"They may have moved to Denver, but our government is still in Washington, D.C., where our Constitution says it should be." Valesco was all but shouting. "This election will tell those who are trying to hold on to power that the people still speak, that the people's will is still supreme, and the people will decide the fate of this country, not the bureaucrats!"

Valesco let the crowds cheer and chant for a while, smiling at them. He started again in a low voice.

"Just before coming onto this stage, I have received horrendous news that touches me personally."

Silence went through the audience.

"It seems that Cuba has designated my church as a terrorist group without justification."

Almost as one, the audience gasped. Hushed conversation and quiet personal denials could just be heard.

"This, again, my friends, is an example of how the world persecutes those who believe the truth. The world does not want to hear the truth. The world wants to suppress the truth. But make no mistake, my friends." He paused for a second. "We will persevere!"

Again the air was split with wild clapping and cheering. People jumped up and down and waved their arms in the air. Valesco let the chaos go on for a while, watching the crowd, suppressing what he really wanted to say. When the noise started to die down, he again spoke in a booming voice.

"That is why I am happy, tonight, to give my endorsement for Sulas Mahe as candidate for the office of the President of the United States!"

A band started playing. Streamers and holographic fireworks filled the air. People cheered and danced. Valesco turned to the candidate, who quickly made his way to the podium and shook Valesco's hand with enthusiasm. When the handshake was almost done, Valesco pulled the man forward to whisper in his ear.

"Don't mess this up."

Chapter Thirty
The Will of (Some) People

"**I** don't even know why they are showing that," Joseph said as he placed his glass back on the table in the bar.

"Because it is the only thing any network is showing. You know how it goes." Wenk scoffed at the display. "At least the sound is off."

"From the reaction, you would think the preacher is running for office." Johan held a humorous smile on his face.

"He might as well be," Joseph replied. "I'm sure that the candidates for every office were either hand-picked or personally approved by Valesco."

"Does he really have that much power?" Johan asked.

"You bet. He's already put all the other alien churches out of business and half the traditional churches. I am sure once he controls the government, he will make all other churches illegal."

"That would be unconstitutional," Wenk objected.

"Don't worry, he'll find some way to do it. Or he will just get the states to declare a constitutional convention and have it changed."

The statement drew a skeptical look from Wenk. "You don't think he'd do that, do you?"

"Yes, I do. I'm not putting anything past this guy. He's after power and there's no one around to stop him."

"What about us?" Johan asked, raising his glass with the statement. "The federal government, I mean."

"We're barely holding onto our own. At least we started early enough to get a part of the population under our protection. I just feel sorry for those we won't be able to help. Left to the wolves and all." Joseph was looking at the table.

Johan turned and leaned toward Wenk. "He seems depressed."

"Maybe the wife isn't in the mood, being pregnant. Nothing wrong with the baby, I hope."

"Hmm, that would do it," Johan said with a nod.

"Not like it's either of you two's business," Joseph said with a stare, but then turned his eyes away. "Besides, you're both wrong. Baby is doing just fine and Mercedes is fine."

"So, dear brother," Johan said, settling into his chair, "what has you in such a sour mood?"

"Mother," Joseph said, looking through the top of his eyes at his brother.

"Yes!" Johan acknowledged the statement with his glass and then again turned to Wenk. "She is not happy with the baby name."

"What's wrong with Julianna?" Wenk asked before a sip of beer.

"She wanted Fenda."

"Fenda? Where did she get that?"

"Family name." Johan downed the rest of his beer and held up the glass for the waitress to see.

"That's asking a lot," Wenk said with a shake of his head. "Fenda! I sure can't see Mercedes going for that."

"Exactly!" Joseph interjected. "Doesn't mean I don't hear it from both sides though."

"Maybe your mother could use it as a special name for your daughter."

"Oh no." Joseph shook his head with vigor. "Mercedes will have none of that. She's made that perfectly clear." Joseph downed the rest of his beer and placed the glass on the table. "Do me a favor, guys, talk about something else."

"Sure!" Johan said with glee. "When are you and Worthia going to follow suit, Wenk?"

"Us?" Wenk laughed. "Probably never. She's still trying to figure out what her triple majors are going to be. Trying to best decide what will cover the widest number of fields, I think."

"That's quite a woman you got there, man." A waitress came with another beer. Johan looked at her as he took the glass, trading meaningful looks.

"Don't I know it," Wenk said.

"Well, whatever you have she likes, I wish you luck. Heavens knows I didn't." Johan took a drink.

"Wait!" Joseph sat forward with a start, pointing a finger. "You dated Worthia?"

"One date," Johan said with melancholy. "Never felt so used afterwards in my life. Since Jenn Swiften when I was twelve, that is, but I didn't really regret that one."

"As much as I like to hear some woman get the best of you, I don't want to hear any more," Joseph said with a wave of his hand. "And I officially regret asking you guys to change the subject."

The field in front of the base gate was starting to look like a parking lot. Dozens of cars, trucks, and other vehicles were parked at irregular intervals in the fields on both sides of the road. Commander Bennett stood just outside the gate.

"Sheriff," Bennett said as the man drew close.

"Commander." The sheriff gave him a nod. "I appreciate you doing this. You can imagine that the McCradys are quite upset about all this." His head twitched toward the vehicles.

"Please tell them that I am sorry they were inconvenienced, but we did not ask the people to park here." Bennett handed the man a bag full of keys with the certificate chips to the vehicles attached. "You can understand that we can't allow them to just drive onto the base without being inspected."

"I understand. I'm just glad harvest is over or McCrady would be really upset. Takes his farming seriously." The sheriff, with a grinning laugh, took the bag.

"Appropriate for a farmer, I suppose." Bennett grinned back.

The sheriff looked past Bennett toward the base. His eyes went up the buildings that had been erected.

"You guys sure went and built yourself some skyscrapers there. How tall is that big one?"

"Eighty-six stories. The two next to it are eighty stories."

"Why you want to build them so high?"

"Efficient use of space on the base. And we need the living space for all of our guests."

"I couldn't help but notice most of those vehicles aren't from around here." The sheriff pointed with his thumb over his shoulder.

"Most aren't. We seem to draw from quite a wide area. By the way, the people will not be needing those vehicles back. I am sure they are quite a boon to your town."

The sheriff's cheeks reddened slightly as he grinned. "Guess I can't deny that. Though we ourselves have people coming to our town from the cities, if you didn't know. At least we will have something to give to them to use if they don't have their own, which some don't."

"Do you have enough vacant farms to put them on?"

"The state has instituted a program to break up the really large ones of the rich farmers and is portioning it out to the newcomers. The new communes, that is. Too risky to just give land to someone who has never worked it." The sheriff nodded with the statement.

"Do they have the power to just take people's land like that?" Bennett's head tilted to the right as he frowned.

"Lots of them already left. Those that didn't seem to see the storm coming, if you know what I mean. I hear tell of a family down in Nebraska that owned four hundred thousand acres of land. Lost all of it but five hundred acres. They up and moved to New York City, so I'm told. The state said something about back taxes and all, but I doubt anyone believes that. Well, some do. It's hard to tell what's what these days." The sheriff shrugged in a carefree way.

"I can understand. A lot of changes going on at the moment." Bennett nodded.

"You guys in there vote in the election?" The sheriff took out some chewing gum and placed a couple of pieces in his mouth.

"No, didn't bother. Figured we knew who would win one way or the other."

The sheriff laughed, which ended in a cough. "That's everyone, I am sure. I hear all sorts of things, like there are a bunch of cities that walled themselves off."

"That's correct," Bennett said without emotion.

"And I hear," the sheriff said between chews, "that there are even more cities where non-church people are movin' to, ones with some big factories that kicked out church people and only hires atheist."

"I have heard the same thing."

"You military guys protecting those too?"

"Some of them." Bennett gave the sheriff a keen stare, as if trying to read his mind.

"I just don't know what all the fuss is about. You just sign up for their church and go to meetin's on Sunday and everyone's happy." The sheriff gave a long shrug.

"Not everyone likes to be told what to do. Plus, we used to have a little thing in this country called religious freedom."

"So you want people worshipping those old religions that were wrong? Sounds like a waste of time to me. We know the aliens exist and they said they put us here, so all that stuff in the writin's must be about them. The ones that weren't polluted, that is."

"And what if the aliens lied?" Bennett cocked an eyebrow.

"Why would they do that?" The sheriff stopped chewing with the question.

"So that we won't fight them."

Laughing, the sheriff replied, "Like that did us any good."

"Just saying." Bennett maintained his even tone and posture.

"Well, unless you want your base disappearing again, I won't advise it, son." The thought continued to bring the sheriff enjoyment.

"As much as I appreciate you taking the time to talk to me, I have other things I must attend to. Please tell the McCradys I regret their inconvenience. Good day, sir."

"Sure thing. Next time."

They shook hands and Bennett turned back to enter the base. He waited until inside to activate voice mode on the interface.

"You catch all that?"

"Sure did," Benitez said. "Trying to pry information from you?"

"Don't know. Maybe he was just being friendly."

"I know which one I'd choose."

"That's your job. Just how bad were the elections?" Bennett saluted the guard.

"Locally, not much changed. Across the country, it was a landslide. Certain areas are going to be feeling real pressure soon. I would expect any state that does not have a no-gun law to have one soon."

"And more messes like Tennessee." Bennett nodded to some passing troops as he climbed into the waiting PCA.

"If they try the same tactics in Texas, there will be a real mess."

"I doubt they will." The PCA smoothly accelerated toward the headquarters building. "Too big of a chunk to bite off. They'll start in the cities, where it will be easier. From what I have seen, not many gun owners there."

"Still, at some point, there will be bloodshed."

"That is a given. Are all the cities secure, at least the ones initially picked?"

"Yes. The last wall was finished just before the election."

"That's a relief." The statement held more emotion than any Bennett had made in the last ten minutes.

"But now there are other towns asking for the same treatment."

"So the sheriff said. Any of strategic importance?"

"How far down the list you want to go?" The statement was said in a way to imply an answer.

"Wish we could do more, but we can barely handle what we have here. Refugees are coming in at an ever increasing pace. I knew this would be coming, but knowing and seeing are two different things." The PCA pulled up in front of the headquarters building. "I'll be in my office in a few. I know there's nothing we can do, but I would at least like to see that list of cities."

"Roger. Everyone's probably curious about the same thing. I'm sure people here still have families elsewhere."

"That's something I don't even want to think about." Bennett sighed as the doors opened.

Chapter Thirty-One
Preliminaries

"**S**hould we really be doing this?" the Governor of Kentucky asked Valesco as he stared at the convention floor from the booth in the back. The booth was outfitted with every form of luxury that would fit. Valesco, though, was the only one who sat.

"We're not making an official religion," Valesco replied. "We are just letting each state decide what constitutes religious freedom."

"States you are sure will define that term as you wish."

"Yes, I am sure." Valesco appeared to soak in the noise of the crowd and each vote as it was cast like a man who drank a fine wine.

"But will the states comply?"

"Of course they will. We have made sure of that."

The man shifted uncomfortably. "If you are satisfied, then I am satisfied."

Valesco laughed. "You will be satisfied with the new power you will wield, I am sure."

"There's that, too," the man replied with a smile.

Both men watched the roll call count continue. When it was finished, the new constitution passed without a negative vote. Valesco drew in a deep breath and beamed. Standing up, he stretched his arms and then pulled them into his chest, then turned away from the scene back into the booth.

"It *has* been a successful day," Valesco said as he picked up a glass of deep red wine and raised it to his lips while the other man talked.

"It will take a while for the changes to take effect, though not as long as it would have if the heretics hadn't already made their move. Less government is always easier to deal with. Plus, we don't have to deal with the military."

"Yes," Valesco said in a sharp voice, "we do need to deal with the military. We can't just leave them out there, can we?"

"But they took all the weapons."

"Then we starve them out." The flip of Valesco's hands spilled some drops of wine in the stark white carpet, but he took no notice.

"They have prepared for that, building greenhouses on the bases and inside of factories that they cleared out for the purpose."

"Then it will just take longer." Valesco seemed unconcerned.

"There is another issue to the matter." The man shifted nervously.

"And that would be?"

"All of the medicine manufacturing and most of the high-tech manufacturing was either located in or was moved to the protected cities. What couldn't be moved was destroyed. On top of that, the scientists who know how to create the medicines and the engineers who designed the machines were also moved into the cities."

"Then we will import the technology from abroad," Valesco said with a shrug, spilling more wine.

"It appears that a similar effort has been going on around the world. It is most noticeable in eastern Asia, where your efforts appear to be going slower than elsewhere. At least as far as we know."

"That part of the world is a problem, yes. Soon, this country will be ours and we can move in full force to the rest of the world."

"But we will not have the military," the man said pointedly.

"It will not be needed. We have truth on our side." It was late coming, but Valesco failed in suppressing a laugh.

"You say that, but you don't seem to believe it."

"Don't worry, my friend. All will be taken care of in time. We will find a solution to the protected cities. Besides, the truth is written by the winners."

"I hope so." The man made a short bow and exited the room.

Valesco's wine glass flew across the room to shatter against the wall. An attendant looked in from their access door, drew her head back in, and re-emerged with brush and dustpan. Garo entered the room.

"Do you need me?" Garo asked.

"NO! YES! NO! Wait!" Valesco paced the floor, fist pounding in the air. "Why wasn't I told what the heretics were doing in the cities?"

"You said you wanted to concentrate on the election. Plus, there did not appear to be anything we could do about it."

"You know how I *hate* to be surprised!"

"You delegated the responsibility to our mayors. They did what they could."

"Which appears to be nothing! I should have them all shot!"

"Which would accomplish nothing."

Valesco turned on the man and stared hard, but Garo did not waver.

"You appear very calm, given the bad news you deliver."

"We only did as you asked." He gave Valesco a very small shrug.

The stare continued for a few moments, but then Valesco returned to pacing, this time with his arms crossed in front of him. He made several passes back and forth without speaking. Garo remained silent.

"How bad is the medicine situation?" Valesco finally asked.

"Total. They were very thorough. They left some simple things like aspirin, but all the advanced medicines, the biologics, and the medical equipment like diagnostic machines have all been moved. Unless we can take the protected cities, people will be dependent on them for medical treatment."

"We still have doctors, don't we?"

"Yes, but without the medicines, there is only so much they can do."

"And I suppose the cities plan on trading us medicine for food." Resignation filled Valesco's voice.

"It would appear to be the plan. As far as other things go, we have many of the large part manufacturing facilities, but the small part manufacturing, in particular the quantum chips and computer parts, were moved or destroyed. With people being moved to agrarian communes, our needs will not be high in the near future, but eventually we will be forced to trade with the cities for advanced technology, unless we can take the equipment back."

Valesco took a deep breath and started to pace. "And how likely is it that we will be able to take the cities?"

"At this time? Extremely unlikely. If we can get some heavy weapons from overseas, we might have a chance, but the military has been diligent about installing defensive works along the fences. An excessive amount, if you ask me. Plus, they have drones: air, land, and sea."

"Sea?" Valesco's head came around to Garo.

"The list of protected cities relies heavily on coastal locations. Islands were of particular interest because they are easier to protect. With far less coast to protect, the density of sea drones protecting the islands is high."

"You sound like you admire them," Valesco said with a huff.

"I was special forces at one time, so I can appreciate a well-designed defense." Garo shrugged, but only when Valesco wasn't looking.

"So you are supposed to tell me how to defeat these defenses." Valesco used his pumping hand to emphasize the statement.

"My professional opinion," Garo said in a slow, steady pace, "is that at this time, we are not equipped to defeat these defenses. We do not have trained men and we do not have the equipment. To try and force our way into the cities would be foolish and costly. The few minor incidents that have occurred show that the military is more than willing to fire on non-combatants. And since they have non-lethal weapons at their disposal, there is little fallout from using them."

"And if we are able to get heavy weapons from abroad?"

"Unless we acquire them soon, the defenses will be even better. The cities are already constructing layered defenses."

"Where are they getting the money for all this?" The question was much louder than required.

"Money?" Garo's eyebrows went up. "People are scared and more than happy to help construct defenses for a safe place to live and basic necessities. A protected city is becoming one large commune, which makes them infinitely more efficient than the old city."

"Why can't you bring me good news?" Valesco's head was turned up toward the ceiling.

"I bring the news that exists."

"So we must trick the cities into giving up."

"That appears to be our only option at this time." His voice did not convey confidence.

"I will have to think on this matter. Leave me."

"Yes, sir." Garo made a short bow and walked out of the room, smiling for once.

Most of the people who stood outside the security gate in Denver were armed, but only with pistols and rifles, and then older models. They were led by a man in a tailored three-piece suit. The man walked in accordance with his opinion of himself—utter importance.

"I am here to serve a subpoena on Mr. Warrence Donnest on charges of impersonating an officer of the federal government!" The man waved a paper in the air. The view behind the security gate didn't change. "Mr. Donnest and his so-called government is in violation of the laws of the United States of America and will surrender themselves and this facility to the rightfully elected government of the United States!"

The people waited. After some minutes, their vision wavered between each other and the fencing in front of them. A wide, one-meter high wall had been constructed just behind the fence, thick enough to prevent vehicles from ramming their way through the wall. In a few locations, the wall was being extended upwards. The man in the suit stood without wavering or looking away from the gate. His patience was rewarded by the sight of Donnest walking out from behind the security building on the other side of the gate.

"Are you Warrence Donnest?"

"Yes, I am."

"I hereby arrest you in the name of the United States of America."

Donnest held a suppressed laugh. "Do you really expect me to come out there and let you arrest me?"

"I am a duly appointed law enforcement officer of the federal government and a citizen of the U.S. of A. You are either a citizen and also subject to the same laws or a foreign entity in this country illegally and thus subject to arrest."

"I am a citizen of this country, but if you participate in the current government that has set themselves up outside this wall, you are *not!* You have given away your rights and your federal government to a religious organization, from which it is illegal to govern this country. You are a Puritan, sir, and nothing else. Everyone in here are still citizens who hold to the Constitution that formed this country." Donnest stood with his hands clasped behind his back without swaying or motion.

"All laws have been made in accordance with the federally established rule of law…"

"Established rule of law! Hell, man, the federal government no longer has a legislature, a Supreme Court, and almost no powers whatsoever. For all intents and purposes, except for foreign relations, the federal government doesn't even exist anymore! Your warrant is a sham piece of paper with no power behind it and means nothing here."

The man shifted his weight. "I am authorized to use force if required to execute this warrant under my discretion."

"You are welcome to try, but I will warn you. Any use of force against this city or against the people in this city will be met with deadly force." Donnest smiled at the man.

The others in the group outside the gate did not know what happened until it was over. The man in the suit, in one motion, slid his coat from his side, drew a pistol, and fired at Donnest. The particle beam went through Donnest, but appeared to have no effect, as Donnest remained standing with no pain or injury from the shot.

"Do you really think I was foolish enough to appear in person?" Donnest asked.

"A hologram," a voice said from the group as a particle beam came from a security turret, vaporizing a hole into the suit and the man wearing it. The man and pistol fell to the ground as one. The paper he had been holding floated down, carried by the wind a short distance away. The rest of the group only stared. When no other beam appeared, two people walked forward, put a hand under an arm each, lifted the suited man from the ground, and took him and the pistol away. The paper was left to its own devices.

*   *   *

"What was the point of that?" Donnest asked those assembled in the room with him. "It only got a man killed."

"Maybe that was the point," AG Benson Tallenson said. "Get it on the news feeds, show the rest of the country how violent we are or something like that."

"Not like it's going to change anyone's minds," Donnest replied.

"There's still the issue of the unprotected cities," Information Secretary Clentin Carmichael stated. "Maybe it's a warning to them."

"Have we devised any further plans for protecting more cities?" Donnest asked.

"We're concentrating on major ports at the moment," ex-Secretary of Interior and now Secretary of Defense Harrow Adams replied. "Of course, Miami will be our big worry since we have no hold there, but the idea is that if we can control the ports, we can control the import of military equipment, assuming they can get their hands on any. We're looking into options."

"What about the smaller cities?"

"We have dispatched the forces we have available, but it's not enough to cover all of them. The fact is that we will lose some cities if the issue is forced and we have to pick and chose which those will be. Of course, if we knew which ones the Puritans will concentrate on first, it would make things easier." Adams looked at Carmichael.

"At the moment, they don't even have a military, though they have started training camps that appear to be doing just that. They are very short on weapons, relying on civilian weapons at the moment."

"Even with only civilian weapons, they could do a lot of damage to a population," Donnest said. "We have an abundance of weapons. How about dispersing them to the city populations, at least those we have no doubts about?"

"What kind of weapons?" Tallenson looked doubtful.

"Hand-held only with one charge worth of ammo. Maybe we can even rig the weapons so that the charges can't be replaced without destroying the weapon."

"We'll look into it. Arming civilians may only draw attention to them and make them a more urgent target, though. The more isolated a city is, the more likely it will be an initial target."

"That might be true. Have some estimates worked up. We need to take our best guess. Even if we're wrong, at least some places need to be prepared."

Donnest turned and took several steps away. He rubbed the back of his neck with one hand and then walked to the balcony. As he leaned on the railing, he looked at the city around him. New construction was everywhere, but the evidence of overcrowding was also there. Even with no cars on the roads, they were full with foot traffic and improvised carts trying to stay out of the way of trucks hauling material and buses hauling people. He didn't hear the people in the room leave as he watched. One person remained in the room. With soft, quiet steps, Donnest's wife walked up and put her arm around his waist.

"I'm worried about how many we'll leave behind," Donnest said softly.

"We're doing what we can. The government was downsized long before you took the job, particularly the military. If you had twice the forces you have now, you still couldn't save everyone."

"Doesn't make me feel any better."

The woman laid her head on the side of his arm. "At least you started early. Without the last four years, we would have really been in a mess. A few military bases would probably be the only things left and who knows if they would have lasted."

"The one in South Dakota would have," Donnest said with a laugh. "I'm sure of that."

"Fate gives you the people you need when you need them." She gave him a squeeze.

"You and that Hutchisonism of yours," Donnest said with fake derision.

"It's kept me believing in you," she replied with a smile.

"Then I have no objections whatsoever." He bent down and gave her a kiss.

Chapter Thirty-Two
Open Warfare

The naval attack ship *Intercept* edged ever closer to the cargo vessel. Two planes circled overhead, anti-ship missiles clearly visible underneath their wings. The cargo vessel, an older wave-riding hull version, was much slower than the *Intercept*, lacking its tri-hull and anti-friction bubble system. Even so, the ship demonstrated no inclination to slow or vary from its course.

"Cargo vessel *Pilgrim*," Captain Harper said into the bridge interface, "stop your vessel and prepare to be boarded."

After a pause, a voice reply came without a visual accompaniment. "You have no authority to stop this vessel."

"Your vessel will be stopped either voluntarily or by force. I would prefer that you volunteer, but am prepared for the other option." The captain cut the verbal signal.

"Do you think they will force us to fire on them?" his commander asked.

"Depends if he is one of those Puritan true believers or not. Let's hope for their sake they are not." The captain turned toward another crew member. "Is there any evidence that their ship is slowing?"

"No, sir. Their engines have not decreased in speed."

"Commander Amster, explain it to them."

"Forward gun," Commander Amster said, "fire at designated target."

The forward beam projector on the ship emitted a red beam that hit the cargo ship on the rear hull quarter above the waterline. The metal warmed to a red glow, but then the beam stopped, allowing the metal to cool. The weapon had fired for less than a second, but it took much longer for the location on the ship to cool.

"*Pilgrim*," the captain said after turning on the mic to the interface again, "I repeat, stop your vessel or the next shot will penetrate the hull and destroy your engine. There will be no further warnings."

The captain again turned the link to mute and waited, standing with his hands behind his back. No one spoke. After several moments, the captain turned once more to the sensor station.

"Any sign of the ship stopping?"

"Yes, sir. The engines are spooling down."

"Good. Rescue teams can stand down."

"*Intercept*," a voice came over the interface. "Air One. Doors are opening on the vessel."

"Monitor the situation, Air One."

It didn't take long for another report. "*Intercept*, I see a plane inside the hull."

"Air One, if that plane takes off, shoot it down."

The whole bridge crew watched the slowing cargo vessel. Before it stopped completely, a plane rose from under the deck and accelerated across the water. The jet dove, following the plane and pacing its progress. A video taken from Air One showed the jet lining up behind the plane. A red beam came from the jet, hitting the plane's engine. Smoke spewed from the plane while it lost the little altitude it had, crashing into the water. Parts of the plane were ripped off by the impact and thrown ahead and to the side of the main body, which sank below the water as if weighed down significantly.

"*Intercept*, the plane is in the water. I repeat, the plane is in the water and sinking fast."

"Any sign of the crew?" Harper asked.

"Negative, *Intercept*. The plane is almost completely underwater. No sign of the crew. If they aren't out by now, I doubt they'll make it."

"Roger, Air One. Maintain surveillance for five minutes and then return." The captain turned to the commander. "Commander Amster, join the boarding team. Search every inch of that ship and confiscate any weapons."

"Yes, sir." The commander saluted and turned to leave the bridge.

"Any regrets leaving that desk job, Commander?" the captain asked as Amster turned.

"No, sir!" Rebecca responded before leaving the bridge.

"*Pilgrim*," the captain said, once again addressing the interface after activating voice communications, "we are sending a boarding party to your vessel. Cooperate with them or they will use force. Once your vessel is cleared, you may continue to Miami. Comms, switch the interface and call Naval Command so I can report the incident."

"Yes, sir."

"With as few ships as we have, let's hope there aren't many more of these smugglers around."

"Mr. President!" General Samuelson all but burst into the living room. President Donnest and members of the Denver City Council held coffee cups while sitting on sofas. The interruption caused several to rattle their cups and one to hurriedly place it on the coffee table before he shook hot coffee from his hand. The interruption didn't phase Joseph and Worthia as they sat on one of the sofas.

"Yes, General." Donnest held his voice steady with effort.

"A convoy has been sighted traveling toward Boise. We estimate about one thousand armed men inside the vehicles."

"That must be some convoy," one of the city councilors remarked.

"It is."

"What forces do we have in Boise?" Donnest asked, standing.

"One company, about one-hundred and fifty troops, plus officers, sir."

"Can we send them any support?"

"We can send two flights of close-air support crafts, but they don't have the facilities to base in Boise, so their over-target time will be limited."

"Can we take out the convoy before it gets there?"

"Not enough time for the crafts to get there, sir. And exo-fighters fly too fast to be effective on ground vehicles, without taking out a whole lot more, that is."

"Get the CAS going. How close is our nearest reinforcements?"

"It will take at least a day to prepare and get there, sir." Disappointment could be heard in Samuelson's voice and seen on her face.

"Which is exactly the reason Boise was chosen, I am sure. Get those reinforcements moving. We'll just have to hope the company can hold out that long."

"Yes, sir." Samuelson saluted and left at a quick pace. Donnest turned back to the council members.

"I am sorry, but it appears our meeting will have to be postponed."

"We understand completely, Mr. President," a woman said as she stood and straightened her clothes. "Not that I expect there is, but if there is anything we can do, please let us know."

"Thank you, councilwoman. Thank you, Mr. Gint, for coming to help the city with their plans. If you will excuse me, I'm sure I am needed in the situation room."

"Good luck, Mr. President," a man from the group called as the president left. He was joined by an aide as he exited the door.

"We might just need it," Donnest said under his breath as he walked. "Has the cabinet been told?"

"Yes sir," the aide said. "They will meet you in the situation room."

Neither man noticed Joseph and Worthia following them.

No more was said as the president, the path clearing in front of him, made his way down several floors, taking the stairs instead of waiting for an elevator. By the time he entered the situation room, the displays were up, with various views of Boise and the surrounding area. The largest tracked the oncoming convoy, which was approaching the city.

"How did they get so close to the town without our knowing?" Donnest asked.

A man in military uniform turned and answered. "They're using commercial vehicles which took different routes to the city, only combining about thirty miles away when forced to by the roads. Up to that point, it looked like normal traffic."

"I assume the company commander was told as soon as we knew."

"Yes, sir. The company has been deployed, but it obviously cannot cover all the approaches or the whole city."

"So what is our strategy, General?"

Samuelson turned toward the president. "Deploy in depth and slow the attackers as much as possible, inflicting as many casualties as possible without fully engaging. The troops will fall back and take up new positions behind the next layer of defenses while it engages."

"Will that work?"

"The men they will be engaging have less than a year's training, so we think our chances are good."

"Has anyone looked for a second wave?" Harrow Adams asked.

"Yes, we are keeping every view we have on the highways, but have seen nothing."

"What about the smaller roads?"

"There are too many to track. The larger secondary roads will be watched with long-range drones as they achieve position."

"What are our options if there is a second force?" Adams asked.

"Not many," Samuelson said with a resigned voice. "We can't afford to keep dumping troops into Boise even if we had them close enough to move there. The city has no defenses of note and is not high on the list to receive support to create them."

"Is there any way the Puritans could have known that?" Donnest asked.

"I want to say no," Adams replied. "But the lack of defenses is pretty apparent."

"The convoy is approaching the town," a voice called out nearer the displays.

The group turned as a unit to the largest display. The convoy occupied all lanes of US Route 84. As the convoy neared the southwest corner of the town, two large pulsators opened fire on the lead vehicles. Two beams cut holes in two trucks that went through the cab and into the trailer behind it. At first, the trucks lost no speed or direction, but then started to drift to the side of road. The following truck slowed long enough to allow the vehicles to drift off the road into the surrounding ditches.

The pulsators paused only long enough to aim again and fire. One caught a truck in the cab, but missed the trailer behind it. The other scored a gash into the side of a trailer that started at the front and traveled halfway down the trailer. The first tractor swerved, causing the trailer to swing around and roll onto the road. The second truck kept driving as if heedless of the damage done behind it.

The trucks behind the lead vehicles started to trail smoke and skid on the road. The remaining lead vehicle drove directly toward one pulsator. It never made the remaining distance as both weapons concentrated fire on the vehicle, ripping it to multiple parts as the beams vaporized metal in two directions. The weapons then turned back to the braking vehicles.

The smoke obscured only part of the vehicles. All doors on the trailers were open and people were already jumping out to the ditches. The pulsators opened up on the next layer of trucks, but it was clear that with the trucks stopped, the front vehicles would obscure the field of fire against following units. Trailers were vaporized as men jumped from them, some of the men on fire or caught in the fire. The pulsators found the other targets in view, but the destruction at the front of the convoy was reaching maximum value. It was only moments until the pulsators stopped firing and those in the situation room could see from their high view that the weapons were being prepared to be moved. Infantry spread out in front of the weapons, taking shots at targets of opportunity, but the position was not ideal and soon the soldiers and weapons left on vehicles into the city.

"Six down, forty-four left to go," Donnest said with derision.

"At least we've managed to get them out of the vehicles," Samuelson said.

"Until they realize the weapons have been moved."

A repeating scene evolved. The military troops would take up positions, some prepared and some made on the fly, fire on the invading forces, and then move back when casualties would slow down the invaders. The company took far fewer casualties, but the accumulated effect could be seen in smaller defenses at succeeding positions.

The CAS vehicles came into the wider-angle view. After circling a couple of times, they managed to take out several vehicles, but it was clear that being inside a city prohibited effective fire. After only a few runs, the planes left the scene.

"This is painful to watch," Donnest said, his voice sad.

"Yes, but they are doing a good job, Mr. President," Samuelson responded.

"Do they know how much we appreciate what they are doing?"

"Yes, sir, and believe me, they wouldn't want to be anywhere else. And everyone who is not there wishes they could join them. It's all down to the ground troops now, sir."

"Is that a train?" Worthia asked one of the soldiers running the displays.

"Yes. It appears to be a cargo train."

"Is it stopping?"

Firm footsteps from Samuelson approached Worthia. "Who is this girl and why is she in my operations room?"

"Because I can just about guarantee that she is smarter than anyone else in this room." Joseph stepped up to the general between her and Worthia.

"Someone get these civilians out of here!" Samuelson looked around for security.

"Doesn't fifty trucks for a thousand men seem like a very low density of men per truck?" Worthia asked the woman, unphased.

"For your information, girl, they would also be bringing weapons, equipment, supplies, and medical facilities with them." Samuelson had the look of a school teacher scoffing at a student.

"But these are civilians. They won't bring more than their rifles, some ammo, and a cooler of beer and sandwiches." Worthia stood her ground.

"So why bring so many trucks?" Adams asked, drawn into the conversation.

"A distraction." The comment came from Donnest.

"Or a holding action," Worthia added.

"When did you learn about holding actions?" Joseph asked the girl.

"Is the train stopping?" the president asked the soldier at the display.

"It is slowing. At this rate, it will stop just outside of town in about fifteen minutes."

"I need to talk to the officer in charge of that company right away.

What about the CAS? Can they take out the train?" Donnest walked back into the center of the room.

"We can't fire on the train unless we are sure it is hauling troops. By the time we know, the craft won't have enough fuel to make it back to base." The man in blue who answered looked sorry about the information.

"Major Green is on the interface, sir," came a voice. The president turned to the display.

"Mr. President." The woman saluted.

"Major Green, you may need to evacuate very shortly. Have you prepared for this?"

"Yes, sir! But I think we can hold off our attackers, sir, particularly once we fall back to our base."

"Major, you very well might have a much larger force coming in on the other side of town. We'll know in about fifteen minutes."

A look of concern covered the major's face. "Shit," was said softly, but loud enough to be picked up by the mic as Green turned away for a second.

"Listen to me carefully, Major. The most important thing about your evacuation is that no heavy weapons fall into the enemy's hands. You must bring them with you or destroy them. Do you understand?"

"All part of the plan, Mr. President."

"We'll let you know in a few minutes what's happening. Keep this line open."

"Yes, sir." The woman turned away from the monitor. "Fall back to the next position," she said into another interface.

Attention in the room went back to the main display. Samuelson gave Worthia and Joseph a dirty look before returning. When Joseph looked at her, Worthia only shrugged. Time ticked by as they waited on the train to stop. Because the view was from so far off, it was hard to see when the train came to a complete halt, but the soldier at the interface added a number for the train's velocity. It finally hit zero. Once it did, the doors on the train cars opened and people started jumping out.

"Major Green," the president said, "our suspicions on the train have been confirmed. You need to exit the town as soon as possible."

"Understood, sir." The major turned away from view. "Operation E starts now!"

The major disappeared. People started pulling back from the front position. Another screen showed other personnel placing equipment into vehicles from buildings at the base. Just behind the front position, a vehicle sat in the middle of the street. The soldiers ran around by the vehicle, abandoning it in place.

"Isn't that a heavy weapon vehicle?" the president asked.

"Yes, sir," Samuelson said.

"Didn't she understand my instructions?"

"She did, sir. If they are going to destroy equipment, it might as well be put to good use." Samuelson smiled.

Donnest slowly turned from the general to watch the scene. As the soldiers pulled back, the invaders advanced. Dozens moved to the abandoned vehicle, gathering around their prize. The soldiers hurried away and the invaders celebrated. In an instant, the center of the view was replaced by a red glow that quickly grew to a block in diameter. The glow lasted only a few seconds before disappearing, replaced by blackened ground. The men on the far edge ran back they way they had come.

"It will give our troops additional time to evacuate," Samuelson said.

"Plus make the Puritans nervous about approaching any other equipment," Donnest added.

"Yes, sir."

The scene at the company base intensified. Personnel poured in as vehicles were filled and filed out of the parking lot. Once formed, the military convoy stopped only to collect the remaining troops and then headed south by way of a two lane road. Small explosions could be seen at the empty base, mostly producing smoke from the building. Then the few remaining vehicles exploded at the same time.

"I hate abandoning the civilian population," Donnest said.

"With the extra personnel arriving on the train, there is no scenario where our troops could successfully defend the town." Samuelson didn't sound happy making the statement.

"I would suggest that they bring as many as they could with them, but I know we are already crowded, if not overcrowded." Donnest turned from the displays and walked toward Joseph and Worthia. He gave them a little smile. "That was a keen observation, young lady."

"Thank you, sir." Worthia gave him a slight bow.

"I have an opening in my cabinet. I would like you to fill it."

"I… what… I'm not even done with my education yet." Worthia stuttered as her eyes went wide.

"You can finish it here. I need all the best people I can find and I think you are one of them."

"She'll take it," Joseph said.

"Hey! You don't speak for me."

"No, I speak for myself and if the president wants smart people, I want him to pick you." Joseph gave her a generous smile. "Besides, you're an American and you have to do what the president says, right?"

"I think I get to choose on this one," Worthia responded. "Besides, wouldn't the same go for you?"

"Nope," Joseph said with a cheery voice. "I'm Dutch."

"But you married an American," the president added.

"So?"

"According to agreed accords," Donnest continued, "any European who marries an American automatically becomes a dual citizen of both, and vice versa."

"Wait! No one told me about this!" Joseph looked genuinely concerned as his eyes went wide.

"Sorry, that's the law." The president smiled at him.

"I knew getting married was going to bite me in the butt sooner or later," Joseph grumped as Worthia laughed.

Chapter Thirty-Three
Strategic Strike

"We need a win." Donnest paced while everyone else sat. "We're losing towns to the Puritans and it looks bad."

"We only have so many troops," Adams protested. "We can't be everywhere and most of the towns we've 'lost' weren't even garrisoned."

"It's doesn't matter. There is a perception that we are losing the war."

"We knew the Puritans would take everything but the protected cities and islands. Okay," Adams waved his hands, "not knew, but expected. And I don't think that the people in those cities are anything but grateful that they live there."

"I am also talking about perception overseas. If we look like we are going to lose the country, it will affect what happens in other places. If we can at least show a win, we can bolster their view."

"Our forces are spread out too much." Worthia made the statement with confidence. "We need to concentrate them to obtain a clear victory."

"That means we will be protecting less people," the president moaned.

"You can't have it both ways, sir. A victory might also make the Puritans pause at further conquest, particularly if we take out something strategic." Adams was more animated, getting into the conversation.

"But which city do we choose to protect and how long can we do it?" Donnest asked.

"Not protect, take out their assets." Worthia was also getting animated. "Find a store house, ammo dump, or something that not only will be a show of force, but set their efforts back."

"Any ideas?" Donnest stopped pacing and turned toward the group.

"What about their headquarters?" Secretary of State Wo Standington asked.

"They're always occupied. We would have to tolerate civilian causalities, and I mean true civilians." Concern over the suggestion was written over Adams' face.

"We're not going to do that. It would allow our enemies to condemn us as the worst kind of people. We need to pick another target and a significant one." Donnest went back to pacing.

"A training camp," Adams said.

"Yes, the largest one," Worthia added.

"Where is that?" Donnest asked.

"California, outside of Los Angeles." Adams started to grin. "Within range of the San Diego base. Everyone there should be a valid military target."

"I want a plan by tomorrow. Dismissed."

"This will give the bastards something to think about," Adams said as they left the room.

"How can you use 'innocent civilians' and 'training camp' in the same sentence?" Wenk asked, brow furrowed.

"When you don't care about the truth." Joseph did not even look at the display, raising his beer for another drink.

"I mean, doesn't that just make you sound stupid?"

"You heard the don't care part, right?"

Wenk put the bottle to his lips but still watched the display, seeming to ignore the comment. His stare at the display was complete.

Joseph decided to change subjects. "What the heck did they use, anyway?"

"Looks like cluster bombs. Shit! They took out everything down to the dirt! Do you really think they killed five thousand people?"

"Probably an inflated number. I would guess more like two thousand at most, but heck, what do I know?"

"You figured out what made that laser of ours tick, that's for sure."

"Particle beam," Joseph corrected.

"Whatever." Wenk waved him off and shook his head. "The advances of science that count on people doing things wrong are historic."

"Science doesn't count on it, it's just that people tend to do things wrong all the time and every once in a while, something is done wrong right, as probability dictates it should." Joseph waved his bottle back and forth as he talked.

"Are you drunk?" Wenk looked away from the display and toward his friend.

"No, just working on it."

"Did I miss a holiday or something?"

"Just giving my brain the night off. It deserves it." Joseph took another long swallow.

"There's something wrong, I can feel it." Wenk turned his chair back toward Joseph and straddled the chair. "Tell me. You having trouble with Mercedes?"

"Mercedes?" Joseph acted surprised at the question, looking at Wenk through the top of his eyes. "If there was problems there, I would most likely be dead."

"So what is it?"

Joseph took another long pull on his drink before answering, finishing the bottle. He set it down on the table, but it tipped over and rolled around before coming to a stop against the others.

"I'm just tired of people killing each other, is all." Joseph's head went back over the rear of the chair.

"You're living in the wrong age for that, friend." Wenk chuckled and shook his head. "People out there are dedicated to killing others, particularly us, in case you haven't noticed." Wenk touched his bottle to Joseph's arm.

"Did I start all this?"

Wenk spit out the beer he had started to drink. "What?"

"Did I start all this killing?"

"How would you have done that?" Wenk's head cocked to one side and his eyes narrowed.

"You know, those people out in front of the base."

"Please, you can't be serious." Wenk added a laugh to the statement.

"I wanted something to start and it did, didn't it?"

"Get over yourself." Wenk gave him a wave as he took a drink. "This was going to happen with or without you. Or do you think Valesco was just sitting in his office thinking, 'You know, if Gint would just start a riot, I could get my evil scheme started'? Give me a break."

Joseph stared up at the ceiling for a while. He started getting dizzy, so he brought his head back around.

"You're right. They had plans long before that. They had to. Just sometimes it feels like I started all this."

"Well, if you want to blame someone for that," Wenk waved his beer at the display, "it was probably Worthia's idea."

The comment sent Joseph into a sputtering laugh. He ended up coughing onto the floor, head down.

"I bet you're right. That is just the sort of thing she would dream up. Zero risk, maximum effectiveness." Joseph laughed some more, holding his belly.

"Have you heard from her?" Wenk's question had an anxious note in it.

"Me? If anyone would have, it would be you, won't it?" Joseph looked at his friend, questioning.

"Barely. Says the president and studies keep her busy. Not like we can have much of a relationship so far away. Guess it was good while it lasted." Wenk's head bowed, then he took a long drink of his own.

"Hey, if I know one thing, it's that if Worthia thinks you are worth it, she'll be back. That girl doesn't let anything stand in her way."

"But how will I know?" Wenk spread his arms.

"Has she told you that you two are done?"

"Ah, no."

"Then you're good, for now at least. You could always ask for some time and go see her. She'd like that."

"But how do I know when is a good time?"

Joseph leaned closer. "For that much effort, it's always a good time. Now I think I need to get home before I can't. Or you con me into a game of darts I can't get out of." Joseph slapped his friend's knee and then stood up.

"The wife waiting on you?"

"No, they're at some play-date thing, whatever that is. Not like the kid doesn't play all the time as it is. That's what Mercedes calls it when the place gets trashed."

"As long as the kid cleans it up," Wenk said nonchalantly.

"Really? Man, have you got a lot to learn. Tomorrow, guy."

"Tomorrow." Wenk watched him go, half to make sure Joseph walked steadily. "Just leave the lonely bachelor all on his own. That's fine, I'm used to it. Not like I can't entertain myself, you know. Even if it's Thursday and there's no game running tonight. Dang." Wenk shook his head. "I need a new hobby."

The fist slammed into the display. The display was interrupted for a moment, but the hologram was restored as soon as the fist was removed, still showing the destruction of the training base.

"Don't they have anything else to talk about?" Valesco grumbled. "It's been more than a day."

"I could tell them to change their story to something else." Garo lifted an eyebrow.

"That would make them only more suspicious and while we control the media, there are still some that can't control their own curiosity." Valesco walked away from the displays. "I tire of this conflict. It goes too slow."

"We are making steady progress. The fact that we started from scratch on troops added time to the process..."

"The process is going too slow!" Valesco slammed his hands down on his desk.

"The resources we are using in this country and the effort we are using to move the headquarters to Jerusalem are slowing our progress overseas..."

"We still haven't taken America yet!"

"We are slowly acquiring larger weapons from multiple sources, but we still do not have any armored vehicles or…"

"We need to do something big." Valesco straightened from leaning on the desk. "How many men do we have trained?"

"Fifteen thousand at the moment. Another ten thousand will be ready by next spring…"

"We need to take Denver."

Garo stood, dumbstruck, looking at the man. "Denver? You can't be serious."

"If we take Denver and the rebel government, the other cities will lose their will to resist. Plus, it will remove any legitimacy that they enjoy with the other countries."

"I'm not debating the benefits, I'm questioning our ability to take the city. Past confrontations have resulted in large casualties…"

"It doesn't matter." Valesco's hand made a sweeping gesture. "We will be moving the headquarters soon and I want Denver taken by the time I leave."

"If we lose a large number of troops during the assault, we wouldn't be able to replace them for several years and it will hurt further recruitment."

"I want Denver! Take it and do it soon!" Valesco was actually shaking.

"Yes, sir. I will make arrangements right away." Garo bowed his head so Valesco couldn't see his eyes.

"Good!" Valesco turned away from Garo, who walked out of the room as fast as he could without looking hurried.

Not acknowledging the assistant outside the office, Garo made his way to his office and closed the door. He started toward his chair, but then diverted to the window. He looked out over Des Moines and the fields in the distance.

"He doesn't care. He doesn't care how many people die in an attempt doomed to fail. Or how much it will set back our efforts to consolidate this country." Garo looked out over the city silently for a while. "Maybe he deserves the loss. He's the one who wanted things 'interesting,' wasn't he? But now that they are, he's frustrated and distracted by his move to Jerusalem so he can be ready for the aliens when they return, presenting himself as king of the world. As if they'd respect that."

Garo put his hands behind his back and rocked on his heels. "So, Mr. Valesco, I will give you what you want. I will arrange an assault on Denver. It will take months, but just about the time you are moving, it will happen. And when we fail, what will you do? Run off to Jerusalem? Blame me?"

The statement caused Garo to pause. He tapped his hands behind his back for a moment, not looking out the window.

"I need a contingency plan. I need something so I don't go down with this debacle." Garo continued to ponder. "I need a patsy. No problem, we have plenty of those. And I need an excuse not to be there. That all should be relatively easy to arrange. We are having trouble with the WPC anyway. It might need my personal attention very soon."

Chapter Thirty-Four
Demonstration and Acting

Fidgeting, Joseph stood in front of the multi-view holographic camera. Behind him was a large block of material. It didn't help that it was cold outside for April with a strong early-morning wind, the reason for the thermal insulating jacket. He was sure he could see a cloud with every breath as a constant reminder. Finally, the light on the camera turned green and the 'eye' holding it nodded.

"Welcome, one and all. My name is Joseph Gint, which you hopefully already know, and we are here to demonstrate our latest particle projection weapon, which I like to call the Particle Drill, for reasons to soon be evident.

"Behind me is our target. A combination half a meter of every type of damage resistant material known to man." Joseph stepped aside and waved at the block. "This block is made of metal, ceramic, and organics. Over here," Joseph waved at the weapon ten meters away, "is the particle drill. A little crude at the moment, but, as you will see, it gets the job done. Let's retire to the bunker, shall we?"

Followed by the eye, Joseph headed to the bunker, still talking. "As you know, particle beams are not visible, so we have added an external color, one I personally selected and I think you will enjoy. There is no real need to move to the bunker and look through three inches of quartz glass, since there is no leakage or radiation effects, but regulations are regulations."

With the door closed, the eye took up a position with a view of

Joseph and the target outside. The control panel in the room had a standard interface and one big red button.

"The demonstration is programmed, so all we have to do is hit the button. My addition to the controls, by the way. Thought it would add to the drama. The timer is set for a three-point-eight-six second burst. Are we ready? Let's light this puppy!"

Joseph walked over to the panel, put his hand on the button, and pushed. A glittery-gold beam came from the weapon. Smoke came from the target. A sizzle could be heard and a fire erupted on the organic material target layer. Soon, the golden light disappeared and Joseph turned back to the eye.

"Shall we go view the result?" Leading the way, Joseph exited the bunker and walked toward the target. "Remember, this target would prevent penetration from all known ballistic rounds and take minutes, if not hours from normal particle beams used today of the same size. Let's check our target after less than four seconds of the particle drill."

Walking around the target, the eye showed the front, where a hole approximately two centimeters wide appeared. When it panned to view the back plate, a hole less than half a centimeter showed, the organic material still smoking.

"And that is why I like to call it the particle drill!" A large smile appeared on Joseph's face. "But, ladies and gentleman, there is more. We must answer the rumors of this weapon being able to destroy the wing material used previously by the aliens. Wenk, if you please!"

Carrying a frame with a small sample held in the middle, Wenk brought the wing material while two others brought the stand for the frame. Placed and assembled in seconds, the camera view joined the four away from the target.

"Now, according to procedure," Joseph said as the others walked away, "we should be inside the bunker for this test, but since the weapon will only be on for zero-point-twelve seconds, let's just get on with it."

Sporting a smile, Joseph raised his interface and said, "Execute." The beam from the weapon was brief. The reaction by those entering the bunker was dramatic.

"What?! What the hell?!" came from Wenk. "Joseph!"

"Let's examine the sample, shall we?" The camera followed Joseph after a pause and more encouragement from Joseph, finally focusing on the wing sample. A clear view of a hole showed in the material with the edges still glowing.

"And thus we have our demonstration. We are currently working on optimizing the design of the weapon for minimal size and maximum efficiency." Joseph walked around the bunker, removing his distraught companions from the background. "I am sure that some of you have heard that we have a power issue, apparently experiencing less power output than input to the weapon. This issue has been resolved. The power output from the weapon was being incorrectly measured. All power usage is now accounted for and within normal parameters.

"Thank you for joining us for our demonstration. I want to thank all the researchers here at Revelation Base for their hard work in helping make this happen. It has been a true team effort. I also want to thank Commander Bennett for his support. Without—"

"We're out," the camera man announced.

"Hey! You cut my credits short!" Joseph huffed.

"No one was listening anyway." The man started moving camera eyes to their stored position.

"Well," Joseph said, throwing up his hands, "no one can blame me if they didn't get credit then."

"What the hell did you think you were doing?!" A lieutenant walked around the bunker.

"There was no danger," Joseph said, dismissing the man. "Besides, it added a little drama."

"We don't do drama here, we do safe!" The man was breathing harder than normal and his finger was waving at Joseph. "This is going into my report."

"I won't expect anything different." Joseph rolled his eyes. "Am I done here or do you need me to oversee moving the weapon back to the research building?"

"I think you've done quite enough." The man turned back toward the test stand.

"He must be new here." The flippancy in Joseph's voice was thick as he started back toward the buildings.

"You could have warned me," Wenk said with insistence as he caught up.

"And miss that reaction? No way!" A laugh accompanied the statement.

"One of these days, you're going to go too far."

"I'm pretty sure I know how far too far is and I make sure I stay away from it. On to more important questions. How was my performance? I didn't embarrass myself somehow I wasn't aware, did I? Mercedes fussed over me for an hour and I really don't want to hear from her that I messed up for days."

Wenk looked at him for a while as if debating within himself. Sighing, he said, "No, not that I saw. I'd love to say you did just to torture you, but I'm sure you'd watch the record if I did."

"You know me so well. You want lunch? I'll buy."

"Kind of early, isn't it?"

"Being on camera makes me hungry. Wings?"

Chapter Thirty-Five
Assault on Denver

Fifteen thousand people could not be hidden from sight and no one tried. The attackers stood as if the sight would instill fear in the inhabitants of Denver. Four thousand were assigned to each of the two secondary approaches. A clearing had been made for two hundred yards outside the gate and walls by the defenders. The troops had been stationed in front of the main gate and into the surrounding city past the clearing. The defenses had continued to be improved every day even while the attackers arrived. A three meter high, one meter thick wall stood behind the fence. Defensive turrets could be seen on the tops of buildings behind the wall. No defenders could be seen, but the few overhead pictures showed that they were there, waiting.

Men took their stations four hundred meters in front of the gate. The strategy appeared to be simple—overwhelm the defenses. The men had been subjected to talks for months on the enemy's treason, his torture of the faithful, and the promise of God's reward. Most had been anxious for blood after viewing the attacks by the heretics on the training camps and depots. The number of civilian deaths claimed had been high. It was time for the heretics to pay for their sins.

Inside the city, all was quiet. The preparations by highly trained personnel had not taken long. Surveillance cameras were everywhere to track the enemy, even outside the city walls. Satellite coverage had been arranged and drones were on standby.

"We should attack first," Adams said as he stood next to Donnest.

"No, they must attack first. We can't be accused of starting this battle." They stood in a room set up with three walls of displays that monitored all directions. The military commanders had a separate room with a direct communication link to the president. The entire cabinet and the mayor of Denver stood in the room, everyone too nervous to sit in the provided chairs except Worthia, now Secretary of the Interior. Not only did she sit, but she sipped a drink casually held in her hand. Wo Standington walked over to stand next to her.

"How can you be so calm?" Wo asked.

"Since they wouldn't give us guns, not much we can do unless the Puritans make it all the way to this building, which I consider highly doubtful." Worthia swirled the liquid around in her glass.

"If they get that far, we're dead." The nervousness in Wo's voice could not be missed.

"Speak for yourself. I don't plan to just stand around and let anyone shoot me."

"And what are you going to fight with?"

"This chair if I need to." Worthia took another sip.

The Puritan troops in front of the main gate started moving. A few moments later, the troops at the other locations started moving.

"When they hit the clearing, assuming they haven't fired before then, our defense will open up." Adams shifted the weight on his feet. "They were informed about the no-go zones and the local population has known about it for months."

"Will two hundred meters be enough to stop them?" Donnest asked.

"It will be enough to cause massive casualties. The turrets are all rapid fire units and set to kill. No need to worry about people getting back up and fighting. The men on the walls have assault rifle models. Some have slug throwers for visual effect."

"The general told me about that. They will create a mess."

"That's the idea. Give them something to think about."

"I'm surprised we had any." Donnest's eyes flared.

"Every type of weapon has its purpose, Mr. President." Adams' statement was made without emotion.

The troops approaching the front gate went from a walk to a slow jog and then a half-run. Unit cohesion started to suffer, but no one seemed to mind. At three hundred meters, the troops let out a cheer, raising their weapons over their heads. The captains tried to get the men back into line, but a close-up of faces showed rampant enthusiasm. The attempts were ignored by the charging men. The thickness of the troops running down the road grew as more men filled in behind the initial ranks from other roads and the staging area. It was an impressive sight, encouraging to the officers behind them and frightening to the people in the room.

At two hundred meters, some of the attackers made a mistake. They starting firing their weapons at the gates and the turrets on the walls. The shots, fired while running, were wild and uncoordinated, causing no real damage. In response, the turrets on the fence and the wall that had direct line of sight of the attacks opened up. Rapid staccato blue beams shot from the weapons to the troops. The weapons higher on the wall fired into the crowd, leaving the front line attackers for the fence weapons.

Men started to fall in the front ranks. Those behind them took no notice except to jump over the bodies and run faster. One man tripped over a body and fell face-first. The fall saved him from weapon fire, but not the feet of those coming behind him. When the crowd cleared the buildings, more turrets were activated by the command computer and opened fire in their designated fields. Some fired down streets one block over. The number of bodies lying on the ground rose quickly.

On the north side of the city, as soon as the fence turrets started firing, thirty aerial drones flew over the wall. Flying erratic patterns, the drones fired into the oncoming crowd. People fell at an alarming rate. Small missiles rose from behind the assaulting troops. Most missed the drones, but a few found their targets. Drones exploded above the troops, which did not help the crowd's progress. Weapons on top of the wall targeted the firing locations of the missiles. Explosions indicated the presence of more missiles that would never be fired.

On the south side of the city, the charge was only met by fence turret fire. Encouraged, the attackers charged at full speed. When they reached one hundred meters, four tubes appeared above the fence. A rushing sound could be heard from the tubes. When the attackers reached fifty meters, streams of fire, thick and gel-like, flowed from the tubes, sweeping the attackers. The streams arced over one hundred meters from the tubes. Everything caught by the gel-like flame ignited: people, weapons, walls, buildings, even the ground. The approach soon became an inferno of fire. The troops behind the inferno stopped and retreated.

"Plasma throwers," Adams said as he watched with Donnest.

"Nasty things." Donnest shook his head.

"Never been used before. They were designed for jungle combat, but as you can see, they are effective in urban combat also."

"Won't that start a lot of building fires?"

"Yes, but that will help prevent further attacks. We're pretty sure the buildings were evacuated, but without going through them floor by floor, we can't be one hundred percent positive."

"Casualties of war?" The question had elements of an accusation.

"There are always casualties." Adams paused. "How many will there be if those Puritans get inside this city to do what they want?"

"Thousands. Tens of thousands." Donnest's voice was resigned.

"At least."

"I never was a combat soldier. I wasn't even security. My specialty was cyber warfare. It wasn't messy like this is."

"If it makes you feel any better, Mr. President, no one wants this, but we also must protect those inside, our friends and family included."

"I know. Doesn't mean I won't have nightmares."

"Soldiers have nightmares, Mr. President."

When the attackers reached twenty meters from the front wall, the soldiers kneeing behind the wall threw grenades into the oncoming crowd. As the grenades reached just above the crowd, they bloomed into balls of energy. At first, the energy blocked the view of anyone caught inside the ball. As it faded, bodies were revealed, burned into charred lumps. The explosions caused the men behind them to pause. It was an amateur mistake, giving the turrets more time to target the attackers. The larger turrets on the wall swept the accumulating crowds, digging gouges into the ground as they swept across.

The total effect was too much for the attackers, particularly when the soldiers with slug-throwers opened up and blood and gore started to spray over their fellow troops. Those in the front started to push those behind them backwards or out of the way. Some ran back into the buildings they had passed, others ran down alleys or entered gaps in the buildings. The turrets kept firing as people tried to hide, gouging large holes into buildings. Those retreating back up the street suffered the worst. By the time the survivors made it back to their starting position, the street was carpeted with men. Some still moved, but most didn't.

As the turrets stopped firing, exo-fighters roared overhead, followed by close-air support. Fire from the planes started to fall farther from the city walls.

"What's the estimate of their casualties?" Donnest asked.

"Fifteen hundred." Adams pointed at a number near the bottom of the display.

"Damn. And that's just at the front gate."

"Yes. The overall estimate is approximately three thousand. And counting."

"Shit! Don't these guys know when they have lost?"

"Apparently not."

As they talked, two missiles streaked from off the screen toward the front gate. One was interrupted by a beam and blew up. The second made it to the gate, which was enveloped by flames and smoke. The wall turrets responded by firing at the launch locations.

When the smoke and flames cleared, the front gate was a wreck of twisted metal. As they watched, one side fell to the ground. Explosive bolts activated and the remaining gate flew from the support and clattered to the ground.

A cheer was heard from the attackers, thousands of voices at once. People ran from the buildings, streets, alleys, and anywhere they had taken cover, heading for the gate. More troops came from the flanks of the attackers in vehicles, non-combat varieties modified to hold weapons and troops. The vehicles drove down side roads between buildings, heedless of anyone on foot who may be using the roads, firing as they came.

From out of the gates came land drones, tracked vehicles each with a turret occupied by a heavy pulsator and two small pulsators. The drones came out two abreast, turning toward the lanes of approach of the enemy vehicles. Firing down the roads, the drones turned the attackers' vehicles into wheeled lumps of hot metal. Ammunition on the vehicles exploded, pelting those standing near them. The results were more dramatic than the fence turrets. Men ran back into the buildings, screaming. The drones pushed the vehicle remains out of the way using their front armor and continued toward the enemy camp. Some turned down other roads, directed by central command to identified targets.

The drones gone, men looked cautiously from their cover. The emptiness inside the gate made a tempting sight, but none moved. Then something moved inside the gate. A large tracked vehicle moved from behind the wall and took up a position in front of the opening. Turning, it aimed its large-bore weapon, half a meter in diameter, down the road as if daring anyone to challenge it.

"They won't really fire that thing, would they?" Donnest asked.

"If they have to," Adams replied.

"A satellite killer?" Worthia asked from the position she had taken up behind the president. She turned to Adams. "Do you know what that thing would do if they fired it?"

"Cause a line of destruction not seen since a comet scored the earth tens of thousands of years ago? Yes, I do, but we can't be choosy here. It would take a real idiot to charge that thing and with the turrets still active, we don't think they will try it. If they did, I doubt it would take more than one shot to convince them otherwise. Besides, right about now they are occupied with the land drones. See?"

Adams pointed at a display taken from an elevated angle. The land drones were causing havoc among the attacking troops and their support systems. All three weapons on the drones fired almost continually. Fires started in multiple places. Confusion was rampant, added by the lack of training. Troops that tried to fire at the fast-moving drones tended to hit their own men instead of the drones.

The planes concentrated on the larger targets, which disappeared quickly. The exo-fighters stayed only briefly. The CAS circled above in case they were needed. The few missiles fired at the planes were easily defeated by counter-measures.

"How much longer can they hold out?" Donnest asked. He looked at the casualty estimation, which had hit six thousand. All three attacks had been driven away from the city.

"With fanatics, there's no way to know." Adams stood and watched.

"Maybe you should offer amnesty for any who lay down their arms and surrender," Worthia offered.

"Amnesty! Are you mad?!" Adams turned to her, hate evident in his eyes. "These fanatics have attacked and killed people! The have stolen, desecrated, burned, and ruined lives! They don't deserve mercy! They deserve to be wiped out!"

"What are you going to do, kill every Puritan in the whole country?" Worthia's voice was calm in comparison.

"If we have to!"

"Mr. President," Worthia said in a even voice as she turned back to Donnest, "we have won this fight, but there is no way we are taking back the whole country. We should use this victory to make the Puritans come to terms. Recover some of the cities or at least make sure they remain free of the Puritans. We can show that we are not the blood-thirsty demons I am sure they paint us as. We can come to an arrangement. Then we can use our technology to slowly regain the other cities. Maybe, over time, people will tire of the church and come to their senses."

"You can't be serious!" Adams waved his arms above his head.

"No, she's right. Harrow, we've all been afraid today, but we have to do what's right for the country, not just what we want to. That means doing what's right for those people outside the walls." Donnest raised his interface. Samuelson's face appeared on a display. "General, make an announcement that we will accept the surrender of anyone who lays down their arms. They will be given amnesty and allowed to return to their homes."

"Are you sure, Mr. President?" Samuelson looked dumbstruck.

"Yes. Call back the drones and the planes and contact their commander and ask for his surrender."

"And if he doesn't?"

"Have a drone take him out and then ask the next guy down the line."

"Yes, Mr. President." Samuelson turned and the display changed views.

"I still wish they'd let me speak in person."

"No way, Mr. President," Adams responded, though the comment was not directed toward him. "Too risky. They are setting up the holo display now."

"Feels a little impersonal."

"That's the point."

The woman running the holo-camera fussed with his setup, ignoring the discussion like a good soldier. After another five minutes, she looked encouragingly at the president. Straightening himself, Donnest cleared his throat and watched for the soldier's prompt, which came after a few more minutes.

"I know you have been told not to trust me," Donnest started, tension in his voice, "and I am sure you have been told awful things about us. This battle was not my idea or anyone's inside this city. We do not glory in seeing so many dead Americans. We do not want war, only to live as we choose, just as you do. We wish to live in peace. That is what I am asking for now.

"If you lay down your arms and swear not to take up arms against us again, you will be free to leave and return home. You may also find any bodies of friends or relatives and take them with you. We will provide passage on any out-bound trains traveling in the right direction. Any surviving vehicles which brought you can also be used after being stripped of weapons." Donnest's voice had started to ease, his body more relaxed.

"I still consider everyone in this country Americans. None of us benefit from fighting each other. All of us benefit by finding some kind of arrangement that allows us to live with each other. You call us heretics and we call you fanatics. Those are only names, words to convey meaning. *Biased* meanings. I only ask for what this country was founded for: respect of other people not based on what they believe or where they come from, but in spite of what they believe or where they come from. Does not the Bible teach love and tolerance in the New Testament? Or do you prefer the society of retribution shown in the Old?

"This government will halt all attacks on Puritan bases as of this moment, but if attacks on cities resume, our attacks will resume. You have lost many weapons today, and we will do all we can to make sure you do not acquire the weapons required to defeat us. Further warfare would only cause many more casualties. Do you want more friends and family members to die? I do not and hope you do not also." Pleading and firm at the same time, Donnest's hands started to motion with his words.

"Take this message back to your leaders. We do not want war and are willing to negotiate a truce, if not a peace. If not, further deaths will be on your leaders' heads. Hold them responsible where the responsibility is due."

The holographic display was turned off. From the monitors, Donnest, deflating, and the others watched the crowds begin to stir. Slowly, most made their way to the waiting military personnel.

"What if some of them don't take the pledge?" Worthia asked.

"Let's see how many that is. Hopefully it won't be many. If nothing else, we can put them to work cleaning up the mess outside. Once that is done, we'll probably let them go too. We don't need the responsibility of feeding and caring for them long term."

"And the people outside of the wall? What about their damaged property?"

"They can take that up with the church, though I would be surprised if it did much for them, given how badly they lost."

"Should we do anything if they don't?" The question from Worthia seemed to imply an answer. Donnest nodded his head.

"We can think about that when it happens. I don't want to make any promises, but I'm not a monster either." Donnest grinned.

"It would also go a long way to raise our stock with the locals." Worthia raised an eyebrow.

"True, particularly if not with the greater church." Donnest looked at the displays and then turned to the group. "I think we can leave the rest of the events today with the military. Everyone, go home and get some rest. We might need it tomorrow."

People started to slowly filter out of the room. Most took one last look at the displays as if expecting something to happen at the last moment. Most looked relieved. Many looked like they needed a stiff drink. The mayor came up and shook Donnest's hand, thanking him for what the military had done. The last to remain was Worthia, who waited for all to leave before speaking.

"Thank you for listening to me."

"You gave sound advice."

"I know I didn't show much emotion, but the sight sickened me. So many dead." Worthia looked down with unfocused eyes.

"It sickened me too. If we keep doing this, we will tear our country apart. We have to find another way." Donnest continued to look at the monitors as if unable to look away.

"You don't think the protected cities can stand on their own?"

"They could, but our country would be much less than it is today. It would also be ripe for losing large parts to other countries who survive the Puritans in better shape."

"You mean the WPC? I really don't think they would do that." Worthia sounded confident, but with a new worry, looking back up at the president.

"They might not claim land, but they could take over economically in areas while we are trying to just survive. Shishiho has shown no inclination to do so, but a target that is too tempting might change that."

"Of course," Worthia said, nodding. "Is there anything I can do for you right now?"

"Get some rest," Donnest said with a laugh. "I might need more good ideas tomorrow."

"One a day is all I promise," Worthia said as she turned to leave the room. "Any more than that and you're pressing your luck."

"One a day I will take."

"And if you don't ask for one, you can't take a raincheck," she said as she reached the door.

"Darn! Now you're getting picky."

"HOW COULD YOU HAVE LET THIS HAPPEN!" Valesco was shouting at the display. "WHY WEREN'T YOU THERE!"

"I put one of your hand-picked generals in charge while I attended to the difficulties in the WPC." Garo was uncharacteristically calm while facing the shouting man. It may have had something to do with the fact that they were on opposite sides of the Earth.

"This is a disaster! Do you know how long it will take to recover from this?"

"I told you not to do this, but you insisted. I predicted this outcome, but you ordered the attack to happen. I provided all the equipment and men we had, but it wasn't enough."

Valesco's eyes stared daggers at Garo, but he did not flinch. Huffing, Valesco clenched his fists.

"You seem to have recovered a large amount of moxie, my friend. You forget who is in charge of this church. I can destroy you and replace you with another in a matter of hours. At my word, I can have you exiled or killed, as I wish. You should be quivering in fear!"

"No, I don't think so." Garo started pacing in front of the display, not looking at it. "You see, when you were so busy preparing to move to Jerusalem, I was making changes of my own. Even more than before, all of your special operation units are under my control, except the few that you took as your personal bodyguard. That means the chances of you ordering my execution are, like, nil.

"Now, I can't remove you as head of the church and I won't want to. Everyone listens to you and I will never be able to replace you. But I can take America from you. In fact, I already have. You could try to tell the churches here that you have excommunicated me, but I already have systems in place to edit your broadcasts, so it won't get through. You can have the rest of the world, I only ask for this one country. Be happy with that deal."

"What?! You can't dictate to me! I am Valesco! I run this church. It does as I say!"

"No, I did as you said. And now I don't." Garo turned back to the monitor. "If you try to take America from me, we will start our own church. I have the men in place to take out pastors loyal to you and replace them with ones loyal to me. You would be surprised at how much loyalty you can buy, but then, maybe you wouldn't." The statement came with a sideways nod of the head. "If you force my hand, people will disappear. If not, they can continue as they are. It's your call."

Valesco steamed for a while, but then his face changed and he started to laugh. The laughter grew louder, his head flew back, and his arms went around his body as if to hold it together. It took a few minutes for the laughter to subside.

"Garo, Garo, how you have grown. Who would have thought that my shy little minion would have grown to become a man of force! I am so proud of you." Valesco wiped his eyes of tears. "Of course you can have America. I have moved on to greater things, greater challenges. I would say I am sorry to leave you with such a mess, but I am eager to see what you do with it."

"You know," Garo said without changing expression, "I still can't tell when you are serious, but I'll take it. If you need to think of this as your idea, then go ahead."

"Well, my friend," Valesco said, slapping his hands together, "I have a lot to do and you have a lot of funerals to attend. Make sure you treat those families good, their men were martyrs for our cause, as I will be announcing in my next speech. Just wanted to warn you it was coming. I will also name you as the head of our American church branch. Quite frankly, you are welcome to it. I foresee more success in Europe and Africa myself. The Middle East will be stubborn, but I expect that once we have them on board, they will be our best asset."

With a single wave, the display went blank. Garo stood and stared at the wall now visible with the display off. Eventually, he turned away.

"Jerk."

Chapter Thirty-Six
Endgame

The room could have been designed by Frank Lloyd Wright. Three sides were glass that gave a view of pine trees with snow-capped mountains on one side and a pristine lake on the other. The fourth wall was glass except for the large double doors of red-stained wood. The table was a dark walnut with irregular edges. Only four chairs were placed at the table, two on each side. They were glide-chairs with thick-padded red velvet linings. To one side was a smaller, plain table that held drinks and glasses of lead crystal. Nothing was allowed on the main table, as if someone feared the negotiators would throw the items at each other.

Waiting at the far side of the table with a view of the door was Garo. He was dressed in a silk, three-piece suit tailored to every curve of his body. The silk was a dark gray with black pinstripes barely discernible. He had let his hair grow and now it came to just above his shoulders, parted on his left side. His hands were clasped together in a position of waiting.

A young woman appeared in the hallway and walked toward the door. She was alone, which caused Garo to tilt his head and furrow his brow. Walking through the door, the woman strode to the table and occupied one of the chairs on the opposite side. Garo looked back to the hallway, but no one else could be seen.

"Good morning, Mr. Garo," the woman said in an even, clear voice. "My name is Worthia Kerala."

"You're the Secretary of the Interior." It was a half-question. "Why would they send the Secretary of the Interior?"

"This is a matter interior to the United States, so it falls in my purview." Worthia removed a three-centimeter dome covered in black mesh from her pocket. "Do you mind if I record our discussion?"

Garo laughed. "No, not at all. Do they think you will distract me with your looks?"

"I have the full confidence of the President of the United States and have been given full power to negotiate this 'temporary cease-fire,' as you put it." Placing the dome on the table between them, Worthia looked the man in the eye. "I must ask you, for my own curiosity, why this is only a temporary measure and not a peace negotiation?"

"Valesco is still the head of the church." Garo straightened himself. "He has stated that there will be no peace negotiated with the heretics. Thus, until he states otherwise, which I won't count on, or dies, there will be no negotiated peace."

"I understand. One item before we start." Worthia took in a small breath and looked at the table for a second. "I shall refer to your group as Puritans and everyone else as Citizens. I would rather avoid name calling such as heretics or fanatics. It will not further our conversation."

Garo smiled and looked at Worthia for a few seconds. "Agreed."

"Also, to be clear, we are here to discuss the conditions under which both of our sides will institute and continue a halt to all hostilities, armed and otherwise, and attempts to acquire territory, towns, cities, or any other property or people who do not voluntarily join the other faction. If either side violates these conditions, the other is free to re-open hostilities without warning. Agreed?"

"Agreed."

"Good, then we can begin."

"I would like to begin with what your government is offering to us." Garo leaned forward and placed his palms on the table. "If you are offering nothing, then I see no reason to hold these discussions."

Worthia took a deep breath and straightened her back. "I have a list of what we are offering. We will not offer more, only less if pushed.

"First, we will defend the national borders of North America, defined as what is known as the United States, Canada, Alaska, Hawaii, and the islands considered to be owned by America and Canada, from all external military threats and acts of aggression. This shall include any attack by sea, air, or military movement over land. This will not include the movement of non-military personnel, criminals, contraband, or other such activities. We will not police your laws."

"We do not expect or desire you to do so." Garo gave a slow nod.

"Secondly, we will represent the United States and Canada in all negotiations and conferences with other entities not represented by a church that deal with military matters."

"Reasonable, since you hold all the weapons." Garo gave the briefest of shrugs.

"Thirdly, we will establish and maintain medical treatment centers outside each of our cities for use by any Puritan who wishes treatment. In areas that require such, we will establish more than one. A record of expenses, reasonable expenses, will be kept and repaid by trade goods such as food, material, and finished goods requested by the city." Worthia kept her pose as if stating the item without emotion. The only change was the occasional tenor of her voice.

"How are we to know that your expenses are reasonable?"

"We will make our accounting available, upon request by qualified personnel, for review. We will not make them available to just anyone. Please make sure they have some kind of credentials that inform us that they have an idea of what they are looking at."

Garo leaned back into the chair. "Agreed."

"Fourthly, we will, by trade, supply finished goods required by the surrounding communities at fair values. We will need to be given an idea of what goods those communities need, at least initially. We will not provide weapons, robotics, or any advanced technology that can be used for weapons or against us."

"I would expect nothing less." Garo's grin appeared genuine.

"Lastly, we will be responsible for all satellites and maintain their operation. Use of the satellites will be allowed free of charge to those in North America. We will also defend against any space-based threats."

"Since you have the technology that controls the satellites, I see no alternative." The smile turned into a smirk.

Worthia eyed the man for a moment before speaking. "Shall we proceed to the conditions of the temporary peace?"

"Of course. Would you care to suggest the conditions?"

"I will communicate what we are willing to accept." Worthia gave him a hard stare. "Would you like something to drink before we continue?"

"I'm fine." Garo returned the stare as if a challenge. "Please continue."

"Let us proceed, then, to the conditions of the truce. Send." Worthia's interface sent a file to Garo's, which displayed it on the table. "This is a list of what will be considered Citizens cities. I don't expect any of them to surprise you. Would you like a minute to read them?"

"Yes." Garo's eyes scanned the list, reading each name without hurry. After reaching the end, he said, "Yes, no surprises."

"And this, send, is a list of what we shall call neutral cities. It is not long, but again, I would hope you will agree that their fates have not been decided at this moment." Another file was sent to Garo's interface. He examined the list with casual ease.

"I would argue with a few of these," Garo said as he listed his eyes, "but you and I both know that they have been more trouble than they are worth. If you feel a desire to claim them as neutral, I will not argue." Garo looked up. "What else?"

"The Puritans will not object to the establishment of defenses in any of the Citizen cities or any future Citizen city."

"If you wish to waste your time and money…" Garo shrugged.

"No Puritans will try to starve out the cities."

No reaction from Garo came.

"No Puritan will in any way or by any agents try to infiltrate or sabotage a neutral or Citizen city. They will not try to infest or spread disease—"

"Is all this really necessary? I get the idea." Garo slumped a little in his chair, leaning to one side.

"Just being thorough." Worthia gave him a smirk. "I'll move on since all this will be in the document we sign."

"Maybe we should just hit the highlights then."

"Fine." Worthia took a breath and slowly let it out. "Puritans will not form treaties with foreign governments, but can establish trade agreements and control the immigration of people into their areas from foreign countries. They cannot control the emigration to Citizen cities."

"So you're saying we can't stop our people from defecting to you." Garo's chin seemed to emphasize the statement.

"Why would you want to keep them if they don't want to live with you anymore?" Worthia raised an eyebrow. "Besides, we reserve the right to reject them."

Garo made a huff of a laugh. Worthia wondered if he would break out laughing, but he didn't.

"You mean you would reject someone if they came to you?"

"I'm saying we reserve the right to do so." Worthia did not change expressions.

"I would assume no less," Garo said smoothly and then waved for her to continue.

"All transactions with Citizens will be done by barter or dollars, whose relative value to other currencies will be set by our government."

"Unless your Citizens agree to some other form during the exchange."

"Fine, but pushing Citizens to agree to such repeatedly will not be tolerated."

"Fine." Garo waved off the statement.

"Diplomatic relations will be established at Denver for official interactions between your government and ours. We will establish a location for such meetings."

"Our person doesn't get to live inside your walls?" Garo asked facetiously.

"You are already living in our country."

"Agree to disagree." Garo spread his hands. "Anything else?"

"It would be nice if you kept your rhetoric about us to a minimum. I know you have no control over Valesco, but what your churches in this country do will have a large effect. Besides, you have plenty of other things to bother with, in my opinion."

"I will mention it to the preachers, but I can't guarantee anything."

"Excessive… demonization… by a preacher could result in detrimental results in their trade negotiations by the representatives of a given city, which is not totally under our control." Worthia gave him another smirk.

"I will convey the message."

Worthia was silent for a few seconds. "That is all the salient points, I believe. Are there any you wish to discuss?"

"Your list was quite detailed." Garo sat back and gave Worthia what he imagined was a pleasant smile. "Would you do the honor of joining me at dinner?"

"Not a chance." Worthia returned the pleasant smile.

Epilogue
Life Goes On

"Daddy!" came the enthusiastic shout as Joseph stepped into the apartment. He bent down so Julianna could jump into his arms. He lifted her off the floor as she hugged him.

"Did you have a good day?"

"Yes! Mommy took us out in the field and let me find bugs! I have them in my jars. You want to see them?" The expression on her face told Joseph he would be seeing them.

"Of course I do, but first I have to say hi to Mommy. You know how she is." Joseph put his arm under Julianna to support her weight.

"She's changing Zhi. He stinks." The girl giggled.

"Well, maybe Mommy can wait a minute more, then," Joseph whispered to the girl, which made her giggle more.

"I can wait for what?" Mercedes asked as she walked into the room. "And how do you manage to come home right after I change your son every time?"

"I put odor detectors in the apartment and check them before I come in." Joseph leaned over and kissed his wife.

"I almost believe you. Here, take your son so I can finish getting dinner ready." Mercedes handed him the baby, who cooed and pursed his lips.

"Is Zhi a clean boy?" Julianna asked. "Now can we look at bugs?"

"Sure, honey, up until your mother says we have to come to dinner."

"Yeah!"

Joseph set the girl down, who ran into the other room. "Did you eat any bugs while you were in the field?" Joseph asked the baby.

"Aaaaa, brrrrr," answered the baby and he pawed at Joseph's chin.

"I'll take that as a yes. Good job on the potty timing, by the way," Joseph whispered. "Keep it up."

"Wenk's going to join us for dinner," Mercedes called from the other room. "Jul wanted to show him her bugs."

"I'm sure Uncle Wenk will really like that, won't he?" Joseph asked the baby. "But no eating them for you. Your sister would be upset if you did."

Zhi pouted and then laughed. Joseph looked at the baby with squinted eyes.

"Has my brother been babysitting Zhi?" Joseph called to his wife.

Bennett walked slowly from the gate, joined by a small crowd of military and non-military personnel. Next to him walked Second Lieutenant Cal Harjo in a new uniform, carrying a box. Joseph walked behind the commander next to Colonel Fred Allin.

"I'm not sure why I'm here," Joseph mumbled to the colonel.

"He's probably punishing you for something you said," came the reply.

"You'd have to be more specific to be helpful."

In front of Bennett was a group of civilians led by the Governor of South Dakota. The group, mostly locals, included one news crew. The group waited.

When Bennett was within arm's reach, he stopped. The governor cleared his throat.

"Commander Bennett, I am here to officially notify you of the end of hostilities between the State of South Dakota and your base. I have been informed through my organization that a peace treaty has been signed between the Puritans and the… Citizens. Let us hope that this will usher in a period of prosperity for both of us."

"Let us hope." Bennett stepped forward and the two men shook hands. "As a token of that hope, I have brought a gift to commemorate the occasion. Second-Lieutenant?"

Bennett motioned to the young officer, who walked forward with the box and then removed the lid. Bennett reached in and removed the item from the box and held it out to the governor.

"What is it?"

"It's an artifact from the battle that took place here forty years ago. We believe it is part of one of the… angels… that was destroyed here. I thought you might like to have it."

The man's eyes went wide as he lifted the piece. It wasn't large and was very light. Its purpose was not evident from its twisted shape.

"Thank you, sir. You do me great honor by your gift."

"We have no need to keep it classified anymore and I figured you would enjoy having it much more than I would."

"It will be placed on my desk for all to see." The governor carefully handed the piece to an aide, who looked almost nervous enough to drop it, but settled after a stern look from the governor. Turning back to Bennett, the man said, "Now you make me wish I had brought something for you."

"Your goodwill and peaceful co-existence is all I require."

"That, sir, I am confident you will have."

The men shook hands again. Joseph leaned toward Colonel Allin and whispered.

"Do you think it will last?"

"I sure hope so."

Read on for an excerpt from *Rebel Earth,* the final book in the *Awakening Earth* trilogy

At the next intersection Tigen stopped and listened. Sounds of gunfire led him down the left hall to find two infantrymen dispatching a creature that had entered a reception hall. He arrived just in time to see the creature fall into several pieces not five meters from the men. Swerving his rifle Tigen's direction, the man's eyes went wide with shock and then fear as he promptly pointed the rifle upwards.

"Sorry, sir. These things are hard to kill."

"Carry on."

Tigen's attention was drawn by noises farther down the hall. A length of flame came through the ceiling and traced a circle, cutting ragged edges into the ceiling. Breaking into a run, Tigen made for the hole, avoiding the circular piece of ceiling as it fell. A creature soon followed, flaming sword ablaze. As it landed on top of the shattered ceiling piece, Tigen grabbed its sword hand with his left gloved hand, twisting it in what should be an unnatural angle, and drove his right augmented fist into the lion face in front of him.

Staggered, the creature brought up its other hand as it tried to focus its eyes. It was rewarded by a metal hand raining repeated blows. The muzzle broke and yellowish liquid flowed from the face. The next blow missed as the head turned, revealing an eagle beak and eyes. A wing swept from behind the creature, causing a cut along Tigen's right arm. He responded by driving his fist into the body of the creature and squeezing his left hand as hard as possible. Rewarded by a sound that could have been breaking bones, Tigen twisted the hand further.

With a screech to pierce eardrums, the creature beat its wings, leaving the ground and kicking Tigen with both feet. Twisting his body, Tigen whipped the creature against the wall and followed with more blows from his right. He could feel the creature attempting to turn its wrist and felt the heat of the sword as it inched toward his head.

"Left hand blade!" Tigen shouted. From its sheath along his left thumb, a metal blade shot from its case and plunged into the wrist of the creature. Holding the body with his right, Tigen wrenched his left and was rewarded by the creature's hand separating from its arm to be thrown down the hall, scoring the floor as it went.

Wings beat at Tigen as he held the creature, driving his left elbow into its throat. As he did, the wings beat softer and the creature sagged until it hung limp against the wall. Backing off, Tigen watched the creature fall to the floor as if a rag doll. Turning, he noticed the sword still flamed. He kicked the body but it did not respond.

"To all combatants," Tigen said out loud. "This is Commander Tigen Tonsten. The sword hilt is the power source for the creatures. Separate the sword from the creature and they soon lose all power."

About the Author

Dale E. McClenning was born in Illinois but has lived most of his life in Indiana. He went to Ohio State for Mechanical Engineering and was an engineer for 33 years mostly doing industrial turbine engines (generator sets). He has a wife of 36 years, two boys (35 and 31), two daughters-in-law and one grand-daughter (9 going on 16). He has been reading science fiction since grade school and writing since junior high. He has also read a lot of history and theology.